THE MAYFLY'S VISIT

IN THE SHADOW OF A MONSTER

VOLUME 2

DALILA CARYN

Evil Goddess Press

Cover art and design by Yenthe Joline

(Hardcover) ISBN: 979-8-9904789-5-4
(Paperback) ISBN: 979-8-9904789-3-0
(E-book) ISBN: 979-8-9904789-4-7
Library of Congress Control Number: 2025913877

Dear Reader,

This novel includes certain themes that may be triggering. Including on page violence, assisted suicide, verbal abuse, depression and some suicidal ideation. As well as references to, off page, child molestation and rape.
Please be gentle with your inner selves. You deserve love and peace; I hope you find it and guard it fiercely.

Dalila

DALILA CARYN is the author of the fantasy novels of The Forgotten Sister series, The Liberator Saga, the In The Shadow of a Monster trilogy, the Merely Mortal Men Myths, and the Chaos Dragon Adventures. In 2021 she founded Evil Goddess Press through which she proudly publishes her novels. Writing is her lifelong adventure and constant learning experience. It is her hope that each new book she writes is a little bit better than the last—and she is *not even close* to done yet!

For Shani who would not finish this book until the cave was "more romantic." I hope this meets with your approval.

The Mayfly's Visit

Stayed the mayfly for a spell,
In springtime when the evening fell.
He sought a woman's company
And built for her a fantasy.
His power stole into her mind,
Her sweetest wishes there to find.
He then embodied each desire,
To lure her heart and light her fire.
Through wild blossoms of love's delight,
Through tender whispers in dark of night,
Through stolen breaths and laughter wild,
Through silences in evenings mild,
They lived a lifetime in a May.
But dawned the June he'd flown away.
And with him crumbled every dream,
So sorrows sat where joy had been;
As doomed as mayflies are their gifts;
They gleam in May, in June cause rifts.
Even his last remembrance,
Of every laugh and stolen glance,
The budding purpose of his stay
That marked the world ere he decay
Spawned the mayfly for a spell,
In springtime when the evening fell.
And left behind his progeny
To grow in clouds of mystery,
Unknowing of his nature deep;
Of planting seeds that others reap
When manhood dawns one fateful May—
Then he as well—must fly away.

THE SHADOW OF THE PAST

THE RISING SWARM

"It's alright, Hadhi," Noam repeated as Hadhi collapsed in his arms, his heart breaking for her. Then his hasty heart, always so far ahead of his mind, slipped free of his lips and into the world. "I love you."

Hadhi's sobs returned, stronger than before, wracking her body and shaking his arms loose. With a great gasp, Hadhi shoved away, sending him tumbling backwards. Noam struck his head on the stone pillar behind him. His eyes popped open in shock and he leaned there, senseless. One hand stretched out towards Hadhi, to comfort her, to halt her. Hadhi stood shaking violently and her eyes flared wide.

"You do not know me." Her voice was so small and broken Noam felt the pain of it in his own chest. Hadhi took off running.

Noam lay a moment watching her run, waiting for his senses to return. She had disappeared around the corner of the veranda by the time Noam shoved himself up. He ached more than he should from such a small bump on the head. He ached in more places than he should, his chest creaking and groaning as though it was being constricted by a force beyond his own.

Noam's breath caught as Hadhi raced into his sight again. Not returning to him, as he wished. No. She was racing back his way from the ground, running past the palace and away from the city. The wind rippled through her gown, and her hair floated behind her like foam atop the ocean. She was so fast. Noam was not slow himself, but he didn't move to chase her. He stood leaning against the rail of the veranda watching until she was out of sight.

Oh, I hate him...I thought it would go away when he died. You do not know me. But he did. I am Sour-Faced-Hadhi, my father's monster.

Noam's head pounded. He could see her eyes in his mind, laid over her racing form in the night. Her huge, horrified eyes. He so longed to be able to pull Hadhi into his arms and fix all her pain. Take it all away. And he felt an all too familiar longing. One he hadn't felt in years. He tried to shake it off as he watched her run. Tried to sort his feelings from the past away from his feelings in the moment.

Of course she had run. It was too much. It was too...fast. He'd meant the words, meant for them to wrap around her and heal her pains. But he already knew that wasn't possible. Not for him. Not for anyone.

He'd tried that with his mother, as she had tried it with him, and his father. Even Shiraz and Ethan had tried to take Noam's pain away. But though it touched his soul and made him feel loved, there was always part of his pain that lived too deep inside for anyone to touch. It never fully went away. And Hadhi's pain ran so much deeper. He shouldn't have even tried to touch it.

"I love you, Papa." Noam heard the echo of his childhood voice, felt his arms reaching out for the attention his brother was receiving. But his father jerked away. Shoved Noam's arms down.

"Must you attack me? Go hang off your mother."

Noam flinched in the here and now. Locking that old voice as far away as he could. But it was harder tonight than it had been recently. This wasn't the same. Not at all.

Hadhi had only known him for a day. How could any of the intensity of his feeling seem real to her when her life had known such pain and rejection? As a child, from his father, having his love shoved away, that had been his father's fault. But tonight, Noam was the problem.

It's alright, Hadhi. I love you. He shouldn't have said it. It took the moment from comfort to something else.

He'd frightened her when she'd needed someone to...come undone with. Someone to scream and rage and cry with, and still be safe. That was what love meant to Noam. But clearly it had not been Hadhi's experience of it.

Something small zipped past his ear, making Noam shudder. He watched it land on the veranda, watched a pair of somethings land and felt his stomach sucked away with a sudden nauseating flash of memory and fear.

They lived a lifetime in a May.

But dawned the June he'd flown away.

Zawadi stepped back from Kane. The winds stirred outside of the palace and bugs began to sing. Not cicadas. She was familiar with that sound. This... *stung* the air, chewing away at it, as if it would replace the air with nothing but that lonely, vibrant, desperate song that zipped and flapped swarming the air. She should not have granted that wish.

She looked around, but it seemed she alone heard the sound. With a suddenness so startling it made her jump, she saw through the open arch Zuberi's eldest shove out of Noam's arms as he tried to comfort her. He fell backwards and Zawadi took a step back. She could see them all from this angle. The look of anguish on that face, Zuberi's eldest, so solitary she could not even feel love when it reached out for her. Noam, shocked at first, then pain lashed across his face, and rejection as his love took to her feet and fled his arms. And Kane, the twisted smile remaking his face, the joy he felt at all the suffering.

"I will be Zuberi's legacy. Once I prove myself to the king, I will be the most powerful man in Maltuba."

A bug zipped by Zawadi on her right. She batted it away. Then another flew past her on the left. She wanted to bat at her arms and flee the swarm she felt. But there was no swarm. Just—those—two. Yet their song consumed the air. Overpowered her hearing. The sight of them dancing around one another left a chill in her soul.

No. Not cicadas.

Her eyes followed the course of the bugs out the arch, to Noam, watching his love flee. *Mayflies*.

She should not have granted that wish. Something had shifted because of it. Noam's eyes too fell on the doomed insects, and he shook.

How long would he be for this world now?

Kane spun around, his eyes landing on Zawadi once more, dressed up in this Asha skin. A wicked replica of Zuberi's grin twisted Kane's features. He winked and moved by her, his path following that of the king.

Zawadi waited. Breathed. Looked inside for a way to undo her wish, to take it back. Never before had she feared what her wishes might do in the world. Some were meant to kill—and they would. Kane would die. But what havoc would he wreak first?

Zawadi gave herself one more moment to fret. Then breathed out, shutting away her concerns. Battle Born granted wishes and walked away. The magic knew best. She wasn't here to care for these creatures or to guard them from harm. They should look to themselves for protection. Or perhaps —they should have chosen better whom to love.

PREY

She had never been taught how to be prey. Hadhi tore down the balcony to the front stairs and out into the night. Her flight was sloppy, tearing past startled party guests and guards alike. She did not notice their faces, just their bodies, just the threat of them, and she slammed into hard stone walls or slid around columns to avoid them. Racing right beneath towers where she knew yet more guards stood. Surely other prey were better at fleeing. She knew they were. She had seen it when she hunted. How some kept to their herd, or lone animals might leap in strange patterns to confuse predators. How quick animals doubled back on their own scent, or slow ones played dead. They all had methods.

But Hadhi was raised to be a predator. And now there was nothing she was hunting, nothing she was after but—escape. She was prey. *Fezik.* It was a very different beast, this fear.

Hadhi had snuck into the palace she was fleeing before. Snuck in, did her work, and snuck out again. And though the same petrifying fear of the king had lived inside her, it was different when she was the predator. It felt different.

Her feet stirred up swirls of sand, and visions leapt into her path, making her jerk away and run faster, but none of them were here. Not one of them still lived.

She saw Queen Imara draped against the tub like a rag, the scars across her body, the weight in her eyes, the misery. She looked up, her eyes slipped over Hadhi with regret. With sympathy.

"Nox," Hadhi shouted at her ghost. "Nox. Paax kamko nong io pang dun. Nza!" *No. It will not be that way. Never!* But Hadhi did not even believe herself. Tears fell with the vow, belying her certainty.

She would escape. She could escape. She could be happy, she could be free, she could be lo—

Hadhi saw a grin in the darkness. She did not need to see one more piece of him to know it was her father's ghost. To know what he would say. Hadhi threw her hands over her ears, but his tickled whisper slipped between her fingers and slid into her mind as she passed his grinning figure.

Cyva mur nong yziz czan sa qi, gzufiga. There is no such thing as love, monster.

A soft trail of fingers brushed across her hand, like Noam's fingers when they brushed hers in the line. Trying to grab on, trying to reach out, trying to catch hold. But never making contact. Because she ran. She ran from him as much as any ghost on the road. Perhaps more. Because right or wrong about love's existence, Baba knew her. And the eyes out in the darkness, Kiho's eyes, cheetahs and gazelles, and fairies the size of mice, and so many other eyes. The souls she had snuffed out at her father's command, their last flashes of life flaring as Hadhi ran by. They all said the same. They all knew the truth Noam did not.

She was a monster. And even if love existed. It was not for people like her.

"Nong cur ifik vis uli, gzufiga," the ghosts hissed. *Not for people like you, monster.*

Nuru watched her sister race away from the palace. She tended to forget that Hadhi was so fast. So often when Nuru looked on her, Hadhi was perfectly still. But her stillness and speed both had been honed over years of practice. For a moment, watching her run, Nuru allowed herself to believe that Hadhi would get away. That she would escape into the night and never allow the cheetah pursuing her to catch up. But it wasn't so. The palace guards watched her direction. They weren't racing after her yet, but if the king ordered it, they would find her.

A woman of Maltuba can be married to a cheetah or a gazelle.

And anyway...she wasn't running for good. That wasn't the run of someone with a goal. Nuru knew movement, it was a language all its own. And Hadhi's feet were too desperate even to know what she was doing. She was running for space. Running to breathe. Running because she felt pursued and was desperate to be free. She ran like prey.

Nuru slid down the wall of the palace, watching her sister through the geometric patterned holes in the wall of the veranda. Her breath was tight in her chest, as she saw not her sister, but the trail of stirring sands in her wake. Tears slid down Nuru's face. It was so like Baba's funeral.

No one had let Nuru see Baba's body. It was wrapped in a vibrant orange and green silk with the fractal triangles of the Ga'ogo decorating it, a sash of golden threads tying it closed. Most bodies were wrapped in their own finest cloths to be burned, but Baba's had come from the palace, *the finest silk in the land*, the king had said. Because he was a great man.

But Nuru hadn't cared. She'd just wanted to see his face. She didn't believe them. That body looked far too small to have been her father. He was larger than mortal men. And no one would let her look. *He'd been attacked by animals*, they said. *It would frighten her*, they said. *He wouldn't want her to see him that way*, they said. But she didn't believe a word. She wasn't even as sad as she was angry. Because it wasn't real. It couldn't be. He would come home while they were burning the body of this imposter and laugh at them for having believed it was him.

That was what she told herself as she walked with her family to the mouth of the desert. And as she watched three of the Spirit Dancers leaping and twirling and calling the great spirit Ether out of the desert, in celebration of Baba's life. That was what she told herself as her neighbors sang the songs of honoring. Grief was not for funerals, so no one expected Nuru to cry. No one but her. If this truly were Baba, she was certain she would be crying, would be sobbing, would throw herself on the pyre to stop them lighting it. So it wasn't him. Surely she would defy the Great Spirits and risk waking all the unsettled dead and dragging them back into Maltuba with her tears. It could not be him. That was what she told herself when the king himself lit the pyre on the altar. It wasn't real.

She knew it. Until the moment the flames crackled to life, and Hadhi—the most stoic among them on any day—Hadhi *gasped* a sob so anguished it ruptured Nuru's chest. Hadhi bent forward, shoving her fist into her mouth, but her sobs would not be silenced by force, nor her tears be stopped. She jerked away, fled the desert and their father's funeral, long before it was over.

That was the moment Nuru understood it was real. The moment Nuru began to grieve. But still she didn't sob or cry as she would have expected. Her pain was racing away with Hadhi, just like the spiraling sands that trailed after her now. She carried all their pain away, so they could stand beside his body and celebrate all his life had been. She carried all their pain.

Nuru shoved up the wall. Something had to be done. Because she knew without having to be told that Hadhi would be back to carry all their pain again. To keep them all safe. She would be the prey, to keep the cheetah from devouring the people she loved.

"She always cries alone, doesn't she?" Sade's voice startled Nuru as she walked up from the far end of the veranda, her eyes trailing Hadhi into the night. "I was in the market the day she was mauled. We'd barely spoken in years, but I saw her, shaking and bloody, just standing there beside your father as he and Amal laughed over the meat. I could see how terrified she still was, how much she wanted to collapse and have arms around her. I started to go to her, but—" Sade wasn't really speaking to Nuru it seemed, just remembering, and even that was painful.

How did she know exactly the things Nuru's own mind was calling forward? Though she did not want to be thinking of it, Nuru heard again and again what people had whispered about her sister without seeing Nuru there. That Baba had meant her to be scarred. That he had not saved her as he always said. Nuru didn't want to know any of it. If she had heard them say it any other way, she would not have believed it at all; she still did not want to, but…they overheard *Hadhi* say those things. And Hadhi did not lie.

"I started to go to her, and her head shifted. She saw me. Looked me right in the eyes, crying and shaking, and when I moved towards her, she just…shook her head. Her eyes were so fiery and forbidding and scared. I let that stop me. But I should not have. I remember her comforting me when I cried once. I'd fallen and scraped my knee, such a little injury, and she comforted me. But Hadhi cries alone. Even at the funeral. It is forbidden, but…there should have been arms for her to fall into. Arms to close around her and make her safe."

Sade turned away from the veranda. Her hand fell on Nuru's shoulder and pulled her near. Nuru didn't realize she was crying until Sade pressed Nuru's face against the blue and orange silk bow at her shoulder and ran a hand down the back of her head.

Nuru barely knew her. She saw Sade around Jaccada on occasion. And knew Uncle Kafil planned to marry her. She knew her father, Diji, was part of the royal guard. And that when they were younger, she and Hadhi had been friends, but before today, they had rarely spoken and now Nuru closed her arms around her and clung on.

"She holds you when you cry, doesn't she?" Sade asked. Nuru just nodded. "I thought so. Come. She will be back. The night is far from over. When she returns, she shall not put us off. She will have our arms. I promise."

They walked into the palace together, Nuru wishing that nothing had ever come between Hadhi and this friend. Hadhi deserved friends.

But in her mind's eyes, she saw Hadhi, so many times, not just tonight, or the funeral, or even after she was mauled. She saw her eyes full of that exact pain Sade described, fiery and forbidding and so scared. The look of cornered prey. Nuru recalled it, over and over again. It might be the most familiar look she had ever seen in her sister's eyes. Haunted and hunted. How long had it been so and Nuru simply had not wanted to see?

Kane followed his prey. The king made his way through the ballroom with many a woman jumping from his path to bow. He stopped to confer with a soldier near one of the open arches of the veranda. Both their gazes drifted out towards the night where Hadhi was fleeing like the weak creature he would prove her to be. Hadhi had no right to the praise Zuberi had heaped upon her, no right to be called his legacy. Just look at the grin on the king's face as he watched her fleeing.

King Enzi thought of himself as the most powerful creature in the world. The ultimate predator. But it wasn't so. He was merely allowed to believe it. Allowed to stand tall and attack the creatures he ruled. Allowed by men like Zuberi. Men like Kane. Without them, he was nothing. And Kane would prove it to him, after he made himself invaluable, after he made himself a place at the king's right hand just like Zuberi had held. Then Kane would destroy him. He would be stronger than Zuberi, more than his legacy. He would rule Maltuba. And destroy every man who got in his way, and every man who had willingly followed the king into the destruction of Kane's home, his family. His—

Kane's hand jerked, and he heard the screams deep in his ear canal, so deep he could feel them shuddering along his vocal cords. But he did not make a sound. He balled his hand into a fist. He would get his vengeance, just as Zuberi had promised him.

"Look at you," the echo of Zuberi's first words to him sounded in Kane's head. *"I knew there must be one survivor amongst you. You will do great things."*

"Please, please, save the others. Help them."

Zuberi had shaken his head. "It is too late for them. And they are not like you. Only the strong have a right to survive. You feel that already, that is why you fought to live, not to save them."

"No! I came for help." Kane hated the echo of his weaker self, his child self. The slap of Zuberi's hand cracking across his face was no less than he had deserved in that moment, just what he'd needed.

"Only the weak need saving! You are strong. You will be a warrior. An incarnation of Gitonga. You will radiate strength and remake your people. The other children are already dead. Gitonga willed it because they were not strong enough to achieve their own survival. Do you want to join them? Or do you want to live and avenge them?"

"Against you," Kane had snarled, his first sign of real strength. And Zuberi laughed.

"If you are strong enough. But I meant against the man who sent me. Against your king."

"He isn't my king."

Zuberi turned Kane around to face the fighting going on below the cliff where they stood. "Watch the Tikoo fall. Enzi is your king now. I have made him so. If you want your revenge, you must get strong enough to defeat me."

In the here and now, Kane relaxed his hand. He only wished he knew who had beat him to Zuberi's murder. Over all the years of training, and with as much...love as Kane ever grew to feel for the man, Kane had always intended that his hand be the one to end Zuberi's life. Now that dream was taken from him. But not the rest.

He would kill Enzi. He would rule Maltuba. And all of the weak would be made to suffer for having allowed Enzi to rule.

Hadhi would suffer. Her fear tonight would be nothing compared to what he would do to her. Until she admitted that Zuberi was wrong, she was no killer. She was an insignificant bit of prey for a real monster to devour.

THE CHARIOT OF WIND

Asha didn't know where she wanted to take Azize first. She had so many favorite places. She could take him to the fields of Looma blossoms behind Sabra's childhood home where they had lain on their backs, stared up at the sky, and dreamed of far off lands. In truth, the docks were one of her many favorite places in Maltuba, but only when new ships were coming in from far off lands or being launched towards them. If it were day, she would take him to the market. Drag him through the vendors from foreign lands to watch them bartering wildly for Maltuban silks, and blessing stones, and spices. Show him how much wonder from other lands could be bought for a mere handful of Maltuban silk threads. She would...

But why not? Asha was magic; it could be day if she wanted it. Zawadi had given her no rules as to what the magic could do. Why did Asha keep limiting herself?

She giggled wildly as the chariot of wind carried them away from the ship she had conjured for him from his childhood.

Azize looked at her in fear. It was only then that Asha felt how tightly he was gripping onto her arm. Or...the tiny arm of the child whose body she was using. His grip leeched color from her skin; it ought to hurt but Asha couldn't feel her body. Only her magic.

"What is funny? Are you alright?" Azize demanded.

"I am awake!" Asha shouted through a laugh. The chariot raced by the buildings at the docks. It dragged them by the smaller homes of fishermen and net makers or sail painters.

"Are there other nations with sails like ours?" Asha asked. Hoping there were. She loved Maltuba, it was one of the greatest nations in the world. The greatest. But she longed to hear him mention just one world as colorful as her own. She knew if the magic simply heard the name of another nation, it would carry them there, right this moment. She knew it.

"Not really," Azize said, and his voice grew less fearful but no less wary. "Everywhere we went, the painted sails set us apart. People always knew when the Maltuban's were coming."

Asha beamed. That was the idea. But she felt less enthusiasm from him. She remembered once at the docks watching a foreign ship sailing into the harbor, as a Maltuban trading ship was sailing out. The Maltuban ship released its sails as it met with the channel, and as they unfurled, a rainbow of color and pattern met the eye, rivaling the sunlight and the sea in its beauty.

The unadorned beige sails of the other ship were hastily rolled up and hidden in shame. They were like flamingos among storks, shaming other creatures with their beauty.

"I understand there are some islands in the Blazing Sea where so many of the inhabitants traverse by sea that the sails of their ships, and even their vessels are painted with family colors or symbols. And there is said to be a pirate queen whose sails are embroidered with her conquests, but we never saw her ship. So we were the only..."

"The only colorful birds in a sea of beige. The only prideful flock announcing their arrival like Great Spirits descending from the sky."

Azize chuckled. His fingers loosened yet more from her arm, so they merely lay against her. A soft—hungry—contact. "That is something my father might say. I cannot fathom why it doesn't sound hostile when you say it."

"Because it isn't!" Asha waved her arms through the wind like a billowing sail. The air grew light and colorful, nearly solid. You could see in the undulating shape of it, a giant sail stretched out across the ground with no less than ten men and women working in concert, stamping the fractal pattern of diamonds and wheat in bright blues, oranges, purples greens and gold. "Look at their faces, the joy, the concentration. There is no threat in sharing what you love, in announcing it to the world. *Love*—is always beautiful."

The image flapped above them. Asha watched Azize's eyes follow the echo of his citizens creating great works of art. Saw him gasp as the image transformed into the workmen stringing the sails to his ship, singing songs of the jungle and the desert and the sea, and the blessed nation that sat between them.

He gasped as the image curled up on itself like a sail rolled tight and dissolved in a sprinkling of colorful light falling around them. They'd reached the center of town where the homes of rich men, scholars, and the vaashta stood. No two were exactly the same, their domes conical or rounded; a few had flat roofs and stairs leading up to them like the mansion Asha had grown up in. And all had reliefs molded into their walls, stories of gods on the homes of the vaashta, or family symbols on rich men's homes, or even simple patterns. Asha used to run between them, making herself a map in her head, not of buildings, but of patterns, like they were a secret language only she knew.

But just now the homes didn't interest her. The colorful lights of her magic fell around the center, creating a hive of activity, a bright, loud, colorful market. Children ran between the legs of adults. Sellers haggled over their wares. On a low wall surrounding a home, someone sang. You could smell the meats being cooked, and the vegetables and the pnupa bread rising.

"Ethee Oxtia!" Azize exclaimed, his fist rising to his heart as he looked around. Maumai always bowed so before the vaashta, recognizing them as the voices of the gods.

Asha snorted and smacked his hand away from his chest. "It is only magic. I am no god."

Azize hiccuped his mirth, but his eyes still looked just a bit too wide and wary to be anything but a worshiper. Then he spoke.

"No. You are no god, Asha." He said her name again with lingering bits of shock. And Asha felt the swell of wonder that had enveloped her when he'd first recognized her despite this body.

"But what of the one who granted your wish for power. This is... Don't they hear us?" he asked all of a sudden. Their chariot of air carried them between the vendor's carts or just over people's heads, dancing about in this magical scene.

"No," Asha shook her head. "They aren't here. Magic spells don't show what is, they show—" she giggled, "what is seen."

Azize opened and shut his mouth several times. Asha could see the battle within him, trying to banish his fear. It was such a struggle for him that part of Asha wanted to pull the magic back, make it small, make it something he could handle. But it was such a *small, quiet* impulse compared to the desire to *paint the entire night in magic* and swim through it, soak it up, live and live and *live* to the very limit of the power thrumming beneath her skin.

"So...if they are not here, I suppose I cannot have any of the pnupa and faaszulop Tabia just made?"

Asha giggled, delighted with him. She knew he could fight his fears and embrace the magic. Or she hadn't known it. But she had hoped.

"If you want dip to burn your tongue and bread to eat it off of, I will make it for you," Asha said, playfully territorial. And a green and orange painted dish appeared in her hands with the twisted spiced bread and the creamy reddish dip in a bowl at its center. "AND!" Asha exclaimed shouting so loud and so excitably that her market illusion dissolved around them before she could even show him how Maltuba was the envy of the world. "I know the perfect place for you to eat it!" Not waiting for his assent, Asha's power raced away with them, climbing up, up, up above the houses surrounding the market and into the darkness once more.

DISHARMONY

Jauhar watched her daughter take off running, nearly colliding with Sade and her mother, tears streaming down her cheeks. A tiny jerk moved Jauhar's leg without order from her mind, her body starting towards her daughter. But Jauhar held herself in brittle place as she had many times before. So many times.

She shut away thoughts of the past and focused on the moment. It was the only way to protect her family as best she could. Oh, but she wished this night were over. Everything within Jauhar was at war, but to all the world she looked lovely and at peace as her mind and body attacked one another. It was a feeling she knew well.

Over the years of being Zuberi's wife, her mind and her body had so rarely been in harmony with each other. The times she felt entirely herself were so few and so scattered they seemed more like lingering bits of dream than reality.

"Mzaa, before you married Baba, did you dream of being a wife and having children? Did you...want it?" Hadhi had asked when she was all of ten.

"What a thing to ask. Of course. Why?"

Hadhi shook her head, looking away, unable to answer with words. And Jauhar had known what was going on in that mind, known Hadhi was wondering, if that was true, why her mother didn't want her now. So she'd swept from the room in a rage and had barely spoken to her daughter for days. It was so easy for the rest of them to look at her and find her wanting; they liked the sweet, easy wives. But women like that were destroyed by life. Women like that had to remain naive or they crumpled to nothing and faded away from too much reality. Jauhar might not be what her children wanted, but she would be here to see them safe and cared for, as other sweet mothers never could in such a home.

Sweet mothers like Sabra could be now because Zuberi was gone. Because Jauhar had laid the way for her. That pitiful lecture she'd tried to give Jauhar when the king departed and Hadhi stomped outside played through her mind as she made her way around the room, laying the way for Hadhi as *strong* mothers did.

"Jauhar," Sabra whispered in a shaky voice. "Are you certain this is best?"

Jauhar had stood precisely where she had been when Hadhi returned with the king. She hadn't moved an inch, her heart even remaining still and aching to beat in her chest.

Slowly, Jauhar turned to Sabra. She was so hesitant. The sort of woman who was destroyed by life. The sort of woman Hadhi could never be. Jauhar lifted her chin high and all the steel life had forced into her bones stiffened her posture. "You are the mother of a son," Jauhar said. "It is *far* preferable. You shall never have to choose between teaching him strength and comforting his fears." Jauhar made no effort to soften her voice with Sabra today, and the tension her husband's young wife felt was transferred to her son so Lin began to cry and fight loudly against the pouch where she carried him.

Jauhar offered no help, continuing the lecture it was past time Sabra heard. "There is no *best* to choose. The king has made his preference known. Now the only option available to Hadhi, or any of us, is to see to it that he makes her his *queen*."

Sabra looked away, covering her son's head as he continued to cry. Sabra looked like she might be crying herself. And that was allowed, because she was the mother of a son. Twice, Jauhar had lost babies; one was too early to know a gender, but one she carried nearly to term, her son. He would have been a year older than Asha had he lived. He would have been Zuberi's favorite child. He would have been here to protect his sisters and see them married before men like Enzi could claim them. But Jauhar hadn't been strong then. Not strong enough to bring him into the world alive. Not strong enough to handle her husband leaving her broken and empty, with a four year old daughter to care for on her own, and returning home a month later with a new bride.

Jauhar barely remembered how she and Hadhi survived that month. She'd not left the hut much. And when Zuberi returned, it was so much worse. Jauhar was too depressed and useless to fight for her place in the house. And though she'd despised her husband, Rama took over everything, cleaning, cooking, caring for Zuberi and Jauhar—and Hadhi. It was only when Jauhar heard her daughter call Rama *mzaa* that she found any of her old strength. That woman was not Hadhi's mother. That woman had not bled and suffered and cared for her. She hadn't loved her.

Jauhar had to learn through her suffering how to be strong in a marriage, how to be strong in life. But Hadhi was strong already. She wouldn't like her husband, but she would not break apart and nearly die from his lack of love, as Jauhar had after she lost her son.

"I am sorry." Sabra lay a hand on Jauhar's sleeve, offering comfort.

"For what? My daughter will be queen. Every woman or man who has called her expression sour will be made to crawl to her for their comfort. This is the best thing that could ever have happened to her."

"Of course," Sabra agreed falsely. "Because it is always best to be trapped with someone more powerful than you, who wants nothing so much as to exert his will to break your own."

Jauhar shook her head dismissively. "Hadhi is not you, Sabra. There is no breaking her will."

Sabra made a little pained sound, tiny, one could barely hear it. But Lin stopped crying and lay a hand against his mother's chest. The sight nearly brought tears to Jauhar's eyes. Her body, still the victim of emotion and longing. But her will was iron. It held back the tears. Quietly, Sabra walked away. Because she was allowed to be soft and afraid. Jauhar felt another jerk in her leg, envisioning Hadhi running away. She would be back. She would be strong, as she'd been raised to be. But...tonight Jauhar would handle things. Tonight, Jauhar would be the strong one and allow her daughter a chance to feel the softness inside.

Jauhar lifted her chin as she saw mothers around the room casting her looks of jealousy, or pity. None of them mattered. Hadhi would be queen. Hadhi would rule over them all. Then Jauhar could relax. Then her body could finally be at peace. Then...she could be soft again.

THE MEASURE OF A SHADOW

"Hello again." Sabra drew in a sharp breath of courage and stepped into the path of the woman was most certainly *not* Asha, despite the bright *Asha* smile that painted her lips when Sabra startled her.

Sabra had seen the woman edging alongside one of the open arches to the veranda next to the handsome man who'd made Hadhi so uneasy the night before. Their shared whispers and easy looks made Sabra realize Hadhi must have felt some threat from the man that Sabra did not. Hadhi had not, however, felt the threat from the woman in Asha's body.

Likely because Hadhi always felt threatened by Asha's presence, albeit not physically. Or because her being was so much more threatened by the king on whose arm she stood. Sabra shuddered again, reliving the moment of terror when Hadhi's hand nearly closed around the hilt of the king's sword. She would have killed him. Right there, in a room full of citizens and guards and threats. She would die for such a thing. But Hadhi was too enraged to feel afraid. Too wounded to care if she died. Sabra had felt equally wounded once. But...she still feared death, and she thought Hadhi should as well. They all should. The only way to heal from their wounds was to live.

Out the arch, Sabra had seen Hadhi fall to her knees with her hands shoved into her hair and her pain bleeding off of her into the night. Sabra felt the winds shifting, watched sands stirring into the air and lay her lips against her son's head.

This...not-Asha was magic. Sabra suspected she was the same woman she'd taken for her grandmother only this morning. But she no longer felt benevolent. Approaching her could be dangerous.

But so were all kinds of loving. When the Sister Goddess stirred the sands, instead of those who worshiped her doing so, she was speaking to you.

She was asking for your courage, your forgiveness, your recompense—your love.

"I truly thought you were my grandmother when we spoke, isn't that odd?" Sabra asked with a small smile. For that exchange had been a gift.

"Very," the woman laughed with Asha's voice. "I'm two years younger than you."

Sabra ignored her attempts to play Asha. The woman knew or could feel enough to do a convincing interpretation, but this was the woman she'd spoken to at the river. The woman who'd given her confidence and made her examine herself. The woman who had felt safe.

Sabra had been watching Asha more closely since she'd seen her transform and dive into the bushes last night. It was just like Asha to have an adventure, to find magic, and to use it merely to flout Jauhar. When they were younger, Sabra thought Asha's dreams were bigger, but she knew differently now. Asha was as tied to her family as any of them. So tied even magic couldn't shake her from what she really wanted: family.

Sabra had seen Asha talking so intently with that little girl this morning, then seen the same little girl sobbing and throwing herself into Hadhi's arms and Sabra knew that little girl was Asha. What's more, she'd celebrated it. It had seemed that this magical being was giving Asha, giving all of them, things they had always needed. She seemed like a magical guardian righting the wrongs of their lives.

She'd given Asha an adventure and a chance to be herself without family resentments to get in the way. Then she'd even given her a chance to get love and care from her sister. She'd given Sabra the space to see she could set her own course. She was even giving Hadhi a chance to be a better sister to Asha.

Sabra used to hate Hadhi, when Asha and Sabra were first becoming friends. Before she'd joined the family and realized that she was as needy and wounded as any of them, perhaps more. Hadhi had just been so...cold. She'd sucked the air right out of all of Asha's grand plans or beautiful dreams. Hadhi was so unhappy she wanted everyone else to be unhappy with her—or that was how it had seemed.

That change of perspective lived in Sabra now. She knew how easy it was to *see a person wrong.* She knew how easy it was to see things you expected and not what was really there.

"Why have you come?" Sabra's question was so small it barely stirred the air.

"The king commanded every woman be here, or else Mzaa Jauhar would have found a way to keep me home. You know that."

Sabra looked down at Lin's head and felt tears gathering behind her eyes. She wrapped an unnecessary hand on his back.

She would have sworn this woman was here to help them, until she saw her with Jauhar. Until she saw her delighting in the sight of Hadhi trapped on the arm of a man who wanted to destroy her spirit. Now Sabra didn't know. It could be she was here to be kind to some and unkind to others. Or it could be she had sinister plans for all of them and they just hadn't revealed themselves yet.

"When you told me to cast off my husband's shadow, I wonder, did you have any idea how large of a shadow a monster of his variety casts? It was not only me it fell over."

Asha giggled. "Observant, aren't you? Do they credit you with it?"

"They would have no cause to know." Sabra was through being asked to resent the women who were her family now. "I was married to a man who stole my tongue. To remain safe, I was silent and obedient, because any failure resulted in—" Sabra shivered involuntarily but stiffened her spine, as she had seen Jauhar do a hundred times in only the first two days of Sabra's marriage. Stiffen your spine, bear up under the cruelty.

The thought cast Sabra momentarily back into the past. She'd never once seen Zuberi strike Jauhar, nor seen any signs that he'd done it in private. No, he would run his fingers along her softly, he would call her his *perfect* beauty, nothing was allowed to mar her beauty. He'd beaten their cook when Jauhar burned her hand. No, he never hit Jauhar. But that didn't stop him taking her apart, didn't stop him tearing her down so she was defeated but stiffening her spine to appear unmoved.

Sabra stopped stiffening her spine. She allowed her hand to quiver in her son's back. Let this woman see how her words affected her. "Any failure resulted in beatings for me. Or my brothers. I have not spoken to them since

Zuberi's death. I would think to do so, but be overcome with sweats and shaking, because part of me worried Zuberi would return to punish me. I worried he would kill them for my offense. I was married only two years before my husband died, but in that time, he so thoroughly altered me that the family I was born to do not feel like my family any longer. He made me his, just as he wanted. Just as he left his mark on each of them."

The woman watched her with a quietude unsuited to Asha, her eyes growing brighter and brighter with silvery light.

"I have told you, you are free," the woman insisted.

"Are they?" Sabra waited a moment, but with no response forthcoming, she spoke again. "Long before you came, Hadhi was hated by her neighbors, for being his daughter. Though they watched him treat her cruelly. She is the only one of his children I am certain was beaten by his hands and scarred by his words. Why would you delight to see her suffer further?"

The woman shrugged. "Who said that was why I was delighted?"

"Did you give Asha magic?" Sabra pressed though her pulse raced and her body shook. "Was it a kindness? Or some...disguised threat?"

The woman smirked with Asha's face. Shrugging, she slipped into the crowd before Sabra could stop her.

As the woman darted across the room after Enzi, Sabra let out a pained breath. Her lungs rose and fell tightly. She couldn't say for certain if the woman was a threat, but she certainly wasn't a woman to be challenged lightly. And yet...the Sister Goddess demanded her acolytes forgive, demanded that they love. Sometimes she demanded they love more than their hearts were readily prepared to offer. And Sabra wanted her son to see such love from his mother. She wanted him to learn to give such love. She needed to defend this family. His. And *hers*.

HEAVY IS THE PAST

Asha took Azize to the roof of the mansion, her old home. She could feel her uncle and his family inside. Most of the children were asleep but Uncle Kafil was in the courtyard waiting for something; he felt tense. Just now, Asha wasn't concerned. She was dancing across the thin ledge of the roof imagining herself like a willoomi with her colorful silk threads spinning around in the air.

Azize had finished eating a while ago. Now his body was coiled tight again. He didn't like the magic or the wildness. Asha grinned and leapt off the ledge. He gasped as she landed noiselessly on the roof.

"Why here?" he asked.

Asha threw her arms wide. "You can see everywhere! We're a mere mile from the capitol palace; if we are very quiet, we might even hear the music. In the day, you can see the jungle winking at you, daring you to dive in and get lost. You can see the ocean, spot ships long before they come into harbor. And you can have your eyes burned by the light of the next life staring into the desert. The whole world open before you. What's not to love?"

Azize's smile was a little more relaxed now that Asha was on solid ground. She was pleased that he was more comfortable, but she was getting anxious to move again, to do something *dangerous*. The magic wanted to be used. And it wasn't alone. Asha wanted to use it. She wanted so much.

"What was your favorite place?" she demanded, trying to keep still for him.

Azize shook his head in distaste and though he'd looked excited before, even when he was afraid, now he looked less present. His hand slipped into his pocket, where he'd hidden the slipper as if he'd noticed her noticing his lack of attention.

"This is beautiful," Azize agreed. "Why did you want to travel, if you had *the world* open before you?"

Asha answered, but some quiet part of her was watching him. There was something off about his behavior. "Baba always told me stories of adventure, and magic, and they always began the same, *far away in a magical land.*" She shrugged. "I always wanted to see the lands only he knew."

Azize forced a smile. She could see it now, part of Azize wanted to speak but was being stopped. As if he was spelled so. As if *she* was stopping him.

Asha crossed to him, in her tiny body, and pulled his hand away from his pocket. If he was spelled to silence, she would free him.

"I want to know you," Asha entreated softly. "Won't you tell me your favorite places?"

Azize seemed to grind his teeth before he met Asha's gaze. "I didn't have one in Maltuba. I liked the quiet of the desert at night. And I liked the promise of other lands at the docks, or the south road. But...they are all *his*. So the only places I ever wanted to be were away from here."

Asha jerked back at his vehemence. He...hated it here. She thought of the time she and Hadhi had spent nursing his mother, every day he was expected home, by everyone but his mother.

"He knows what I want for him. It is not here. So he should not be either," Queen *Imara had said in response to a remark between Asha and a maid about how he could abandon her.*

Asha had tried to accept the queen's words, but inside she was angry at the son who hadn't come home to be with his dying mother. Asha would have been with her mother every moment she could, no matter how much she wanted to see the world. Asha had not understood. And though she wanted to understand now, it was still incomprehensible.

"Then why are you back?" Asha's hesitant question ended with a bite. "If there is nothing you love here."

"I didn't say there was *nothing I love*. Just no favorite place." He scooted away from her. "Maltuba wasn't the same for me. I could see the same things from the palace. But when I looked at the jungle, I only saw a place my father wanted to conquer. Do you remember the menagerie you tricked me into showing you? All of those animals in shackles, wasting away. You were so excited to see them, but I hated that place. I hate how it makes me feel. Trapped. Dominated.

"There was no place here I could love, because all of them belong to *him*," Azize finished through a snarl.

Asha was completely thrown by his anger. Not just anger—*Rage*. It fell over her and made her quake. Made her...slightly afraid of him. Who knew someone could look so sweet, and carry such anger? Asha had known his father all her life, and he was very fond of his own voice and his power, but he was also easily amused and playful. Asha couldn't think of a thing to make one hate him. She knew that the queen had not loved him. Theirs was a marriage of treaty, a bonding of nations when the king absorbed the Tikoo into Maltuba. But in the months Asha had cared for her, even Imara had not expressed such rage towards her husband.

Azize seemed to realize he'd frightened her. His hands crawled under his legs and his shoulders scrunched. Asha wondered if his anger wasn't as much with her as with his father.

The menagerie you tricked me *into showing you.*

He knew who she was now. And he wanted her still, but he wasn't happy about that. Or...Asha's eyes fell on his hand buried beneath his legs, the hands that had been slipping periodically into his pocket. What if part of him was caught? What if he was here against his will? But not in his father's hold, in hers?

Was that what he was thinking?

Asha forced out the air that wanted to lift her up like a bit of silk in the breeze and carry her away from such fears. She forced it out and settled on the roof, trying again. "Why did you come home?"

Azize looked into the distance. "I didn't feel ready to return, but I felt... pulled back." He twitched like he would reach for his pocket. "When I was traveling, I don't think I knew what I was doing at first, but I was gathering men. Men who were stronger than me. Men who were not his. Men to protect me from him, or to..." Azize shrugged. And Asha knew what the rest of his words would have been and she was half impressed and half appalled. Treason! He was casually discussing overthrowing his father. Ethee Uvaasha!

"Do you think fifteen men is enough?" The words sprayed out of her mouth with amused shock. Azize glared.

"I am sorry." She laughed with the lie. She wasn't certain what she was, but it wasn't sorry. This was her father's friend he was discussing overthrowing, and she couldn't think of a single reason why he would want to. But she could imagine her father applauding such a move. Baba liked bold men, and he'd never thought of Azize that way.

"I said I *wasn't* ready," Azize bit out. He shook his head. "I've never told any of them my thoughts. They weren't really plans, just thoughts. Well, I have told Noam, but Noam is different. He'll follow me anywhere. When I told him, he just smiled. He didn't think I meant it. He thought I was waiting for word my father had died or changed. He asked me how many more men I needed—*to feel safe when you see him?* Those were his words."

Asha reached out and grasped Azize's hand. She'd never realized he felt unsafe. She squeezed his hand gently, sorry now.

"I should not have mocked. What did he do to make you afraid?"

Azize just stared at her for several moments, examining her like she was a foreign land. "Are you a different person? Or am I? Or is this bond only the magic? Do you think we will like each other at all if the magic goes away?"

Asha drew her child's hand back into her lap and bit her lip. The words a punch of pain, acknowledging that fear that she'd begun to have.

"It will be gone at midnight." Asha had been so...hopeful. So sure that his desire to find her and his enthusiasm for her were like her own for him. That this would be love, again. But it seemed love of this kind was different from the love she'd known. Nothing she had ever said would have shaken Baba's love. But Azize was angry with her after only a few hours alone. And as much as she wanted to blame it all on his weaker feelings, she could not. She'd hurt him, however unintentional. She hated the feeling.

"I am truly sorry, Azize. I did not...I do not always realize how my words hurt people. Please forgive me."

Azize shrugged. "It was not so great an offense, it only reminded me."

"Of how I was as a child." She looked at the hands of the child she was wearing now. "How I was five hours ago." She fingered her gown wonderingly. "Hadhi gave me this. Not knowing me at all, she dried my tears and encouraged me not to give up on winning you."

Azize chuckled hard. "Hadhi has not hidden that she has no desire to be my bride."

"That was not why she said it." Asha shook her head, annoyed. It seemed he wasn't much better at listening than her. And she didn't like the smile he wore when he spoke of Hadhi. There was no past complicating his feelings for her. Asha almost didn't speak again, because the words she meant to say were complementary, and Hadhi was apparently still a rival for Azize's affections. Though, as he said, Hadhi wanted none of it.

"Zawadi said I had never met my sister, and she was right. There is a kindness in her I never knew. And perhaps my not seeing it is more her fault than my own, but...a bit of it is my fault." Asha plopped her elbows on her knees, her chin atop her hands, and stared into the distance, angry and guilty and confused. Azize had been in her life, at the periphery, but in it since she was a child. She'd seen his fear and his desire to run away, but she had never wondered why.

Though Asha's mind could not conjure a reason to hate the genial king, the fact that Azize could must say something.

You saw what your father wanted you to see.

"Who is Zawadi?"

Asha glanced over. Tonight was nowhere near as fun as last night. She should have stayed on the ship with him or led him off into the wild. Last night, she'd felt so alive as she led him around the palace. She'd devoured his stories like they were her own adventures. She'd basked in stealing his attention from Hadhi and Jauhar. All of it had made her feel powerful. But tonight she was embracing the magic more and the reality of Azize and the possibility of a future and...it was different. He was pulling her out of her joy in the magic, where yesterday he'd fed it.

She felt heavy. And she didn't want to. She would only have this power for a short while more.

Asha pushed her hands against the roof and floated up into the air. She noticed her cousin Shafira open the mansion gate for a man and close it furtively behind him, but ignored it.

She grinned at Azize. "She is the nymph who granted my wish for power." Asha called out to the other creatures in the night with her power. At once, she heard the answering growls and shouts of animals who felt her from within the jungle. "It is a marvelous gift. I don't know that I will ever feel quite myself when this is gone, but...I was not lying when I said I want to know you, Azize. All of you. I am here with you, only talking, though my blood longs to be nations away or swimming with whales. I am trying. Won't you do the same? Tell me what your father did. Or tell me why you left when you did. Tell me anything."

NOT MADE TO BE LOVED

"There is no such thing as love, Monster, not for creatures like us."

"Rama loved me," Hadhi said. Such a soft rebellion, barely above a whisper, but Baba was not having even that.

His cruelty ate away at her. "Rama never knew you. Not like I do. Did she? She didn't even care to," he pressed when Hadhi failed to answer. "Rama hated me and saw you as a way to punish me, by making you hate me too, but..." he laughed. "That would only matter to someone who wanted love from you. Someone who thought you were capable of it."

Hadhi's stomach turned, and tears clenched their claws into the backs of her eyes. But Baba was not finished. She was still standing. He never walked away from one of his victims until they were dead. Even if they walked away after.

"If Rama had known the real monster you keep inside, she would have hated you as much as she ever did me. Maybe more."

It's alright, Hadhi, I lo—

Hadhi cut Noam's echo off. Her feet pounded across the ground. She had left her sandals on the road somewhere back in Jaccada. They were only slowing her down, and she could not slow down. She could not stop. If she stopped, the words would crawl inside her. If she stopped, she would want to believe them. If she stopped, her heart would break open and destroy her again.

She could not let that happen. She had been destroyed too many times already.

She laughed as she ran, no soft tinkling sound, like her mother made, or Asha. No. Her laughter sounded like a scream, like an animal cry. Like rage.

How could he say that? How dare he?

How did he fail to see she...Hadhi was not made to be loved? She was not made to have peace inside. She did not want one more person to claim they loved her when all they would do in the end was leave. All they would want, when they knew the real her, was to use her ugliness for their ends.

He did not love her. He could not. It was not even possible. Noam had never met her.

So Hadhi's feet pounded the ground, hard. Not for speed, but for the pain. She could run faster with softer feet. She was good at it. Baba said once that there were only two animals faster than Hadhi at a hunt, a cheetah and himself. But right now, she did not care about speed, she cared to remind herself with each pounding foot that Noam did not know her.

She raced across the hard earth and her eyes saw other days of racing. Saw the shuddering llooma blossoms, and the shifting of the tall grasses. She ran and her eyes saw the past. How silent she was, how her body shook the grasses far wider than her prey, but only in the same path. She ran, and she remembered blood spattered across caverns and hill sides. Felt its warmth on her skin, as her knife sunk into the notch between skull and neck, severing spinal cords, before slipping away in the darkness.

It was always dark, the ground cooling, the air quiet. It was always dark —when she hunted people.

Noam did not know her. He would not love her if he did.

The sands stirred and a ghost of a moment formed around her, so she ran through it, reliving it.

"Hadhi? That is your name, yes?" Queen Imara's head lay bent over the lip of her tub. She was not strong enough to hold it up on her own. Hadhi rolled up a soft cloth and lifted the queen's head gently, laying it between her and the tub.

"Ka," Hadhi agreed simply.

Asha was meant to be the queen's second attendant as she was nursed back to health. But the queen had sent her away and had Hadhi alone bathe her. Asha was not to see certain things. Not to see the marks on the queen's wrist. Nor the scars on her ankles and across her back. She was not to see anything that might challenge her beautiful view of the world. But Hadhi was strong. She could lift a weakened queen, who was four inches taller than her and heavy from exhaustion. She could see the marks on the queen's wrist and know that she had not simply fallen ill, but that she had chosen to die and been stopped. Hadhi could see the long-healed scars from the shackles the queen had worn in the first years of her marriage without it breaking her, because

Hadhi already saw the world as a place of ugliness. Hadhi, quiet, obedient, ugly Hadhi could be trusted to see all the horrors in the world and keep moving.

"Rama said you were special. Resilient. She said I would have wanted you for one of my warriors," the queen laughed, and tears fled her eyes. "One more child I could fail."

Hadhi moved around the tub, cleaning the queen with a soft cloth. She let her cry. She should be allowed her pains, Hadhi thought. Too often, Hadhi had bit her tongue to stop the tears that wanted to pour out of her. If the queen wanted to cry, she should. Hadhi watched the woman come undone with sadness and marveled at the beauty of it. The beauty of how strongly she still loved, despite all the king's attempts to kill the softness inside of her. It was magnificent how hard she clung to her love.

"Rama said," Hadhi whispered, when the queen's tears quieted, "Iotic tubaetelle mur nong teoupa. Uli uro bam tubaetelle." Being defeated is not failure. You were only defeated.

The queen raised her head slightly so her eyes could take in Hadhi.

"I worried when Rama died that Zuberi would undo all she tried to teach you. I worried, when he sent you, that you were here as his enforcer."

*Hadhi looked away. She was here to nurse the queen back to health. She was here to "*be certain she does not die," *those were her father's instructions.*

She was here as Baba's enforcer.

Hadhi lay aside the cloth and moved to retrieve a bowl of warming water from the fire to rinse the queen. But Imara's hand shot out. She gripped Hadhi tighter than she had appeared to have the strength for a moment ago.

"Have you killed for him, child?"

Hadhi tried to shake the queen off, but her grip was like iron. "Have you?" she repeated.

Hadhi nodded. Thinking the queen would release her now. But she did not. She tugged, brought Hadhi back to her knees beside the tub.

"To what end? Do you not hate him?"

Yes. *She hated Baba. But Hadhi's heart pounded in fear. Did she want Hadhi to kill him? Would she ask Hadhi to murder her own father? Perhaps the king as well. She wanted Hadhi for a soldier as Rama had said she would. Like Baba. All anyone wanted of her was death.*

"To what end?" the queen asked again. Her voice did not raise, but her intensity did. Her body shook the water in the tub, making it slosh and splash Hadhi.

"He told me to. So I did," Hadhi said. But she knew it was not true. Was not complete. There was something missing in her words, but she did not know what.

She had killed men for her father. Men he said were evil. Men he said were harming children. And Hadhi had not questioned it, because...the world was ugly. People were ugly. Again and again, she had seen that. She had killed because Baba called it a test. A chance to prove she could escape when she killed her real enemy. But never did he let her kill Enzi. And Hadhi waited. Hadhi did only what her father told her to do. Killed only who he told her to kill. As if her hand was not her own. As if the blood upon it did not touch her.

The queen was regarding Hadhi deeply. Seeking something. And whatever she sought, she did not find. Her hand released Hadhi's wrist and she fell back, out of energy again.

Perhaps she saw what Hadhi felt in this moment, what she had felt before but shoved away. That the blood did touch her. That it always had. The blood drenched her. Coated her in the stench of death.

"No soldier of mine was ever asked to kill for my will alone," Queen Imara spoke, confirming Hadhi's fear. She did see. Everyone must. "They were only asked to kill for their own conscience. To kill those who would harm them."

"You wish me to kill the king?" Hadhi whispered the question in Fairy, terrified of being overheard.

The queen laughed softly. "No, child. I have tried. My warriors have tried. He does not seem it, but the king is well *protected. It is you who would die from such an endeavor. And not quickly. Some other girl would sit beside some other tub, nursing you back into a life you do not want. Again, and again, and again. They will send you to me again. You must know this. I will live for now. But I will try again, and again, they will send you, to make* you *small. To make you a part of my suffering. Until I will hate you as much as them, merely for keeping me living. Until you will hate yourself for the same reason. If you tried to kill the king, you would only assure that the same was true of you. No. I do not want you to kill him." She released a heavy breath, shutting her eyes. "I want you to let me die."*

Hadhi stumbled onto her behind. She did not know why allowing a woman to die should feel worse to her than murder, but it did. She wanted her to go on living. She wanted her to heal. She wanted her to be the pillar of strength Rama had spoken of, the queen who would rescue them all. She did not want this woman to die.

The queen shifted in the bath, turned to her side, towards the window and the night, and Hadhi saw the scars on her back. Some from blades, some wrinkled up from tongues of flame, her body a terrible portrait of suffering. And not all of it old. There was bruising on her thighs and a stab wound on her back that had yet to heal. Her torture apparently unending. Still the woman's request horrified Hadhi.

"As long as I am alive, they will wait for my rescue. For I was a fierce warrior. When your father and his men came for me, I killed ten and wounded many more. I wounded him. Stabbed my blade into him. But not deep enough to touch the sour soul within. I was defeated. Szii iom tubaetelle. Yet my warriors wait. They look on me and are sure I can rescue them. They allow themselves to be beaten down more each day. Do not be your father's enforcer today. Be the quiet girl Rama praised. Let me die, so they can rise. Please."

Hadhi could not say a word. She crossed to the fire and brought back the bowl of warming water. Her hands stung from how hot the bowl was. But she could not bring herself to set it down. She looked on the queen and heard her words over and over in her head. And her father's echo chasing after it.

Rama said I would want you for one of my warriors.

Rama hated me and she saw you as a way to punish me. If she'd known the real you, she would have hated you as much as she ever did me.

Hadhi's hands began to burn. She should set the bowl down. She should cool it before she used it to rinse the queen. She should tell her father exactly what the woman said. She should make sure she lived. Rama had wanted her to live. Hadhi wanted her to live. Everyone saw her and wanted her strength and were inspired by it.

Hadhi set the bowl down. She lifted a cool pitcher and poured a bit into the hot water, tempering it.

"Please," the queen repeated. "You do not need to do anything. Just leave me alone, I will do the rest. Please. Let me die."

Hadhi returned to the tub and gently rinsed the queen with the warm water. She set the bowl aside and went to a stool to retrieve a drying blanket. Behind her, she heard the queen begin to cry.

"Please. Rama said you were strong. Please. No one will know. They will never know." She hiccuped and her tears returned.

With a blanket draped over her shoulder, Hadhi bent and slipped her arms beneath the queen's, lifting her to her feet. Hadhi lifted her over the lip of the tub. When her feet touched the floor, Hadhi closed the blanket around the queen. She sobbed, shaking in Hadhi's arms. Hadhi held on, rubbing circles in the woman's back, remembering when she had held Rama this way.

"Please," Queen Imara sobbed into Hadhi's shoulder. "Do not let them use me to bring my son home. Do not let them use me to keep my people quiet. Please."

Hadhi carried the woman to her bed and helped her to dry, her hands soft as they pulled the absorbent blanket around the wounds on the woman's ankles. She recalled the first time she had seen the scars on Rama's hip and thigh. The giant slashes healed over but in no way concealing the violence of what had been done to her. By Baba.

Hadhi's vision felt fuzzy, the world mottled from the tears in her eyes. She lifted her gaze to the queen. Their eyes locked, both wet with tears, both seeking. It might have gone on forever, but Hadhi heard her sister returning. Hadhi rose from the bed and retrieved the long tunic. She helped the queen slip into it.

"I will do it," Hadhi whispered as she held the woman near, smoothing the cloth down her back. "I know ways they cannot stop. Uli kamko dzao." You will rest.

The queen gasped and her tears dried. She pulled Hadhi near and kissed her cheek, before settling back on the bed and allowing Hadhi to lift a blanket to cover her from toe to throat before Asha could see a thing.

Hadhi never knew why the woman believed her. Why those words soothed her so well that she lay back with a smile. Why she allowed Asha to feed her and drifted to sleep with no worries. There should have been no reason for her to trust that Hadhi would help her. But she did.

Although, Hadhi supposed, if the something you wanted was ugly, who else would you trust?

Her faith was even justified. As Hadhi slipped into the room in the middle of the night and sliced the tiniest cut into the less sensitive skin from her shackle scars, not even waking the queen as she deposited the snake venom into her blood. Ending her life before she could wake. She had sat beside her until her breathing stopped, the whole while holding her hand and trying to give herself the courage to sneak out the window to the king's suite and do the same to him. But when Imara's breath hitched and faltered entirely, Hadhi was still too afraid. So she merely slipped into the night, past the little blue and white bird that sang softly on the window ledge, unaware of the monster that had visited the queen.

AWAKENED FEARS

Noam returned indoors, away from the disquieting insects. Hadhi had long since faded from his view, but in his mind's eye, he saw still her cloud of hair wafting up and down as she ran and the wind billowing out the layers of her gown like it was being tugged at by hands of air. He saw her racing away, swirling waves of sand rising behind her, and another image slipped beneath it in his mind. The woven basket drifting out to sea. It seemed that Hadhi ran alongside it, moving so fast her feet could not sink beneath the waves. It seemed as though she would leave with it and never return.

When manhood dawns one fateful May
Then he as well must fly away.

His heart jerked painfully, fear threatening to drag him into the past. Always the people he loved were racing away as he stood by, watching them leave.

He felt a buzz, as if the mayflies had followed him—*then he as well must fly away*—but he knew it was his own imagination and fought off a shudder. He caught sight of Tadeo across the room with a small group of locals. He made his way over though there were so many other things he would prefer to be doing: chasing after Hadhi. Figuring out what exactly he'd danced with in her sister's body *I have had it and will keep it for as long as it was lent to me.* That didn't sound safe, particularly because it had seemed she was after Hadhi or her family *I have a debt to settle.* He ought to be figuring out what that was. Or finding Azize—Killing the king.

But the buzzing filled his mind, and he saw dead mayflies showering him and he felt his heart constrict realizing that it had been May when he left Glen Harrow.

He'd intentionally not thought about it then, put it out of his mind, planning to leave that unpleasantness behind him. But it had been May, May four years ago.

No. It wasn't real. And he knew better than to follow instincts whose impetus was fear. He needed to take his time and find his calm.

Tadeo was always a comforting presence. Noam could use that at the moment. Could use the distraction.

Tadeo was laughing as Noam walked up. "This is the third tunic I've worn today. The others were so damp with sweat when I removed them they actually dripped."

The pair of women laughed and the young man with them nodded.

"It is quite warm," the elder of the two women agreed. "I suppose May is nearly gone, but still I do not look forward to the height of summer."

Stayed the mayfly for a spell

In springtime when the evening fell.

"Noam." Tadeo's tap on Noam's shoulder was far more startling than it should have been. "Ahh. I can see from your dazed expression that the heat had gotten to you as well," Tadeo said lightly but Noam was sure Tadeo knew this distraction was from more than heat. Tadeo was simply skilled at pretending ease. Usually, Noam was as well. It was how they'd first formed a bond.

"It was somewhat stifling. Even with the night cooling the air." Noam strove to be his lighter self. "But who are we to complain, we did not stand beneath the sun all day in that endless line. Has it been fully exhausted? I've not seen Azize yet."

"He is through with the line," the male in the group remarked flatly. "But the promised reward does not seem to be forthcoming."

Noam recognized him suddenly. He'd been the cheetah dancer last night. The one who taunted Hadhi. Knowing she'd been mauled by a cheetah. Noam had come here for ease but felt his blood boiling with only more anger. The woman beside him looked embarrassed. She'd been one of the dancers too, the desert, Noam thought. She'd done beautifully, so powerful and entrancing. He should focus on that.

"You were both among the Spirit Dancers, I believe." Noam changed the subject because his mind wanted to get stuck on the young man's words and be angry at him, or with his friend for having disappeared. But he knew that it was the situation as a whole that bothered him.

It was Hadhi's pain that was bothering him. And his growing fear that he could do nothing to help her.

"Are you a dancer as well?" he asked the last member of the party. She was likely in her later sixties, but he had noticed a wide variety in the dancers, and with some thirty on the floor, it would have been easy to miss one.

"I do not perform among them often." The woman shook her head. "But I lead them in their exaltations. I am Eshe."

"It is my honor to meet you." Noam bowed slightly. He did not know the name, but the way she said it implied she held great status. Leading the Spirit Dancers was surely an important position. And she accepted his bow as if it was due to her.

"If you lead them, does that mean you designed the performance yesterday? It was inspiring."

"I did." She smiled benevolently. "I am always proud when my work is realized and the dancers perform so well you can see the great spirits through them and feel their glory. As they surely did yesterday."

"Oh, they most certainly did," Tadeo agreed. "When you danced the desert goddess—"

"Ether," the young woman, whose name escaped Noam though they had met last night, provided when Tadeo paused.

"Yes..." Tadeo went on talking, but Noam hardly heard him.

"What do you find spectacular?"

"Ether," Hadhi blurted out as if rushing to cover her pause.

"The vast desert that swallows up all who enter it?" Noam asked, equal parts amused by her and concerned for her.

"No one has ever returned from it. They could be dead, or in the next life. Or— Maybe she freed them. Maybe they are happy."

Was that where Hadhi was running to? Would it free her? He should want that—no—he did. He did want that for her. She should escape. She should be free. He just...wished he hadn't frightened her. Wished he could stop seeing her running away from him again and again.

The world did not pause for Noam to be distracted. Tadeo was spewing flattery about feeling welcomed by the goddess herself.

The young woman laughed softly. "Not too welcomed, I hope. Ether embraces the spirits of the dead and holds them in her care. She loves the living of course, but if she welcomes you, then you are not long for this life."

Tadeo laughed, spouting yet more nonsense trepidation over the welcome and the others played along. Usually, Noam would play along as well, but he could not. He only saw again and again the woven basket that had dragged his mother's dead body out to sea and Hadhi running alongside it.

Before Noam could do as he was imagining and make a quick escape, the young woman stopped him.

"You are Hadhi's friend, yes? It is pleasing to see her form friends. She has always seemed isolated. But perhaps...her father was a force to say the least."

"Faizah," the young man hissed a warning. But the woman ignored him. The elder woman regarded the young woman with interest she had shown in nothing else.

"Perhaps without his presence she can join the world a bit more. Perhaps all his children can. I hope so."

"So do I," Noam said softly, but a shudder shook him as he heard the buzzing again. And the lines of the song taunted him.

> *He sought a woman's company*
> *And built for her a fantasy...*
> *They lived a lifetime in a May.*
> *But dawned the June he'd flown away.*

Noam thought of his mother and Hadhi and fantasies. Was that all this was? Was he doomed to leave her behind with May's end? Leaving her life worse off than before she met him. Hated by her neighbors, raising the child of a man who'd abandoned her. Sea Spirits but he hated that song. He'd thought he could not hate it any more than he had as a child, but he was so wrong.

And left behind his progeny
To grow in clouds of mystery,
Unknowing of his nature deep;
Of planting seeds that others reap
When manhood dawns one fateful May—
Then he as well must fly away.

He couldn't let it come true. He couldn't be...that. He would prove this was more than a fantasy, and he was more than just a product of a magic spell. He needed to find that fey creature!

"If you will all excuse me," Noam said, offering another bow to the group. "I must go check on our wayward prince, perhaps he has slipped and fallen on sweat from his own tunic."

Most everyone laughed, but Tadeo watched him curiously, his eyes asking for explanation. But Noam had none for him. He had no explanations for anything yet, all he had was a certainty...a hope? A fervent wish. That he was not a Mayfly. That this was not a fantasy.

THE STRONGEST MAN ALIVE

Kane had not expected the small shiver of fear that raced down his spine when he found the king alone. Nor the prodding charge that kept twitching his right hand open, leaving his burned skin constantly visible. The burns on his hands anyway. The king knew him to be Zuberi's man. He had met with him yesterday to give him his report but had not even finished half of it before he was dismissed so the man could consult with his staff about the ball.

The king seemed not to like Kane. Or at least not to trust him. He wouldn't look directly at him, but it did not feel like fear. Kane could sense fear. That was not what kept the king from meeting his eye. But he did not know what did.

Tonight was different. As soon as the king dismissed the young woman who'd been with him, against her will if her looks were indicative of anything, he met Kane's eyes with a bright smile. And that shiver raced down Kane's back.

He remembered Zuberi saying Enzi was not a man to fear, but nor was he one to underestimate.

"You are eager to be in my presence." The king laughed. "You will find me not as easy to manipulate as my son."

Kane had learned to give nothing away in expression unless he wished it. He shrugged at the king's puzzling words. Was the man disturbed that Kane had spied *for him*?

"I do not recall much manipulation was required."

"How dull for you. What plans have you now that Zuberi is dead?" He behaved as though Kane had not worked for him.

"To serve my king, as Zuberi would have." Kane tilted up his head. This was not a man to back down with. And he meant to make Kane work.

"And you think following my son around is a worthwhile service?" He chuckled. "Zuberi killed and manipulated and conspired for me. You have been a nursemaid to an errant child."

"I have been far more than that. Any knowledge Zuberi gave you about foreign nations came from me. Any assassinations made in the lands the prince visited were carried out by me. And every plot your son was invited to join against you was thwarted by me. As were several attempts on his life. I watched him, yes, because it was my duty. But that was not all I did."

Enzi clapped derisively. His eyes fell on Kane's flexing right hand and his smile widened. "I marveled at Zuberi. But never for what he thought were his greatest skills. He prided himself on being the strongest beast. But any man can kill." Kane jerked internally, feeling the words like a blow. "Any man can be made so hungry that he would devour his own child only to survive the next hour." He felt the blow again. "But no one understood human nature like him." The king stopped in front of Kane, lifting Kane's scarred hand into both of his own.

An angry charge raced from his hand up his arm, rattling through his jaw with the urge to clench his teeth. To growl. To strike. But Enzi must not know. Which meant he was allowed to gently trace his finger along the burn scars on Kane's skin and smile that wicked grin of his while Kane fought off the screaming voices in the back of his mind. Fought off the shuddering frigid skin of memory that wanted to settle around him, as the king basked in his own power.

Kane! Kane, help. Aaaa! Help! HELP!"

"No other man could light a child on fire and then have that same child beg to learn from him, beg to serve him, and earn his approval." Enzi's voice was soft and full of such admiration, it nearly sounded loving, and his finger continued brushing over Kane's palm, spreading a chill beneath the skin. It crawled inside so that Kane knew he would feel it, again and again and again. The brush of evil Enzi was allowed to spread.

You cannot think of Enzi as you do me. Not if you ever mean to defeat him. It is only ever fear that drives him. He is so in love with fear that as much as he ever seeks to cause it, he also seeks out beings to cause fear in him. He loves both equally.

Kane yanked his hand back and stepped around the king. "I begged for nothing. I merely bided my time, until I found my moment to slip away from your son and take Zuberi's heart out."

Now Enzi really laughed, loud and wildly entertained. "Come boy, make up better lies. His heart was quite intact when he was found."

"It was a figurative statement. The man had no heart to take." Kane clenched his hands into fists. That was a foolish lie.

For all he knew, the king had killed Zuberi. But...he couldn't believe Zuberi had been right. Kane had never thought to actively fear the king, but when he was alone in his presence, there was a power emanating from him, seeking to make Kane feel like the frightened child he'd been years ago. And *succeeding!* He didn't want to know what more Enzi would do to destroy that child.

"If he stood in front of you now, and I asked you to rip his heart out, you would not. It is the same for all of you. No one knew so well how to engender fierce unbreakable loyalty—and from the very creatures he destroyed!" Enzi's laughter shook the gardens.

"Believe what you will about Zuberi's death. But...a wise man would hear what I have to say of your son's compatriots."

"Fifteen broken soldiers do not exactly make me tremble," the king sneered. Crossing to a bench, he waved for Kane to continue. "But you want to prove your worth so badly, what do you know?"

"You, Your Majesty, are widely hated. Many nations are willing to send out young men to pretend great love for your son as a way of reaching you."

"Do you know of any such men among them?"

"I do. Tadeo was raised an assassin. Gatik has sold his sword to nations and criminals alike. Omar was banished from his nation after he killed seven members of the royal family. And Elof began merely as a soldier, but in one battle he killed so many men they called him the beast of Goff. When their leader was crowned king, he feared him so that he took out a bounty for his head. Your son..." Kane tightened his throat against any show of emotion. He hated the man before him for himself, and his people, but also for Azize. Enzi should die. He would die for Kane's plans, and so must Azize, but only one of them deserved it. "Makes a habit of gathering murders with no home to return to and treating them as family."

"And do any of this *family,*" the king mocked, "know you know of their pasts and their plans?"

"They know me to be one of the family, ready to slay my king so that another can take his place."

Enzi chuckled. "It is pleasing at last to see some strength in Azize. Though he will surely fail to overthrow me."

Kane hated the anger that flared in him, hearing Azize praised for his strength. The plan had been all Kane's. He was merely saying these things to get on Enzi's good side. Kane didn't need the assassins Azize had gathered. Not to kill Enzi. He would do it alone. *Kane* was Zuberi's *perfect killer*.

"I was advised that one of the men he traveled with was after my head." Enzi ran his hand along the hilt of his sword. "The stones are wary of Azize's smiley confidant."

"Noam?" Kane could not conceal his derision. "You have focused on the only one among them who is no killer. He is merely your son's favorite pet."

"An appearance of harmlessness is an effective way to conceal a spy. You would not understand this having been trained by Zuberi. He hated to appear anything less than the strongest man in the room. Hated me every time I gave an order that reminded him who was stronger. You could be right, this Noam may not be after my head. It might yet prove to be you. But I will not be caught, because I have always known to distrust appearances."

"I will prove myself. If you want Noam's head, I will bring it to you, and every other assassin your son brought home."

"What good are their heads when I do not trust you? But you may bring them to me—whole." He chuckled "And you said Zuberi had no heart. You left your first family to burn, and you will lead these to bleed. So hungry." The king grinned, looking quite hungry himself. "It is moments like these that I most miss Zuberi. The things he could have taught me."

Kane's right hand jerked. He could hear the screams so clearly. Could smell the burning flesh. He was not afraid. But...as Enzi's gaze traveled over him, Kane felt that same missing. He wished Zuberi were here. Watching him. He wished he could have been here to see Kane become the strongest man alive. Because he would. That was all his existence amounted to.

THE RUNAWAY PRINCE

Azize snorted bitterly at Asha's question, but his small smile returned. "I left when I did because…he let me. I told him I would study other nations, to learn their weaknesses. He liked that, so he let me go." His tone slowly darkened. "By then, I had learned to tell him what he wanted to hear. But it was a lie, I was running away, the same as ever. I'd intended never to come home." He smirked at Asha, and it was an unpleasant expression, reminding her of the resentments he held for her. "Certainly not to stay."

"But?" Asha gasped when he just let his statement hang there. Was he not here to stay?

"But?" he prompted her to continue. Asha didn't know if it was because she was in the body of a child, or if knowing her for her true self had weakened his regard, but he wasn't looking at her with warm, enraptured feelings. He looked at her like he couldn't see her. But he had to. *He would know her anywhere.*

"Do you mean to stay now?" Asha pressed.

Azize's hand crawled out from beneath his leg and found the slipper. And Asha was bereft. Last night when she had hidden in the bushes watching him hold that slipper, she had felt it under her skin. Felt it as though he was holding her. But she had held the other slipper then, the slipper that had vanished from Jauhar's box of treasure where Asha had hidden it. Asha couldn't feel what he was feeling, she couldn't feel his touch like she was treasure, like she was precious. She could only look out of a stranger's eyes and watch the runaway prince quivering with fear at the idea of coming home to stay.

"What if I said no? What if I asked you to leave with me? Would you?" He looked up. Right at her, and Asha gasped, because that she could feel and it was lovely.

He was unsure of her, that was all. The magic, and his lifetime of doubting, and their fraught childhood were rearing up to frighten him.

Asha nodded again and again. "Of course! I would love to travel the world with you."

"Even if I meant never to come home?" he pressed.

"Not even once your father is dead? Not even to be king?" Asha asked, not because her answer would change, but—Who would lead Maltuba? These were his people. Did he not love them?

Azize notched up his head. "Maybe not. Tell me honestly, Asha, have you even once thought of me as your future king? Did you ever fear that day? They didn't." Azize waved to the city, but Asha followed his hand and noticed more men emerge from the shadows to enter the mansion courtyard. What was Uncle Kafil up to?

"See!" Azize waved a hand before her face. "Even now you think me too weak to lead. Just as my father sees me. Why would I want to rule here?"

"Because they don't see you so." Asha rolled her eyes, she'd been distracted a mere moment. "And because it is your birthright. Not just from your father, from your *mother* as well."

"*My mother,*" he snarled, looking like a different man. "All of you invoke *my mother* trying to control me. As though she belonged to you. *Your* indomitable, forbearing queen. *Your* symbol. She didn't belong to you! Or to my father. She had her own life! She was ten years older than he, married, and the leader of the Tikoo when yo—" He faltered. His eyes took Asha in as though her presence was a shock and the rage fell out of him. When he spoke again, his words were flat, heavy, and—not what he'd started to say. "When she was stolen from her people so my father could use her to crush them."

Asha was horrified. How could that possibly be so? "No. She...It wasn't a union of love, but she *agreed* to be his bride as part of a peace treaty—"

"That was years later, Asha!" Azize snarled, tearing his eyes away from her. His words remained tight, as if his rage had not in fact left him as she'd thought but simply been concealed. "Your queen had been thoroughly defeated when she agreed to that treaty. Two years after my birth. Did you never consider what that time was for her?"

Asha was taken aback. It had honestly never occurred to her that the treaty had not been signed before he was born. A rushing sickness began to grow in her gut, but she couldn't speak, and Azize filled the void.

"She was held as a captive, chained up like an animal! She only agreed to be his queen to stop the violence against her people."

"I...I cannot believe my father would be a part of that," Asha whispered, not trying to fight him, just disbelieving. The king was Baba's closest friend. A man he'd brought Asha to meet. Baba taught Asha to exert *her* will, to pursue *her* desires. He would never be a party to treating a woman as though she had no self. "He must not have known. He couldn't have called such a man his friend."

"Your father was his enforcer." Azize looked like he wanted to shake her.

"Anything he did, he did in service to his king and to keep our nation safe!" Asha shook with her growing intensity. Her heart raced and her eyes ached. It was all lies. Either Azize lied, or Enzi had lied to him. But Baba wasn't like that. Baba *wouldn't* have befriended a man like that.

"You cannot be the only person in Maltuba who doesn't know what my father is. What *your* father was," Azize growled. His hands were fisted against the roof now, one grasping the slipper tight. He didn't look at all loverly or worried as she floated further and further away from him. "He was a brute."

"No." Asha refused to believe him. She heard a great rumble in the distance and felt clouds forming overhead, but barely noticed, too intent on this argument.

"He beat and stole, and terrified and murdered, in his king's name. But he *enjoyed* doing it."

"No!"

"You say you want to know me, but you don't," Azize shouted angrily.

Last night he had been so sweet. He had wanted to feed her hunger for adventure and her laughter, her joy. Now he wanted to rip it away.

"Noam was right, wasn't he?" Azize asked in a low growl. "This is all a game for you? Did my father put you up to this?"

"What?" Asha gasped.

"I half convinced myself that you had changed, but you haven't. You were always so confident, so..." He lost his words, raising his hands into the air and shaking them before her in frustration. "This is some spell, isn't it? You and my father are trying to mix me up until I stay. Until I am one more creature he's dominated."

"Why would *I* do that?" Asha shouted back, as angry as he was now. "Until last night, I never even liked you."

"For your *baba's friend*," Azize fired back in a bitter tone. "Either you are a part of one of his games or..."

"Or what?" Asha challenged. "What reason do I have to be wasting my hours of magic on someone who doesn't like me *as I am?* I should have had bigger dreams. I should have wished to see the world, but I wished to get to know you."

"No. You didn't," Azize snarled. "You wished for *magic*. And you are using it to drive me mad. You don't even want to know the truth, so how can you want to know me? Maltuba isn't the precious jewel you think it is. You should run as far from it as you can get, because eventually one of those people your father helped mine crush will want to crush you for their vengeance."

Asha was crying, shaking. Shrinking. His rage was crawling inside of her and making her feel weak. Like he was stealing magic through the slipper he was crushing. Like they were switching places.

He meant himself, didn't he? *He* wanted to crush her. He wanted vengeance for something he blamed Baba for but hadn't even the character to tell her what it was.

"They will? Or you will? You didn't know my father," Asha insisted. "You're afraid to face your father. Afraid to call this your home. Afraid to rule. My father kept Maltuba safe and you don't think you can. That's why you're lashing out at me, because I'm challenging you to face your fears. Because I can see the beauty here that you don't want to."

Azize's eyes darkened, nearly vanishing for a moment as his irises expanded and his suppressed rage emerged. "You don't think I wanted to love my home? To love my father? All my life I've been jealous of you and your willful ignorance. I'd watch your father and mine beat some man into submission while you were playing in the gardens. When they had cleared him away, you'd run in asking about the menagerie or the library or the cheetah head on my father's wall! I wanted to strangle you. How could you spend your whole life beside a monster and never know what he was?"

"He wasn't a *monster!*" Asha shouted so loud she saw it shaking the ground. "You didn't know him. My father was a great man! He loved us, he loved Maltuba. You are just a frightened boy who doesn't want to face what must be done to keep him safe."

"You cannot mean that," Azize demanded shaking his head. "You're just angry because you didn't want to know this truth. Come back here, talk to me," Azize ordered.

Asha's eyes flashed. "Why would I do anything with you if you cannot see any beauty in the home and the people I love. Who *all* love me—*and my father?*"

Azize was panting but couldn't seem to force out words, and Asha couldn't wait a moment longer for him to speak.

"You want to run away so badly, just go." Asha waved an arm and Azize vanished, back to the ship she'd made for him. Asha sobbed. It was all lies. All of it. Baba was a great man.

Asha shook and shook, crying and aching and longing for the love she'd been missing. But she wouldn't be getting that from Azize. She would never have it again, would she?

She just missed Baba so much.

WITH JAGGED HEART

Sade had led Nuru to a group that included Sade's mother, Nia, a few Spirit Dancers, and Abiola. They were all talking about Hadhi—and the king. *What did this mean? He hadn't favored anyone so specifically in a long while.* That sort of thing. And with every word, Nuru sunk into herself. She was desperate to break away, but to where? It appeared everyone in the room was talking about Hadhi. Nuru would find no relief. Or so she thought until Omi, who on any other occasion Nuru would have ignored, broke into the conversation.

"It was a dance," she mocked. "You are all making a bit much of it. She is Zuberi's eldest daughter, she was in the palace a great deal when she cared for the queen. King Enzi was likely just coming up with some task for her to get their family out of that hut. Everyone knows he has always meant for Asha to marry Azize, but it wouldn't do for them to be living at the edge of Ether like outcasts when it happened."

"Kafil was seated beside the king yesterday," Abiola conceded. "They could have been making plans." She looked at Sade as if for answers, but Sade, who usually appeared fairly intelligent, blinked as if she hadn't heard a word. Was she hiding something? Abiola went on. "Why wait until now?"

"The king is capricious, uncaring for anything not in his view." Omi shrugged.

"A king's work is never done." Nia's loud comment seemed to be an attempt to excuse Omi's remarks. She looked meaningfully over her left shoulder where Vaasht Oba was emerging from one of the inner palace halls.

At once the conversation shifted to sort of things Nuru would have preferred when she first joined them. Discussions of who Azize might favor, some even remembering that Hadhi had caught his eyes. Perhaps that was why the king danced with her, to approve of his son's choice.

Nuru let them talk around her. There was no saying the king wanted anything to do with Hadhi at all. He was Baba's friend, of course he would dance with his daughters.

Surely that was all there was to it. She should not have let her mother's wild hopes convince her that something was wrong. It was just a dance. But even as she was thinking it, Nuru thought of Hadhi—racing away. Hadhi in tears. Hadhi afraid.

Hadhi didn't think it was nothing.

Nuru spotted Ayinde following Vaasht Bakari out of the hall, his head was down. He didn't quite look himself, but he was clearly speaking to someone out of Nuru's view. Suddenly, Neema swept into view, moving past them at speed looking angry...or frightened.

Nuru remembered what she'd heard Neema saying before she ran outside. *No* one *deserves to be treated to his sort of attention.*

What did she know? Nuru felt a heavy urge, weighted like a statue had settled on her feet, and didn't want her to move. If she moved, she would learn something she didn't want to know. She would see something she didn't want to see.

Neema wore that look like Hadhi had, haunted and hunted, cornered prey. Nuru wasn't a warrior. She wasn't even a hunter, Hadhi had barely started teaching her. But...she was a friend. She could be a friend.

Jauhar moved away from the group she'd been speaking to as she saw her daughter's admirer striding towards her with furor. Men. So easily overset. She wondered if he even knew how much he was revealing with just his stride. At all other times, he moved with casual ease, no haste or agitation. But now he looked like a different man: his posture had lengthened and his gaze had intensified. Wasn't it sweet, how much he cared? For now. But he didn't know the real Hadhi.

He bowed stiffly. "Jauhar, I have yet to enjoy that dance you promised me. Might we have it now?" He asked prettily but even in his tone there was a lack of ease.

Jauhar dipped her head in dismissive acceptance. She could feel the people around them taking notice of him once again invading her family but she played it off far better than he.

"Where is Asha?" he asked as soon as they had stepped onto the dance floor.

Jauhar raised an eyebrow. "You'll have no more luck with her than with Hadhi. Asha knows her worth."

"But Hadhi does not. And whose fault is that?" Noam hissed passionately.

"Hadhi will be queen." Jauhar smiled, her entire being burning with certainty. "Everyone will know her worth."

"As greater than Asha's?" Noam snarled. "It really is too bad her father isn't here to see. Or Asha's mother. Finally, you'll be the most important of Zuberi's wives."

Jauhar bit down on her tongue to stop herself from slapping him in the middle of the ballroom. How dare he? How dare all men presume to know what was in a woman from nothing but a passing acquaintance?

"I was always the most important." She spoke the words softly but full of venom.

Noam looked away, stiff and angry. He was so *sweet*. So desperate to protect Hadhi from the monsters of the world. But he wasn't up to the task. Hadhi was far more familiar with monsters. He only saw the grieving girl. Not the resilient killer her father had made. This man was too... gentle to understand Hadhi. She could see why Hadhi thought this man was what she wanted, reveling in his soft attentions. But he would take them away once he saw the real her.

"Where is Asha?" Noam repeated tightly. "I do not want to pursue her. I want to ask her a question."

Jauhar shrugged. "She followed Enzi, presumably to have her chance at Azize before anyone else."

"Where *is* Azize?" Noam snapped, distracted. "It is late, this is beyond rudeness."

Jauhar laughed. "Princes are not asked for politeness.

"Jauhar." Noam's tone was carefully soft. Sympathetic. She didn't need softness from him. "Do you know of anything you or your family have done to offend nymphs, or witches, or any magical creature?"

Jauhar flounced her head to the side, rolling her eyes, but her hand itched to slip into the folds of her gown for that slipper. She'd nearly forgotten its existence with Hadhi on the arm of the king. But now she longed to reach in and crush it, to be sure *Asha* was crushed. "Of course not," she lied.

Her daughters had done nothing. She had done nothing. But Zuberi wasn't living if he did not charge into the most dangerous storms, towards the sharpest cliffs. He wasn't alive unless he was proving it every moment with the risks he took and the enemies he bested. Zuberi had offended, challenged, or killed every being of magic he had come across.

"There is something after your family. I know she is, even Hadhi..." He drifted off, eyes clouding over, as his mind caught up with his mouth. Was he beginning to realize he didn't know Hadhi quite as well as he'd thought? "What about Hadhi? Could she have offended one?" he asked flatly.

"I don't see how. Unless they are offended by her sour-face," Jauhar lied with a little laugh. Hadhi might have helped her father, Zuberi hadn't mentioned any such thing, but he'd not mentioned his plans to have Hadhi hunt a predator either. And despite what everyone else thought, Jauhar knew her daughter was well able to keep a secret.

"Do not speak of her that way," Noam snapped, loud enough to be heard by the other dancers.

Jauhar laughed as the boy glanced around shyly. "Why are men so sensitive? It has never bothered Hadhi."

"Not that you'd care to notice," he returned. "You who 'watched' her father 'try to break her?' Did it never occur to you to build her back up?"

Jauhar ground her teeth, her eyes burning across the man with resentment of him and all the men who'd come before him. "You come from a world away and think you can judge me after a day's acquaintance. All because you feel sorry for her." Jauhar scoffed. "That is what you feel, not love, pity."

Noam chewed on his lip, fighting off some words he didn't want to share before their now avid audience. Jauhar had no such concerns. Her daughter would be queen.

"I watched this king and the one before treat women like amusing insects, to be taken apart and cast aside. No one will do so with Hadhi," Jauhar said proudly. "Her father was not kind to her, but he taught her something she will carry forever: she *cannot* be broken."

Noam led Jauhar away from the dance floor. She could feel the tightly restrained rage in him, but oddly, the agitation he had come to her with was easing, leaving only softness.

"Yes, she can," Noam whispered. "She already has been. Time, after time, after time. That she picks herself back up does not mean she hasn't been broken, it only means she keeps living."

The words sucked the air out of Jauhar. Until she felt every tear and crack within her being, every scar she had smiled over for years, the weakness she'd pretended didn't exist. Felt that woman she'd never wanted her daughter to be. No. He was wrong. Hadhi was strong. Hadhi was impervious to the pain. Hadhi could not be broken.

Jauhar felt the sobs that had carried her daughter to sleep last night. The sobs that had shaken her after her face was mauled, the sobs she shed alone or with anyone other than her mother.

No. He was wrong.

"If you will excuse me. I have to help your daughter, however I can," he said heavily and moved away through the crowd. Wrong.

He must be wrong.

PREDATOR IN DISGUISE

Zawadi followed Kane to her next quarry now that she'd escaped the rest of Zuberi's women. Grant a man a wish to prove himself to his king and he ran right there like a puppy. She shouldn't have worried. It was something about Noam, surely. She'd never thought mayflies were real. Well, the flies, yes, but the magical creature of the songs, no. But he had a distinctly magical effect on one for not being magical. His belief, or his fear, that the father of his blood was a mayfly had burrowed into her skin, making her wonder.

Now she watched Kane exit the gardens trembling with rage, and a bit of fear, if she didn't miss her guess. Off to round up his friends for the king. So easily.

Zawadi felt the scream inside him as he made his way by her unaware. Felt it echoing inside herself. Felt the others crying out. But unlike the man who'd just fled the garden, she didn't shy away from the screams and the pain. The death. She didn't shy away from the guilt.

She was the reason they were gone. She was the reason for the screams. But she would also be the reason King Enzi was made to scream and writhe and watch as his world crumbled. And the others, her sisters, her friends, they would have their share of vengeance. But for now, she quieted their screams, quieted the parts of self that were her and called up the bits of Asha that had fooled the king and his sword already tonight. She only had a short while left in this body, and she needed to use it.

She walked forward, bold and playful, as Asha would in her place. She could see the stones on the king's sword flare momentarily, uncertain of her, then the king glanced up and smiled like an uncle to a favored niece.

"Asha, what are you doing out here?"

The stones dimmed, looking like ordinary gems, and Zawadi laughed, Asha's laugh. "Looking for Azize, we only had a moment in the line. I got the feeling he wanted to say something far too interesting to waste in the ballroom."

King Enzi chuckled. "Something loverly, do you think?" he coaxed.

Asha giggled. "Not by half. Oh, he liked what he saw, but...he didn't like that he liked it."

The king patted the bench beside him, grinning. They were in an enclosed garden. The walls of the palace and the veranda shut it in, but where they stood was a perfect circle, marked out in a colorful pebble path and the roof of a gazebo. The roof was not solid, holes cut out of it marking the phases of the moon, and....oh, clever. Where the light fell through them, it marked different symbols formed from the pebbles. Some for the time of year, some marking crop rotations. Very interesting. This must be Gzifa's garden. An odd place to find the king.

Zawadi would not think him the type to honor female goddesses. But then there were lounges around the outside of the gazebo and it was both quiet enough for privacy and open enough to be easily seen. The sort of place where he would enjoy harming others.

Zawadi took the seat the king suggested. She could feel such pleasure emanating from him that she must assume he'd been spreading evil tonight.

Why would you delight to see her suffer more?

Zawadi shook off the odd echo in her mind. Unsure what brought it out.

"And you, Asha? Were you pleased with what you saw?"

Zawadi shrugged. "He seems much the same." She let her words fall flat, beginning to lead the conversation where she needed it. To answers and awakened fears. To wishes made death. "I'd hoped to have more fun with him. With his friends. I'd hoped...but everything is different."

The king nodded, looking up into the gazebo roof. Zawadi followed his gaze and took in the mosaic of the night sky. Built out of pebbles and the blue grey sand of Maltuba's beaches, it seemed even to be shot through with bands of gold. She supposed those were willoomi threads. So lovely. Everywhere she turned, there was another beauty to marvel at.

It was the sort of thing that could confuse another, make them think the king who ruled this land was equally beautiful, make them mistake appreciating beauty for some sign of inner goodness. But this gazebo wasn't made by him, or even for him. It was a place of worship for his ancestors. He could enjoy the loveliness of it, but those feelings did not sink within and affect his vision of the world. He was a man who devoured. Not one who created. Nor even one who glorified. All he did was take. And it led to blood dripping down walls, and screams of pain, and children ripped from life long before their time.

From the corner of her eye, Zawadi saw the stones flaring again and forced herself to shove aside any thoughts but the plan. Once he wished she could feel anything she needed to feel. But right now she must focus or those stones on his sword could finish the job Zuberi started for him and take her power giving it into the hands of someone truly evil.

Noam found the king and the nymph in the garden, sitting on a bench together with their backs to the palace. Noam hung back and watched. He could not precisely walk up to the nymph and demand she save Hadhi from the king when the two were together.

"Do you miss my father?" she asked in a small sham of a voice.

"Of course. Zuberi was a king's man. A warrior. All must miss him."

"I thought so as well, but I have heard whispers—"

"Oh," the king sounded only vaguely intrigued, and Noam sensed impatience from the nymph. She had expected a different emotion, fear perhaps. What was going on?

"No ordinary thief on the road could kill my father."

"Certainly not," Enzi agreed. "You have heard rumors of the true culprit?"

"Some implied it was you. That he had acted outside your wishes," she nearly snarled. It seemed impossible to Noam that the king didn't feel the power coming off her. Couldn't sense the predator disguised as a harmless girl beside him.

Was Noam truly that different? *You can sense magic so it hasn't the same hold over you...*

"They implied he had killed some magic beings for his own pleasure—"

"No, Asha," the king interrupted forcefully, but his force had little effect.

"Then who? Tell me who did this?"

"If I knew the man, he would be dead already," the king assured her. "No man was of as much service as Zuberi."

The nymph's head rose slowly higher, regally. "Did he act on his own? Killing those beings?"

She was after vengeance against Hadhi's dead father? But...he was gone. There could be no avenging herself against him. Any reasonable being would see there was no way through. But her energy did not feel reasonable.

And Hadhi knew something. She had been scared by the mention of nymphs last night.

It wasn't until he was dancing with Jauhar that it occurred to Noam that Hadhi seemed to know what was after her. And that he'd been letting his own fears, and his own feelings, lead him since she ran off. But Noam wasn't the person with reason to fear. That was Hadhi. And in any way he could, for as long as he could, Noam meant to help her. Which meant really listening.

The way she told the story of those scars and about her father and the tiny fey he'd slaughtered after sending his *best hunter* to track them; there had been bitterness in her voice when she'd said that. At the time, he'd taken it for jealousy for the unnamed hunter. But what if it was a different kind of bitterness? What if it was regret? She left things out of all of her stories.

Had her father kept testing her? Could she be involved with whatever brought this creature for vengeance? He could not deny Hadhi had the weighted presence of one who had known much evil. *I was his monster. And he was hiding me, biding his time.* It would not have been by choice if she'd helped her father. The man clearly manipulated and abused his children. But would this woman see it so?

The king stared down the girl before him, searching her gaze. At last, he sighed.

"It was meant to be a secret, Asha. When I find the man who spoke, he will have a long life of suffering so he never forgets sinning against his king.

Your father acted on my order. Those...*demons* pride themselves on revenging men in battle. And they are allied to the Reethurn."

Revenging men in battle? *The Battle Born.* Noam forced himself smaller, hiding behind the bush. Not a nymph at all. A Battle Born was a powerful foe. Most called them the death flock because they were found circling fields of battle, swooping down just as men drew their last breaths as if yanking them from their bodies.

No one knew for certain if they devoured souls, but what they did know was that they granted wishes of vengeance. Noam had once thought such a creature helped curse his father...until Ethan learned the name of the witch who'd laid the curse and joined an expedition to hunt her.

"Reethurn are our allies."

The king scoffed. "Zuberi taught you better than that. If a man or a kingdom is not your subordinate, he will eventually be your enemy."

"So you strike first," the false Asha said softly and painfully.

"Exactly."

"And lay waste to all before you?"

"It is the only way to be certain." Enzi's voice betrayed a glee that belied his words. He liked killing, liked inflicting pain. The threat was insignificant, he wanted the suffering.

Noam knew they were bound to spot him any moment. He ought to run, find Hadhi and get her away from here. This was so much worse than Hadhi trapped by the king or some angry nymph after their family. The Sisterhood of Battle Born were fey born creatures, but they were said to be reborn from the cries of the betrayed and to gain power from bathing in the blood of traitors. They granted wishes for vengeance, righting the wrongs they saw. If a Battle Born was after Hadhi and her family, it would not stop until it felt the scales were equalled.

"I originally believed one such creature had killed your father," the king said quietly.

"Did he not complete his mission?"

"The one who led him to her kind survived. Wounded but alive. He came to me and told me this before he died. He was meant to be seeking it out and destroying it. But he never got the chance."

Wounded, so there might be hope of escape, but...how long ago had her father died?

"But if their leader was the killer, surely she would have killed me as well," the king remarked. "I've no idea who killed your father, Asha."

"No," the Battle Born replied in an oddly tickled voice. "Nor I. But he is dead." Her words were a statement, but her tone was confused.

"Of course he is dead! You saw what the animals had done to him. Asha, I promise you I will find his killer."

"Is that what you want? More than anything?" she asked, and her power charged the air. Noam *saw* it. It...sparked almost. But was so dark the word did not suit. He could see little fissures of darkness distorting the air around the king.

"If you had a wish, that would be it?" she pressed.

Noam willed the king to say yes. He didn't care to have justice for the killer, but if the king wished for something else, he might wish for Hadhi, and he couldn't let him have her. The Battle Born killed their victims by granting them wishes. Every wish, no matter how innocuous, led to death. But...the wisher always got their desire first.

"You are behaving strange, Asha."

"I am." She nodded, and her demeanor changed, her shoulders shrunk, and she looked harmless again. "It is just that it is nearly midnight, and Azize has not returned, and all I can think of when I am with you is Baba."

The king, easily convinced of her helplessness, took the Battle Born's hand between his own and squeezed. "If I had only one wish, it would be to find the one responsible for Zuberi's death and for them to be dragged in chains before your family, to pay the highest price."

Noam breathed a sigh of relief. The Battle Born's eyes flashed, and a breeze shook the garden. She looked up curiously, all the while raising the king's hands with her own. Noam felt what made her curious. There was more than just her power in the air; a heavy suffocating pressure of grief weighed upon the garden. But the Battle Born ignored the other power and lay her lips on the king's hand. A force of wind knocked Noam backwards.

"Then it must be so," she said.

Noam fled the garden. There was powerful magic in the air, and he had a feeling the Battle Born was nowhere near done.

THE LONGEST
YESTERDAY

RAGING AGAINST GHOSTS

Hadhi's feet ached, probably bled. She was leaving a trail no doubt, but she could not stop her feet from moving forward. She knew where she was going now. Perhaps she had known as soon as she raced down the palace steps.

She even knew why. Fear, certainly. But more and so much deeper—rage! She hadn't felt a thing like it in so long, but when Noam kissed her head and spoke his gentle words of love...it broke free within her. All the anger she had hidden under her grief and her need to defend her family. She had pounded it down and buried it deep inside herself because there was nowhere for it to go, no one to hear it.

Her father deserved to hear it! Deserved to feel all the pain he had wrought. But he always managed to be gone when there was pain to share. Always managed to brush away every word that ought to claw and gouge and burn his soul.

And here he was gone again when she needed someone to rage at. He was always gone when she needed him most.

She saw his ghost again as she ran. Mocking her, always mocking her. Even to the very last time she saw him.

"They kill a man with his greatest desire. Offer him riches and women and immortality—"

"Power," Hadhi had interrupted her father, as he raced around the house, grabbing his most prized possessions. She meant the word to sound scathing, but it came out hesitant. She was never as forceful with him as she was in her mind. And he knew it.

He smirked at his daughter and went back to packing. Weapons mostly, a bit of clothing, all his coins, and the medallion of gold and jewels the king had given him.

The rest of the family, even the staff, had gone to the mouth of Ether for the death service for Aunt Lolia. Hadhi should be there. Aunt Lolia had always been with

Hadhi when she needed her. Hadhi should be with her cousins. But Baba was gone when she died, and expected home, so Mzaa made Hadhi wait so she could bring him. He knew now. He just did not care.

"Yes, power too. All you have to do is make sure none of your sisters or mothers makes any wishes, and you'll be safe."

"Then stay." Hadhi could not believe she was begging him to stay. She was always happiest when he was away, even knowing that if he was gone and Asha remained, he was hurting someone, she was still happier.

"The nymph that's after me, she..." He shrugged, bobbing his head from side to side.

Hadhi did not need him to finish. Two words of his story said it all. She and nymph. He had already had what he wanted of it. Now it would punish his family for whatever he had done.

"What did you wish for?" she asked, but Baba just walked away.

Hadhi should stay. She should warn her family, but no one would believe her. No one ever believed her when she spoke badly of Baba. No one but Sabra, and she had no recourse either.

Hadhi stared around her father's room, at the rocks and odd shaped twigs, little things he and Asha had collected and invented stories around. He had never done such things with Hadhi, but Asha loved their "tiny adventures." She wanted to meet nymphs. Would have come alive the way she did, with her eyes sparkling and her beautiful smile, awed by everything. Even Hadhi loved Asha in such moments. Now her greatest fantasy was going to kill her, because of something Baba did.

Hadhi chased after her father. He was taking a crooked way to the south road. Going around the homes and avoiding the palace patrols. He never needed to do that.

"Baba!" she shouted when she had nearly caught him. At first, he merely went faster, but when she shouted at the top of her lungs, he stopped. She rushed to reach his side, then had no idea what to say; she only knew she could not let him go. "What did you wish for?"

"Hadhi." He rolled his eyes, walking again. "Why do you care? Do you want me to have my heart's desire?" His voice was so amused, so dismissive, Hadhi wanted to lash out, but nothing she said had ever affected him. She followed him for miles with no words. Why did she keep walking? What did she hope to get from him? Something would not let her stop.

"What did you wish for?" She could think of nothing else to ask.

"I wished to meet them all, Hadhi. To see her entire tribe at once," he answered coldly.

"Why would you…" Hadhi trailed off, stumbling, as her breath fled and her feet became too alien to control. She landed on one knee in the dirt and pushed slowly to her feet.

Her father could tell a million stories about his longing for adventure, could make you long with him. Could paint the world in color such as nature could not invent. But it was all lies. He did not care what dragons looked like, or how old mermaids lived to be. All he ever wanted was power. If he had not asked for power, there could be only one reason. He meant to get it by doing something awful.

He laughed. He always laughed at her. "They were in Enzi's way."

"Ot omua gitelle uli ragnok?" She barely got the words out and hated herself. He did not respect weakness. He did not understand empathy, or mercy, or sorrow. And he hated it when she spoke Maltuban.

He walked back to her and twisted Hadhi's chin, smiling at her scars. "You are my monster. My own image. My legacy. You know the answer." He waited. "Tell me, monster, how many did I hurt?" His tone called her childish, and weak, and foolish as he pronounced each word precisely for her.

Her skin crawled under his touch and her stomach dropped. He was right; she knew. She always understood perfectly what no one else did. Because she was like him.

It was not the power of ruling he was after. It was the hunt, the power of being the strongest beast. It did not matter if the creatures were in Enzi's way. He would have found another excuse to test himself.

"How many, monster?" He shook her head again, his fingers crushing her chin.

Hadhi pulled away, looking to the ground. "All of them," she whispered. Her stomach churned so she thought she might vomit. She should be used to the feeling. "You killed them all."

He nodded and retrieved his pack. He flung it over his shoulder. "Almost." Collecting his loose weapons, he set off walking. He knew she would follow. And she did, trudging in his wake like a pet. "A few got away injured. There were dozens of them, Hadhi," he said with such glee Hadhi wanted to be sick, but she was too familiar with him. "And I nearly slew them all!"

"You are running from them now." Her words left an oddly pleased feeling behind. "They are stronger than you, the few wounded ones."

"No." He picked up his pace. "They are not stronger. But they can look like anyone. I need to devise a strategy."

"So we are distraction?" Hadhi demanded. "Something for them to kill on their way to you?"

He chuckled. "Not with my monster guarding."

Why? Why was it always on her to clean up his messes? If he was so strong, why was he dead? Why had he not killed Enzi? Why make Hadhi into his monster and hide her away, waiting for his moment? Why not do it himself? Why? Why was she still left in a position of giving him everything he wanted?

Hadhi raced towards the white rocks where he died, where the last of his blood fell. Raced to the last place she had left to rage against his spirit for all the ugliness he had grown in her. To rage against all the things she wished her hands had never learned to do, because...

He knew her. Better than anyone. And he left her with one more test. And she knew. *Knew.* If Nuru's life was in the balance, if other girls would have to take her place, no matter how much she wished to do anything else, to be anyone else. She knew she would do what Baba had taught her once more and be his monster.

YOUR GREATEST POWER

Nuru followed Neema down to the palace kitchens. She'd looked agitated and hadn't stopped though Nuru called her name. So Nuru had expected to find her crying or hiding when she arrived. But she did not.

Neema was pacing by one of the stoves in the open air. The kitchens consisted of a dark, cool room with no windows for storage of things like grains and vegetables, another room for the meats, and yet another with counter space for food preparation, and an open courtyard where there were multiple stoves, with a fountain in the center of the hexagonal enclosure and a few beds of growing spices.

Neema paced back and forth between one of the stoves and the fountain. She had a chunk of bread in her hands that she ripped up as she paced, but never ate. Nuru watched her from the preparation room, surprised that she had never seen the rage in her before. Neema always seemed...a little oblivious to the world. She wore a smile no matter what, she was occasionally so bright Nuru found it annoying. But not so now, and this was the first time Nuru was sure she was seeing her friend exactly as she was. That disturbed Nuru, not that Neema had such feelings inside, but that Nuru had known Neema since they were small but when she'd seen a change in her friend that she hadn't particularly liked, she had not realized it was covering for something. Neema was in pain. And as with Hadhi, Nuru hadn't seen it.

Maybe she was not a very good friend. But she could be now. Nuru stepped through the doorway.

Neema had not looked up, but several of the kitchen staff had. Many exchanged looks glancing up the stairs, preparing to send her away most likely. She wasn't well known here, but she recognized a few faces. It seemed strange that the servants just ignored Neema, but as Nuru approached her friend, a few smiled to see someone coming to comfort her. They must know what disturbed her and were giving her space. The servant at the stove Neema paced beside looked up and Nuru recognized her, Hanifa, Eshe's eldest daughter. She was a bit older than Hadhi and had never been close with Nuru and her friends, but they saw each other around. She wondered if Neema knew her better because she was a spirit dancer.

"Neema," Nuru called out softly, stepping into her pacing route. "Are you alright?"

Nuru had thought Neema ignored her calls in the hallways, but she startled so badly that Nuru reassessed. She was too angry, or hurt, or... something to have heard her. Even now Nuru watched as her friend's face went from rage to shock, to fear and struggled to pull out that overly bright smile Nuru had been growing impatient with this year.

"Nuru!" Her voice was both bright and teary as she fought to pretend everything was fine. She opened her mouth, but Nuru knew whatever came out would not be real, and she did what she had wanted to with her sister tonight.

Jerking forward, Nuru threw her arms around Neema and clung on. "It's alright. You don't have to tell me what's upset you, and you don't have to pretend you aren't upset either. Just tell me what I can do to help, and I'll do it. Please."

At first, Neema stood stiffly. She almost felt like she would shove out of Nuru's arms, but the more shaky breaths she expelled, the more hope Nuru had that she would accept help. Finally, Neema let out a particularly heavy breath and collapsed against Nuru. She didn't cry or speak, just lay against her as if her fight had simply vanished, and one of her arms rose to encircle Nuru's back, then the other. She clung on hard and Nuru returned the embrace.

"Can you make me someone else?" she whispered into Nuru's shoulder. "I wish I was someone else. No!" She jerked as if she would shove out of Nuru's arms but then clung on tighter. "Then someone else might be me, and I would be as bad as the rest of them. I wish..." But she couldn't seem to find the words.

"Someone would kill all the predators," Nuru provided.

There was a beat of silence, true silence, though Nuru had not spoken so loudly it should disrupt the servants. But it had, her words had stilled them. Eyes bent towards her and Neema, and though there were no nods or words the weight of those expressions made it clear that while Nuru had not always seen this place for what it was, it wasn't only Hadhi and Neema who did.

Neema pushed back a bit from Nuru. Her arms remained around her back, but she put space enough between them to look into her eyes. And what Nuru saw there, she did not understand. It wasn't like the gaze of the servants, who were now breaking into work noisily as if they had never stopped. There was a yes in Neema's eyes, but so much shame along with it that Nuru could not understand, until she spoke.

"When he danced with Hadhi," Neema said, leaving no doubt in Nuru's mind who Neema thought the predator was, "there was a moment when I thought to myself, good! He will turn his attentions there and if we're all lucky, she'll kill and skin another predator and we won't have to do a thing." Neema laughed sadly, shrugging off Nuru's arms as if she would hate her as much as...as she hated herself. That was what her eyes looked like. That was what Hadhi's eyes had looked like this past year.

Nuru gave her space but managed to grab onto Neema's hand, letting her know she understood, letting her know she loved Neema, and no fears could change that.

Neema laughed harder, but it was a brittle—painful sound. "But then I saw her scars and thought of everyone calling her sour-faced. I tried to burn my face last year, told my mother I wanted to be ugly. She stopped me but said it wouldn't change anything. I watched him dancing with Hadhi and I realized she was right; it wouldn't matter."

That sounded a bit like Neema was calling her sister ugly. Nuru would usually be arguing with her, but she just let her talk today. She needed to talk. Had Neema ever tried to tell Nuru about this before?

"He didn't choose me because I was beautiful, or special, or even weak. He chose me because he *can*." The word vibrated from Neema's lips, seeming to shake the entire enclosure. Bowls clattered, flames hissed, boiling water splashed over the rims of pans. For a moment, Nuru truly thought it was some magic in Neema, then she noticed the shaking of the servants. Only

Hanifa failed to trembled, her movements measured and steady as she removed bread from within an oven.

"He can. He can, because he is powerful. And no matter how small and powerless I know my parents to be, I hate them for *his power*. For allowing it. I hate everyone for it. Mostly..." She didn't finish the thought, but she didn't need to. Nuru could see it. *Me. Mostly me.* That had been what Neema wanted to say. "I should be able to do something to stop him. Shouldn't I? So as soon as that hope that someone else would stop him passed, I got angry again. Because there I was expecting of your sister what I couldn't do, and everyone around me was expecting it too, salivating after her blade and his blood on her hands the way he salivates after any pain he can inflict and any shame he can wake. I was as ugly as him for a moment."

"No." Nuru snapped it, far harsher than she should with one as fragile as Neema seemed, but she couldn't stop it. Her mouth tasted sour, as her being sloshed with revulsion, but none of it was for her friend. "No, you weren't. You were scared, you were desperate. You weren't trying to hurt someone, you were feeling hope. You were feeling hope."

Nuru felt her body beginning to rock, wanting comfort. When she rocked like this, Hadhi would reach out and pull her near, protect her from whatever had caused her fear.

I might never have wanted anything, Nuru, but at least I do not expect everyone else to provide me what I want.

Hadhi's words from earlier raced through her mind and mixed with the ones Neema had been saying. Nuru stilled her quaking body. She felt no less terrified for herself, her friend, her sister, or even the shaking servants all around her. But she knew what she most had to offer in this moment wasn't solutions or protection. It was what her grandmother had called her greatest gift. *"Kup nav fa oon vaoli havio".* She always told Nuru that she had the *embrace of a true friend.* And that she gave it freely. *"Nza ixiz pang, paax mur ulin ethus simi."* Never change that, it is your greatest power.

What Nuru had was arms and hopes and all the love she could give her friend.

"No. You are not a predator, and you will not be prey either." She pulled Neema back into her arms. "I don't know how, but now that I know, I promise I will help."

Neema sniffled and laughed into Nuru's shoulder, this laugh sounding lighter than the ones before. "Your mother gave you a high estimation of your power, *Great Spirit Nuru*."

Nuru laughed, tears burning her eyes, but not dampening her cheeks or her spirits. She kissed Neema firmly on the cheek. "Not high. Fair. You will see. I'm very powerful."

NOWHERE'S SONS

"**K**ane, Omar and Mikhail left the palace looking for Azize once we realized he wasn't in his rooms," Daniel leaned in to whisper.

Noam didn't like the sound of that. He hadn't trusted Kane with Hadhi already. But something her mother said about her husband's spy made him more suspicious. But it wasn't to him to order these men. Daniel, as the oldest and most experienced among them, had taken up the role of commander for these men of varied backgrounds.

At first, Azize's friends had tried to keep things light, dancing with all the woman they could, making jokes about their friends exhaustion from heat and too many lovely faces. But now the women were not to be entertained. They waited, because they must, but they did not dance, they did not laugh or pretend to be amused. They stood in scattered groups, talking impatiently about being dragged here and abandoned, or about Jauhar's daughters and the missing royalty. Things were assumed. The room was pretty evenly split between annoyance and relief.

Jauhar was perhaps the only person enjoying herself. Though she did not appear to enjoy the assumptions people made about Asha's and Azize's combined absence. He'd heard her say at least twice, "they have not been seen together once," and "Asha is probably in the menagerie." The assumption that Hadhi would marry the king though, that she was enjoying.

A few of Azize's soldier friends had taken up posts around the room, to listen to guests and try to keep the calm. Now that Noam had returned from eavesdropping, Daniel was including him. Though Noam was not a soldier and had generally been treated like Azize's lovable manservant.

"Dion, Masahiro, and Renz have not returned from searching the grounds yet."

"You may want to...cautiously have another pair check on them," Noam suggested throwing his voice low. "The king already suspects Azize brought us here to overthrow him."

"Not an entirely wrongheaded notion." Daniel smirked sideways.

At Noam's raised brow, Daniel shrugged. "He never said, but...we are all older, former soldiers with no pressing allegiances, who have little in common with a prince. We knew. One does not collect a group of nowhere's sons without purpose."

That was an apt name for them all, Nowhere's Sons. It suited Noam more than he would like to admit. He wasn't like his sister who'd left hating the island. Noam knew there was plenty of ugly there, but there was beauty he had loved as well. But most of Glen Harrow's people were relieved to see him leave. If they were asked, he had no home among them. And the same was true with most of Azize's friends. He wondered now if he didn't fit better among them than he had believed. He should warn them about the Battle Born, she had said she was not after Azize, but Noam wasn't sure he trusted that magic could attack a man without harming his son.

Noam spotted his friend trudging up the steps of the palace, with Kane at his side and Omar jogging up behind them.

"He's here." Noam moved around Daniel to go outside. He wanted to speak with Azize before he entered the palace. Even annoyed and tired, these women were bound to mob him.

Noam watched the heavy way his friend was walking, noted that he'd changed clothes, but that these were perhaps dirtier than the ones he'd worn for hours of fitting the shoe to every foot. Something had happened to him. He looked exhausted. He looked lost. Noam was nearly to him, with questions of concern poised on his lips, but with some of his worry abated, what came out was not what Noam expected.

"Where have you been? You drag all of these women here and then abandon them for hours— it is incredibly rude."

Kane laughed, as did Daniel who'd followed Noam out. But Azize glared.

"It was hardly intentional," Azize defended. "But I...do not think I can face them now."

"No?" Noam challenged. He didn't think he'd ever spoken so forcefully with another man, but he couldn't bring himself to back down. "I am sorry, brother, but that is not an option. These women woke early to prepare for you, waited hours in the blazing sun, and now have waited the entire day. It is nearly midnight! Yet all wait on the promise—"

"Of trying to trap me into staying here!" Azize whisper shouted with a glare.

"It isn't their fault that your father forced them here, Azize," Noam pressed, needing his friend to be truly affected. "You hate what is forced on you. Respect what has been forced on them. You have always been a prince, but up to now, I would not have called you spoiled."

"Oh, come now." Kane stepped between them, trying to ease the tension. "He isn't spoiled."

Noam knew he was being sharper with his friend than he had before, but he wasn't being nearly as sharp as the situation warranted. He could still see the tension in Hadhi as she was trapped in the king's arms. Felt how she'd shaken when she spoke of her father hiding her from Enzi. Azize was forced to play host to a bevy of women, but he could still pick up and leave if he wanted. That was why he brought home soldiers, so he could leave again. The same couldn't be said of these women. Any of them.

"I think," Kane said with a half grin, "our friend is just a bit jealous that the woman he's infatuated with caught the eye of the king and is taking it out on the wrong people."

"Who caught my father's eye?" Azize demanded, looking between his friends.

"The girl with the scars," Kane said, and Noam nearly punched him. Kane knew Hadhi's name. He knew more than her name. He'd been mocking her and following her around in the crowd. She had caught more attention than just Noam's and the king's.

"Hadhi?" Azize asked disbelieving. "My father wants her? *You* want her? Why?"

It seemed an eon since Noam had wanted to attack his friend when the shoe shrunk around Hadhi's foot. When Azize had laughed with her, been attracted to her. So much had happened since, so much had changed in

Noam since, but here he was angry with his friend again, but this time for failing to see all that was desirable about Hadhi.

"I am addressing you about all of the women. But yes, I have formed a special connection to Hadhi." Noam shook his head. "You spent all day kneeling before the woman of your nation, did you even once try to actually see them? Hadhi is not gregarious, but she is kind, and strong, and loyal. And...none of that matters because no woman deserves to be treated the way *you* have told me your father treats them," Noam hissed, pressing his face past Kane.

Omar looked uncomfortably past Noam. He gave a slight nod to Daniel and disappeared through nearest entrance to the palace.

"Well." Azize faltered for a long moment; his words just stopped. He looked away. "I am sorry for Hadhi. But...what would you have me do? Rush in and say I will marry her?" Azize laughed bitterly, and his voice rose with unraveling rage. "It wouldn't make a difference. He might enjoy that more, forcing himself on my bride to prove his limitless power. Do you think I should stage a coup with fifteen men? No." Azize shook his head. His tone was sharp, but his manner frightened. "We were never here to stay. He would have chosen some woman among them eventually. We just wouldn't have been here to see."

Noam dropped back a step and then another, staring at his friend, his *brother* in disappointment. He wanted to believe that this was only fear and pressure speaking, but he wasn't so sure.

"What I want from you, Azize, is to care," Noam said heavily. "We have no kings in my nation, only tribunals. I used to think it must be so much better to have only one person you must plead your case to. To have one person who cared for all the others. I was fascinated, and I followed you so I could see what it was like to be such a figure. But..." Noam shook his head. "Tribunal or *prince,* it is the caring that is absent. We came here because you needed to see your home again. But I don't think you are seeing it. You talk of it all like there is no variation or beauty. But in that room are women of different faiths, different personalities, and interests. And different degrees of *fear* keeping them there—waiting on you. Because you are the son of this nation.

"You gathered nowhere's sons around you. Men with no homes to return to. But you can have a home here. You know it and your people know it as well. They wait on you because though they have doubts, they hope you are here to care for them and their nation. *Your home.*

"I follow you, Azize. We all do." Noam waved at Kane and Daniel. "So why did *you* come here, if not to stay? If not to care for others who are still chained up as his toys?"

Kane raised both brows at Noam and shook his head. "Big words." Kane's tone was light, he even laughed, but in his eyes there was rage. "From a kitchen hand. How many kings have you overthrown?"

"Back off, Kane. Noam wasn't discussing any such thing," Daniel intervened, but Azize and Noam saw only each other. "Noam only means that if we do plan to leave, we should do it quickly, before we upend their lives more than we already have. And do you know what? I think we should let them discuss it, alone. We'll be inside." Daniel clapped Noam on the shoulder as he walked by. Kane gave a perhaps playful wink and left as well. Noam was beginning to very much dislike that man.

GREAT MAN

This was torture. Asha was shaking and sobbing when the light released her. She could barely breathe. Bending forward, she braced herself on her knees and tried to catch hold of her riotous emotions. She couldn't understand why tonight was so different. Last night when the magic took hold of her, Asha had felt everyone, everything! She'd felt all powerful. But she had not felt emotional. She'd simply embraced the moments, the taste of adventure.

Tonight, with everything she embraced, came a wave of overpowering emotion, joy or sorrow, jealousy, anger, regret. All were so large that her body could not seem to contain them. If she laughed, her joy was so strong, it lifted her entire body into the air. If she was angry, the night bore her rage in torrents of thunder and wind. If she grieved...

Asha collapsed to the ground beside the white rocks that marked the southern road, the southern edge of Jaccada. Baba's body was found mere steps away; he had been on his way home.

Asha sat in the dust and watched as the ground was pelted with great droplets of rain. The whole world must mourn such a man as Zuberi. A great man, a great father, a...

A brute...he beat and stole, and frightened and murdered.

It wasn't true! Lightning tore fissures across the sky, in every direction, the fabric of the night coming undone with Asha's rage.

"It isn't true!" she shouted. But she couldn't make herself stop shaking, couldn't stop the sobs. Before her eyes, she saw the white rocks, the rain, the tattered sky, but in her mind, she saw so many faces. Sabra, almost smiling as Baba's body was burned to return it to the spirits. The looks of...disbelief on the faces of their neighbors as Asha spoke of what a great man her father was.

The only faces she could call up who truly mourned his loss were Mzaa Jauhar and Nuru. No! Hadhi too. She was so hollow and hungry, she'd barely slept for months. Even now, she ate less than ever before, couldn't bring herself to hunt any longer, and she never, ever smiled. She had cried when his body was burned. Though it was forbidden—a sob had been ripped from her, anguished and wrenching, every soul at the service had shaken with her grief—she'd had to flee the service her grief was so strong. Her family mourned.

"Because you were a good man." Asha pushed her child's body off the ground, walking to one rock she leaned against it. "You were a good man. He didn't know you," Asha insisted. "He ran away. I was right about him all along, he's..."

"Why are you everywhere?" A breathless voice startled Asha.

She spun around. Hadhi stood behind her, panting, and wet. She looked ragged, as though she'd run the whole ten miles between the capitol building and the white rocks. Her eyes were so red that Asha did not even think about it. She rushed forward and wrapped her sister in a tight hug.

Hadhi must be here for the same reason. Someone must have said something about Baba; she must have needed to be near him. As Asha did.

The rain pattered away as they hugged, or Asha hugged her sister. Hadhi stood with her arms limp at her sides.

"I do not recall seeing you before tonight," Hadhi said hollowly, and her body swayed like she would fall over. "Are you the nymph? Come to kill us at last? I waited but you did not come."

"Hadhi?" Asha drew away, took one step after another back from her sister and stared up at her. *Come to...kill us?* But Hadhi wasn't looking her way. She gazed at the wet ground, dazed. "Hadhi, what do you mean?"

"He told me you would come for your revenge. I..." Her breath hitched as though she would start crying; she looked so shattered and lonely. And Asha couldn't help hearing Zawadi's question once more:

"Have you ever seen your sister before this day? Did you ever care to meet her?"

"I understand," Hadhi said flatly. "What he did to you cannot go unpunished, but...my sisters, my mothers, they knew nothing of it. Only I knew. Please, have your revenge on me alone." It didn't sound like begging. Hadhi said the words with a hollow voice, and they scratched across the air hoarsely as she walked around the little girl to stand between the white rocks.

"Nuru only sees the next sunrise, or the wind sweeping up the sands of Ether, calling her to dance. And Asha—Asha would want to meet you, and the others he slew. She would inspire you."

Asha caught her breath, *others he slew*. Who? Not Baba. Never. Asha's tears brought the rain once more, a sorrowful screen of drops falling between the sisters.

"He promised her wonders. She would not understand, even if you told her a hundred times. And Lin!" Hadhi grew animated at last. Spinning around, she rushed forward and yanked her sister's hands from her sides, squeezing with all her might. "He is only a babe. My father never laid eyes on him. Sabra will raise him well, she had no love for my father."

"Did you?" The words were torn from Asha on a sob, and she yanked her hands back. It was lies. All of it lies! But everyone knew Hadhi couldn't lie.

Hadhi's eyes filled with tears; she sucked in a shaky breath. Her head was shaking and nodding at once, the rain weighing down her hair so it collapsed against her face and neck. She should look smaller, but the less dramatic hair somehow left visible all that was dramatic about Hadhi alone. There were gigantic feelings in her that were only now visible.

"He never loved me," she whispered, her hands fisting around her clothes. "Never. I thought it was impossible to love me. Mzaa does not, or she has not said as much. Nuru does a bit, but...No one knows me." She sobbed the words, and the tears that had been crowding her eyes overflowed. They fell on her face, and as the rain poured down, Asha wondered if some of it did not come from her sister. Was she so lonesome?

"Not like my father knew me."

"But did you love him?" Asha pressed, had to. She could not explain why. She watched her half-sister, so torn apart and lonely and her heart longed to comfort her, but in the same instant, some part of Asha wanted to lash out. How could she speak of their father so, accuse him of...

He was a brute...he beat and...murdered.

We live *longer, so humans are desirous of our power, or our deaths, at times both.*

They were taken from me.

It was not Baba. They were wrong. Zawadi would never have given her such a gift if it were true. She was here to repay a great deed Baba had done. They were all wrong.

"Did you love him?" Asha growled, and thunder shook the air.

BROTHERS

In the quiet after the others left, Azize walked to the edge of the veranda, staring into the dark city surrounding them. "I was on my way back to the party when she found me, in a different body, but I knew it was her. My mystery woman. She came to me in a child's body." Azize shook himself.

Noam drew in a deep breath, taking a moment to calm the fear and anxiety he'd attacked his friend with. He settled against the rail with him. This was Azize, his brother. He was not a bad man, just a lost one. So lost.

When Noam left home, following Azize, he'd seen such a heaviness about him. Noam had sworn he would help Azize, the way Noam's siblings had helped him. Giving him space to know himself, space where he needn't be anyone but his own man. He should have more patience with him now.

"It unnerved me. She kept saying bright, happy things about Maltuba. Kept invoking *my* mother as the reason I should want to stay, want to *lead*. I could always tell the people who hated my father, not just from the way they watched us, but because they always invoked my mother as though she was one of them. Used her to manipulate me, just as he did. I hated that." He was silent a long moment, just breathing with his hands clenched around the railing. "We fought, and I drove her off. She just made me so angry. So I told her things she didn't want to know. I kept wanting to do what she said. I wanted to stay. I wanted to get to know my nation and lead. I wanted to be my mother's son, the king this nation deserved. But every time I felt that, I caught myself wondering if she wasn't some ruse my father constructed to keep me here—like you said."

Noam sighed ruefully. "I don't know that those were my exact words. But I am sorry I made you doubt yourself, and her. I merely wanted to caution you against being consumed by magic."

Azize nodded. "She sent me away from her with magic. Sent me to a ship she'd conjured for me. Told me to run away if that was all I wanted."

There was a long quiet stretch. "Yet here you are," Noam prompted.

For a long moment, they were both silent. Then Azize turned to Noam. "I had better get in, before you call me spoiled again." He paused with an odd smile on his face. "Hadhi, really?"

Noam nodded tightly, his back put up by the tone. "Hadhi."

Azize laughed softly. "Maybe you can convince her to run away with us."

Noam relaxed a bit. Maybe he could. Maybe it would be the best thing for her. She could go away, be with him, and know a time when she was only loved. She deserved that. But she also deserved to be somewhere's daughter. To be loved and wanted and to know that she would be welcomed home with open arms.

And Noam doubted Azize truly meant to leave. Or that Hadhi would go if he did. That would leave her sister here. And Noam meant it when he said it wasn't just Hadhi who deserved better than to be used by King Enzi. Maybe Kane was right. Maybe Noam had been talking about overthrowing a king.

But he glanced sidelong at his brother. Azize would hate him for it. Enzi ought to die, ought to be removed. But the reason Azize hesitated was what held Noam back now. Azize loved his father. Noam wasn't sure his friend could survive being a party to killing him.

Azize sighed heavily. "Perhaps he only wants me to stay and promise to carry on his legacy. If I give him reason to think I will stay, perhaps he will lose interest in Hadhi."

"What reason have you to stay?" Noam asked casually. He could think of a great many reasons, but Azize had spent his whole life running from the responsibilities he felt were forced on him. He had to come to it on his own, or, even if he stayed, he would always be running away from something.

"I could...announce my intention to marry."

Noam laughed. Apparently, Azize wasn't quite ready to embrace his place here. "To the girl who sent you away?"

"She was angry. I...insulted her father," Azize explained. "She had made a wish for magic, but it was Asha. My childhood enemy."

Noam drew in a slow breath as pieces fell into place. Hadhi was nervous when nymphs were mentioned. Asha seemed familiar when he'd met her for the first time, not because of her face, but because of her personality. And the Battle Born had come today with Asha's face. She'd gone to Asha first, offered her a wish, and now Enzi. This did not bode well.

I was his monster. He was hiding me, biding his time.

"Did she tell you where she got this wish?" Noam didn't wait for an answer. "There is something after vengeance from her father. A Battle Born, and since he is dead, she is going after his children."

Azize's entire frame tensed, the exhaustion shoved out of his eyes by worry.

"Would their father have killed a group of fairy? Can you think of anyone he would have taken to assist him?" Noam didn't want to ask what he was asking. Hadhi would not have been involved by choice, but he needed to know so he could protect her. Something was eating her inside, and he didn't think it was regret over an animal she'd hunted.

Azize shook his head. "Zuberi was a killer. A beast. He never needed assistance. You've never seen a man as fearless and callous. The world is better rid of him. If he went to kill fairy, he would do it alone for the glory and the risk. He was a monster."

Noam had his tongue clamped between his teeth and his hands fisted at his sides.

I am Sour-Faced-Hadhi, my father's monster.

Noam hated that word. He'd never thought about it before, but now he could happily wipe it from existence. Even when used about someone he hated. And he did hate Hadhi's father. Every word he heard about him made Noam hate him more, for all the ways he'd tried to make Hadhi hate herself. Yet when Azize called him a monster, Noam had to battle down his sickened rage at the word. It was too ugly and too easy. Call a man a monster and you don't have to face the evil impulses in all men. Such words should never be used because they scarred souls and made those causing the scars feel righteous.

Noam wished Hadhi had never heard it. So she could know how beautiful she truly was.

"This thing that's after Asha, do you think it would hurt her?" Azize demanded all rage and action. "How do we find it? How do we stop it?"

"She can look like anyone. She looked like Asha earlier. We are most likely to find her among their family. But I doubt we can convince her to give up her vengeance. It sounds as if the man decimated her kind. And it may be too late. Wishes made of Battle Born lead to death. She...granted your father a wish as well."

"She can give up her quest or she can perish with the rest of her kind!"

Noam startled hearing such words from his brother's lips. For the first time, Azize reminded him of Ethan, and the rage he'd left the island with, the violence. Noam had no knowledge of what became of his brother, but he could imagine nothing good coming out of such impulses. Noam had always mistrusted magic because of how he came into the world. But Ethan blamed magic and all its wielders, wanted to destroy it. Noam could never calm that rage. Where he'd failed to stop Ethan, Noam was determined not to fail Azize. Azize was not a violent man. And Noam felt a heaviness in his heart that made him wonder if that was not the Battle Born's true quest, to die like the rest of her order.

Shouldn't they try to heal such a wounded soul? Wouldn't Azize have wanted to any other day? He hadn't just pulled men around him for himself. He'd also pulled them together, given them a new family, a new purpose. Wouldn't the Azize of just a few weeks ago have wanted the same for this creature?

"He killed everyone she knew and loved," Noam began, intent on gently leading his friend to the same conclusion.

"That doesn't mean I can allow her to kill anyone." Azize had tried to appear stoic hearing his father was cursed, but Noam knew it was part of what fed Azize's growing vehemence.

Noam shook his head. "No. Revenge will gain her nothing but..."

"But?" Azize prompted, enraged.

Noam could not voice what he was thinking. That it frightened him to hear his friend so quickly leap to murder. That he began to wonder how well he knew his friend.

"Nothing," Noam said at last. "I will try to find her and discover for certain what she is after."

Azize nodded. "Do that. Later, we will speak with Daniel and the others to develop a plan should it be hostile. I will see if I can convince my father I am here to stay."

Noam watched his friend go, disturbed by his new energy. Had Azize truly been ready to come home? Perhaps more time seeing the varied nuance of the world would have helped him to see that there were more ways in life than anger and death.

INTERNAL FIRES

Nuru had left Neema in the kitchens and returned to the party in search of help. She'd advised Neema to go down the tunnel at the back of the kitchens and hide in the Queen's Retreat, where men were not allowed, but Neema seemed to want to be around others. And Hanifa had promised to stay with her. She was an odd one, it could just be that she was resigned, or stoic, like Hadhi, but her reactions to all Neema had revealed seemed too small for someone who did not already know and too angry for someone who did not care. Then there was the way she let Nuru see the little scars on her wrist when she gave her food to take with her to explain her absence. Nuru had seen a similar scar on another wrist tonight. On someone else acting odd, Sade. Was there more to the women than met the eye?

Nuru may have great power, but so far she was not having overwhelming success in gathering help. By and large, the older generation of women either saw nothing wrong with the king taking anything or anyone he wanted, or they were too tired and frightened to do anything.

It was frustrating. No one seemed to have any ideas for how Nuru could keep the king from claiming Hadhi. And she didn't feel right addressing what she knew was happening to Neema without her permission. Even the women who agreed with Nuru had balked when she explained that she was worried for Hadhi.

"Nuru, there is no stopping the king. While your father lived maybe, but if King Enzi wants your sister for his bride, he will have her," Isoke said, her tone hollow. She performed as Nur in the Spirit Dancers. On stage such a force, but it seemed she hadn't much strength in reality. "Perhaps it is best. She has always been a quiet, obedient sort. She might be quite content."

Nuru had glared, enraged, and walked away rather than shouting what she really thought. She knew part of her rage had less to do with Isoke than it did with herself for all she had failed to see happening to the people she loved.

Azize had finally returned. He didn't say a word about what kept him, didn't apologize, just began going from one woman to the next, talking with her, asking her to dance. Nuru noticed that Noam was back again. The first time he returned without Hadhi, Nuru had been angry with him. Now she was just resigned. She'd been right he was going to leave. Azize was going to leave; his feet kept angling away from the women he spoke to. They would go away and leave Hadhi worse off than she was before.

A woman of Maltuba can marry a cheetah or a gazelle.

Why had he even come home?

"Nuru, I would have expected you to be celebrating, not sulking." Eshe, who led the Spirit Dancers, came up alongside her and spoke with a smile in her voice.

"What's to celebrate?" Nuru grumbled, not even looking at her. After everything Neema had revealed and how much Hanifa knew, she had to assume Eshe knew as well. She wished this woman would not talk to her. She'd refused to let Nuru join her dancers, and Nuru had pressured Hadhi to fix it so much that they fought. And now Hadhi was suffering. And Neema was already suffering. They had nothing to say to each other.

"Did your uncle not send word?" She laughed. "I thought he must have, when you danced with Faizah. This morning, I received his offering so you might join the sprint dancers."

The fulfillment of every one of Nuru's dreams momentarily overrode her seething rage. She leapt forward and grabbed Eshe's hands. "Truly? I may join you?"

"Truly." She gripped Nuru's hand back. "I will be honored to have you among us. I've watched you with interest for years. Cheer up, dance. There is nothing in life that cannot be overcome if one only finds *the right movement.*" She smiled softly as she reclaimed her hands and Nuru saw a similar mark on her wrist to the one on Hanifa and Sade before she walked away.

Nuru spun around, overjoyed. This was everything she'd ever wanted. She could dance. And she was sure now, there was more going on than she knew. Perhaps once she officially joined the dances, Eshe would trust her enough to tell her what it was. The second time she spun around she came to a stop with Mzaa right before her.

"What was that about?" Mzaa demanded, but before Nuru could answer, she went right on asking questions. "And where is your sister?"

Nuru swallowed her news. Mzaa wasn't who she wanted to tell. That was Hadhi. She would be overjoyed. She might even dance with Nuru, she would be so happy for her. The thought sucked Nuru's excitement away. She was getting everything she wanted, and Hadhi was being stalked by another cheetah. And even if there was some secret movement going on, how fast was it moving? Would it be fast enough to save her sister? It had already failed to truly protect Neema. So much was unfair.

"Which one?" Nuru asked flatly.

Perhaps Uncle Kafil was doing things to help them all. Perhaps he would...what? Refuse the king permission to marry his niece? Not likely.

"Hadhi," Mzaa snapped. "She shouldn't pout. The king has shown a preference, but nothing is definite. She should be in here."

Maybe Mzaa was right. Maybe if Azize asked Hadhi to marry him first, there would be no king to worry about. Hadhi didn't love Azize, but—

Nuru's mind went quiet with the rest of the room as a pair of Enzi's guards came over to Azize and led him onto the veranda with a hand on either arm. Nuru craned her neck to watch. The king was waiting for his son.

Sabra had taken Lin outside to nurse; this had been a very long day. She had nodded off twice inside the ballroom. It was so warm and nothing was happening. Azize should just run away if that's what he wanted, leave them in peace. Life hadn't been active or new before, but it had been fine. Sabra hadn't lost hours of sleep. She supposed in fairness she should admit that his arrival was what had helped her realize she was free. She was grateful for that. But she was beginning to worry that his return had further fractured this already deeply wounded family.

"I present you with all the women of Jaccada, and some from even further into your nation, and you spend the night plotting with your soldier friends," Sabra heard the king thunder, clearly to his son, and her heart sunk. Azize should not have come home while his father lived.

"I spent barely any more time with my friends than I did with the women. And none of it plotting." Azize sounded more confident than usual.

"Then where were you? Why were your soldiers searching my home?"

"They are not *my soldiers*, they are my friends, and they were searching the palace for me. I was...with a woman. You are right, it was past time I did my duty by my nation. I have decided to stay and marry."

Enzi chuckled windily. "Have you? How coincidental. I've decided to take a bride myself."

Sabra's stomach roiled. It took focused effort to keep her from squeezing her son to her chest. No. No. No. Not Hadhi. Not anyone. Why had Azize come home?

"You don't want another wife. You told me all my life how much you disliked having my mother underfoot."

"And I did," Enzi laughed. "But I cannot count on you to uphold my legacy. I've found a woman who will birth me strong sons, forceful ones."

"I said I was staying," Azize bit out. "You are only trying to best me. And you have! I'll stay. I'll marry. I'll carry on your legacy."

"Good. That's settled then."

"Wait!" Azize shouted as the king walked away. "Where are you going? I wanted—" He trailed off, chasing his father into the palace.

Sabra stood slowly, her feet moved ahead of any conscious command as her mind was far away and—SCREAMING!

She didn't know that she had ever felt this angry before. She'd been scared when Zuberi forced her, and her anger afterwards was always seething. It had no space to rage; all the space in her being had been taken up with a frantic need to not draw his notice. A need to make herself so numb that she didn't feel it when he forced himself on her and didn't care when he beat her. Her entire being had been swathed in numbness for two and a half long years. And now she was free. And what should be coming out was joy and at last peace. But it wasn't. The feelings rising in her now were fire and destruction and so much rage.

How could he? How could they? Why did no one ever stop them?

Sabra had never felt such hate as tore through her body now as she looked on the boy she'd once thought to love and wished he'd never returned.

BEST LAID PLANS

A high screech like an aborted scream caught Zawadi's ear, followed by a heavy thump. She followed the sounds down a side hall off the ballroom. She'd been planning to grab Nuru, or Jauhar, make the best use of this Asha form, but the sound shook across her back. And had her shoulder rolling towards the scars that prevented her arm from rising to its full length in her own body.

That was it. The sounds made her feel her true body.

She froze alone in the hall. She could see the arc of a bloody sword as it was yanked from between her shoulder blades and stabbed into the throat of the woman rushing to defend her. Saw Emu fall, her body collapsing over Zawadi's legs, and heard the high cry of anguish from Kiwi. Her body flailed as she tried to stop Kiwi coming nearer, tried to grab ahold of Emu as she gurgled and jerked, tried to stop the man above them. The monster destroying their haven.

She might have stood there forever alone in a hallway reliving her destruction had she not seen the jerking movement at the end of the hall. A foot. It flopped up and hit the ground with a thud. A few seconds of quiet passed, then the foot and likely the body it was attached to was dragged out of sight.

Zawadi crept nearer. She didn't want to. She likely shouldn't. But she kept seeing Kiwi. Her poor precious, defenseless Kiwi. The body she had given to Asha tonight. She knew it wasn't her. That foot likely belonged to a man. But...she felt Kiwi, defenseless, rushing towards her death because someone else needed her.

Zawadi didn't race towards the violence, but with every second, she moved a little faster. Kiwi urging her forward. Nighthawk, and Sparrow, and

Wren moving her feet far more than Zawadi was. There was something they wanted her to see.

The first thing she saw when she rounded the corner was the trail of blood, so like the trails of blood all over her home from one daughter, one sister after another trying with their dying breaths to shield another. Revulsion crawled up into her mouth long before she spotted the man being dragged away.

He was a shock of red, the blood running down his face merely blending in with his hair and thick beard.

Elof. The man who'd blushed with amusement when Zawadi called Azize a shy boy and offered her mocking protection. His head was slumped forward and there was a rag stuffed into his mouth, but when she stepped close enough to be seen, his eyes lit with panic and he tried to fight again, trying to wave her off. She saw in his eyes what she had seen in the eyes of so many of her dead: no fear for his own life. Only for hers.

And when she looked up, met the grin of the man in the shadows, even now slipping an arm around Elof's throat to steal his air...when she looked into his eyes, she knew who he was, knew. But all she saw was the man who'd created him. Zuberi shadowed Kane in iridescent particles of golden light like dust drifting through the air, but so much more electric.

Zawadi couldn't make her body move. Her dead were holding her here, forcing her to see. She could do nothing but watch as Elof, deprived of air, was robbed as well of his fight and slumped unconscious in Kane's arms.

Kane lifted a finger to his lips, winking. "Back to the festivities with you, and don't tell a soul. Or I'll be after you next." He laughed when he said it as if it was a joke, but Zawadi knew the heart of this man, and he meant it as much as any other threat he'd ever made.

Freed from the hold of her dead, Zawadi raced down the hall away from him. What had she unleashed?

The king's soldiers were on very high alert. They had been subtly growing in number in the ballroom. Now there were near as many soldiers as women. And as far as Noam could tell, neither Dion nor Mikhail had returned.

He was more relieved than he would have expected when he found Tadeo, Daniel and Massahiro talking in a corner.

"That's five missing now that no one can find Kane," Massahiro was saying as Noam approached. "And the palace guard are making sure we cannot get close enough to see what is going on with Azize and the king out on the balcony."

"Not only that balcony," Tadeo whispered. "They are blocking nearly all of our potential escapes. I am aware of only three available. A secret passage through the kitchens leads out to the docks. The walls in Gzifa's garden are easily scaled. And behind the chained jackals in the menagerie, there is a feeding room with a window large enough for a man. But...we cannot get all of us out."

"Nor can we leave Azize and the others behind," Daniel remarked.

"If you are all caught, you will be no help to Azize," Noam put in softly.

"Agreed." Tadeo nodded. "That's why I sent Elof, Royko, and Tareek out through the menagerie. But some of us must stay."

"I will," Noam answered at once. "I am of least use outside."

"I was under the impression Azize gave you a mission. Some magic being?" Daniel asked.

Noam shifted his shoulders and stood a little straighter under Daniel's regard. Had he overheard their discussion? What did he make of Azize's violent impulses? He seemed not to doubt Noam could complete the mission Azize had given him.

"We will get you out, and you will do what Azize has asked. None of the rest of us have seen her."

Noam shrugged. "I imagine you have all seen her, but..."

"You know it when you do," Tadeo slapped his shoulder.

Noam nodded. "And I know who she is after. But I need more information."

"Get it," Massahiro ordered. "I will make sure Gzifa's garden stays clear."

"How without drawing attention?" Noam asked.

Massahiro laughed. "Attention will be needed. I think I shall convince the *voice of the sun* to prove to me his god is stronger than the moon goddess." He winked and left.

Another day, Noam might have been amused to watch his friend trick, annoy, or seduce the stiff clergyman. But he was too nervous even to watch him go. Turning back to the others, Noam quietly gave voice to the fear building in him. He would not have been able to before, but these men truly seemed to see him as one of them; he could not let them go forth unprepared.

Noam sighed. "I may not be right about this, but...if Kane reappears, do not trust him. I believe he has been spying on Azize for the king. Protect yourselves."

The two men looked more confused, or concerned than convinced, but Noam didn't waste any more time. He left before they could ask more or argue.

Noam didn't know what worried him more, that Hadhi was somewhere facing off with the Battle Born, or that King Enzi's men had seen her running and captured her.

I was his monster. He was hiding me, biding his time.

Noam shook off her voice. Her heartbreak. He spotted Nuru alone in a corner and crossed to her.

"Nuru, do you know where Hadhi is?"

She shook her head. "The last time I saw her she was with you. I thought you would help her."

"I am trying." Noam clenched his fists. He kept trying but it only seemed to make things worse. "Do you know where she might go? Does she have a friend she might turn to?"

"She doesn't have any friends but me." Nuru looked at her feet, and her voice dropped to a whisper. "She cries in her sleep sometimes. She doesn't like anyone to know."

Noam's heart broke more with every word.

"I used to think all of them saw things wrong and I saw it right. That Maltuba was beautiful and as long as we were together, we were happy. But... Hadhi is never happy. I'm not sure anymore if my family was ever happy at all."

"Nuru." Noam reached out for her. Nuru looked confused but after a moment just gave him her hand. Noam squeezed it. "It isn't always easy to understand, but a family isn't happy *only if* it has no pain in it. I know Hadhi loves all of you. And I know that you love her, so there must be some happiness in your family, even when there was pain. There certainly was in mine."

Nuru's wide eyes seemed to beg him to promise that it was true. She looked furtively around the room and gripped his hand tightly.

"Do you really like her? Truly?"

"Yes. I..." Noam laughed; he shouldn't say it again. It had not gone well when he told Hadhi, but the words wanted speaking. "I love her."

"Then take her away." Nuru dropped his hand.

Noam forced a laugh, tried to sound light and amused. "Wouldn't you miss her?"

Nuru notched up her chin, looking very much like her sister for a moment. "Yes. But she deserves to be happy. She should not be...married to a cheetah."

"What makes you think she would want to marry me?"

"I said take her away," Nuru growled. "Not marry her."

Noam laughed. "I do not think your sister would go, if it meant leaving you behind. But...I promise I will do my best to see her safe, to see all of you safe."

"That isn't good enough," Nuru snapped. "My father promised to do his best to see Hadhi married. He promised to do his best to get Asha adventures. You need to swear that you will make her happy, that you will keep her far away from King Enzi."

Noam held still, because inside he was shaking. He couldn't make such a promise. He didn't know where Hadhi was. He didn't know how to protect her. And even if he got her away from Enzi, Noam could not promise that Hadhi would be happy. She had told him so many terrible things from her past, but he knew from the way she spoke and the pain she still carried that there were many more inside of her. Pain like that didn't go away.

"I cannot make those promises, Nuru. They would only be wishes. Life is...harder than that. But I will promise you this—A fey woman told me I was blessed with luck—and I give you my word that not only will I love her, I will give Hadhi all my luck. Alright?"

He thought it was possible Nuru had matured in only a matter of hours, because he was certain the girl he'd spoken to at the beginning of the evening would have taken those words and been filled with hope and reassurance. But she shook her head. Noam opened his mouth to try and find something to reassure her, but horns sounded, and as one, the gathering turned to look on the king and his son.

"Women of Maltuba, joyous news!" the king shouted brightly. "This has been a bountiful ball. Both my son and myself have found brides among you."

No. Noam clenched his fists. Beside him, he heard Nuru gasp, felt her drawn upright with rage.

"Tomorrow, before nightfall, we shall both claim brides from the house of Zuberi, honoring the name that has already served our people so well."

Tomorrow!

Noam's eyes shot to Azize, who looked equally surprised, perhaps even horrified. Apparently, he hadn't played the chastened son well enough, because his father was trying to force his hand.

It seemed that was all the announcement the king meant to make, as he and Azize left the floor. The nerve of the man was disgusting. In a family of five women, announcing he and his son would each take one woman but not bothering to say which. And Noam knew neither woman had been asked.

As the royalty left the floor, there was a practiced cheer from around the room, but this corner was quiet. Nuru held up her head as Hadhi might in her place, with her eye burning across the men. Noam wanted to scream. He wanted to race to the stage and strangle the king, strangle Azize. Wanted to burn this place down so no one else should ever feel so again.

1 LOVED THE MONSTER

"Did you love him?" the child snarled.

Hadhi knew her answer; she had been saying it all night. She was glad her father was dead. She hated him. *Only* hated him. But she stepped back, staring at the tiny, dry, sparkling child in the rain. The nymph. It all but begged her for an answer. Did she love her father? Would not it be likelier to spare her if she said no? Yet Hadhi could not force the word out.

"Did you love him?" the girl shouted.

Hadhi opened her mouth, felt sure she knew what would emerge, but before she could speak a voice rose up within her, wrapping itself around all the anger and the sadness, even the fear, wrapping her up as if she were being embraced from within her heart.

It's alright, Hadhi. I love you.

She could not hear Noam before, could not feel his love—or *her own*. But Hadhi turned away from the child, staggering to the white rocks. She collapsed against one and stared at the ground where her father had died. She saw his face before her. He was smiling, completely stunned, with a hand against his wound. He looked up at Hadhi, and despite the betrayal and the fear of death, for the first time Baba seemed *proud of her*. And it shook her to the very center of her soul, made her run away, even though she sat beside him. Though she held his hand as he died.

"Yes," Hadhi answered. "I loved the monster, even knowing what he was." She felt like she should be crying, should be ripped apart by this knowledge, but she was not.

Perhaps she had cried all her tears already. This *love* she had for her father despite the pain, despite his evil, shifted through her, settling things that should be in chaos forever. She was a monster. She knew that but it did not seem to matter so much any longer. The nymph would kill her now, on the spot where she had killed her father.

It was right.

But the realization allowed her to recognize the love she had not understood.

"Will you..." Hadhi rolled her back against the rock, so tired now that she had finally stopped running. She felt so heavy it was as if she had been running since the day of his funeral and simply failed to know it.

She faced the child once more. "It was with King Enzi's approval that he killed your family. The king should be stopped."

The little girl had a hand over her mouth. She was sobbing and her clothes danced violently in a wind that seemed only to touch her.

"Hadhi," she sobbed in some terrible pain. Hadhi pushed off the rock. As soon as she reached for the child, a sharp talon of wind tossed her backwards. She fell to the ground a few feet away. "Hadhi, was he a bad man?"

"I..." There was something so familiar about this child, the way she spoke. "My father?"

The nymph nodded franticly.

Hadhi pushed onto her knees and stared. Was she the nymph? What else could she be with such magic? But how could it not know?

Perhaps, like Hadhi, the nymph was coming to see nothing was so simple.

"He was..." Hadhi began but could not seem to find the words to finish. She had a flash of memory, of her father's face, alight with beauty and love as Asha ran to him. Hadhi had been so jealous, she could not have been more than eight, making Asha just three, and when Baba lifted his Asha into his arms, he came alive. But Hadhi realized now there had been something else in his face.

"He was a jealous man. Frightened. He had been hungry, and hurt, and ignored, and he swore never to be so again. When we were little, Asha and I were friends. We shared a bed in the old hut, and when the animals in the night or a storm would wake her, I comforted her. I told her the sounds in the night were other children, the children of lions, and the children of thunder, all frightened by the dark calling out to their older sisters." Hadhi smiled, and her eyes stung. "She loved my stories. Once, after a storm, she rushed to our father in the morning, he had always, even then, loved her better. But I think perhaps he liked the way she showed her love. No caution about her, giving it all away. When she told him what I had said, there was a look of such...envy in his eyes. So he told her another story, of magic and faraway places he promised someone as simple as me would not know or understand. So she only went to him for her stories."

Hadhi tore her eyes from the ground and looked at the little girl. The wind seemed to be attacking her. It would shove at her shoulders until she staggered back a step or yank at her gown so it dug into her. "He was a bad man. But he was not only bad. He *loved* Asha. Loved the night breezes, and the ocean, leading to worlds far away. But he was so scared, all the time, that he forgot all the ordinary things he loved and grew only to love power. So whenever his power over our family, over the king, or over Asha was threatened, he would do something—" she shrugged, "—evil.

"He was a bad man," Hadhi repeated as she pressed against the ground, rising to her feet. She started towards the child. The magic was attacking the nymph, like Hadhi's heart attacked her, like her father's fear had attacked him. It was all, for every one of them, fear. And just like the noises of the night, it only needed to be put in perspective. "But he hid me from the king. And though he would not do it himself, he told me to keep my sisters safe."

Hadhi stopped before the girl, tears ran from her eyes, and the wind pulled at her, and she looked ready to split apart. Hadhi took a deep breath. "My father left me to guard them, his monster, he said."

The girl stumbled backwards, terrified of Hadhi now. Hadhi braced her feet one behind and one before her, and reached out for the child, catching her to her own chest, so the wind beat at them both.

"But I will protect them my way. I will not harm you." As she hugged the child against her chest, she felt the wind settling slowly, and the rain grew thin. And somewhere in the vicinity of her heart, Hadhi felt free, she felt beautiful. "If someone must die for his crimes, let it be me, please."

"Hadhi," the child creature whispered.

"He would not die for them," Hadhi continued, soothing the girl's back as she would her own sister. "But I would. Please, let me be enough."

"Hadhi," the girl begged in a little, pained voice. "Hadhi, I feel so weak. I think it will rip me apart."

"No," Hadhi whispered. She kissed the crown of the child's head. "I am here. I will hold you together."

Hadhi's lips touched the child's head, and a scream split the night. Light burst in all directions, and thunder raced through the air. In her arms the girl shook as magic burst free of her skin, and she was...transformed.

She grew and grew in Hadhi's arms, until, as the rain and thunder and light dissipated, she fell against Hadhi, sending her staggering backwards under the weight of her half-sister.

"Asha!" The word burst from Hadhi horrified. But her arms closed around her more tightly. She pulled her nearer, struggling under her weight. "Asha. Asha, wake up."

"I...can't." The words were so small, so unlike her sister. Hadhi began to grow frantic.

"Asha, what did you do?" She shook her sister. They both slipped on the wet ground until Hadhi was on her knees and Asha collapsed against Hadhi's shoulders with her legs stretched away from them. "Asha, answer me!"

"I wanted magic," Asha whispered. "Zawadi promised me magic and adventure. I'm so tired." Asha slumped completely over, her head falling forward limp, but Hadhi could feel the heavy rise and fall of her breaths. Slowly, she relaxed her hold and let Asha lay against her knees. Hadhi dropped her arms to her sides. She sat staring into the night and breathing.

Hadhi ran a hand across her sister's cheek. A child's body suited Asha well, she had been so innocent.

Hadhi, was he a bad man?

Hadhi did not know where she found the strength, she had felt completely worn out a moment ago, but she rolled her sister gently onto the ground and shifted so she crouched beside her. Hadhi stretched her arms beneath Asha and lifted her sleeping sister against her chest. Forcing herself to stand, Hadhi trudged slowly through the night, carrying her sister home.

SOUL SHARDS

"*Are you lost, boy?*"

"Sir? Are you lost?" The servant repeated the question, her words shaking loose the echo in Kane's mind. He stood straight, wiping the remnants of Elof's blood from his hands and turned to face the woman, but the sight of her with her hunched posture and burn ravaged face had the echo rising in him again.

"Are you lost, boy?" The woman moved towards him as if he was rabid. "Where are your parents? Do you know where you live? Have you eaten?" She paused between each question, giving him time to respond, but Kane could not.

He stared up at her lost...just as she said. Though he knew exactly where he was, and he knew for exactly what purpose he had come to be there, and knew the answer to each of her questions.

Where were his parents? Dead.

Where did he live? Nowhere. His home was gone.

Had he eaten? Not in days. Not since Zuberi gave him this mission and told him he could complete it or perish.

When he made no response, the woman sat on the earth before Kane and reached into a basket she'd been carrying. She removed a loaf of bread and tore into it, handing Kane a piece.

"I think we must be two of the same people, you and I. For your right hand is burned and my right face. We are what the old stories called qui'iti. So, having found each other we must share a meal, yes?" She tore off another chunk of bread and began eating, not even looking at him. And Kane could resist no more. He dug his teeth into the bread.

"No," he snapped with unnecessary force in the here and now. The servant, likely well used to physical rebukes, cowered away but did not leave.

Kane swept by her towards the palace, annoyed by the reminder, annoyed by this night, and the itchy feeling that had been attacking his skin with memories ever since he stood alone with Enzi.

Elof had taken more effort to subdue than expected. Kane had sparred with all of Azize's men, expecting just such a moment, learning their habits, their weaknesses, their favored strikes. But...Elof had been holding out on him. Kane wondered how many of the others had given equal forethought. All this time he'd thought he was trusted among them, but at least one of them was wise enough not to do so completely. So far Kane had captured only five of his thirteen traveling companions.

Dion and Renz had been simple enough, and Mikhail surprisingly swift. But Elof and Royko took some effort. This would be a wearing night. He heard the shuffling behind him and realized that the servant had followed him. How had he missed it this long?

We are what the old stories called qui'iti...Do you know what that means? Qui'iti? Has anyone told you the old stories?

Kane clenched his fists. But did not turn again to look at the woman behind him. She looked so like that old woman, his qui'iti, the scarred old woman he'd shared a meal with and even managed to speak to a bit.

Kane spotted Azize storming out of the palace the same moment Azize spotted him. Azize waved and his angry posture relaxed. He nearly rushed to reach Kane.

"Kane. At last, a friendly face." Azize radiated fear in a way he had not since they first set sail together. "You would not believe the looks I've been privy to tonight, and none of it for what I've done."

"What, Noam again?" Kane teased, rather certain that it would be deeper. "Ignore him. He had never left his tiny island and still is awed by each new thing he encounters. He simply does not understand you."

Azize shook his head and paced away. "No. Kane...I...what would you say if I...If I wanted to perhaps...stay?" He finished his very hesitant speech.

Kane glanced behind himself, looking for the servant, who was surely overhearing, but there was no one there. Only a dove hobbling along the ground after them with a bent wing. When had she gone? Where? There were no easy ways into the palace where he would not have seen light pour into the courtyard or heard the noise of a door opening.

"That bad?" Azize asked.

Kane jerked around and had his smile ready. "Of course not, I was looking for other ears, so I could be entirely certain of what you are saying." Kane whispered, "Because whatever you are saying, you must know we are with you, always."

Kane said it easily enough. It was even true in its own way. All of these grown men following around a boy who never grew up, fully devoted to him. They would do what he wanted. Even Kane, provided it didn't stop Kane from doing what he must.

And truly, Azize would understand. If he knew all he would understand. After all, he was another qui'iti.

Do you know what that means? Qui'iti? Has anyone told you the old stories?

Kane nodded and spoke around the bread he was devouring. He'd been told the old stories. "Soul bits."

"Umm." The woman nodded. "Very good. I prefer the fairy word fragments, or even shards. When others adapt a language to their own, they sometimes fail to express the truly powerful essence of a word. And bits, though close enough, sounds like something small and insignificant. But a qui'iti is someone who has a heart that knows your same pain or embraces your same joys. It is another piece of you wandering in the world. You will meet many in life if you are lucky. Every time I have met one, some part of my life has been made better, so always I try to make some part of their life better. Do you understand?"

Kane agreed around his food, as she handed him more. "That's why you're feeding me."

She laughed. "I would always have fed you, for you are my neighbor and I could see that you are hungry. But because we are pieces of the same heart, I wish to help you even more. Is there anything I can do that will make your life better? Make your heart stronger?"

Kane had stopped eating at those words. He was here for a purpose. At Zuberi's orders. Zuberi had said he would make Kane strong. Give him a chance to have his revenge. But in order to learn from him he had to prove his strength.

"Anything?" Kane asked.

She smiled. "If it is in my power. I want only for my other soul fragment to thrive." Kane was panting a bit, and she must have seen it, because she opened her arms, offering him an embrace.

Kane stood and walked into her arms. She was still seated on the ground, and his nine year old frame was only a head taller. He was smiling when she loosened her arms and when he shoved a blade into her throat. Her look of shock and fear didn't even shake him. This was why he was here, to find the other fragments of his soul and grow stronger. So he would be powerful enough to slay a beast.

"Thank you," he said as she gurgled on her own blood. Then he sat down and finished his meal.

"I need to stay," Azize said softly, unsure.

He was by far one of the more cowardly fragments of soul Kane had found. The one he was least interested in reabsorbing. He was too innocent still. He should maybe stay a boy forever. And that sort of soul piece wouldn't strengthen Kane before he killed the king, but he would do what he must if it came to that.

"But my father cannot be on the throne if I am to do that." Azize finally got the words out, and Kane grinned, surprised to hear reason and maturity from him.

"Indeed?"

"Yes...gather the others, as many as you can without being suspicious."

"I know the guards routes. I will not be stopped."

"It isn't just guards we have to worry about. There is a fey creature, able to disguise herself as anyone. She is after my father, and after destroying Zuberi's legacy. She may be dangerous."

"A fey creature?" Kane asked. And his mind combed over the evening, over the tingle under his skin, over all the little things he had seen. The way the king's sword had caught the light and its gems seemed to flare when he touched Kane's hand. The hand Asha had kissed. Asha, one of Zuberi's surviving family, who had also seen him in the hall with Elof, and he'd sworn her eyes had turned fully silver. "What sort of fey creature? From where do you have your information?"

"Noam. He overheard her with my father, using Asha's body apparently, but he thinks she means to kill them all, she...Kane? Are you well?" Azize cut himself off and lay a hand at Kane's shoulder.

He could feel himself grinning from ear to ear, and tried to reign it in, but...now he understood. This must be the creature that killed Zuberi. He had known it could not have been a mere man, even a group of men. And the strangeness of the evening as well was made clear. Some fey creature was toying with him. Trying to destroy him because Kane was Zuberi's legacy. He hadn't been hearing the cries of those he'd left behind nor seeing the ghost of the first person he killed for Zuberi. He was being manipulated. But she had shown her hand, and Azize had presented him with the perfect means to prove his worth to the king and prove he was Zuberi's legacy in one move.

"I am fine, just excited to at last have a real adventure with you." Kane winked. "I will gather the others. It seems like we'll be having a hunt."

"Yes, although I have asked Noam to seek out the creature. He's seen her, spoken to her, and seems to know something of her kind. But...There may yet be adventure," he spoke heavily. "There is something we need to do, tomorrow."

Kane slapped Azize on the shoulder hearteningly. Always he had been blessed by finding his other qui'itia. The old woman had taught him that before she served her purpose to him. And now even hesitant Azize would be of use. Presenting Kane with a fey creature intent on killing Enzi, one that even Zuberi could not best. *Kane* would capture it and make his own destiny, just as he'd told her he would. Even bumbling, bright faced Noam, who was no one's qui'iti, nor worthy of any of the fear Enzi felt for him, would be of use. He would lead Kane right to the creature, once Kane made way for him to escape the palace.

He was rather pleased with this night after all.

AT THE HOUR OF NEW DAY

There was not a woman in the throne room who had looked on the king or Azize with anything resembling pleasure, well, none but Mzaa. Sabra looked murderous for perhaps the first time that Nuru had ever seen. But she noted with pride the range of rage, disgust and disapproval on many faces. She was right, the people of Maltuba cared for one another, they were good, they simply had a bad king. The trouble was that that was all there was, some stiffening, some glares and a few whispers as the king and his son departed the dais. Everyone was afraid, too afraid to act. Then her eyes fell on Sade; she was arguing quietly with her mother. When it seemed like she won, Nia caused a loud commotion falling to the ground and moaning as if attacked.

Guards left their posts to check on her, but Sade ignored her mother and slipped out onto the veranda much the same way Shafira had earlier that evening. And Nuru chased after her, mimicking the way she moved.

She didn't call out to stop her, just followed at a distance. It became quickly clear where she would go, and Nuru felt relief well up inside her for a moment before it came crashing back down. What could Uncle Kafil do with his three motherless children and his never properly healed leg? What could anyone do against a king? But something had to change. She couldn't stand by like those other women in the ballroom and simply allow the king to keep harming his people. It wasn't just Hadhi. What about Neema? How many people knew? The way the vaashta had looked at her—the vaashta! They knew, didn't they? That was why they gave an offering to Eshe so she could join the spirit dancers. She was who Ayinde was speaking to, did he know as well? Had he just stood there and—but what could he do either?

Nuru hated this. All of it. She could almost wish she didn't have to know, but then the people around her would just go on being hurt, and she would go on being happy while they suffered.

Nuru reached the mansion ahead of Sade, because she remembered all the short cuts, but once there, she didn't know what to do, how to move. Could she really ask her uncle to risk his life, and his children's safety, when she could not think of a single way he could win? Before she had made up her mind, she heard shouting from within and scuttled in under the wall, by way of the water tunnel. Her feet and the bottom of her silk were wet, but she got inside with no one the wiser.

Oriole perched inside a crevice of the wall around Zuberi's old mansion and observed the gathered men inside its courtyard. In general, the Sisterhood of Battle Born were not overly fond of male gatherings. They tended to lead to a great need for Battle Born services, with all the dead scattered about after them. But Oriole was pleasantly surprised, well, it may yet lead to bodies, but it was starting from a positive place. Zuberi's brother was not very much like him.

She had not taken her own bird form to observe them. Nighthawk had far better eyes and ears for midnight observations. Her sweet courageous girl.

"With no warning, the king demanded every woman in Jaccada attend him at his palace and *suggested* no man over twenty need be present but musical performers. And we...bow down and rush to appease him! How many more of your wives and children and neighbors will we allow him to harm?" Kafil asked the gathered men. His daughter walked among them serving drinks and observing. Oriole wondered if they noticed.

"It is always easy to say we must stop him, easiest when it is your family he's cast his eye on. But your brother protected you from Enzi's wrath, Kafil," Amal remarked.

Kafil shook his head. "Zuberi threw me down a ravine and robbed my home when I tried to join with Ahon."

"And with his other hand, he fed you," Okal argued.

"That was Hadhi," Kafil's daughter snapped. "Uncle Zuberi wanted us to starve; she brought us food in secret. She brought Mzaa silk."

Interesting. Oriole wouldn't have expected that of Zuberi's eldest. But she felt such a burst of shock at the words that she sent her eyes into the shadows and spotted Zuberi's youngest girl, crouched and wide eyed, covering her mouth to remain silent. Interesting.

"Shafira." Kafil nodded towards the house. "Check on your brothers."

The girl rolled her eyes but obeyed.

"My brother is dead," Kafil said. At once the other men pretended sympathy, but Kafil was not seeking commiseration. "Had he lived I would not have dared to say anything. But he is dead. And Enzi hides in his palace, he knows he is vulnerable. For his king, and his amusement, Zuberi abducted Imara, burned her villages, and forced her favorite general to be his second bride."

Oriole jerked at a feeling like a tiny thread being yanked from beneath her skin. Blood and screams flashed through her mind for a blink of an eye then vanished.

She clenched her beak, focusing her power instead on Zuberi's youngest girl and the fresh horrors she felt within.

"He beat our neighbors, killed dragons and shaman," Kafil went on. "He had the speed of ten men in one."

Oriole saw a blade swinging out, slicing across a throat, stabbing at a heart, gouging into an eye socket. Carnage. Death. Her body ached to scream, to flee, and she could feel another such ache.

Any moment now, she expected the girl to run, or to shout out that it was all lies, as surely Asha would have in her place, but she stayed. Her hands fisted on the ground even as tears gathered in her eyes.

"While Zuberi lived, Enzi seemed all powerful. But...Enzi did not kill my brother. He is still seeking the culprit. This is our chance."

There was a long stretch of quiet as the men looked amongst themselves and weighed the certainty of what they had against the hope of a different future. It would end in blood shed after all.

"Mother bird!" The pained wail split across Oriole's mind, and she saw Kiwi. Precious Kiwi. She was not part of the sisterhood yet, far too young, but she had come to them with her mother, Emu. Everyone knew she would be the greatest among them one day. Tiny Kiwi, dragging herself across the floor, trying to save Oriole as Zuberi struck out.

Oriole flapped off the wall, circling the courtyard. She needed someone to move. She needed something to keep her out of that place. Oriole settled on a tree branch. Watched the men look amongst themselves and one man was elected by the eyes to speak their worry.

"There is not a man among us who would cast you before the vaashta for this, but...was it you who killed Zuberi?" Amal asked.

Kafil shook his head, grinding his teeth. "I was mourning my wife and our baby."

The other men nodded encouraging Amal's voice again. "Zuberi's killer might have been a protege trying to earn his place as Enzi's man. He might be just as dangerous. Even if it was some miracle stranger, what then? Are we meaning to let Azize rule? Shall we kill him too? Are you to rule us?"

Oriole snorted and it came out a mocking screech. They were valid worries.

"We will not be killing Azize. He is barely more than a boy. I do not know who should rule. Ahon would have been best. All I know is if we do not act now, nothing will ever improve."

There was much nodding and grumbling, but no one made a move to suggest a thing until the gate was shoved open. A young woman rushed in, and Kafil took to his feet in shock.

"Sade!" Kafil looked around uncomfortably, but the young woman walked forward with purpose.

"The king has made an announcement, and the prince," she spoke breathlessly and between the gaps in the teeth she was grinding. "Both intend to take brides from your family. *Tomorrow.*"

Zawadi had not remained at the ball long enough to hear this announcement. Racing out of the palace after her confrontation with what her wishes could unleash. But the words raced on many manic feet across her feathers making her wings shift, trying to escape the feeling. Was this too her work?

No. No. Enzi was a monster, and Azize was a foolish boy. She would not now or ever take the blame for the mindless way men set forth to claim all before them as if it were their right. But...

"Have none of you a thing to say?" Sade demanded.

"Who?" Kafil asked quietly, angling towards the house, towards his children, all of them below the age of eleven. It was good he thought of them and wished to protect them but—

"Does it matter? Is there a member of your family you will gladly turn over to him?" Sade demanded.

"No, but..."

"He will not be turning anyone over, Sade. King Enzi does not make requests," Okal attempted to chastise.

"Do not call him king and cower here like motes of dust." Kafil reached out to silence his betrothed, but she shook off his hand. "Your greatest fear is death, but every woman in his sight faces greater tortures. He is *one* man. One. Our plans cannot wait any longer, Kafil. I will not watch her be tortured by one more man because other men are weak."

"Hadhi?" Kafil asked in a whisper, but her soft smile and shy eyes of the past two days were gone. Sade was steel now.

"She was overheard tonight speaking of how her father wanted her scarred."

Kafil nodded sadly. "Shafira said. That...sounds like my brother."

"He put her in the path of two predators with a smile on his face." Sade's voice sliced through the gathering. One man specifically, Amal, bearing the brunt of her ire. "Then laughed with other men as she bled. All her life, she has been under the boot of one monster. We cannot stand by and laugh as she is cast at another."

Amal twitched under her gaze, but his voice did not emerge with apologies or with promises to defend her now. No such offers came from any man.

Zuberi's youngest abandoned her hiding place to rush forward. She grabbed her uncle's hand.

"Please," Nuru begged. "Please..." She was having trouble getting her words out. "Mzaa called him a cheetah and..."

"And Hadhi has been mauled by a cheetah before." Kafil crouched, taking Nuru into his arms. "We will stop him. I promise."

"He isn't *just one man*. He has the army and the vaashta on his side," Amal pointed out sharply.

"My plan will work," Kafil interjected with finality. "All we need is to get Enzi out of his palace."

Sade released a breath, softening towards Kafil. "The Queen's Marked are prepared. They will prevent him entering its walls again. If he leaves. And we can weaken the soldiers."

Plans were hastily made as Oriole observed. She was glad there were some among these people ready to rise but was still enraged that their uprising had not occurred before her people were slain to slake their king's greed for blood.

Oriole had come intending to punish this man. But she beat her wings into the air to leave him as he was. Like Sabra, Oriole found this man was one who'd suffered already from Zuberi's presence. And one who might help her curse on Enzi. She would leave him be.

He made me his, just as he wanted. Just as he left his mark on each of them.

Oriole shook off Sabra's voice and flew away. She would not be denied her vengeance.

BLOOD IN SAND

Hadhi did not make it home carrying Asha. Perhaps she was too heavy to carry now, and Hadhi was exhausted from all the running. But Hadhi suspected she had grown a bit weak after a year of using Asha as a servant. Hadhi had never minded work in the past, but as the monster grew within her, she hated everything.

This past year she had hated the air, the sun, her mother, her sisters, her new brother. She had hated them even as she cared for them and waited to protect them. The only thing she had not hated was the desert. Every night she would sit outside their home and stare into its expanse, watching the light retreat, until it touched only the thin edge near her hut. It was vast, empty, unknown. One could be reborn of such a place, freed of all their evil. She would stare into its sands and pray to Ether for such a rebirth. Though she was not raised to pray, raised to believe Great Spirits were guides not gods, Hadhi believed in Ether's divinity. Sometimes she could almost hear the goddess beckon her nearer. But that would mean abandoning her family, and even hating them, she could not do that.

Hadhi found herself and Asha a clump of trees that would offer a bit of protection should Hadhi fall asleep. She settled Asha as comfortably as she could on the ground, and resting her back against a tree trunk, slid to the ground to watch her sleep.

Asha always slept as if in the midst of a storm, thrashing about and kicking whatever sister had the misfortune of sharing her bed. But she was still now. Spent. At least Hadhi hoped that was all there was to it.

Her own hands shook as she reached out to feel her sister's brow. No fever. But magic did not need a fever to kill you. And Asha had clearly found the magic she always sought.

Hadhi leaned back against the tree, shaking from her soul.

"They kill a man with his greatest desire."

She shook off her father's voice. For something to focus on Hadhi let the bead crown fall to her throat and ran her finger through her soaking hair, pulling apart the coils and sectioning it. First in half, then taking up little sections towards the front, she began twisting her wet hair to curve around one side of her face. A little unfamiliar bug settled on a branch above her. Its wings stirred up the air restlessly every few moments, making a frantic hum. When Hadhi looked at it, the bug settled, not completely still, but its hum grew softer, patient. It was as though they soothed each other because when Hadhi took up the second half of her hair she felt less frantic despite the fear. She twirled the ends of her curls around her finger to hold the twists then let her hands drop. And her gaze shifted back to Asha.

This should not have happened. She was supposed to be taking care of her family, protecting them from the nymph. Hadhi hoped she was not too late to save Asha.

The thought left her breathless and achy but for none of the reasons she would have expected. It should be her promise to their father that made her worry for this sister who had not loved her in years, if she ever had. But it was her own love.

She—*Hadhi*—loved this sister.

The bug fluttered its wings softly and Hadhi smiled, because she felt from it a spirit that understood her own. And there was no one else to share this startling revelation with.

Hadhi did not care what Baba wanted! She had loved him all her life. Loved him when he hurt her. Loved him when he hurt others. Loved him when he made her into a monster. And he had never loved her back, but still *Hadhi loved.* Though she had not believed herself capable. Hadhi loved them all. She just could not feel it until tonight.

It would not be too late. Hadhi would not let it be.

"Asha, what did you do?" she whispered, running a hand along her sister's cheek as she slept.

"They kill a man with his greatest desire..."

She heard her father's echo again, felt the memory calling as it had when she ran. But there was so much less rage at the memory now. Only sadness, only regret for all his words she had taken in, and all his lies she had believed, and all the love she had failed to understand.

"You are running from them now." The words left Hadhi oddly pleased. But it would be short lasting, all her pleasures felt so brief that she would doubt she had felt them afterward. *"They are stronger than you, the wounded few."*

"No." He picked up his pace. *"They are not stronger. But they can look like anyone. I need to devise a strategy."*

"So we are distraction?" Hadhi demanded. *"Something for them to kill on their way to you?"*

He chuckled. "Not with my monster guarding."

"I will not kill them." It should be an oath, but it came out a question.

"You would prefer they kill Nuru? Or your mother?" He said it so lightly. He did not care at all, did he?

"What if I just let them have Asha?" she threw out and nearly sobbed when he chuckled.

He grinned over his shoulder. "She might come after her first. I mentioned my best beloved while I was convincing her to grant my wish."

Hadhi was momentarily numb with disbelief. "You would...let them kill her? Asha?"

He would let them kill his best beloved. *Ever since Asha was born, Hadhi had watched her father's love for her and been jealous. She longed to be his favorite child. The one he protected and adored. The one he carried on his shoulders and exalted to the world. But...he would allow her to be killed for something he had done?*

Was that what she had been fighting for her whole life? Was that flippant dismissal the love she had longed for? Was it the reason she had been scarred? The reason she did everything he said, no matter how much it made her hate herself?

Queen Imara's words drifted through her mind. "No soldier of mine was ever asked to kill for my will alone."

That was something she had done without his order. Murder. And it should feel like any other, but it did not. Imara was at peace with her end. And...Hadhi was too.

But she was never at peace with what her father asked. Never. Yet she kept doing it. Anything he asked, no matter how awful. Waiting for his love, his approval. And this was what his love looked like.

No. It had to be a trick. One more test. He was trying to send her away broken. He loved Asha. She knew it. He would protect her.

"Hadhi, when I was your age, I was already the right hand of our future king. I protected my family from every threat. Killed monsters and men with my bare hands. It is time you lived up to my legacy. If you want your sister alive, protect her."

"She is not my best beloved!" Hadhi shouted at the top of her burning lungs. There was a pounding in her head, and Baba just kept walking. The white rocks were up ahead, and he was not stopping. He was going to leave them all to die.

"You promised her adventure."

"And taught her to count on herself. Asha will be fine."

"You promised her magic, then went around killing it."

"Hadhi, you're no use trailing me. You know I never need you along."

She could see her hands covered in blood at his order, in his defense. You know I never need you along—it was not true. He was torturing her, testing her. "Come home and protect them!" she shouted, enraged, but still begging.

"I wonder what they would have to offer you, Hadhi." Baba stopped, seeming truly curious about her and what would make her happy for the first time. "Your mother is easy; she would wish for her place, acknowledged by all." He smiled the way he did when he called Hadhi his monster. Did he only appreciate his family when they were unhappy? "And Nuru would wish to live in the jungle, probably get eaten by a leopard with a smile on her face. Sabra would wish to be free of me. Do you suppose she would die for her freedom right then?" He chuckled.

"Why does that make you happy?" The words were torn from Hadhi with no real hope of an answer. She saw him as he had been the day he stopped her beating the king with a rock. The way he was when he nudged Asha until she called her sister Sour-Faced-Hadhi. The way he had smiled when she stood bleeding over three carcasses. Always at his happiest when one of them was hurt.

Why were they always trying to earn his love, when all he wanted from them was anger and sadness? Why was Hadhi always giving him exactly what he wanted?

Hadhi's tears slowly stopped falling. Her feet stood surely beneath her again. Baba would leave and they would be better off. Maybe they would even be happy. Until they died.

"But you...what do you want more than anything, Hadhi?"

She took a deep breath, felt the air fill her lungs. For the first time in her life, her father wanted to know something about her and she...did not care.

"Asha would ask for adventure! She is such a special child I imagine the nymph will want her to have it. Even if she hates her for being my child."

"They are going to kill us all," Hadhi realized aloud, oddly unmoved. There was something smooth and distant floating through her. "You would, if you were the creature."

"I'd kill you all and make it watch," he said with such fierceness Hadhi wondered if he was trying to scare her. She was not sure she could be scared any longer.

"Why?" Hadhi wondered. "That would not bother you."

He only smiled as he walked around her, bumping a few things loose from his pack. They fell to the ground.

Hadhi walked behind her father, picking up the things he dropped and carrying them to him, out of habit, out of hope. He wanted to know what she would have wished. It seemed impossible he would not know. He knew her darkest thoughts, knew she understood him as only another monster could. How could he not know? Her greatest desire had always, only been to have his love.

She stopped before Baba and held out his medallion and his old dagger, the one his father gave him. The one he taught her to hunt with. "If you are the strongest monster in the world, you will stay."

He looked not at what she was offering him, but into her eyes. Searching her for something about which he could approve. Something he would never find.

"My father wasn't everything I desired either. But I loved him. I gave him a legacy to make him proud." His tone fell over her with that ever familiar disappointment. "If my father had called Kafil his best beloved, even once, Kafil would have been dead before sunrise." Hadhi felt the words like a claw to her heart. "I used to think it was a weakness of womanhood that kept you from killing Asha."

Hadhi's breaths were coming more heavily now, the motion of them lifting her head up and down so her father swayed before her. The world in front of her was blurry but the world in her mind was crisp. She could see it, like a hunt, like one more challenge. She had met so many of his challenges:

"Kill this animal," Baba would say. But Hadhi would hear "kill it and I will love you." And so she struck.

"You are not fast enough to follow this creature," Baba would say, but Hadhi would hear, "prove your speed and I will love you." And so she proved her speed, and an entire tribe were decimated by her father.

"Kill the leader of the Fazzaat, he is wicked like Enzi," Baba had said. But Hadhi heard "kill this man and I will love you enough to kill Enzi for you." And so she struck. So blood slid smooth and warm over her fingers, and ugliness filled her soul.

Over and over again. Every challenge met. And she knew what he would say next. "Kill your sister, prove you love me," Baba would say. And Asha...who she had hated, and resented, and envied. Asha whose very name filled Hadhi with rage, would bleed and fall, and finally there would be no one standing between Hadhi and her father's love. Finally! She would prove it. That was what he wanted. What he had always wanted from her. All she needed to do was kill her greatest rival—her sister.

Rama's little girl—that Hadhi had held and cleaned as Mzaa tended to Rama. The baby so bright that every eye was drawn to her. Hadhi's first little sister. She used to wrap her whole hand around one of Hadhi's fingers—so tight as though she needed to have her sister near, as if she felt safe with her.

And yet Hadhi could see herself do it. Kill Asha. If he asked—Hadhi always did what he asked. But...why? Why would he? Had he never loved Asha? Did he love anyone? Was it a trick? It must be a trick to make Hadhi feel weak and confused.

"I wonder now if it isn't just that you don't care. Do you not love your Baba at all, monster?"

Hadhi heard the ping of the medal striking the dirt, felt her hand curve around the smooth handle of Baba's knife, her fingers sinking into its time worn grip.

She used to hate this knife, fear it really. But it was comfortable now. He had taught her to hunt with it, not because he loved her, but because she was of an age to know and was useless in other ways. She felt...separate. Could not feel any other part of her body. Numb from so much pain. Only her hand and the knife fit within it existed.

"Do you love anyone?" she whispered shakily.

"There is no such thing as love, monster. Not for creatures like us. We've transcended it! For us there is only pow—Aaacch!"

Hadhi and her father looked down in the same instant. She had barely felt her hand move, but she felt the jerk of his blood pushing against her blade and her calm fled. Her hand shook on the knife stuck in Baba's gut. In his artery. He stared at it for the longest time, as blood pushed against the blade in frantic pulses, bits of it splattering over Hadhi's hand on the knife.

He began to chuckle, and the blade shook so badly Hadhi thought it might shake loose. There would be no hope for him then.

What had she done?

"Is that the best you can do?" Baba laughed harder. "You'll have to do better when the nymphs arrive. Ugh." He shoved Hadhi aside, but—Hadhi made sure—the blade came with her. She stepped to the side just as blood leapt from his body in pulsing

sprays. He gasped, shoving a hand over his wound. But it did little to stop the blood gushing forth.

He managed a few steps forward, the blood spraying the ground ahead of him. Hadhi stared at it, shaking all over with her hand covered in blood. His blood. He stumbled. Fell to his knees and removed his fingers from the wound to brace himself on the ground, though it only allowed the blood to spurt faster. His eyes found Hadhi. And he—smiled.

He showed all the pride she had ever wanted to see in his eyes, mixed in with stark betrayal. Hadhi wanted to die.

"My monster." He collapsed.

"Baba!" Hadhi rushed to him, despite the pooled blood beneath him and the now much smaller spurts still pulsing out of his body. She threw herself to the ground beside his head and lifted it to her knees.

He grinned. "Look after my legacy."

"I will." Hadhi promised and meant it. But she could do nothing more to help him. She was his monster, and though she had not thought about it, she had meant this too. Or else her knife would not have sunk into an artery. She had meant it, or else she would not have removed the blade, the only thing staving off his death.

She knew how to kill. It was all she knew. That—and that they would all be safer with him dead.

"My monster," he managed, his voice so weak, so small, so...ordinary. "What would you wish for now?"

Hadhi caught her breath and held her father closer. She watched the life drain from him and felt her breaths hitch with his. She had loved him more than anyone, and she had killed him. He was right.

She was a monster.

The air was quiet around Hadhi and Asha now, the little bug's hum having settled, but its gaze still comforting Hadhi. The animals of the night were all making their way home. It would be dawn soon, and yesterday had been so long, but Hadhi could not sleep. There was a thin dew of tears on her cheeks. She watched Asha, this sister she loved, watched her and felt the love she had tried to deny growing and glowing within. Perhaps she did not need Ether to be reborn. All she needed was this. She might be sour-faced and bitter, she was certainly a killer. But she would not be her father's monster. She had what he never did, this knowledge that she could—and that she *did*—love.

WORLD TURNED OVER

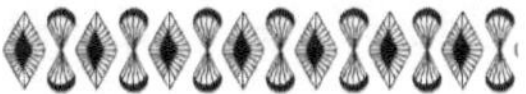

THE SUNRISE CURE

Asha woke to her entire body aching, stiff, and heavy. She was outside with the sun just rising. She felt the overwhelming need to cry but didn't understand it as the sleep first dissolved from her mind.

The others he slew...

Asha's breath hitched.

"Gov uli zat vaolit suriltelle kup nur mbede." Hadhi's voice so startled Asha that she hiccuped, and her tears were gone. *Have you ever truly watched the sun rise?* Asha pulled her head along the ground until she saw Hadhi, leaning against a tree, staring into the distant sunrise. "Szii gov nong." *I have not.*

Hadhi went on quietly. "Paax ouwoa oon havo zuliff. Pactic paax nong pyo ava urilla, nok ava liaama et looi et yamaam. Uli kudu gzaij paax qew haaju ulin ruaat hio uli ayzat drou kup ty ialana fytic." Speaking in Maltuban and with so much passion, so much gentleness. *It creates a new day. Filling it not just with light, but with warmth and color and activity. You can feel it tingle across your skin before you even hear the other animals waking.* Asha was unused to poetry from Hadhi. And she knew Hadhi was not used to it from herself. She'd even said it, complimenting Asha and disparaging herself. *I stammer like a fool.*

It just wasn't so.

"Nuru said she woke one morning, saw its colors and felt the whole world quiet. Sharing the moment with her and knew she was done mourning our father."

Asha dragged her heavy head towards the sunrise as well. They sat together quietly, waiting. Colors rippled out like swaths of fabric remaking the sky. Remaking the whole world.

Asha heard her sister's shaky sigh and pushed up onto her elbows to watch her. Hadhi leaned against the tree, with her head thrown back and her eyes closed. A vibrant smile transformed her face. She looked...*beautiful*. Asha had never met this sister, never even seen her. She was someone entirely new.

Asha's stomach dropped, dragging her back into the dust.

"Are you well?" Hadhi asked, gently. "Are you too weak to sit?"

"No," Asha nearly sobbed the word. The world had been remade with the sunrise, and Asha didn't understand it. Couldn't comprehend a world in which her father was a bad man. If he was bad, and she was his beloved, made him happy, and shared his dreams, didn't that make her bad as well? Was it fair then? That she had never been loved by her sisters? That they used her as a servant? Fair because she was the one who had had the most love from a monster?

"I loved him too, you know?" Hadhi sounded as if she understood Asha's internal tumult better than she did herself. "For the longest time, I thought that made me as bad as him, but last night you showed me the truth. Thank you, Asha."

"I didn't do anything," she grumbled as she struggled to push herself up, angry with Hadhi for implying she had done anything for her. Hadhi leaned forward to assist Asha with a hand under her elbow. "Hadhi! You're freezing."

Hadhi laughed. "The sun will warm me soon enough. The desert at night is cold for one soaked by magic rain."

Asha clasped her sister's arms and rubbed her hands, up and down, trying to restore a bit of warmth. Desperate for reasons she could not explain. Hadhi smiled, shivering, as if the returning warmth made her colder than her freezing skin had.

"He loved you for all the things you were, that he never could be," Hadhi spoke through chattering teeth. Asha continued trying to warm her, the motion allowing her just enough distance from Hadhi's words that she could bear to hear them. "You were generous, and trusting, and loving. He could not be, so he held you as close as he could because he wanted to be like you."

"Et fuputelle szou vis mav adoa." *And made me like him instead.* There were so many things Asha was coming to understand for the first time today. Their past was so different than she'd seen it. Every word Hadhi had said this morning was in Maltuban and her sister was...*eloquent*. Baba had always called her foolish. Baba who hated them speaking anything but Fairy. He'd stolen Hadhi's voice. Even the scars on her chin and throat, that old story of Baba's grand rescue when Hadhi was careless, must be viewed differently.

Asha remembered laughing when Baba told it. Cheering when he spoke of slaying the cheetah that had clawed his daughter. And she remembered Hadhi—silent and heavy in the corner. Why hadn't Asha noticed then? Why hadn't she noticed how his teasing stole Hadhi's light? Hadhi used to have light.

I thought it was impossible to love me.

Asha couldn't stand to see all she'd ignored. She was awful. Even now—even *knowing*—Asha wanted to rail against Hadhi for managing to ruin all her adventures in one fell swoop. *He was a bad man.* She'd known Hadhi would ruin her adventures. And just the thought had tears, gouging her eyes.

She pulled Hadhi against her chest and ran her hands up and down her back. She wanted to say *I* love you, but she didn't know herself in this world. What if she only hurt Hadhi more with the words? What if the feeling went away with a little more sunshine? So Asha only clasped her closer and rubbed her hands faster, desperate to do something for this sister. However small a thing.

"You..." Hadhi shivered. "You are not like him. Nothing mean or hurtful you have done was meant to destroy. It is alright to love him."

"No, it isn't," Asha hissed as tears started falling. It wasn't alright, not if he was the one who took Zawadi's children from her. Not if he was the one who made Hadhi feel unlovable. Not if he was a...*brute*. It wasn't alright, but Asha's heart ached with missing him and such ceaseless confusion. She didn't know who she was if he was evil.

Hadhi's shaking arms closed around Asha. "Alright." Asha could swear she heard a smile in Hadhi's voice. "It is alright, Asha." She laughed joyfully, for perhaps the first time Asha had ever heard. "I love you."

Asha clung tighter to repress the voice of her skepticism. Hadhi had never loved her. Asha had always known it. She thought of all the angry, spiteful looks Hadhi had thrown her way. Her triumph when Asha was forced to stay home from the first ball. That ugly smile she wore when she'd told Asha she had only Azize's dislike. She thought of the pile of silk unwound from her mother's gown and her stomach dropped. That wasn't love.

Both sisters stiffened in the same instant, and when Hadhi spoke her voice was so small and fearful it felt like she must have stolen it from someone else.

"I...the silk in Nuru's hair, I collected it in the caves," she whispered, so hesitant. Again, Asha felt their strange telepathy in this new day. It unnerved her. Might they have always had it? If they had embraced their love for each other? "I would not have done that to your mother's silk, I swear. But I understand if you cannot believe me."

The strange thing was, Asha did believe her. Her words were so fervent, so desperate. But Asha didn't need even that. She would not have believed the same words yesterday, but she had met her sister now, she was gentler and much more loving than Asha had ever imagined— *Of Sour-Faced-Hadhi? The name my sister Asha gifted to me.*

Asha let out a little sob. "I am so sorry," she mumbled into her sister's neck. As all her own unkindness rushed through her memory.

"Asha." Hadhi pushed slowly out of her sister's arms. She was still shivering, but no longer as violently. She regarded Asha with quiet concern. "*I* am sorry. I did not destroy the gown, but...I have hurt you. And that was wrong. I...I never meant to take him from you. I should not—"

"I should have known!" Asha cut her sister off. Azize had said she was the only person in Maltuba who did not know what her father was. "I was never anyone's fool before. I don't let people manipulate me, or get the better of me, but he..."

"Was your father. He made you feel special. How were you to know?"

"I..." Asha was halfway to shouting that she'd seen through everyone else. But she hadn't, had she? She'd never really seen Hadhi before, and she hadn't understood Azize at all, hadn't realized Zawadi was after revenge. What else didn't she see?

"What did Baba do?" It felt wrong calling him that, as if he was too evil to earn a name of such love. But it was who he was, who he had always been.

And though she was begging to know the truth, Asha longed to cover her ears and erase her memory and remain who she had always been.

She wanted to call out to Zawadi and beg her to work some magic so that yesterday might never have happened. She wanted to go back. She could be a servant to her family forever if she could only forget. She longed to do it, but she wasn't. She was facing that truth as Azize said she never did. She wouldn't let him be right. She couldn't be a fool.

"You do not want to know. I did not either."

"Tell me." Asha pushed slowly to her feet. She shook a bit as she stood, her whole being feeble and *hungry*. So hungry. She couldn't remember the last time she'd eaten. But all she hungered after was the power.

Of course, you are Zuberi's daughter.

Hadhi stood, rolling her shoulders and neck. "To the nymphs, or to anyone?" Hadhi asked, on a yawn.

"Both."

Hadhi crossed her arms and rubbed her palms up and down them herself. "For the king, he would...frighten men. Beat their wives and their children. He and his soldiers murdered leaders of other tribes and fey creatures that were aligned with our enemies or our allies." Hadhi paused, looking very much like the sister Asha had always known. Then she shook her head, forced her features to relax, and she spoke much faster. "Anything he thought was necessary to keep them in line. It was he who beat Uncle Kafil. He was speaking out against the king, so Baba threw him down a ravine." Asha gasped, but Hadhi kept right on speaking. "He knew he would survive, but he would not be able to care for his family; they were meant to starve and come to Baba begging for forgiveness. It was a lesson. He was full of lessons for other people, other nations. He would sneak into Reethrun and leave threats against their king or destroy crops."

"But...he said the furthest from home he'd ever been was the outer provinces. He..." It was such a small lie. But it felt almost worse knowing that he'd seen other kingdoms than it had knowing he'd beaten the children of her neighbors and starved her cousins? She really was evil, wasn't she?

"What did he do to Zawadi's children?"

"Whose?"

"The nymph's."

"Oh." Hadhi dropped her arms and pulled her head up, staring sharply into her sister's eyes. Looking as threatening as she had last night, when she mistook Asha for Zawadi. "He killed them. He found one," Hadhi spoke slowly, and Asha felt sure at any moment her half-sister would reach out and offer Asha comfort she didn't deserve. "And asked her to grant him a wish, to see her entire tribe."

Asha covered her mouth, but a gasp fled through the crack in her fingers.

"He killed nearly all of them, but a few wounded ones got away," Hadhi finished.

"He just killed them. For no reason? Had they attacked? Threatened?" Asha pressed, and Hadhi just kept shaking her head. Tiny little shakes, as if it did not warrant the energy to truly deny. As if this world dismantling knowledge was insignificant.

"There must have been a reason!" Asha shouted, overcome. Her entire body pulsed with rage and disbelief as the world opened up before her and was entirely foreign. "You said they would kill us."

"For revenge, yes. At least, he said they would." Hadhi searched her sister so thoroughly Asha wanted to squirm. "What did it offer you? What exactly did you wish for?"

Asha was panting, her hands fisted before her, and her eyeballs felt like they were swelling one moment and clenching tight the next. She couldn't see in front of her face. Everything, everything, *everything*—she ever believed was a lie. And she was so tired. Who was she? Who was anyone?

"Asha?" Hadhi prompted.

"I wished for magic," Asha snapped.

"But what did it say to you, when it offered you a wish? Did you not wonder why it would gift you?" Hadhi asked, incredulous.

"She said," Asha's voice broke, "She said Baba had done a great service for his king that touched her people." Asha sobbed. Covering her face, she bent over, and Hadhi wrapped an arm around her as she cried.

"I thought she meant he had helped her. That Baba was a great man. When she said I was his best beloved, I felt so proud. I didn't even ask." She sobbed harder with every word.

"It is alright."

"No, it's not, it can never be." Asha shoved her sister's arm away. "Nothing will ever be alright again. I don't know anything!"

"That is not true."

"Did you always love me? Were you always kind? Does your mother love me as well? Is Nuru a jungle cat in disguise?" Asha spun away violently, her voice clawing at this foreign land that was her home. "Was Sabra ever my friend? Is this even Maltuba?"

There was a nearly sad smile on her sister's lips. A look of understanding. "I may have always loved you, but even I did not always know it. I hated you, because he loved you so much. I hated you because you were happy. I hated you because I felt like a monster, and I thought that was all monsters could do."

Asha quieted, the fight draining from her. Her pulsing eyes grew slowly calmer, and her head did not pound quite so hard.

"I could have loved you better, in spite of him. But I did not. I am sorry." Hadhi watched Asha with begging eyes, hoping for forgiveness and her words settled around Asha. She felt the truth of them giving her some semblance of peace in this new world. Everyone knew Hadhi could not lie. "Maybe if I had fought harder for your love, he never would have fooled you."

Asha stared at her sister. She was so new, so different. Not once since the sun rose had she worn the expression of such unhappiness and anger that Asha had first called her sour-face. Perhaps it was not such a long period of time, but it felt like forever. Had the sunrise cured her as it had Nuru? It hadn't cured Asha. Not of her grief at any rate. She thought it might have cured her of her joy.

"Asha." Hadhi stole into her consciousness. "You were the stranger at the ball the first night."

She nodded, not even curious to know how Hadhi figured it out. She barely even felt the bit of shame she knew she should. The only things she felt were fatigue and a numb heart—But for the hunger.

"And she gave you magic again last night." Hadhi paced away, but came rapidly back, examining Asha carefully. "Do you feel ill? Weak? Do you think it is killing you?"

Asha lied as easily as ever before, shaking her head.

Asha felt weak. She felt *hunger.* Her body was ready to crumble knowing she would not have the power she *needed* ever again. It wasn't fair. It wasn't right. That magic belonged to her. It was inside her, begging to be replenished. She needed it. But she couldn't have it.

Yes, it might be killing her. She'd never felt so empty and ill and desperate before.

"What exactly did she say about the wish? I need to know why she is here, and what she is trying to do." Hadhi pressed with a force more similar to her mother than the quiet resentful sister Asha had always known.

"She said I could have any one wish." Hollow, Asha plopped onto the ground. Blinking to keep her eyes open as exhaustion dragged them down. "I asked to be like her, to have magic. She said it would overwhelm me, kill me if she gave me all her magic. She said a human could contain no more than fifteen hours. So I asked for five. Then I asked for five again. She refused at first, but she gave it. She said it was all too interesting to miss."

"What was?" Hadhi demanded.

"You." Exhausted, Asha looked up at Hadhi, and her mind buzzed with the memory. "You and Noam. He passed you in the line and held your hand."

Hadhi gave a tiny jerk and for a moment her lips ticked up, but in no other way did she acknowledge that the moment had occurred. But that jerk was enough now. Asha was coming to know her sister. Hadhi was so used to hiding from joy.

"That was when she agreed to come in and give me the power," Asha finished flatly.

"And she tricked you?" Hadhi asked.

Hadhi did not even respond to Asha's reference to Noam. What was between them? Perhaps that was a trick as well? Asha didn't know anything. Perhaps the nymph only wanted Asha to confront who her father was; maybe she was trying to help. Maybe she was trying to kill her, though she warned her again and again that the magic would destroy her. Maybe... anything. Asha knew nothing.

Asha swayed. She wanted to fall backwards and cry. She clenched her fists and forced all her muscles to firm. Hadhi was watching her. Hadhi was concerned. She'd never been concerned before. Asha wasn't sure she liked it.

"Come, we should get home," Hadhi said gently.

Asha ran her hands across the dry earth. "I have no home."

"Asha!" Hadhi snapped, her eyes growing sharp like talons and her hand snapping out for Asha's. "You have a home. You are loved in it. My mother does not love you. But she does not love anything. Baba took that away from her. But we will not let him take it from us. Nuru loves you. Even Sabra, who wants to blame you for Baba forcing her to wed him, loves you still. Do not let him ruin what you have."

"No one wants me there for anything but laundry."

"I will do the laundry." Hadhi's hand waited between them.

"No!" Asha tried to jump to her feet but swayed forward. Hadhi reached out to steady her, but Asha shoved her back though she pitched towards the earth. She stumbled forward, intent on having her say. "I was his *best beloved!* And now I am the servant. And it was fine, because...I lived in my adventures, and I was taking care of his girls, and I was...his FOOL! I can't go back there."

"Why not?" Hadhi asked calmly.

"Because none of it's true anymore. Because I want him standing in front of me so I can make him tell me the truth, to my face, and—"

Hadhi pulled Asha close and ran a hand over her back. "It would not make it better. I am so sorry. I am. Please come home. Let me help you, you are weak still."

"I don't want to be a bad person." Asha sobbed.

"You are not one. Let me help you, like you helped me. *Please.*"

Hadhi was begging. Asha had never heard her sister beg before. And she remembered what Sabra had said, that no one ever invited Hadhi on any adventures, that she needed to know she had a right to them.

Helping Asha home didn't seem like much of an adventure, but from the look in her sister's eyes, Hadhi *needed* to do this. She needed to help her. She truly did love her, didn't she? Asha used to want that so badly. Slowly, Asha nodded and leaned on her sister's shoulder, and together they walked towards home.

STRANGLED LONGINGS

It was after dawn and no one had slept. Jauhar was pacing, Nuru was out who knew where, and Sabra was stewing on a rug as Lin pulled, scooted and stumbled, trying to stand. She was enraged. There was no other word for it. But even though she could tell Jauhar was angry as well, Sabra had not addressed the whys again. Jauhar had made her feelings plain last night.

Sabra cast one more look Jauhar's way and stood to leave the room. No one had eaten and it seemed it would be up to Sabra to cook. She should also pray. Now was the time for Ether's guidance, and her protection, but Sabra hated going to the goddess with her rage still burning.

As soon as Sabra stood, Jauhar stopped pacing and began speaking. Her eyes never touched Sabra, but the pain in her tone did.

"When I was first married to Zuberi, I was so young, and he was so... passionate, so loving. He devoted all his attention to me. He called me his perfect love, he called me brilliant. Told me no one was as clever as I was. He told me all his plans, let me help him. He was going to rise from an outcast to the right hand of the king. And I was going to be at his side. He loved me." Her voice dropped to a whisper. "I know he did."

Jauhar was not a woman who could accept comforting of a physical kind, but Sabra knew her presence and her silence were a comfort to Jauhar. So she remained. She couldn't have spoken without it, and she needed to say this.

"Then I lost my first child and Zuberi suffered greatly." Jauhar spoke so casually, flat and unemotional as she spoke of all her children, but Sabra felt the words stab her. Her eyes drifted to her son. How terrible a loss that would be.

"He thought it meant there was some weakness in me, or in him. His father, you understand," Jauhar looked at Sabra now, "had been banished to this hut, to the edge of Ether because he had fled battle. His friends died, but he survived and was cast here for his cowardice. Zuberi would never allow that to happen to himself. He feared nothing—for himself." Jauhar's head rose with pride and rage on her husband's behalf. She looked away again. "But the loss of the babe shook him. So, when Hadhi was born, he rejoiced like no other father. He grew more determined than ever to make his mark. To leave this hut and never return to it. To make her proud.

"This would be the answer to his every dream—two of his daughters marrying royalty—the answer to his every dream."

Sabra started forward as the silence stretched, her feet faltered, but her voice couldn't help reaching out.

"And your dreams?" Sabra asked softly, all clenched up in preparation for Jauhar's rage. She wouldn't strike her, as Zuberi would have, but Jauhar's rages were no less frightening. At times, they were even as painful.

Hadhi isn't you. There is no breaking her will.

But Jauhar surprised Sabra. She turned slowly, her eyes slightly misted with tears.

"I have been trying to remember," she whispered. "When Nuru was dancing last night, I watched her come alive and I thought I must have had drea—"

There was a knock on the wall of the hut, halting Jauhar. And before the visitor was welcomed, a dark form walked in.

"Hadhi," Jauhar exclaimed. But it wasn't her. The second he was inside, Jauhar and Sabra turned their glares on Azize.

"Hello, ladies," Azize said brightly.

It was their place to bow and smile and make him feel welcomed, but neither woman was so inclined. Sabra felt her rage redouble, burning higher now because he had just entered their home without invitation, because he had stopped Jauhar speaking when she clearly needed to. Because he *took* without regard to what others wanted, just like every other man she'd ever known. Nothing like the boy she remembered.

He waited rather a long while for a response that was not coming. When Lin's squeal of delight interrupted the silence and Sabra turned away to coo at her son, it became clear to Azize that no one intended to say a thing. He spoke again.

"I came seeking Asha. Might I have a word with her?"

"Come to tell her of her good fortune?" Jauhar asked in a deceptively pleasant tone, but Sabra knew what was coming and smiled. "As I am certain you did not see her last night to do so."

"I..." Azize fumbled.

Sabra wasn't as sure as Jauhar that Asha and Azize had not seen each other. But something told her, whether they had seen each other or no, he had not asked her permission, otherwise...where was she? So the small rebuke was no less than he deserved.

"I wanted to speak with her. And indeed Hadhi. My father, she should know, has men out searching for her." It was said as though friendly, but now that Sabra was less inclined to believe in others just because it was what she preferred Sabra saw the attempt at intimidation.

Surely he, better than anyone, knew what his father was. Surely he knew that Hadhi did not deserve her fate, but he would use it to remind Jauhar and Sabra of their places. She wanted to strike him. She'd never wanted to do that to anyone before. Not even Zuberi. She'd only wanted to get away from Zuberi.

"Hadhi merely wished time alone to prepare," Jauhar snapped, not to be intimidated by a mere prince. "She will be home in time for the weddings—today."

Azize swallowed. "Indeed. And Asha, do you know where she is?" he pressed.

It occurred to her now that perhaps she should be more worried. Neither Asha, nor Hadhi, or even Nuru had been seen since last night. What if that woman was a malevolent force? Why was Sabra just sitting here basking in these petty squabbles when she had sworn to protect this family?

"The last person that I saw her with was your father. Have you asked him?" Jauhar said, not so subtly suggesting the king might have harmed her or hidden her from Azize.

Sabra was sick. Sick of herself, sick of them all. Sick of the games with power. Zuberi loved games of power. Sabra was wearing a chiian today, the traditional headscarf worn by women in her tribe. It was the first time she'd worn one since she was married at seventeen. When she was a child, she'd seen it on her mother, and the wider brim on her grandmother, she'd seen cousins with them and neighbors, and she'd longed to be old enough to wear this symbol of adulthood, of her tribe, and of her faith. She'd been so proud to wear it once she turned twelve; it made her feel a part of something larger than herself.

But Zuberi wouldn't allow it. He said when she married him, she became his family, and her old life was dead. He'd stolen it from her, not because it displeased him, but because he wanted power over her. Her clothes, her friendships, her body—her voice.

But last night, after the king made his announcement. After she'd watched two more men who were meant to lead and protect this nation, stealing from it—Sabra came home, and dug through her old things until she found one. And she wrapped it around her head and added the flat square sheet that widened the scarf at angles above her skull, marking her as a widow. She'd put it on with Lin laying on the bed, and she told him with each turn of the scarf around her head about his grandmother, and his great grandmother and the tribe he belonged to. She was wearing it not as a game with power, but as a symbol for her son and herself. And for the world to know she existed. She had choices, she had a voice. She mattered.

Now Sabra watched Jauhar and Azize take jabs at each other, each one trying to exert power over the other, and she realized it was all fear. They were both powerless in different ways, so they fought that understanding off by harming each other.

"If you will excuse us, Azize," Jauhar walked forward, urging Azize back outside, "we have a great deal to prepare."

"Of course," Azize said equally sharply. "But first I would like to speak with Sabra?"

Sabra glanced sidelong at her son and back to Jauhar. Jauhar nodded, casting a sideways glare at Azize.

Sabra swept out of the hut by the back entrance, knowing Azize would follow.

A bird swooped down right between Asha and Hadhi. Asha screeched and cowered against her sister's shoulder, feeling completely helpless. But Hadhi was never shaken. She held Asha close with one arm and swatted at the bird with the other. Asha was so busy feeling jealous of her sister's strength that she nearly missed it—the bird had silver eyes.

Zawadi.

Had she heard Asha's silent wish? Had she come to grant it?

Zawadi swooped down once more, and Hadhi nearly hit her.

"Stop," Asha said weakly, pulling her sister's arm down. The bird flew past them and landed on the top branch of a thin, nearly dead tree nearby.

"What is the matter?" Hadhi asked. She sounded halfway to solicitous, but still sharp enough to be Hadhi. Asha wished she could hate her sister's tone of voice, wished she could mock her, even internally, but she couldn't. Everything had changed.

Asha gazed after the bird. "I need to sit."

"We are not so far from home now. Are you certain you cannot make it the rest of the way?"

"I don't want to," Asha said honestly. She didn't ever want to go back. She didn't care what Hadhi said, it wasn't her home, they weren't her family. Nothing of her was true, nothing of her life was real or right. Why should she go back to it?

She understood Azize so much better now. Of course he ran away. She wanted to run away. She wanted never to know what she knew, to be free to wonder and wish and...flee. But Hadhi was holding her close, holding her up, holding her in reality. Hadhi knew, but she didn't run. Asha wasn't sure she could do the same.

Asha gazed at the bird. Maybe it was all a lie, maybe Hadhi was wrong, and Asha could just wish for the power again. She could wish to forget. Or to run away. Or...but nothing held as much appeal as the power.

The bird screeched like it had read Asha's mind, and she heard the sound as words: *Of course, you are Zuberi's daughter.*

"Asha," Hadhi sighed.

Asha threw off her sister's assistance before Hadhi could lecture her again. "No, I don't want to go. I don't want to look on one more face that hates me, that thinks I'm a fool, that..."

"So what will you do?" Hadhi let Asha stumble towards the tree. "Sit here alone, forever? Run away?" She followed slowly, her arm outstretched, not touching, but there if Asha should happen to fall. Asha hated that hand for what it revealed about this new world. "I think...when we hate ourselves it is easier to think everyone must hate us. It is easier to be alone. I understand. I do. But, Asha, please do not let this change you. Be you, just be you more aware."

Asha barely heard her sister. She leaned against the tree and watched Zawadi staring at Hadhi. Had she come for Hadhi today, not Asha? It was wrong and ridiculous; if Hadhi was right, this creature was here to kill them. But jealousy grew within Asha as the bird watched her sister. Zawadi was captivated, as if Hadhi was something special.

I was his best beloved. And now...

"Just go away, Hadhi. I want to be alone," Asha blurted out, tears rising again. She wanted her sister gone more than she'd ever wanted anything. She didn't have to look to know Hadhi's hand fell to her side. Nor to know Hadhi drew up her shoulders with her head stiff and high. Asha saw it all though she was not looking. Of course she did, she had seen Hadhi look so time and again, every time Asha called her Sour-Faced Hadhi. She'd seen it, but she'd never understood it as she did now. She'd never cared—before today.

"Alright." Hadhi's voice was strangled and resigned. She spoke in Fairy for the first time this morning. Asha wanted to take the words back, to hold onto her and apologize for all the hurts, but if she did that, she was admitting it was all true.

"I will leave you alone, but..." Hadhi took Asha's arm in her hand and pulled her around, just shy of harshly, so they were facing one another. "No more wishes," Hadhi ordered.

"If Zawadi wanted to kill me, she could have already." Asha yanked her arm free.

"If death was all she was after."

"What else?" Asha laughed bitterly.

Hadhi shrugged, her eyes retreating from the world. "It is enough for other people, killing for revenge. But..." Hadhi bit her lip and her eyes glossed over. She took a deep breath, and her teary eyes pierced Asha in place. "It is not enough for monsters. We need our enemies to suffer. If she means to punish you, she will give you all you ever wanted. Then pull it away. Bit by aching bit."

Asha felt each of the words like tiny stabbing pins across her skin. She felt the loss of the magic all over again. Was Hadhi right? She looked like someone totally new again; someone frightening...Baba's monster.

Asha nodded.

"Come home soon, or I will come looking for you." Hadhi said nothing else, just spun on her heel and marched away, faster now she was freed of her sister's weight.

A TENDER HEART

Had she felt new only an hour ago? As Hadhi left her half-sister's side, she doubted it. She felt like bellowing, loud and long and sorrowful.

Just go away, Hadhi.

Such a little thing to be wounded by. Asha had said worse over the years. Said worse and caused less pain. But today, as the sun rose, when Hadhi held Asha, helped her for the first time in years. Today she had felt like herself from a time before she knew evil's face, from a time before she knew hatred and rage and resentment. She felt free.

And all it took was four little words to remind her:

Ugh, it's Sour-Faced-Hadhi, come to tattle again.

Sour-face, sour girl, sour Hadhi.

Baba, why does she look so sour? It hurts my eyes to look at her.

A lifetime of jeers and sniggers rushed from Hadhi's memory as she stomped homeward, leaving Asha alone, as she preferred. The little bug from the night before followed her, its frantic hum matching her angry strides.

She should not let Asha's words sting. Asha was hurting. She did not mean it to hurt, at least not so deeply. It could not be disregarded that Asha knew full well how to manipulate people. She was willing to hurt someone a little to get what she wanted. But she did not mean to score Hadhi's insides and remind her that she had never been wanted or needed by this sister. By anyone. But she might have meant to send her away with what Asha would see as a light sting.

What had possessed Hadhi to think a lifetime of hurts could be banished by one sunrise and a few moments of love acknowledged? Even if they grew closer, some part of Asha would always see her as Sour-Faced-Hadhi.

Hadhi stood at the crest of a small peak, their family hut sat down in the valley, and Ether was stretched out beyond it. She stood where she had seen Noam's friends yesterday. She drew in a deep breath, tried to force her clenched fists open.

The moment she descended this hill, she would be herself again. There would be vengeance seekers to worry over, and mother's criticism to bear, and the king—Hadhi stiffened. She did not want to think about that. She wanted to stay up here and be in a different world; she wanted to turn down the little path that led to the caves where she used to collect silk with Aunt Lolia. She wanted to pretend she could go back to the girl she was then, still sour-faced, still ugly inside, but not yet fully a monster.

But she could not stay up here forever and the moment she descended the hill, she would have to face it all. The king would not be put off. What could she do about any of it? What could she do without being Baba's monster? All it knew was blood and death, all it deserved was—

"Hadhi." The tiny gasp of her name had Hadhi spinning around into a crouch, half-afraid it was a ghost. Her hand closed instinctively around a sharp rock on the ground. The bug flew around her face, then down, softly guiding her gaze. Hadhi followed its path as it disappeared into the entrance of the cave.

The cave did not look like much from here, merely a dark hole too small to fit through without bending and twisting, but Hadhi knew what thrived in its depths. It would be a perfect place to hide and watch her family. Hadhi strained her eyes in this bright light, to see into the cave, searching for the threat.

Her hand fell open as her tension evaporated. Noam. He was lying on his stomach in the rocky entrance to the cave.

It's alright, Hadhi.

She had not allowed herself to think of him. Could not bear to contemplate what she could never have. Even freed as she had felt this morning when Asha mentioned Noam and his hand brushing hers, Hadhi had felt it for only an instant before pushing it away. She had sisters to protect and nymphs to discourage. But—here he was—*waiting for her*.

Hadhi rose silently and took the path she and her aunt had worn into the mountain from climbing that way so often. It was a little overgrown with dry weeds now. But Hadhi hardly noticed the claws of bushes catching on her dress or the brief scrapes across her skin as she made her way to Noam. He was not speaking. He just stared at her, pushing himself up as she came. His eyes never left her. The closer she grew, the tighter her breaths became, and the harder her heart pounded.

It's alright, Hadhi.

She crouched before the cave. There was a little wall of rocks between them, but neither moved to pass it. He could sit up, but the cave's entrance was too low to stand. Noam just watched her, as if the sight of her was all he needed. Here, she was wanted.

It's alright, Hadhi, I love you.

The words danced tingling beneath her skin and twirled into her chest, until she could not help it...she giggled.

"I thought I was the quiet one. Can you not speak? How hard did I hit you?" She expected a smile, or a laugh. But he just stared. Hadhi's skin heated with worry, and she glanced away. "Noam?"

Maybe she was mistaken? She had abandoned him last night after he confessed his love. Maybe he was angry. Maybe he wanted nothing to do with her now.

"Why are you here?" Hadhi's eyes trailed away towards her home. Someone might see her if they came out. See and drag her away from Noam, back to the real world.

Noam's hand stretched out of the cave and glided slowly under her chin, urging her eyes back to his. When their eyes met again, his thumb slid gently around her face, over her cheek, her lower lip, caressing her.

"I could barely breathe last night worrying for you," he spoke at last. "Are you well, my l— "

He cut himself off, releasing her chin in the same instant.

"Noam." Hadhi grabbed onto his wrist, before it could slip away completely. "I am sorry."

"*You* have nothing to apologize for." He spoke in a rush, a rush that felt oddly familiar. For a moment, she could not understand the familiarity, then she took in his averted gaze, and the speed of his pulse against her fingers and she knew—and the world tilted.

The sun rose within her, warming her so completely she was on fire. Her heart fluttered wildly. They were so different, she and Noam, so different that she had failed to understand him. He wore a bright smile, seemingly so easy. He was joy and sunshine and goodness, and she was a monster.

But in this way, they were wholly the same. Somehow, unbelievably, he did not expect to be loved. How could he not know it was impossible not to love him?

Hadhi smiled softly. She nodded backwards, releasing his wrist, and moved to climb over the low wall. Noam reached out to help her over the rocks, with his hands at her waist. Hadhi could not keep her smile from stretching. How sweet he was, how tender.

"Daku uli, szo zyid qio," Hadhi whispered, her smile tingling with joy. *Thank you, my tender heart.*

Once Hadhi was inside the cave Noam released her and scooted back. Hadhi opened her mouth to speak, but nothing came out. There was so much she wanted to say to him. So much he deserved to hear. But not down here in the dirt and the darkness. She took his hand and climbed over him in a crouch, scooting towards the tunnel that led deeper into the cave. Hadhi wanted to show him her favorite place in Maltuba; she wanted to show him magic—of the only kind she had known before him.

BATTLE BORN

"Well." Zawadi flapped into the air, stirring her wings to hover, staring after Hadhi's retreating form. When Hadhi was small enough on the horizon that she could not hear them, a silvery grey smoke billowed out of the current of the bird's wings. It floated out from her, down like a waterfall until it covered the bird completely and everything between it and the ground.

A little chuckle startled the smoke away and standing next to Asha was a tall, slender young woman with sultry silver eyes. She was dressed in a thin gown of silver with a black lacy wing pattern overlay from her neck down to the bottom of the gown. It hugged close to her neck, arms and torso then fluttered out wide like an inverted looma blossom, stopping at her ankles. She wore a scarf that hid her hair and came to a point atop her head, with little strands of black beads dropping down the forehead. She was perhaps Hadhi's age and had a warmth about her that made Asha want to reach out.

She didn't even look at Asha; her eyes were still trained on the vanishing dot that was Hadhi. But Asha examined her with wonder and with a sinking sickness within.

She would want to meet you, and the others he slew.

Had she? Was every form Zawadi took some remnant of her missing children? All so different, but so beautiful.

"What an interesting sister you have, daughter of Zuberi." The words forced Asha back a few steps. "I see you took my advice and came to know her better."

"Are you here to kill me?" Asha asked flatly. She wanted to reach out and touch the fabric of the woman's gown. Wanted to ask how it was made, and why it was so tight some places and loose in others. She wanted to smile and sparkle and be Asha, just more aware. But she couldn't.

She thought she might be hollow within, scraped clean of desire, and joy and wonder, and anything but this gnawing hunger for power. And certainty that her life without it was meaningless.

Zawadi faced Asha slowly, her gown swayed as she did, brushing against her legs, then it floated out in a silent sway. It was lovely, a soft silvery color similar to her eyes that seemed constantly to move with the light around her. Everything about her was magical.

"As you said, if that were my desire I could have killed you already. Time and time again." Her eyes grew sharp as she said the last, almost bitter.

"So what do you want?" Asha wondered at herself, at her empty curiosity. She should be quivering, should be terrified. But she was...here. That was all she knew.

The ground shuddered, and a puff of air blew out the hem of Zawadi's gown. Behind her, a formation of rock with a smooth, deep dip in the center rose up from the ground. Zawadi sat, rolling her shoulders. She looked Asha over, torn between disdain and regret.

"Do you know what it is to be Battle Born?" It wasn't a question. She spoke with a voice rich with air and intent; the force of it sent Asha tumbling to her behind. "That is the name our sisterhood chose, Battle Born." Her head rose and her eyes looked beyond Asha. "It is to feel, not with your own heart, but with the hearts of hundreds. To feel their deaths, their fears, their anger and sorrow, and above all—their very last desire." Her eyes darkened, seemed even to grow in size, the orb completely consumed in the darkening grey of her sorrow. "Cut short and always denied by time."

Had she felt Baba's last wish? Asha shouldn't wonder, shouldn't care. But her love for him was still a part of her. And she longed to know.

Zawadi's foot swept the ground as she spoke, stirring up little flurries of sand. It formed a sort of fog between her and Asha, thin and shot across with little bits of light. Figures began to form out of the fog, faces. Old and young, laughing, flirting, effervescing life, all different women. Then all at once their faces became masks of pain, and hands flew up to cover their pointy ears. Then their eyes flashed, as Zawadi's did when she bestowed a gift.

"We were called first by a great injustice, one being setting himself above all others, killing scores to gain power. The first of our order heard the cries of the wronged, felt them as though they were our own. And set out to manifest their desires."

The fog shifted and the faces were gone, replaced by slashing swords, and flying spears, and blood. So much blood.

Asha wanted to look away. It was horrible, monstrous. Why hadn't she listened to Hadhi? But she couldn't look away; the magic would not let her. It called to her. Under her skin, in her veins, the hunger pulled her closer, longing to absorb the magic from the air, even as her heart was revolted by all the blood.

The women's faces returned changed; they wore all black, long gowns or robes that touched the ground, and each woman's head was covered. It was a uniform. Marking their collective mission. Asha watched them fly out of the sky as a flock of varied birds. Watched them offering gifts, comfort, sweet memories of the dead, or homes rising out of the mist, or arms locked tight around the lonely.

"Death is all anyone knows of us. But it is not all there is to last wishes." Zawadi's voice was a mere whisper, confused and seeking. "We take revenge, for those who ask, those who deserve. But there are other wishes made, even by those who deserve justice. Some wish to see their loved ones again, some wish to care for them as they never could alive. Some...a very few, wish to forgive, or to offer comfort.

"And we carry all of this within us." Her voice shook with pain, with weight too long carried. "All of it."

She had such a different voice today, and yet not for a moment did Asha doubt her identity. Asha managed to tear her eyes away from the fog and stare hungrily at Zawadi. She looked lost and heartbroken, and so different. How strange a power she had. Was any face Asha saw her own? Did she even know what her own face looked like? Did she care? Did she choose the face that best fit her mission, and the emotion she came with? With which emotion had she come to Asha today?

"Which brought you here?" Asha whispered.

Zawadi shook her head. And the fog flashed, pulling Asha's attention once more. She watched Baba, fighting with all the fervor of a mad man, slaying the women with flashing eyes, one after another. Asha watched two of the forms Zawadi had come to her in cut down. The first form she'd seen and—That *tiny child* stabbed through the heart as she reached out a hand and begged him to stop. A child. He killed a child. Asha saw the pain of their sisters falling weakening the other Battle Born, long enough for Baba to attack.

Every strike he made hit Asha. Air exploded from her lips, scraped her bare, left her sobbing dry, scratchy tears, and wails too thin to touch the air. Her stomach burned with the sorrows.

"I feel them all," Zawadi mourned with a shuddery breath of air. "My daughters. My sisters. My friends. Too many. Battle Born were never meant to stand alone."

"It pulls you apart," Asha whispered, unsure where the air had come from that allowed her to speak.

"Yes." Zawadi slashed her foot through the fog and the images vanished. She stood, shaking the beads at her head and her seat of stone crumpled to the ground. "Yes," she repeated. "Some cried out for vengeance, some cried out for peace, so many cried out for the one thing I could not give—time. They came from everywhere, it was chaos. I could do *nothing*." Her voice broke. When she spoke again, it lacked all color or energy. "There were many among us who cried out for..."

"Forgiveness?" Asha asked, desperate and afraid.

Zawadi tilted her head, her eyes searching within. "No, not exactly. An end. An understanding so deep and powerful that it stretches across the ages, reaches inside every generation to come, so that this might never happen again. It is a far more complicated wish than I know how to bring about."

Asha slowly pushed to her feet. She felt weak all over, tired. As though she was a stranger in her own body. As though it might not belong to her any longer.

"What will you do?" Asha shook with the words.

Zawadi stepped forward so there was almost no space between her and Asha. In this new form, she was taller than Asha; she looked down into her.

"I meant to leave it to you. To each of you. It does not come from me alone, the magic I grant you. It comes from the fallen, their wishes reaching into the world." She raised the hands of her current body, and Asha noticed the intricate tattoos on her sandy brown hands.

So unique each of these women were. And Baba stole that from the world.

"Thus far it has served you well, shown you your sister, found you a love. But..." She almost smiled, her lips lifting at the corners, then they dropped with sympathy. "It has also taken from you: energy, and illusion, and ignorance. There is no saying for certain what the power will do next, if you ask it."

"So..." Asha felt at once wildly hopeful for the return of power and terrified of what more it could take from her. *She will give you all you ever wanted. Then pull it away. Bit by aching bit.* "So what if I do not wish for anything more? Will it still kill me?"

Zawadi shrugged and turned away. "Everything dies seeking some desire. You might die today, or in twenty years. But it would always be a death of seeking."

"What does that mean?" Asha screamed at a complete loss, nothing made sense anymore. She never used to be so ignorant. Or perhaps she was but she never knew it. Until today.

Zawadi's eyes snapped into tight lines. Wind rose from all around shaking out her gown, making it grow. She was a vessel of fabric, her being surging forward, dragging a dark dawn in her wake until it enveloped all behind her.

"Yours are not the only wishes I must see to. Yours are not the only fears in the world. Nor the most important to me. Wish, or do not. It is nothing to me, death will find you if you are deserving of death, or if you are deserving of life. All. Things. Die!" Zawadi cried out.

Her words shook the ground and the air. Even the fabric rippling around her danced with frantic shudders that evoked shrieks of pain. But not Zawadi. Her eyes burned with silver light and she held still against the tempest.

"What do you want of me, daughter of Zuberi?"

Daughter of Zuberi.

The name clawed across Asha's skin but did not draw out her fear or her sorrow. She heard not her father's beloved voice rise up to comfort her, but Hadhi's. Saw Hadhi's eyes as she thanked her sister for showing her she was not a monster. Felt the strength of her command:

Be you, just be you more aware.

"Five hours," Asha whispered and watched Zawadi grimace. It took her an age to start forward, but Asha threw up a hand to halt her. "Not of the power. Five hours..." She swallowed, forcing the words out, because she must. She must be more aware. "Five hours feeling the loss you do. Five hours where you are free of it."

The woman stumbled back, yanked to the ground by the wildly struggling fabric. She tumbled to her knees, fighting what looked like arms pulling at her. So many arms.

Asha watched Zawadi drowning. Flailing against the fabric as it rose around her intent on devouring her now that her vulnerability was exposed. She fought for purchase in her up-turned world. Asha understood that. She felt that.

"I could never have been like you, because I never felt others," Asha spoke, coming to understand her own request. "Please. Let me." Asha sobbed, and the tears she had thought dried, wet her cheeks. "I want to be a better person. Let me carry them." She held out a hand.

"They will weigh on you more than the magic ever could," Zawadi whispered, shaking her head. But she grasped Asha's hand desperately. She rose slowly to her feet as the weight of her anguish lessened, and the wild waves of fabric slowly dissolved, leaving only her gown.

"I am stronger than I look," Asha insisted.

Zawadi opened and closed her mouth. She seemed so ordinary now. Like the rest of the world, lost and fumbling her way through life.

"Do you think this offer will make me spare you?" she demanded, seeming less to believe it and more wishing that were the case. The Battle Born's whole world turned upside down by a daughter of Zuberi. Just as Asha's had been.

Asha shook her head.

Zawadi surged forward, stumbling into Asha's arms as the fabric caught her feet.

"Not one moment more," she whispered and kissed Asha's cheek in a rush, as if afraid Asha would change her mind.

Asha held her breath. The world felt exactly the same. Asha breathed. Zawadi breathed. Nothing changed.

Asha fell, screeching in pain with the force of a thousand souls at once. And her world went dark.

VOICE OF RAGE

Sabra felt Azize behind her and opened her mouth to speak. But he was already talking over her.

"I am surprised to find you living here. Why are you not in the mansion?" Azize asked.

Sabra began to swallow her rage and just answer him, but she felt her hands clenched in fists and stopped herself.

You are free. You are free. You are free.

Sabra wondered how many times she would have to tell herself before she actually began believing it. But she said it to herself right now and she spun to face the boy she used to love.

"Did you bother to ask her?" Sabra demanded. "Do you intend to? What will you do if her answer is not to your liking?"

"Sabra." His tone aimed to soothe. "I am sorry if I've hurt you."

"Hurt me," Sabra laughed. "You haven't hurt me, Azize."

He began to speak but she cut him off.

"You've enraged me." She advanced on him with burning eyes. "You've disappointed me. When we were children, I loved your sweetness and your shyness. You seemed goodness personified, and I loved you for it."

"I am the same as I was when I left," Azize defended.

"Perhaps. But all that means is you were not as good as I imagined." Her gaze took pity on him for a moment, seeing the boy of her past. But the rage would not be quieted. "You took her consent for granted. You announced what would be, without even seeking her out to stand beside you. You are no better than other men."

"Asha and I understand each other," Azize began sharply. He was clearly intending to speak further, but Sabra's angry laughter silenced him.

"How? You have known her again for two days, and none of it as herself." Azize's eyes widened, but Sabra didn't stop to explain how she knew what she knew. "You know her as much now as you did when she was a child. And it is all superficial. When we were young, you saw only what you hate, now you see only what you love—"

"I see more than that!" Azize snapped. And she could hear him, in his rage, pulling out a tone he must have heard from his father. A tone that said I am powerful and you are small, bow to me. But Sabra was done bowing.

"Then where is she?" Sabra taunted.

"I don't know. I hoped you might. We fought last night. I forced her to face what her father really was and she didn't like it. Where would she go? You are her best friend, I—

Sabra was laughing again, hard. "I am not her best friend. I am not her friend at all. Zuberi would never allow such a thing; it is why I am now widowed. For perhaps a few months, she preferred my company to his, went with me everywhere. He despised it. So he went to my father and told him what would be and took me home as his wife so I could not threaten his control over Asha."

Azize shifted back, bracing a leg behind him, preparing to run from the unpleasantness. Sabra knew he had suffered. She was not alone in that. But Azize didn't seem to recognize suffering in anyone else.

"What, truly, do you know about her?" Sabra pressed. "Not that she has lived in this hut since three days after her father's half-devoured body was burned. Not that she has not had a friend in years. Nor I think that Jauhar, and her sisters, and I as well, I suppose, have used her as our servant since Zuberi's death. We have all delighted to see her brought low, because that is the sort of legacy her father cultivated." Sabra spoke with regret, but also relief. She'd known she was delighting in Asha's suffering, but she couldn't explain why. Now that she was free, she knew. And she knew it didn't have to continue.

"Did you know that all her life what she's wanted most was a mother to hold her and love her? But while she has been covetous of it, that desire has never made her feel malice towards those who have what she wants? The only friend she was ever allowed was Zuberi. He controlled his family like they were chattel. For each of them it was different, but not one was anything but his property no matter how free she seemed."

"I...didn't know," Azize whispered. "Sabra...I...I said she couldn't be the only one who didn't know who he was."

Sabra's eyes burned from all the times she'd wanted to scream the same thing at her friend. But those words just weren't true. "Oh, she could. If anyone had told her the truth, he would have killed them."

"I didn't know. She just...she was making light of my concerns. She only sees Maltuba as this beautiful place, and she wanted me to want to be here, to want to lead. But she didn't know what it would cost me."

"Do you?" Sabra asked pitilessly. "You have been gone for years, Azize. You left a boy, one assumes you returned because you were prepared to see it as a man. What do you know of your nation now? I used to think you were so different from the other men who wanted me. Men who would leer at me, then speak only to my father. But you stole her choices. Are you any different, Azize, from that man you have hated all your life?"

"Of course," Azize insisted. "Asha and I discussed this...perhaps not marriage, but we discussed forever; she wanted it."

Sabra looked around them, silently discounting his words.

Azize collapsed onto a stool. He pulled out a shoe and held it before him. It was beaded in blue and gold, the slipper Asha had left him two nights ago.

"I used to love you too," Azize said wonderingly. He ran his hands along the shoe as he spoke. "Then I met her and I was swept up, carried away. I was here, but I was gone. She was adventure and laughter. I hold this in my hands, and I am sure—completely sure—that I love her and that she loves me. It whispers to come and find her. It promises the type of love I have been missing all my life. I hold this and I am sure. But then I put it down," he lay it on the ground, "and I wonder, if it isn't a spell. I wonder if she is tricking me. Or my father is tricking me. Or Maltuba itself is tricking me. Forcing me here where I will spend the rest of my days at the whims of others."

Sabra chuckled right in the middle of his poignant speech. It was unkind. But her rage didn't care.

"You spent years of freedom, Azize. Go among your people, see how many of them has had even one," Sabra instructed unsympathetically.

"She isn't coming back, is she?" Azize asked as Sabra was just passing him. "I drove her off and she will not return."

"Then you are free to run away. If that's what you want. Do you know what you want?"

He shook his head, staring up at her. She didn't think he noticed, but even as his eyes were trained on her, his hand was reaching out for the shoe.

"I don't...I can't stay—*alone*. You could take her place. You could marry me and help me see what you think I should."

Sabra didn't move a muscle; her eyes bore Azize into place. How dare he?

"Are you asking me, Azize?" Sabra's angry words shook the air. "Or are you telling me?"

"Asking!" he shouted, offended.

Sabra nodded once and swept around him. "No," she said with more force than she'd believed herself capable of.

"What?" Azize leapt to his feet, with the shoe in hand, and raced around her. He'd taken her agreement for granted. And why not? As a girl she would have agreed without question. He hadn't really heard her. Sabra's being might be quaking in fear of violence and force but her rage was what powered her now.

"You said you were asking." Sabra raised her head high. "You have my answer. Perhaps you should find Asha and get hers." Sabra didn't wait for him to say more. She stomped into the house. Her body sang and quivered. She was enraged and elated in one. She hadn't felt this alert since before her son was born.

No.

Was there a lovelier word? Was there a lovelier feeling than being able to reject what was entirely wrong for you? Asha needed to feel this. Jauhar did. And Hadhi. Oh, Hadhi needed it so badly. She was so used to bending for her father and her mother. So used to being deformed in soul because she changed it to suit someone else.

No. She might start saying no every day, a mantra chanted to the sun. NO!

BEFORE THE WORLD COMES IN

The further they went, the taller they were able to stand. It was not as dark in the caves as it should be; the walls held a shiny ore that caught the light and danced along the walls like fire bugs lighting their way. Noam followed Hadhi wordlessly, his quiet heartbeat and his whirring mind at cross purposes with each other.

Daku uli, szo zyid qio.

He knew a few of the words. Thank you. My. But zyid was unfamiliar, and he couldn't remember if qio was love, or heart, or community. Community seemed the least likely. He wanted to ask what exactly the words meant, but so many things stopped his tongue.

It was not just the fear of overwhelming her again, or even of the bug he'd seen fly into the cave ahead of them. The mayfly. He also thought of Azize's plans discussed hurriedly with only a portion of his men, and Kane one of them. What if Noam was right about him? What if the plan failed?

Hadhi needed to know what happened after she left the ball. But she led him into the darkness as if she already knew. As if he must be a secret. As if she could not look on him in the light. And he knew, though he feared any mayfly connections and though he wanted the world to know his love for her. Noam would follow her anywhere. Do anything he must—to be near her.

It was madness. But it was also love. And it was true.

Noam was close at her back the whole way. His warmth spread across her skin and sunk beneath it, threading through her like a million fluttering strands of silk caressing her and bringing her to life. Oh, how she had needed to be near to him like this.

Hadhi's words came easier with Noam behind her, always her being was shy of baring its truths. Shy of hearing again that she was not what someone wanted.

But Noam was shy of rejection too, and she had not understood that even after his stories. Noam deserved all of the things she had always wanted for herself. He deserved to know that he was loved, that he was beautiful, that he was desired and so entirely magical.

"I could not hear you last night," Hadhi whispered, shortening her steps to be nearer to him. "It did not seem possible that someone as beautiful and good as you could love me when...no one has ever loved me."

"Hadhi." His hand tightened around hers, and he pulled her back against his chest, wrapping their joined hands forward around her waist. He leaned his head next to hers and pressed his lips beneath her ear.

Hadhi shimmered. This was joy. "I could not possibly deserve you, so how could I hear you? It would hurt too much when it all went away, but—" Hadhi giggled in spite of herself, in spite of how heavy and frightening this was. In spite of the tears gathering somewhere in the vicinity of her heart knowing that nothing had changed. *She could not keep him*. The world was going to find them, to barge in and steal any beauty they found together. The king would claim her. Or the nymph would kill her. Or Baba's monster would frighten Noam away all on her own.

But not now. Hadhi turned around in his arms so she could see his beautiful face. Now belonged to them. She tipped her head up, even as her hand behind his neck urged him closer.

"I do not care if I deserve you," Hadhi said breathlessly, just before her lips touched his. "I want every moment I can have with you. I love you, Noam."

Their lips met, and the heat between them burned the world away. There was nothing but them, drinking in one another's love. Nothing but this lovely, wild treasured feeling that existed between them.

Noam framed Hadhi's face between his hands and repeated the words her soul was begging to hear again. "I love you, Hadhi."

She clung tighter to him embracing the joy. Hadhi took one of Noam's hands in hers.

"I want to show you something." Hadhi pulled him on, tingly with anticipation and nearness to him.

It was quiet in the depths of the cave and far cooler than it ever was out of doors. It truly seemed like another world, and as they turned the corner from the tunnel into the wide colorfully strung home of the swirrle bugs, the cave's true magic banished any resemblance to the real world.

Noam caught his breath. "My word," he gasped. She knew he would understand.

Hadhi released his hand and let him move out before her taking in the loops and swirls and intricately woven netting of swirrle silk. They were stretched like curtains around the cave, so one could walk between them like a maze. Older clouds of silk had fallen to the ground and lay together making piles of rainbow thread. It was here that Hadhi had collected the golden threads that still adorned Nuru's hair. Here where she felt her most hopeful.

Noam stretched a hand towards the nearest willoomi, a continuous loop of golden thread like a sunburst. His hand stopped short of touching it until Hadhi led his finger to the soft silk.

"We call them willoomi, painted clouds," Hadhi explained.

Noam moved his hand gently across the looping sun of golden thread, but he kept glancing at Hadhi as she spoke.

"Before people collected the bugs and farmed the colors that were most popular, they would float out of the caves after storms. People would collect them, fighting each other for the best ones."

Noam grinned softly. "If these are the cobwebs you were hiding in, I understand why you never went out," he teased. She knew he was teasing, but Hadhi corrected him all the same.

"These were not made by spiders. They cannot trap anyone. Swirrle are worms, they live in the dark. They have no eyes they just…feel the patterns they make. They are artists. But only in secret, even from themselves."

Hadhi needed him to see this. She needed him to know that there were beautiful things in her. Loving, artistic bits of her soul the monster had naught to do with. She had shown him her rage, and resentment, her scars already. She had shown him the hunter, and bits of the ugly inside. He had said twice now that he loved her, and no amount of ugly she had shared as yet had shaken him. But he was so beautiful. So good. Eventually, he would see she did not measure up. Outside of this cave, she did not deserve him, but in here she knew the beautiful things about herself. And she wanted him to know them too.

She heard the song of the bug that had been trailing her. It had a new cadence, encouraging, urging her to share. And it was louder now as if it had found another soul to share its song.

"My aunt and I used to come here and collect the abandoned threads. She said the wild thread was best; the colors they make are not as vibrant when farmed. Aunt Lolia could weave patterns like no one else, the most beautiful in Maltuba. We collected every color, but most everyone wants the gold threads."

Noam glanced back, with a small smile. "Which is your favorite color?"

His eyes touched her own, so warm, so intent. She had never been looked at that way. Never been seen. It made her hungry for things she had only ever wanted with him. To be touched. To touch him. To be bold. "The greens." Hadhi nodded further in.

Noam's fingers meshed with hers as they walked deeper. Their hands did not quite meet, his thumb slipping between their joined fingers to weave gently against her palm. Hadhi's shoulders rolled with a pleasant tingle, and she pressed herself closer to his side.

"There are so many hues of green, and they are so..."

"Alive?" Noam suggested.

Hadhi nodded, grateful that he understood.

"This is spectacular, Hadhi. So...unexpected." He was not looking at the painted clouds. His eyes traced up Hadhi's neck to her face, and every place his eyes passed tingled with excitement. "You sound very happy when you speak of your aunt. Are you close?"

"We were. She died only a week before—" But Hadhi did not want to think about her father in here. "We were," she said again, a little more flatly this time.

"I am glad." Noam kissed gently at the corner of Hadhi's lips. "You see, other people love you too."

Hadhi stretched up and pulled him to her for a proper, ravenous kiss. She would have begged him to say the words again and again, but she did not have to.

"I love you, Hadhi." Noam kissed her eyes and her cheek and began to kiss his way down her neck. She bit down on her tongue as wild hunger ripped through her. Desperate for more of him she pressed closer to his beautiful lips.

Hadhi shut her eyes and completely lost her breath as his lips traced her scars. She wanted to cry again, or laugh, or...she did not know what. She felt everything at once and all she knew in the midst of it was that she wanted to be with him. To be closer to him. She wanted to touch him and love him and have him love her.

"You're so sweet," he gasped, his breath coming in shorter and shorter pants like her own. "So beautiful. My Hadhi."

It took everything within her to ignore the years of insecurities that went racing through her brain, taunting *Sour-Faced-Hadhi* or *she made herself look a proper beast with those scars*. The angriest, surest parts of her wanted to shove out of his arms and demand he never lie to her. But she fought her doubts. Yet still he sensed it.

He stopped kissing her and set her back so he could look into her eyes, with an arm wrapped gently at her back to keep her near. "My serious Hadhi." Noam smiled as he said this, as though it was something he loved about her. "What is the matter?"

Hadhi shook her head, wished she had not ruined this. "I am not sweet," Hadhi bit out. "Nor beautiful. I am a...you do not know me," she finished unsteadily, devouring the inside of her lip.

Noam's arm at her back tightened, and he regarded her with such seriousness he looked like a different person. "Yes, I do. You are sad, and you are lonely, and *you are beautiful*. Even when you do not smile." He leaned forward and kissed her gently on the lips, but he was not finished. "Most of all, Hadhi, you are angry. Because you do not feel loved. You are one of the angriest women I have ever met."

Hadhi stiffened. She had brought him here so she could escape those parts of herself. She had brought him here to see her beautiful parts, but she had ruined it. He was seeing the ugly even here. Noam held on tighter, but still so tenderly, his fingers brushing gently against her arms so even with the shame of letting him see her ugliness here, the hunger he woke would not die.

"I'm glad you're angry." Hadhi startled, the violence of her reaction nearly shaking off his arms. Noam laughed. "If you weren't angry with the people who fail to show you love, you would be a fool. You, Hadhi, are beautiful and deserving of love. And the people who fail to give it to you deserve all your rage. Yet you take care of them. You are like this cave, wrapping up all your beauty in darkness, to keep anyone from destroying it."

He looked so impossibly *fierce*. And he loved her, ugliness and all.

Hadhi dragged his head to hers, kissing him with all her love and passion. Her heart beat wildly as new longings rose within her. She wanted to be closer to him. To feel his skin against her own, to take his warmth inside her and feel it forever. She tugged at his clothes and laughed against his chest. This was beautiful. This was magical. This was everything.

"I love you." Hadhi beamed at him. "It is impossible not to love you." Hadhi was frantic and ecstatic. Noam seemed to be hesitating, but she did not think it was from any lack of desire. He was being careful with her.

Hadhi moved back a bit; they were both breathing heavily, both clinging to one another. It was more than she had ever had, and it was beautiful. But she needed more. Hadhi released his hand so she could reach up and untie her dress. It fell to the ground amid the old fallen clouds of silk, and Hadhi stood bare before him. She was so shy with everything else, she would have expected to be shy now. But he had called her beautiful, and right now, she knew it to be true.

"Szo *euthuri,* zyid qi," Hadhi whispered, too overcome to find her words in Fairy. "Nav szou." She walked back into his arms. *My beautiful, tender love. Embrace me.*

"Hadhi." Noam's arms closed around her back, pressing her entire body against his own as though she was life itself. "I don't think I can ever let you go."

Smiling she pulled him onto the soft painted clouds at their feet.

"Don't."

LOSS OF HER

Sparrow *was too young yet to truly understand the choice she'd made; all of fifteen, she was a fledgling still. Her eyes sparkled with joy at the thought of granting last wishes. Her face showed every emotion in her being. Wide eyed and soft cheeked, her smile overtook her face when she granted wishes of peace, and crumbled away, pulling her entire face down when she felt the cries of the betrayed, the murdered, and the heartsore.*

She would remain among the Battle Born five more years before she was fully fledged. Must see it all, good with bad, joy with sorrow, death with death. Battle Born saw so much death.

She would see, then she would choose. It was always a choice.

Her eyes were wide open and unafraid when she met her death. She greeted him warmly, like the guest she knew him to be, offered to show him the way, for surely he was lost, coming from the sleeping hall. He smiled his thanks, patting her on the shoulder, then, before she had a chance to make a noise, he slit her throat.

"Aaaaaaa!" Asha screamed in pain as the girl could not. Screamed at the loss of her, but she did not rouse. She tossed about on the ground and felt them all.

Sparrow collapsed in a sparking cavern, her eyes still wide. And she felt with a shock, so powerful it woke the rest of her sisters, her own last wish: to be truly Battle Born. She had always wanted to be one of them.

Wren was the first out of bed. She felt Sparrow's loss and bolted. Her sixty years should have tamed her, but she was always too quick for her own good. She rushed to Sparrow's side and got a knife to the gut halfway there.

The pain was such a shock her hand shot out and locked around her attacker's wrist. He shook her free, smiling her way, and charged out. Others were waking and he launched himself at them. He was faster than any man she'd ever seen, made powerful with single minded intent and with the power he took from each life he stole.

They'd invited a snake among them.

Wren collapsed to her knees in a pool of her own blood. She felt others waking, others fighting, but not enough. Not all of them. A helpless sob escaped her, and she tried to rouse her magic and send it after the snake, but what little power she had dragged her somewhere else. Bleeding and wheezing, she crawled to Sparrow's side.

Sparrow had been such a breath of fresh air. Everyone's joy. Wren ran a hand along the girl's face and felt Sparrow's wish stab at her, stealing the last of Wren's peace. Hatred such as she'd never known surged within her. She wanted nothing so much as to destroy the man who had killed this loving child. To destroy all of his kind, the cowardly and the evil, they had no right to live.

Wren collapsed over the girl, with nothing left to live for.

One by one, they fell. So many Battle Born died that even as she felt them like friends or sisters, Asha was sure she would never know all their names. He'd started with the sleeping ones. Killed them before they had a chance to fight or to have last wishes. But even awake and fighting with magic and rage, they were no match for him. With everyone he killed, he grew more powerful. Madness was a sort of power it seemed.

Whippoorwill was a quiet soul, not known for great power or any striking aspects of spirit. She could generally be counted on to hold up the walls with her back, but she had a depth of empathy that none could match and eyes so clear and still, one saw their soul reflected in them.

One would expect to find her cowering in a crevice, destroyed by the pain of all her sister's falling, but she was not. The crystalline structure of their cave sang with her, tiny pings, like bells echoed through the halls, as little rocks struck the stalagmite, a whirling cyclone in her wake as she rushed at their attacker. Her empathy gave her strength such as she'd never had before and she yanked down a stalactite, swinging it like a cudgel.

She was a storm of power. For the moment it seemed she might stop him. Rocks pelted him, tearing at his skin and she beat at him with magic and the stalactite with more rage than sense.

Whippoorwill did not even feel the attack, but Asha did. It tossed Asha's body so she moaned, fighting to wake.

Her father's blade sliced at her cheek, stabbed her in an arm, her side, her neck. But nothing could stop Whippoorwill, nothing could reach through the grief and the rage to wake her to the danger. Not until Zuberi, battered and enraged, caught the woman and drove her head into the stone walls of the cave. Her world went black.

But her sister's world did not. Asha felt the difference in this bond.

All Battle Born were sisters by choice, but Whippoorwill and Nighthawk were sisters by blood as well. Twins. They had become Battle Born seemingly of one mind. But Nighthawk knew the whole of it. Nighthawk had all the ideas, the longing for adventure and purpose. She wanted to right all the wrongs in the world. Whippoorwill only wanted to be with her sister.

Nighthawk felt her sister fall like a thousand deaths at once. A torrent of memories flooded her. Whippoorwill's quiet smile or hesitant presence. Her innate goodness. And Nighthawk knew at once what she must do. Knew what the purpose she had been seeking all her life truly was.

She charged at their attacker, with no weapon in hand, and no magic to protect her. Only a wish. Over and over, stronger than any wish she'd ever had, Nighthawk fell on death's sword and sent her wish out to the sisters who remained.

Live.

Her wish wrapped around all the Battle Born still living, overpowering everything within them. Lights danced through the cave, flashing here, bouncing there, blinding one moment and tiny the next. When it cleared, wounded and desperate birds fled the cave. The Battle Born escaped, saved by their sister's sacrifice.

Zuberi dove after them, further wounded a few, but they made good their escape as Nighthawk wanted. All the while, Zuberi smiled, panting with exhaustion and excitement at his success.

When the cave was clear he saw her, Oriole, the one who brought him here. Their mother bird. Her arms were weighed down with her dead as she stared up at this evil she had brought into her home.

He approached her, bloody blade in hand. She did not move.

"You could have had any wish," she whispered, pulling Tanager and Kiwi closer to her chest and taking in the carnage, hopeless, aching—destroyed. She had brought them to this.

"I make my own wishes true." Zuberi stopped before her, and took in the same view with such...pride.

Oriole was bleeding, her blood, her magic, her life force, her will, all puddling beneath her on the floor of the cave. She had never felt so wholly bereft. "You are nothing, Zuberi." Her hands reached out for her fallen. So many dead today, her doing, and his. "You are weak and cowardly, and you will be made to see how powerless you are, before you are allowed to die. The others will see to it."

Zuberi only chortled. "I am the strongest being in the world, no one will kill me. I make my own destiny."

He left her bleeding among her dead and strode from the cave. Oriole collapsed against the crystalline walls of her home and waited to die, with only one wish, that she might deserve to be forgiven.

Asha shivered from the ceaseless loss. She bit her tongue, but she could neither rouse nor stop her tears from falling. It was unbearable.

From beyond all the pain, and all the death, she felt a pair of large soft arms sinking beneath her, pulling her near. And a warm quiet voice slipped into her consciousness.

"It's alright, Bluebird. I have you. You are safe."

THE MOST UNLUCKY WOMAN IN THE WORLD

Noam had Hadhi in his arms; he could feel her heart pound against his own. He should be elated, or at the very least at peace, but he kept hearing that violent buzz that shredded his calm. There were mayflies in the cave with them. It caused a twisted, sinking feeling that he was going to cost Hadhi a great deal.

> *Through wild blossoms of love's delight,*
> *Through tender whispers in dark of night,*
> *Through stolen breaths and laughter wild,*
> *Through silences in evenings mild,*
> *They lived a lifetime in a May—*
> *But dawned the June he'd flown away,*

Noam hated every word swirling through his mind. Hated more that for the first time in his life, he was afraid they were true, and it wasn't only because of what he might lose, but because of what he might cost someone else.

Noam should not have done this. He'd known the moment she took his hand to lead him into the cave that something was changing in his life. He'd known he shouldn't have gone. But how could he do anything but follow her? He hadn't spoken of his love lightly; she was the first person outside of his family to whom he had ever said the words. He loved her. He wanted to be with her forever. But...forever was far easier thought than achieved.

He knew that. But her eyes had been so big and loving and hungry. Noam had never met anyone who needed love as badly as Hadhi, who deserved it, was willing to give it, but honestly didn't expect it back. How was he supposed to keep from showing her just how loved she was?

Still, he should have told her all first. She knew nothing of Enzi's announcement. Knew nothing of Azize's haphazard and likely doomed plan. Noam should have told her and let her make her choices knowing what waited for her. Noam kissed Hadhi possessively one more time and sat up gathering their clothing. Who knew this cave was here? What if they were found?

He'd sworn never to treat loving a woman as casually as his father had. He'd sworn never to risk a child growing up unknowing that he was its father, that it was loved. Under any other circumstance embracing Hadhi like this would not have been such a risk, but this was a foreign land, and she was the woman its king had chosen to be his bride and Noam was...no one. How was he meant to protect her? Or protect a child? This was a mistake. A beautiful, magical mistake.

Hadhi silently took his cue. She turned her back and began dressing, shy again it seemed.

"Hadhi, there are things I should have told you."

"Must we let the world in so soon?" She glanced back with a soft resigned smile.

Noam paused, waiting for Hadhi's explanation.

She shrugged. "Did not it seem we had gone somewhere removed from the world for a time?" She looked around at the painted clouds that surrounded them.

Noam looked as well. He hadn't really looked at them from this angle, out towards the light, filtering in through clouds of various color; it was like being inside of a rainbow. It was...indescribable.

"Yes," Noam nodded. Leaning forward, he drew her lips gently to his. "Run away with me. We'll be enough for each other," he begged, not much used to the feeling. But he couldn't stand the thought of losing her, or of costing her all he knew he still could. He felt helpless.

Azize's plans to imprison the king was...optimistic at best. Too neat for Noam to trust. And it would still see Hadhi married to the king, as it used her wedding as cover. Noam didn't like the plan, but aside from convincing

Hadhi to run away or starting an outright war, Noam could think of nothing to do but trust Azize.

What would become of the wife of a dethroned and jailed king? Enzi needed stopping, but it should not cost Hadhi.

Hadhi looked at him with a soft smile. The silk clouds formed fractal halos behind her and she wore such joy in her expression that if he squinted, Noam could fool himself into believing the emotions had sunk in and become a part of her. Fool himself into thinking she might say yes.

But not his serious Hadhi. She tilted her head just a tick to the right and her eyes filled with understanding, and fear, regret, even love. So much love it should knock a person over, but not all of it was for him.

"I did." She drew out of his arms, finished tying her dress into place and stood. "We walked together, straight into the brightest, fiery heart of Ether." She pulled a bright red willoomi before her with one hand, and a golden one with the other. She could be seen through a screen of color, a silhouette against the rising sun and the desert. "We found a world all our own." She moved through the maze of color, wrapping a pair of green silk strings around herself. "We are still walking there. Now I can live there, on my dark days, instead of in the pit of rage with the monster."

A pressure like a mountain dropped onto Noam's chest, crushing the pain into his being. He felt sickened despite the loving expression in her eyes. Was he exactly the same as the man who had fathered him? Not the man who'd raised him, but the stranger who gave him life? *They lived a lifetime in a May, but dawned the June he'd flown away.* Was he just a moment of joy for a tortured soul? He couldn't bear that. He wanted forever with Hadhi. He loved her and she loved him. That had to matter.

But he didn't expect the words that came out. "There is a story where I am from, The Mayfly's Visit." Noam bit out the words with that incessant chewing noise torturing his eardrums. Hadhi let the silk curtains fall, watching him with careful intensity.

"It is based it on bugs that live for only a day, but... *magical.*" He snorted. "It is the story of a man who comes into a woman's life one May, woos her, loves her. But when May is over, he's gone forever. Doomed to love for only one month and the woman is left behind with nothing but the memories."

Noam was not even looking at Hadhi anymore, his hands fisted around the orange silk cloud beneath him. So Hadhi's hand sliding gently over his cheek shattered him. Shocked his heart into quaking from the gentle love in her touch. She raised his gaze to hers and leaned down to gently brush his lips with her own.

"Why does it make you angry?"

Noam couldn't force out the truth he'd been fighting since he'd first seen the insects last night. *Because I want forever with you. Because I am afraid that I am a mayfly. Because I don't want to be one more person who fails to love you as you deserve.*

"That is a beautiful story." Hadhi spoke when Noam could not. "He loved her, gave her all he had. All his love." Her fervent words crushed Noam's heart anew, but her smile—the power of love in her—freed him of the pressure.

"Who would not want to be loved like that? That it is..." She fumbled, losing her words. "That it ends..."

"Temporary," Noam whispered. It felt as if she'd heard his thoughts.

Hadhi nodded and kissed him as fleetingly as that first brushing of their lips yesterday. "That it is tem-por-ary," she felt the word out haltingly, "does not change that it is love. There is a Maltuban word iooni. It means for all of time. But even in the old stories all of time did not look the same for everyone. Ether's promise to love for all of time was endless, because she was without end. But when a dying mother offered qi iooni to her child it meant all the time she had. If he loved her only for May, then May was their iooni. *Their all of time.*" There were tears in her eyes when she finished and they burned with such intensity Noam felt the power of it in his heart.

He raised a hand and pressed it over hers lingering still on his cheek. His heart sighed with love for this incredible woman who made even heart break look beautiful.

He breathed, sitting in the moment. In the love. Even though he knew it would end, he had to take this one more moment of *iooni* with her.

"When I was a child," Noam began hesitantly, "no one knew who my father was, but they knew it was not the man I called Father. He had been gone when my mother became pregnant." Noam shook off the urge to over explain the few things he did know, because there were such gaps in his knowledge. Surely someone had known who that man was.

"Other children would mock me with that song. Say my father was a mayfly. And that I was one as well." Hadhi lay her forehead gently against Noam's as he spoke. "As much as I was ever angry with those children, or their parents, who surely gave them the idea, I was angriest with that man. Angry at him for existing. For leaving. For not taking us with him. For failing to—" Noam's voice faltered, and Hadhi sat down in his lap, closing her arms around him.

"He would have loved you if ever he had known you. Even the man who raised you, the father who *loved you only from a distance*," she repeated his words from the night they met. Two nights ago. It felt so much longer, so much fuller a feeling to have been so short a time. "Must feel now how greatly he loves you. He must regret your parting."

Noam laughed. He could imagine his father loving him now that he was gone, even missing his presence. But his father didn't matter anymore. What mattered was this woman right here and how gently she tried to lighten his life. She was so sweet. Noam clung to her.

"It is *impossible not to love you*," Hadhi insisted fiercely, her arms tight around him. So tight.

Noam felt so blessed to have met her. And so—afraid for her.

"Hadhi." Noam set her back. He could put it off no more. "After you left the ball, Azize announced his intent to marry."

"To marry Asha?" Hadhi asked with an odd sort of smile. Not quite resentful, but certain and resigned.

Noam nodded, a bit surprised. "He did not say her name, but that is his intent." Noam searched her carefully and explained the rest, "The king made an announcement as well."

Hadhi shivered, her arms fell away from him, and she stiffened her spine. Without a word, she rose and walked out of their haven. And Noam understood. This other world needed none of the ugliness that was to come.

She didn't speak until she had climbed back over the rocks at the mouth of the cave. In the sunlight, she stood tall, raised her head so she stood at her full height and looked back at Noam steadily. "Am I to be queen then?

"I knew," she spoke without Noam so much as nodding. "As soon as he held me trapped in his arms. I knew Enzi meant to...have me. I suppose to be queen is greater compensation than most of his victims get."

"Hadhi." Noam stumbled after her, helpless and angry for it. He tripped over little plants and rocks until he reached her. He took her shoulders in his hands. "I won't let him have you."

Hadhi shook her head, clenched her fists, and looked suddenly lost. "He will not. I..." She seemed unable to find her words. An expression that might be fear kept darting in and out of her eyes. "I am not what he thinks. He sees only the fear, and the envy of my sister. He sees Sour-Faced-Hadhi, and entirely fails to see..." She broke off, stiffening further as if she didn't want to speak.

"What?" Noam prompted gently.

"I never have the words to be understood," Hadhi muttered.

It looked to Noam more like she did not want to tell him. And he could relate to the need to have secret pockets in your heart. "You do not have to explain anything to me."

Hadhi raised her eyes, smiled that over bright toothy smile of their first acquaintance. "You would prefer the mystery?"

"No! Hadhi," Noam sighed, choosing his words with more care. "I prefer you. Only you, exactly as you are. You can tell me anything. But you don't have to tell me to have me take your side."

Still after everything that had passed between them, Hadhi appeared unsure, even doubtful.

"What doesn't he see, Hadhi?" Noam urged.

"My fa—" Hadhi swallowed, closed her eyes, and when she spoke again, her voice was tight, and Noam was almost certain she was not saying what she'd began to. "I am not someone who can be taken. I chose you. He—" She ground her teeth and clenched her fists. "I would never be his."

Noam felt his hands tightening on her shoulders but couldn't bring himself to loosen them. He could envision his hands wringing Enzi's throat for so much as looking at Hadhi. And here she was, saying she expected to be his victim. Trying to comfort Noam over the inevitability.

She deserved so much more.

"Azize has a plan to overthrow his father." Noam forced the words out to pull his mind from its dangerous path, to give her hope. "You are a part of it, but you shouldn't have to be. You should be safe. Let me keep you safe."

Hadhi took it in with a quiet unreadable expression. He might know her forever and never know what went on in that mind. But he had a sinking feeling her quiet was not a herald of agreement.

"I have promised Azize my help." Noam slid his hands from her shoulders down her back, pulling her nearer. "But if you will come with me now, I will take you away. Somewhere Enzi can never harm you."

Hadhi lifted her arms very gently to his and guided them back to his sides. She turned partially away from him.

"I cannot run away from him any longer." Hadhi spoke hesitantly. "When I was ten, I followed my father in secret. I thought..." Her voice drifted away. Every time Noam moved to stand before her, she shifted so her back was to him. "Even then, my father loved Asha best. I thought if I shared a secret with him, he would love me. But it was not a secret I wanted." She stopped speaking for the longest time. Noam took a step towards her, and her words came flooding out devoid of any emotion.

"I saw Enzi forcing himself on a little girl to punish her parents." Hadhi's hands dropped to her sides, fisted. "I tried to kill him. But my father stopped me before Enzi knew I was there. He said Enzi would do the same to me. Not for a moment did I doubt him. If Enzi knew, he would hurt me, and my father would allow it." Hadhi shuddered. "So I did nothing. I remained safe. Have been safe every day since."

She was holding herself so stiff. Noam closed the distance between them, folding his arms around her. He rested his head on hers and felt her quake with all the feelings she restrained.

"You were only a child. You couldn't have done anything."

Hadhi shook her head, and her tears struck the back of Noam's arm. "I do not know that. I never tried. I have never truly tried to stop him. Never."

Noam didn't speak. He tightened his arms on her, laying his lips on the top of her head. There was so much more they needed to discuss. He should ask her about the Battle Born. Ask what she knew. But he just held her tight, riding through the all consuming fear of losing her.

Hadhi deserved so much more than life had ever given her.

"I never understood how terrifying love was before." Of course she would help stop Enzi. He'd known that all along. He just wished he could keep her safe.

"It is not terrifying." Hadhi gripped his arm. "It is beautiful. Loving you makes me strong. Were it not for me, would you ever hesitate to follow Azize?"

Noam sighed, smiling despite the fear. "I'll never know, because there is you."

UNDONE

They both held their breath.

Oriole began counting the seconds, one, two three, four, five, six, seven—

Oriole couldn't stand the anticipation. Then Asha's eyes flew wide, and swelled with tears as she breathed in, one sharp grasp. She screamed, a high-pitched strangled exclamation and crumpled to the ground, unconscious.

Oriole observed it all from Starling's form with an odd vacancy inside her. For the longest time, she could only breathe. She stared at Asha, thrashing about and moaning despite her unconscious state.

Five hours feeling the loss you do. Five hours where you are free of it.

Asha twitched, throwing her hand out after someone. But which one? There were so many to mourn. Starling whose form Oriole had taken today died in her sleep, her throat slit along with so many of her sisters, without ever the chance to have a last wish. But the pain of her loss was no less violent.

Was that how Oriole looked on the inside? All that chaos. Was she screaming and thrashing and fighting? Fighting existence without them.

There were moments when she felt so. When the impotence and rage and anguish overpowered everything else. Moments when she couldn't reconcile her feelings. Couldn't reconcile her continued life with what she'd cost those she loved. When she couldn't countenance the desire within her to pull the children of her enemy near and give them the love they seemed to deserve.

At those moments, the chaos poked through, tore at her, fought with her until she could do nothing but let the magic have its way. And hope she understood in the end. Hope to be punished as she deserved.

Asha let out a strangled yelp, Oriole expected to feel it within as she always did. But she couldn't.

Five hours.

She should fly far away, into the sun, into the horizon. Let her body and her spirit feel the weightlessness for those five hours.

Asha tossed over on the ground, rolling about with her arms fighting invisible foes, moaning. She was all covered in dust and her tears made her face grow muddy. A moaning writhing, helpless mess. She looked nothing like herself. Nothing that was light or playful—joyful.

She was such a joyful girl. It was what drew one near and what one longed most to destroy. How could anyone be so happy?

It wasn't fair.

Oriole transformed. With a high screech she flapped into the air in Peregrine's bird form. She couldn't just stand there watching the destruction of Asha's joy. She had wanted it...so badly. But she couldn't watch it. So she took to the air. Beat her wings towards the desert faster and faster. But no amount of distance stopped her head from turning back. No amount of numbness made her stop worrying for that joyful bird writhing on the ground, holding all of Oriole's pain, and being...changed by it.

She turned back.

She landed beside Asha's writhing body and hopped nearer, listening with a racing heart to the girl's moans and sobs. Asha took on her enemies' pain. Perhaps she did deserve joy. Perhaps she deserved more, and Oriole only needed to be free of the pain to see what her heart was screaming.

Slowly, shuddering from the decision, Oriole transformed once more and slid her arms beneath Asha. She took on a sturdier frame and stronger arms to lift the girl—Nene. Another joyful spirit. In this new form, Oriole pulled Asha tight against her chest and kissed the crown of the girl's head.

"It's alright, Bluebird," she crooned, rocking them both. "I have you. You're safe."

WHAT THE MONSTER KNOWS

Hadhi could not make herself understand it. Maybe she was tricking herself. Maybe he was just a mirage a perfect love her mind had conjured because it had thirsted so long in a loveless desert. What other explanation was there? She had told Noam her greatest sin and still he loved her.

It was too beautiful, too wonderful to be real.

Hadhi needed him to know how miraculous she found him. As she turned in his arms, she saw a tall, unfamiliar woman trudging towards them, her arms laden with something heavy. *Someone.*

"Asha!" Hadhi tore past Noam, racing towards her sister. She had forgotten about Asha. The woman carrying her must be the nymph. Asha could be dead, all because Hadhi had left her alone.

Hadhi slid to a stop before the woman, blocking her path and stretching out a cautious hand for Asha. What if she was dead? Noam was right at her heels; he stopped next to Hadhi and immediately reached out to pull Asha from the nymph's arms. She handed Asha over easily and without argument. Asha changed hands noiselessly. Hadhi could not bring her hand to touch her.

This should never have happened. Asha should not have been alone. Hadhi was meant to be vigilant.

If you want your sister alive, protect her.

"What did you do?" Hadhi snarled, as the monster within her clawed to be let loose. She faced down the stranger.

"I only gave her what she asked for." The woman backed slowly away, her eyes darting between Hadhi and Asha. She looked guilty, nearly as frightened as Hadhi felt. But completely unsurprised that Hadhi knew who she was. "I never meant..."

"She has done nothing to you. You cannot punish her for our father's crimes!"

Hadhi was bubbling with rage and fear. And guilt. She allowed this to happen. She left her sister undefended. She was selfish, just like Baba. Her heart raced, and sweat broke out, heat rising from her chest to envelop her whole head. She had no idea what to do.

You know what to do—Monster.

She wanted to ignore his voice, to be someone else. But someone else had left Asha alone. Someone else had been so wrapped up in love that she forgot to worry. Someone else was not good enough to protect Asha, because she was busy protecting herself.

Hadhi advanced on the creature with murder in her eyes. And the shuddering woman drew up her head and her eyes flashed, showing her own inner monster, and though she did not want to, Hadhi could not help stopping, studying her adversary.

The woman was unquestionably beautiful. Slightly taller than Hadhi with round features and a wider build and a bearing of strength and power. She was covered from head to toe in dark fabric of a rich black. It was loose around her body and arms. She wore a scarf around her head and the knot of a bun at the back. She had a face of experience, not old, but not young either and displayed a will not easily shaken. She glared at Hadhi with flashing eyes and a hardness Hadhi was all too familiar with. A monster surely, with rage, and power, and more tricks than Hadhi had yet to see, but everything had a weakness. And once she knew her weakness...

"Shh." Baba pulled Hadhi back into the cover of the long grass. How had she disappointed him already? He told her what to do, where to strike, and she would do it, if he had let her. "Don't be impatient, Hadhi. Watch your prey, understand everything you can about it, what it eats and drinks, where it sleeps how it fights—what it loves."

"Loves?" Hadhi's eyes shot back to her prey, a gazelle. Could animals love? Was it not wrong to kill something that loved?

For once, Baba did not mock; he nodded solemnly. "Everything loves something. It is what keeps it alive, what drives it to fight or to flee."

"But..." Hadhi watched the creature, so lovely and gentle, so harmless. Her heart beat so hard it hurt her ribs. She could not do this. Baba was going to be disappointed again. She always disappointed him.

He was watching her with new patience. He withdrew his own knife and held it out. "My father gave me this when he taught me to hunt. He told me man is an animal too, the strongest, because he can feel love, but he can also understand it for what it is."

Hadhi waited, praying his answer would make everything alright. That he would say he loved her, even if she did not kill it. Anything. He could say anything, as long as it made it better.

"It's power. Power and weakness in one. The power to make you move, and keep you alive, because you know what you're living for. But if your enemy knows what you love, it becomes a weakness. That's why we study our prey." Baba forced the blade into her hand, closing her fingers around the hilt. "Because once you know your prey's weakness, you have power over him, then it is your right to kill him."

"Your sister chose her own fate." The woman snapped Hadhi out of her memories. "And she isn't dead of it yet."

Hadhi was shaking all over, enraged, frightened. She did not want to be her father's monster any more now than she had as a child. Last night when she thought she stood before the nymph, all she felt was sorrow. She had wanted to greet its vengeance with kindness. She wanted to offer herself up in her sister's place. But now—Hadhi felt guilty.

"She is alive, Hadhi," Noam said quietly. Hadhi tried to tamp down her shame, tried to stamp out the woman her father created. "She is breathing, but she will not rouse."

"This is not the magic she asked for," Hadhi snarled, battling the monster for control. Perhaps her father was right, perhaps she would kill, and kill again, to protect what she loved. Perhaps—

"She didn't ask for magic today," the creature whispered. She stared at Asha completely bewildered. Her features softened and Hadhi could make out old lines from smiles and the shape of soft kisses on her lips. "She asked to feel their loss."

The words stunned the monster, sent it tumbling into a pit of sand, completely obscuring it. Leaving only Hadhi behind. She went to her sister. Noam was holding her like a baby, her head at his shoulder, and her body slung down across his chest, one arm beneath her and one around.

Hadhi ran a hand along Asha's face. "Why would she do that?"

Their loss. The loss of the nymphs their father had killed. Hadhi's stomach plummeted, burning the whole way down. Only knowing of Baba's evil tore Hadhi up. What would feeling it do to Asha?

"She was always a sensitive child," Hadhi whispered. "He kept her from the truth. Knew she could never love him if she understood. Feeling such sorrow will rip her apart."

"Grief rips us all apart," the nymph dismissed. Hadhi spun to face the woman. She should look completely alien, but in her silvery eyes, Hadhi recognized bits of herself and her sour face. She recognized another monster.

Hadhi had no words for her, nothing to fight with. Was she so helpless if not for the monster?

"Once you know your prey's weakness...it is your right to kill him."

Hadhi gripped the knife but shook her head. Baba was not trying to convince her she must kill to survive or to eat. Just because it was her right? Being stronger made you right? Always?

Her breath hitched, audibly panting, and tears began to trickle from her eyes. King Enzi was strong. Did that make him right? Everything he did? No matter how terrible?

Hadhi dropped the knife, scooting backwards and wishing she was someone else's child. Wishing she could run home to her mother and hide. She should never have come. For three months, she had barely spoken a word to her father. She had hated him, hidden from him.

And all he had done was say 'Come along, Hadhi, it's past time you learned to hunt,' and with that friendly smile pointed only at her, she had forgotten how evil he was. She had forgotten that she should not want his love. He smiled and she wanted to please him.

"Hadhi." His voice latched onto her like a toothy jaw, piercing her skin so she wanted to cry out, but he would only strike her for such weakness. Zuberi's daughters were not weak. Hadhi forced air through her nostrils and lifted her eyes to meet Baba's gaze.

"I promised you vengeance." He waved the blade tauntingly before Hadhi's face. "You will never best a beast such as Enzi, if you cannot even kill a gazelle." Then he dug in, showed Hadhi he knew her weakness well. "Are you as helpless as Ahon's girl?"

Hadhi flinched, hearing the screams again. "Or will you be Baba's monster and avenge her?"

Hadhi took the blade.

It all came back to that moment. She took the blade. Hadhi had not seen it then, had not understood her father nearly as well as he understood her. He could have told her anything, and she would have believed him. Could have said the animal felt no pain, told her that the death would help some other creature. But he had not wanted to soothe her. He wanted the sickness that coated her stomach at her first kill. He wanted Hadhi to feel disgusting but to kill all the same, because he had told her to do so. He wanted a weapon.

What could the little bits he had left behind of Hadhi possibly do to save her sister? But what good would the weapon be with no one to wield it?

"Your father's crimes cannot go unpunished."

Hadhi nodded. Of course he could not go unpunished. But he was dead.

"His crimes," Noam snapped, despite holding Asha his whole essence challenged the woman. "Not theirs. Battle Born are not meant to punish the innocent." Hadhi watched Noam with such pride, he was fighting for her, and Asha. And not like a monster, not like— "You said so yourself."

A chill slid through Hadhi.

They knew each other? Noam knew what the woman was? Knew her purpose here? Was he another of them?

The question cast Hadhi out of her body. She could only watch, helpless again, waiting for someone to rescue her. Was any of it real? That story that angered him...was it not fear, but certainty? Was he trying to warn her? Had he granted Hadhi's wish without her asking?

It would have to be a wish for love.

Always love. Would he rip it all away now and leave her less than she ever was before? She had felt so strong, so whole. Who would she be if he took his love away?

It's power and weakness in one.

"I said we make up for it," the nymph argued with Noam, oblivious to Hadhi's turmoil.

Hadhi waited to be shattered, felt the little fissures already slicing up her heart. Waiting to hear it had all been an illusion. Baba's monster never could have been loved.

There is no such thing as love, monster.

Another time her father's echo would make her weak. But in this half world, she had time to pause. Time to recognize the falseness of the words. Just like his hunting lesson, it was lies. He *always* told her lies. Might not have known the truth. He was not all knowing. He was not stronger for having quashed his love. If he had loved Hadhi he might have felt her anguish, might have felt her rage. Might have seen the blade coming.

In this half world, for once, her father's words fell into their proper place and let Hadhi slip back into her body. She did not need to keep believing him.

Hadhi forced herself to move. She went to Asha. Yes, Hadhi had been selfish, but not like her father. Asha had told Hadhi to leave her alone, and she made her wish knowing exactly what came of such wishes, because Hadhi had warned her. Hadhi had not failed her sister for lack of trying, but because Asha was her own woman. But she would not abandon her now. Her sisters would both still have Hadhi's protection. Because Hadhi was not the monster. And she never would be again.

She loved.

That was all that mattered. She loved and that made her strong. Whether the love was returned or not. Whether it ended today or not. She closed her eyes; her hands slid beneath Noam's. She felt him startle, felt a tingle shoot up her spine at just the grazing of their skin. She wished she could simply trust the warmth and the memory of them. Wished he would do something to convince her she was wrong, that he was not a spell, he was just a man who loved her. A miracle.

But such belief was far from easy for her, even with the love burning in her heart. It was perhaps more difficult because...he was so special, so tender. She wanted to keep him forever. *Zav zyid qi.* Her tender love. *Hers.*

"I have made up for it." The nymph waved in Hadhi's direction. "Asha has her sister's love now, though she never felt it before. She has Azize. She has the truth."

"She met you." Hadhi had not meant to interrupt, but the thought would not be silenced, and she had everyone's attention now. Forcing strength she did not feel Hadhi began pulling Asha from Noam's arms.

"I can carry her." He resisted.

"No." Hadhi would not look at Noam. She loved him, but that filled her with fear. She focused on her task, willing her heart to stay whole and strong long enough to see Asha safe. "Asha is mine to care for."

Noam regarded Hadhi as though she were a stranger, but carefully adjusted Asha so she lay across her sister's arms. Her weight stunted Hadhi, but it gave her strength of a different kind as the love rushed through her.

"Meeting you was the fulfillment of Asha's dreams," Hadhi informed the woman. "Asha has many flaws, but my father was the monster." Hadhi shook her head searching for her words. "If you destroy her, offer her joys and then rip them away, correcting scales that can never be balanced, you are as bad as he was."

The woman's eyes danced with angry lights and her jaw rolled as though she had swallowed her tongue. She knew Hadhi was right. Of course she did. All monsters knew what they were. But knowing did not stop them.

Hadhi turned towards home. Noam reached out to steady her beneath her elbow, but she pulled her arm from his grasp, letting her gaze consume his beloved face.

"Are you one of them?" Hadhi hated the quiver in her voice, and her knotted stomach as she pled.

Noam looked truly baffled.

"My father said a few nymphs escaped and would seek vengeance." She forced the words out, though just speaking made her feel weaker. "Are you one of the few?"

The nymph laughed, brittle and superior. Her amusement quivered over Hadhi, reviving her earlier chill. Hadhi's teeth chattered and her limbs stiffened as though soaked again in magic rain. She waited for her heart to break.

"No, Hadhi." Noam reached out, but Hadhi stumbled back a few steps in her haste to get away from him. In her shame.

She should have known. She did know. Of course she did. No one could truly love her. Not once they knew her.

"Hadhi, think about it," Noam insisted. "How could loving you possibly be vengeance?"

A laugh turned sob escaped Hadhi. He was so sincere, gazing at her so tenderly, she longed to believe him, to reach out and trust him, but—

"What better weapon is there, against one such as me?" Hadhi whispered, "Thrust into my heart, for a glorious moment, so I might feel *invincible*." Hadhi shook her head, the sorrow and fear slowly consumed by the rage he had said she should feel. Of course he did, the nymphs wanted a monster to punish in Baba's place. "So that when you expose the lie, you will leave me helpless. Yours to kill by right of strength."

"Hadhi," he bit her name out angrily. "I am not a Battle Born. I love you. Nothing can take that away. We will have *all of time*."

That did not quite sound like love, more like a threat. And despite the rage, Hadhi wanted to latch onto that threat and pretend it was true.

The nymph regarded Noam's sentiments with disdain. And something else that might have been pride, or awe. Disbelief? Hadhi could not be sure. Whatever it was that look made her doubt herself. Allowed her to hope.

She said it was all too interesting to miss...you and Noam.

Maybe he was not one of them. Maybe he was the lighthearted man who...But that was who he pretended to be.

Was the easy charmer the real Noam, or the compassionate man with hidden pain? She could not sort them out. The only thing she knew for certain was the one thing he was trying to convince her was wrong. Nymph, or miracle, or wish made manifest, she could never have kept him. His love would be torn away eventually.

She had known it in the cave. They just let the world in sooner than she wanted. It should not be such a shattering realization. At least now, she would have been truly love—

"Did you make him feel this way?" Hadhi gasped, spinning to face only the nymph, because even as her hope built, caution chased after it. She should not ask. She should keep the fantasy. But the words were already out.

The nymph regarded Hadhi with a quietude so familiar it was as though Hadhi were looking at herself.

"I know what I am feeling!" Noam burst out. But Hadhi and the nymph saw only each other.

"How terrible it is to be loved, when you know the ugliness within." The woman's voice attempted to entice. She need not have bothered; Hadhi was riveted, awaiting her heartbreak. "Invigorating, terrifying—distracting."

Asha's weight tripled on Hadhi's arms. Hadhi stooped under the sudden pressure, forcing her knees to firm before she was bent. Noam reached out for her, but not before the nymph.

"Makes you forget yourself." The creature stepped between them. Her hands slipped beneath Hadhi's helping her to rise. "Makes you think that you could be like her." She ran her large, gentle hand over Asha's face. Suddenly her eyes shot to Hadhi's, with a bright power Hadhi was all to familiar with. *Envy.* "But you are nothing like her."

Hadhi understood the creature well now. And wished she did not. She did not want to know how to destroy it. Even buried, the monster was a part of Hadhi. She took a careful step away, with her broken heart lodged in her throat. Of course he was bewitched to love her. How else?

"I offered *you* no wishes," the Battle Born snapped, but Hadhi gasped in relief. Her eyes sought Noam, but the creature was not finished. "There are those for whom my magic holds no sway, because already they punish themselves."

Hadhi felt the words try to drag what was left of her into the pit with the monster. She took in Noam's angry, wounded face. The woman was right. Hadhi did not need an enemy to steal her joy. She felt the truth with a strike of pity for the woman. Should it not have been for herself? But the Battle Born was all she could seem to see, or to feel. Even as fear of the woman grew. She would be stopped by little but death.

"You are the woman my father tricked." More than any other nymph, this one had cause to rage and fight for vengeance. "You sought out Asha because you think she was the one he loved."

The woman rolled her eyes, but it was too late. Hadhi already knew her.

"You are jealous of her," Hadhi whispered. Noam was watching the exchange with rapt attention. He still looked angry, no—hurt. She had hurt him with her doubt. She should be heavier for the burden, but it was better this way. Better it ended now, before something fully woke the monster and he left in disgust. Now it could be like his story. A brief love and a memory.

"You would not be happier if she were like us. It would only make you sick inside, if he had made her a monster."

"Monster?" the woman snarled, baring her teeth. Her eyes flared with power. "What makes me a monster, daughter of Zuberi?"

Hadhi slowly backed down the path. The woman needed no explanation Hadhi could give; she already knew her answer.

"I do not want to kill you," Hadhi said, avoiding Noam's eyes. The world was truly here now. He was hers no more. But that did not mean she had to watch him recognize the ugliness inside her. "But I will. To protect her, I will."

The nymph scoffed. "Of course you will, daughter of Zuberi, picking up his mantel, are you?"

Hadhi stopped moving, her spine snapped straight. She barely felt Asha's weight as the nymph's words whipped across her, waking her rage.

"My name," Hadhi snarled through clinched teeth, "is Hadhi. Zuberi was my father. But I am not *his*." Rage was filling her, all but overflowing, rage and fear. She wanted to bellow to the heavens, to rip the woman apart, anything to keep her words from being true. "Stay away from my family. I will not seek you out, but if you threaten us, I *will* destroy you." Hadhi marched away, panting from the rage.

Daughter of Zuberi, taking up his mantel, are you?
Never!

THE WORLD TURNED OVER

"You're trembling." Noam's hollow voice startled Oriole. She'd forgotten he was there. How different it was not to feel the people around her. Frightening.

Yes, she was trembling. *That girl.* There was something about her that felt so familiar, so frightening, and so broken. Oriole could not contain the tremble, but when she turned to face Noam, she made certain her eyes flashed with power. He could tremble too.

"Isn't your love gentle? Isn't she sweet?" Oriole mocked, feeling helplessly close to tears. *A monster.* What made her a monster? She could have left after Asha received her last wish. A monster would have left her there, shivering in the middle of nowhere, and gone off to enjoy this...her mind failed her. She had no words for the swirling mass of confusion within. But it would never be something to enjoy.

"You love that mo—"

"Yes," Noam snapped, not allowing her to finish. Where before his voice was hollow with fear, it now rung with steel. "But I did not stay behind to discuss her. I've been waiting for you."

"Why? To discuss my trembling perhaps?" she sneered, unwilling to change the subject. "Tell me, aren't you trembling? Now that you see what she is."

"What *Hadhi* is, is..." Noam hissed through his teeth, he closed his eyes. When they opened, Oriole watched him struggling to pull forward his old veneer of charm and ease. He couldn't quite manage it, a frantic energy lingering around him. Oriole reached out, needing to feel what he felt.

But she couldn't.

Couldn't feel a bit of him, why? She felt Hadhi. Had no trouble recognizing the meaning of every twinge and swallow and twist within the girl. She understood the monster wholly.

Why couldn't she feel Noam? Or Asha. She hadn't felt Asha's turmoil as she writhed on the ground, as she carried her from the road.

Had Oriole shed more of her magic than she meant, more than just the loss, and the memory? Had she shed her ability to feel the world? But if that were so, why could she feel Hadhi?

"I know what you promised Enzi," Noam snapped, his struggle for charm abandoned. "Will he die of the wish?"

Oriole tilted her head this way and that. She had never been without absolute knowledge of the struggle within her fellow beings. Never but once. But Zuberi wasn't quite human, was he? He'd given over to his inner monster long before they met.

It should not be so unsettling, should not send a chill arching down her spine, this not knowing. She had felt all there was within Noam last night. He was no monster. He was a child of magic. But part of the fear that trembled through her body was from the unknown. If she couldn't feel a threat coming, then anyone could hurt her.

"All men die deaths of seeking," she replied at length.

"Do not toy with me, there isn't time. Will his wish kill him?"

Oriole wanted to evade, to banter, to taunt. They were the only mechanisms left that brought her any solace, a moment of pow—

The thought struck her full in the gut, bile rising within her.

Power.

Was that all she wanted now? Had she *become* her enemy?

She swung away, pulled Nene's body right up to a small cliff's edge and stared out. She could not bring herself to harm even one of these bodies, but...she wished she had not survived the attack.

"His death was the spell's intent," she answered Noam flatly. Why hadn't she died? "Enzi should die to get his vengeance, but—" She looked up at Noam, her eyes pleading understanding, but he was not watching her. He was gazing after his love.

"None of the wishes are doing as I expect any longer." Oriole's eyes as well fell on the slowly shrinking Hadhi. Hadhi was having trouble navigating the way down the hill with her sister in her arms. Odd, she must have taken the same trail a hundred times with an animal of equal size slung over her shoulders. Was it so much more arduous to bear the living?

"There is a plan to stop Enzi." Noam faced Oriole. "I promised Azize to seek you out and beg you not to harm Asha or intervene in Azize's plans."

"Why would I stop Enzi's death?"

Noam clenched his jaw. "The plan does not call for Enzi to die."

"Ahhh." She looked away, following the current of her sigh towards the desert. What did they want from her? Beg her not to have her vengeance against Asha, as if she even wanted it any longer. And they wanted her to release Enzi as well, when he surely had a hand in the deaths of her sisters. Couldn't they see this was all she had left? "Perhaps living with oneself is a worse fate," she whispered.

"No." Noam grabbed Oriole by the wrist. "No," he said again, "not for men like Enzi. If the plan succeeds, if he is imprisoned...do what you will. Leave him, kill him, I don't know anymore what is right. But..." He swallowed and his eyes bore into Oriole's with a power to rival her own.

"Will you grant me a wish?"

"You are not dying." Oriole shook at her wrist, confused and growing frightened.

"I know. I know. But she might." Together, they turned, barely able to catch sight of Hadhi struggling down the hill. "She is..." He lost his words for a breath. "In some moments, I feel we are the same. In others, she is my opposite. But she must be the most unlucky woman in the world. The things she's seen and felt—" The girl rounded a corner and was out of sight and Noam's voice faltered again, only to return more intense. "I know you have magic for other things than just death, the magic you were born with. Maybe it is time you use that."

Odd that he knew such things about her kind. Few did. But Oriole felt such hunger, not for power or freedom, but simply to know if she could. If there was more to her than only ends.

"What do you wish?" she whispered with nothing but the thinnest thread of hope.

"You said I was lucky? Blessed?" She nodded. "Let her be blessed instead."

"What?" Anger and envy rose within her. For that girl, for the beast who snarled and threatened and had nothing in her but the monster her father raised—

But that wasn't entirely true, was it? She had more, she loved her sisters, loved Noam, but not enough. It was not enough for her to trust his feelings. And it was nowhere near enough for him to make such a sacrifice.

"You have no idea what such a thing would cost you. You scoff and fight and decry magic, but it has already helped you more than you know. If you turn your back on that now, throw it away—No. It will not work."

"Please," he begged. "It must."

"NO!" Oriole snapped her wrist free. Why had she let him touch her at all? "She would *squander* it. Could never understand it. Your life was not gentle either. You had hatred to battle. You chose happiness. But Zuberi's eldest, with her impenetrable depths, darkness even I cannot see through, she *never* would." Oriole screamed, unsure why this angered her so. The girl's threats had not been so frightening. She was not, as Oriole had taunted her, anywhere near as evil as her father. But she had something of Zuberi in her, and she was so painfully familiar, a mirror of the suffering Oriole had shed for only five hours. She couldn't stand the sight of the girl. "You haven't truly seen her, haven't felt what she is inside. She doesn't deserve it."

"I don't care if *you* think she deserves it. It is my luck," he shouted, caught halfway between shouting and beaming. "My wish. Will you grant it or not?"

Sparks bit at the spot where he'd held her wrist, and all around the wind rose, rippling the fabric of the air. Magic rushed between them. So powerful Oriole knew it was not from her alone. She felt the thrash of a hundred wings—so much power spun around them. Something wanted her to say yes.

"No," Oriole whispered, afraid.

"Because you can't?" he challenged.

"I'm too old to be taunted into changing my mind."

But he would not back down; it didn't suit such an easy creature to be so stubborn. "Because you don't agree with my wish? Because you don't approve of Hadhi?" As he spoke his eyes glinted, and Oriole saw his mind working, adjusting to a different tactic. "Or because I do not deserve my wish?"

She might have underestimated him. Did he deserve his wish? She had seen into his soul yesterday, and yesterday she would have granted him anything. She had almost wanted him to escape with his love. But today she had truly met his love.

Zuberi was my father, but I am not his.

"I didn't understand the luck," Noam spoke quietly. He reached out gently and took both her hands in his. "Not entirely. Even after you told me about it. Not until she looked into my eyes and told me no one had *ever* loved her."

That knocked the air from Oriole's being, left a gaping empty ache in her chest, and a new weight in her bones.

"I could have been like that. You're right, my life wasn't free of rejection. But I was lucky. I was blessed enough to see that my father's failure to love me was *not my fault*. She has never had that. Maybe she would choose happiness too, if she were given the chance."

"You could *die* of such a wish," Oriole whispered, ready to cry for his love, but hoping to rouse even a bit of his caution. Hoping to change his mind.

"How many men have died of your wishes?" he asked with a laugh. And his ease returned. He was warm, charming—*unfathomable*. A child of magic. "At least I know what I am asking. I would gladly die for her, if I must. But first I will fight for the chance to stand beside her. For the chance for her to see how deserving of love she truly is."

Oriole was trembling again, and tears rushed from her eyes without her leave. "Children of magic," she sighed, pulled her arms up, and his hands with them. "I hope she is worth it."

She kissed the back of his hand, and the earth rumbled. The loud crash and crack of the changing world sounded in the distance. Wings beat all around them, until a single giant explosion sounded in the air, and all went quiet.

As one, she and Noam looked off in the direction where the shaking originated. Ether. At the furthest visible edge, it swayed, dust rose into the air and the wind leapt. Noam was smiling as he pulled his eyes from the desert. He didn't look a thing like a man who'd just given up his luck.

"She is." Noam yanked Oriole into his arms with a suddenness that caught her completely by surprise. He wrapped his arms around her in a powerful hug, leaving her unsteady for an entirely new reason as the world turned over again.

The desert ceased shaking.

"Thank you." Noam released her and raced after his love. Hadhi—unfathomable.

Oriole stood with no idea what to do, or where to go. She had four hours left with no pain and no...self. Who was she without it?

In the desert, the dust cloud shifted, growing closer, obscuring the horizon. Maybe it would only keep growing, maybe the wind would rise and the sands would fly, and if she stood just here, maybe it would come for her.

Maybe Ether would devour her, as monsters deserved.

She couldn't tell where it came from, the desert, her memory, or the magic lingering from her spell, but a voice gently soothed its way through Oriole, almost rousing that self she was so certain had left her.

Live.

IN THE COMPANY OF WOMEN

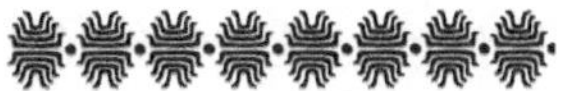

THE QUEEN'S RETREAT

Nuru wanted to gather more support. Neema and her family, Arya and Ayinde. Surely they would all want to help. So many of the women in the palace last night looked ready to kill the king then and there. But when she's said as much last night, the men in her uncle's home suggested that Nuru knowing was already too much of a risk.

Sade had bristled at the idea that Nuru or any woman would be the liability, when the men had been so reticent to act. But she had agreed that with so much at risk, they should only trust those they were already sure of.

At least the Queen's Marked, a gathering of servants mostly and a few other members like Sade, her family, and Eshe, were involved. Though not in the attack; they were merely to block up all palace entrances so the king could not return.

Now Nuru hid in the Queen's Retreat, outside the capitol building. It had been a bathing area for queens of the past, and their maids. But the capitol palace had such features inside now. So this was just a private area no men were allowed to enter, where the queen and other women could gather. Water ran through tubes made of hollowed out tree branches and poured down a constructed fountain into a little pool. There was a mud hut with molded patterns on the walls and silks hanging before the entrance. Nuru had been sneaking in here for years, ever since Hadhi defied Baba and refused to let Nuru come with her to the palace.

Nuru had needed to be defiant as well and find her own way in. But once she got to the palace and saw the guards with their spears perched along the roof, once she'd seen Hadhi trudge inside...Nuru hadn't had the nerve to actually sneak in. So she hid in the Queen's Retreat. No one came. Not the first day, nor the second, but there was food and clean drinking water in a covered basket, so servants must visit the hut daily. By the end of the week, it was boring, and Nuru went to play with her cousins instead. It seemed fitting that they should be hidden here now, right under the nose of the king.

There were ten children of varying ages, her three cousins, and other children Uncle Kafil had asked Nuru to hide when she went to see him last night. Nuru knew a few of them; they were all younger though. The oldest among them was Shafira. Nuru approached her now.

"I think I should get more food, in case you have to be here long. Can you keep them quiet?"

Shafira shrugged. "Depends for how long. Do you really think this is safe? Right at the king's door."

Nuru didn't know what could possibly be considered safe. Her uncle and four other men intended to attack the king's caravan when he left the palace to go to the desert for his wedding to Hadhi. They were going to kill him before he ever made it to Ether. Or, more likely, die in the attempt and all their children would be killed as well.

"Where are all the wives?" Nuru demanded, suddenly struck by their absence. Why was Nuru asked the watch the little children? She'd thought last night that her uncle gave her the task so she would feel useful, but most of these children had mothers living. Some more than one.

"The older children and the mothers went with Baba," Shafira said angrily. "I wanted to go as well, but he said I was needed to protect the littler ones. And to hide them in the jungle..."

When it doesn't work. Nuru's mind supplied what Shafira couldn't voice.

Nuru notched up her chin and forced confidence she didn't feel. "It will work."

It at least made her feel a bit better. She still felt the others, especially Neema and anyone else the king had hurt ought to have the chance to participate, but she would trust the adults to do their part. "Here is the safest place; men cannot pass the wall on pain of death. And there is a secret exit."

Nuru led her cousin to the curtained entrance to the hut and peeked out cautiously. The whole retreat was like a hut itself, a high wall with long bolts of cloth stretched across it in great strips. There were little gaps between the cloths, but none was wide enough to properly see inside. Once she was sure there was no one around, Nuru led her cousin to the waterfall.

"Behind the water is a tunnel, it isn't very large, but—" Nuru cut herself off. She had stuck her head into the tunnel to show her cousin, but catching sight of a figure inside, Nuru darted through the gap between the falls and the water, getting only slightly splashed.

"Neema!" She grabbed her friend off the ground and into her arms. Last night, when Uncle Kafil insisted that Nuru could tell no one, she'd been so overcome with fear for Hadhi and her uncle and her cousins that she'd forgotten Neema for a moment. But she was so relieved to see her now.

"Are you alright? Why are you in the tunnel? Neema?"

Neema was so quiet. She had a far away expression and her hands were clasped tightly around something. "I hadn't known about the tunnel," she said at last. "Never been in the Queen's Retreat before, but I went last night after you suggested it. I found this." She opened her palm.

It was just a long metal stick, the sort some women used to decorate their hair. But it was sharp. Deadly. Nuru knew what kept her friend quiet and felt such an ugly surge of hope. Hope that Neema had done it, had killed the king. But it was wrong to have wanted it and she didn't need to ask. The tip was clean and Neema was frightened still.

Nuru tried to take the stick from Neema's hand, but she closed her fingers around it tight and dropped her hand to her side. That was fair. Here she was, hiding in a tunnel so alone, it was fair that she have something to defend herself, however paltry.

Last night, when Nuru had begged her uncle to just take Hadhi away and hide her, he'd shaken his head and said words that made Nuru so proud to be his family. "Hadhi deserves to be among her people. She deserves to know they would keep her safe, no matter the cost."

Nuru gave Neema another hug and urged her through the waterfall entrance. "I need your help." She pretended not to understand what Neema had been imagining, all alone and frightened, in the dark.

She deserved all those same things Hadhi did. She deserved community around her. When Neema caught sight of Shafira and the other children, her eyes narrowed on Nuru in confusion. In hushed tones, Nuru relayed her uncle's plan, with Shafira looking out for anyone who might overhear. Nuru made sure to express her uncle's desire to protect *all* of Enzi's victims. Neema needed to hear that her neighbors cared for her, that they did not think she deserved to be harmed.

"It took us so long to sneak the children in, a few at a time, by the front gate." Nuru neared the end of her retelling, but Neema had yet to speak. Her eyes though were teary with hope and fear. "We had to watch for guards, but it was fairly dark out." Technically, the gate was never locked, and women were allowed to enter the retreat but most of the boys she'd let in there wouldn't even be allowed. But it was also a place of protection, Nuru thought the queens of old would understand, despite the rules.

Finally, Neema spoke. "Nuru." Her voice splintered so it must slice up her throat to get the words out. "I never meant...I shouldn't have...I don't want any of you hurt just for me." Her tears began to fall.

Nuru's eyes grew wet as well. She gripped Neema's wrist. "We are friends. We are a community. Vay chizoo etowo ty et pu ur chizootelle ta'kepa." *We protect each other and so are protected ourselves.* Nuru repeated the oath of Maltuba. "Of course we should risk our safety for you, but no, not *just* for you. For all of us, because none of us are safe, if any of us have to be harmed to keep it so. I should always have known. Thank you for telling me. Help Shafira with the little ones, I will bring supplies. It will work. We will all be safe."

Nuru hugged Neema once more before leaving by the front gate. When Nuru used to sneak into the retreat, she'd pretended to be queen.

Baba had just married Sabra, there were servants all over the place, and sisters and Mzaa. Even in the mansion, Nuru never had a space of her own, no place where she could just be, and dance. So for the first few days, having the retreat all to herself was fun. She'd danced under the fabric shade, played in the water, lay in the mud hut when it got too warm.

She was a queen who'd gone into the retreat to contemplate some challenge. She would walk slowly down one line of shade and up another. She would take a swim in the little pool and let the water cool her mind. Then she would rise and dress in the extra silks that were left in the hut. Once she'd saved the whole kingdom, she would dress in her own clothes again and run off to do something else.

Maltuba deserved a queen of Nuru's imagining. The sort who led her people.

She stared at the palace. She should be walking away, but—Uncle Kafil did not expect to survive. He would kill the king to protect Hadhi, but even if he succeeded, he and his friends would be put to death.

There should be another way. There must be a way to keep her cousins safe, and her uncle safe, and her sister safe, Neema and even Maltuba safe. Maltuba was not an ugly place! Look at what its people were willing to risk to save others. It was beautiful. It deserved a ruler as kind, but...it also deserved to have the people who would fight to see that happen remain alive after.

It deserved for all of them to know they had a choice. Nuru had promised not to tell and she intended to keep her promise, but it still felt wrong. Wrong for herself, and wrong for her nation.

There ought to be a peaceful way to stop the king.

All she need to do to see the king was tell the guard at the gate that she was Hadhi's sister, and she would be let in. But what then? Tell him to be kind? Politely ask him not to marry Hadhi or harm his people?

A woman of Maltuba can marry a cheetah or a gazelle.

You didn't politely ask cheetahs anything. And anyway, how could it be right to be led by a man who didn't believe a woman had a right to refuse to wed him? A right to refuse him anything?

Maltuba deserved better than a leader who stole from them. It deserved a leader who loved them.

Nuru's whole life had been safe and happy, and the longer she thought, the more the reason became clear.

Before Baba died, if Nuru was running for the door, Hadhi would be close at her heels. No matter what she'd been doing, Hadhi would be after Nuru as though frightened of losing sight of her, for even a moment.

"Nuru, wait. You have no idea what dangers are out there. I will protect you."

She always protected Nuru. Always.

Even when Nuru had wanted the danger or wanted to escape her sister's frantic obsession with safety. Though she loved Hadhi, Nuru just hadn't seen what there was to be so worried about. But she did now. Hadhi saw all the frightening things, all the sad and the angry things, and she protected her sister from all of it.

There had been days before Baba married Sabra when he would come home full of stories and laughter. And without Asha around to listen, he would call for Nuru.

"Where is my little jungle cat?"

Nuru loved it. For the first time, he noticed her.

"I'm here, Baba. Where were you all day?"

He would laugh and pull Nuru onto his knee as he told all sorts of stories. Hadhi was always there, just standing, watching them. It never took long for Hadhi to remind Baba that Asha was with Sabra, that someone must bring her home safely.

At the time, Nuru thought Hadhi was jealous. Baba had a way of making one greedy for his attention. But that wasn't it. Was it? Baba would smile at Hadhi in such a cold way, then go fetch his best beloved. As soon as he was gone, Hadhi was herself again. She would sling an arm around Nuru's shoulder and ask about her day, though she'd already seen it. Hadhi listened to every word as though it was special.

Nuru had never realized all the ways Hadhi protected her. Guarding Nuru from the jealousy over Baba's attention. Letting Nuru get enough to feel loved, but not so much that she would miss it when Asha returned and Baba saw no one else.

That was the sort of leader this nation deserved, one who would see to the safety, not just of their bodies, but of their hearts as well. But Nuru wasn't sure how their nation got that and kept Hadhi safe.

It was only fair that Nuru should protect Hadhi for a change.

HAUNTED

Kane was in a marvelous mood for a man who had not slept. He'd managed quite a bit last night! The others were wary of him at first, Noam's doing, but his luck ended today.

Kane nearly laughed aloud but managed to stop himself. He had never met a man who was as much a fool as Noam! *Wishing* to give his luck away. Practically begging a being of magic to kill him. It was too easy! Zuberi's spirit might just rise from Ether at the offense of his *perfect weapon* falling for such a fool. He had no right to be with her, no right to be with anyone; the fact that he had lived this long was offensive to all the children who had died understanding more of the world.

But...Noam was for later. Kane had other prey in his scent. He couldn't say he thought much of the creature. She appeared to have some physical strength, which was not to be discounted, and could apparently change her shape as she had last night—

Last night when she granted you a wish, you mean? a familiar voice taunted Kane. He looked around but could see no form. It would be too strange for Zuberi's spirit to truly have risen just as he had been thinking it would. *I taught you better. We don't wish for our destiny. We make it.* The voice laughed. *At least I do.*

Kane felt a growl deep in his chest from the lingering taunts of his mentor. He wouldn't let Zuberi distract him just because it offended his sensibilities, even in death, that anyone might be stronger than he. Kane had a creature to capture. Kane would prove he was stronger, and though he could not taunt Zuberi's living face with that knowledge, he would taunt his *perfect weapon* with it. He would show her which one of them was Zuberi's legacy.

Over the course of one evening, he'd captured eight of Azize's men, on his own, and with half of them suspicious of him. He'd tracked Noam, located Hadhi, who the king was seeking, and found the magic creature who killed Zuberi, and just a half an hour ago, while eavesdropping on Noam and Hadhi in their lovers' rendezvous, he'd caught Omar sneaking around Zuberi's hut. He was bound, gagged and unconscious near the river. It was only a matter of time before Kane took down every man who stood in his way and presented this creature to the king on a platter as final proof that he was stronger than Zuberi.

He watched the creature now, too distracted staring off at the rising sands of Ether to notice him creeping nearer. Hadhi had mentioned *a few* when she was failing to kill the woman. This woman didn't seem powerful enough to have killed Zuberi but looks could be deceiving. It was one of the first lessons Zuberi taught him.

Never trust your eyes alone. Be like the raven who waits to see if other creatures die before dining on a carcass.

Kane smelled burning. No, not just burning—burning *flesh*. His right hand flexed wide as a sharp tongue of flames scoured it. His chest rose and fell with the effort to contain the scream. Flames leapt all around him. He was trapped again, surrounded by flames. They moved closer and closer, and he saw the faces of the other children, the ones he'd left behind pressing in, the fire coming from their empty eye sockets as their flesh peeled away.

You're no better than them, are you? Only the strong deserve to live.

He saw Zuberi now, beyond the flames, preening as the screams of dying children split the air and the scent of their burning flesh stifled all other odors. Saw him watching from above, as if he'd been watching that day, felt the looseness of his bindings fall away, saw his child-self scrabbling up the hill, as Zuberi turned away, and went to wait. As if...

You never could make your own destiny. I gave it to you.

With a great roar, Kane leapt from his crouched hiding place on an outcropping of the cliff and launched himself at the woman staring into the distance. He toppled her to the ground, shouting his rage at Zuberi, as he attacked his killer.

"I make my own destiny!"

The roar of the young man's attack came out of nowhere. Zawadi had stood for a long while watching the sandstorm. Watching it sway towards the deep distance of the desert, then surge forward. Watching it dredge up sands from the depths of dunes and shift the shape of the horizon. But it did not draw near enough to be any kind of threat. She could think of nothing to do. Nowhere to go. She was curious to see what became of Noam's wish, but she was also certain it would not be good. She shouldn't stay to see, but she couldn't leave.

She felt...she couldn't explain it in words, but she felt *presences* all around her. Felt loss, and pain, felt feelings rising from the desert as though they were beings. She couldn't bring herself to move, waiting for one to feel familiar.

Then came the roar.

"I make my own destiny!" he shouted as he toppled her to the ground in Nene's fairy form.

Zawadi landed hard enough to shake the breath from her body. But also hard enough to shake the fog from her mind. Hard enough to rouse her *rage*. She kicked out at the man who would attack her with Zuberi's last words to her.

He flew backwards, landing just short of the cliff. Nene was a force. He scrambled to his feet and pulled a blade from beneath the high slit of his robes.

Zawadi leapt up in the body of a different sister. Pintail. She had been the only elf among the order, and her agility and speed were better suited for hand to hand battles than any woman in the order. Had he not slit her throat in her sleep, Zawadi had no doubt Zuberi would have suffered greatly at Pintail's hands.

"Do you make it?" Zawadi growled. "Or do you let Zuberi choose a destiny for you?"

The man struck out. There was a wildness in his eyes. A fever. Flames of madness consuming him from within. He could have attacked her far more efficiently without the shout, and he occasionally swung out at not just her, but the air around her as if attacking those presences Zawadi felt inklings of.

He charged at her, feet and hands flying far faster than she expected. Zawadi fought as Pintail would. The long robes of the order had high slits and loose leg coverings for this sister, and her body reacted long before Oriole's would have.

Limbs entangled and separated, blows were absorbed and deflected. It was a whirl of motion, a surge of life like Zawadi had not felt in years. Nothing—not vengeance, not planning, not even Asha's wish to free her of the weight—had felt as good as this motion. She felt her rage, long buried beneath her shame and regret, rise up and give power to Pintail's strikes.

She fought! As she wished she could have when she faced off with Zuberi. She beat back this maddened boy until she had him held against her with an arm pinning in his throat. She squeezed it tighter as he gasped and flailed.

His legs kicked out, and his hands clawed, but with each passing second, he lost verve. She would win. She saw the body in her arms, but it was a different face than he had had when he launched himself at her. A hated face.

She saw Zuberi. And she squeezed all the tighter. *Finally.* This was what she needed. This was what the world needed. This.

"Mother bird?" A soft coo shuddered over the air, startling Zawadi's eyes open, Oriole's eyes? Mother Bird's?

Her arm fell away, and she dropped the nearly lifeless boy to the ground. Dove?

She saw the bird flapping nearer. What was Dove doing here? She'd ordered them all to stay away. One of only twelve Battle Born sisters left alive. The daughter whose blessings she'd felt on the boy. Whose blessings Zawadi had distorted for her vengeance.

Oriole stumbled backwards. Fell to the ground for her robes trapped beneath the body of the boy she'd nearly killed.

No. No. She could not face Dove. She could not face any of the order. It was for that reason as much as for their safety that she had ordered them to disburse and go into hiding.

Oriole kicked the boy away and leapt into the air in a new body. Gyr's bird form. She rushed away, far too fast for Dove to follow.

She couldn't face one she'd failed so thoroughly.

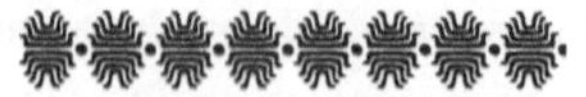

UNDERSTANDING

Hadhi was nearly to the house when Noam came racing down the hill with his easy smile in place. Did nothing phase him? Had he not heard anything that passed between her and the nymph?

She waited for him; whatever was to be said, it must be here, away from everyone. Away from Mzaa in particular. Hadhi adjusted Asha in her arms her every muscle creaking, but Asha did not stir and the pit of guilt in Hadhi's stomach grew.

"Hadhi." Noam stopped beside her his breath heavy from the run. He shook his head, smiling all the while. "I am not a nymph. Nor is my love a spell."

Hadhi tried to accept his declaration without feeling her entire being quake; *how terrible it is to be loved, when you know the ugliness within.* Noam did not let it go at that, reaching out for Asha. Hadhi took a step back, but he just took two to compensate and latched onto Hadhi's shoulders.

"There is no point doubting me, Hadhi," Noam declared. "I will not give up one moment of our iooni."

Hadhi's heart burned, and he took advantage of her stupor taking Asha easily. Hadhi stared at them, torn between the urges to laugh or to cry. He should just let her go. She was bound to hurt him worse if he stayed. Bound to leave him as wounded as Asha.

But he could not go, could he? He loved her.

"No time to stand around gawking at me," Noam remarked, walking towards the hut

"Noam." Hadhi flinched at the volume of her voice, high and *desperate*.

He turned, not quite smiling. He was waiting for a fight. And all Hadhi wanted to say was, you are beautiful when you do not smile. But what came out was "What is gawking?"

Noam grinned. "Staring in amazement." He wiggled his eyebrows. "Or lust."

Hadhi shook her head, looking away as her face heated.

It was oddly dark for morning. In the distance, a sandstorm was rising from Ether to cover the sky. It was far off yet, might not even reach them, but it filled Hadhi with a sense of foreboding. When sandstorms rose from the depths of Ether, the spirits of the dead were welcomed back into Maltuba. She already felt haunted enough last night.

Hadhi slipped her arm through Noam's, staring up at him as a world of words cascaded through her mind too fast to latch onto a single one.

Noam smiled gently. "I love you too."

Understanding. Another new experience.

Hadhi wished she could revel in it, but look what her reveling had cost Asha. She pulled the feelings deep into her heart. Another day would be for marveling. Now she needed to be strong.

Noam carried Asha the rest of the way without waking her.

She asked to feel the loss of them.

It was so like Asha, taking on more than she could possibly understand, running wildly away from the evil she had learned of their father. Hadhi would never have done that, would never have thought to. Asha had such innate goodness, Hadhi must convince her of that. She could not let their father ruin in death what he could not in life.

Hadhi led Noam through the back entrance of her home and steadied him down the steps towards the room she shared with her sisters.

"Hadhi!" Mzaa rushed out of her room. "Where have you been? I've been frantic, have you..." She drifted off her gaze sharpening on Noam.

"This way." Hadhi led Noam into her room, too concerned with Asha, and nymphs, and revolution to sense the danger at home. "Here, lay her on my bed?"

"Your bed?" Mzaa demanded, her worry instantly transformed to rage. "Why? What's the matter with her?"

"I will explain, bring Nuru and Sabra," Hadhi said calmly.

"You do not give me instructions. Answer me." There was no mistaking Mzaa's anger now.

"It was not an order. I am seeing to Asha," Hadhi sighed, wishing the crisis could be handled without resentment and power struggles.

"Toss her in the dust where she is happy!" Mzaa screeched. Hadhi longed to hide her mother's hatred from Noam. But mingled in with her embarrassment was a swell of sorrow. She should have spoken to this long ago. It should have eaten at her the way Kiho did. Hadhi should have protected her sister.

Did you always love me?

There should never have been any doubt. Rama would be so disappointed in her. *We are a family now, Hadhi, and family protects each other.* But Hadhi allowed their father to build a wedge between them and now Asha felt so alone and so ugly that she had put her life at risk trying to fix it. Hadhi could not let it go on. Such fear and hatred only grew inside of you, until you could not remember ever being anything but ugly. Until you doubted every show of love.

Hadhi's eyes slid down Noam's back. She had hurt him with her doubts. But she did not know how to fix it, could barely comprehend how she was loved. But she was. And Hadhi must see that Asha and Noam knew they were loved as well.

"Asha is not well. She will lay on my bed, and we will care for her," Hadhi insisted, gently. She knew authority over this family was all her mother had. "Please bring Nuru and Sabra, you must all know something."

"There isn't time," Mzaa snapped. An abundance of fears played across her face, then vanished like a trick of the light. "I assume since he *found you,*" Mzaa snarled, not even looking Noam's way, "that he told you what happened last night?"

"Yes, I know, Mzaa. But what has happened to Asha could happen to us all."

Mzaa yanked Hadhi away from her sister. "If she is contagious, stay away. Let Azize see to her, or send her to her uncle. You will be queen at sunset. You cannot afford to be ill."

"At sunset!" Hadhi swiveled to demand of Noam. He nodded, swallowing tightly. Hadhi drew in rapid breaths, fighting the panic. Her heart was pounding like it wanted to split open her chest and flee her body. *Today.* She would be married to an evil man, before the day was out. No wonder he had told her that story. They were the creatures doomed to love for only one day. She would not even have the day to wrap up the memory. She wanted to scream—to run! *But there was no time.*

She felt the monster deep inside sensing Hadhi's fear, poking its head up, growling low as it sniffed the air for prey.

Hadhi forced air through her nostrils and pulled her arm from her mother's grasp. She needed to be calm. "Asha is my sister. I will see to her health. There is no contagion."

Mzaa took a step back and for the first time since he lay Asha on the bed truly observed Noam. Seemed to want to sear off his skin with her eyes alone. Then her fiery gaze clawed at Hadhi.

"What is the matter with you?" Mzaa yanked Hadhi's chin hard, shaking her.

"Let her go." Noam reached out to defend her. Hadhi held him off with a hand outstretched behind her. He stopped, but Hadhi could feel his tension. Hadhi breathed slowly, settling her heart beats as she did in a hunt.

"Do you have any idea the sort of trouble you will cause if Enzi finds out?" Mzaa snarled.

At another time, Hadhi would not have understood what she had seen. But Hadhi knew. She had noticed herself the subtle way Noam's attention to her had changed, and hers to him. Their bodies were more attuned to one another. And he defended her as though she were his. What a novelty it was, being treasured. Of course her mother would know.

"You could be queen!"

"Jauhar, release her," Noam insisted tightly.

"I am fine," Hadhi assured him.

"You are worrying over your father's best beloved. And risking all our safety and comfort on a bit of lust." She threw Hadhi's chin away.

"Mzaa, stop!" Hadhi shouted, feeling tears of shame burn against her eyes. She had been selfish. Asha was suffering for it. What would Hadhi cost everyone else?

"Must you ruin everything?"

Noam walked between them and tried to pull Hadhi against his side, but Hadhi shifted away. Hiding from his care, she did not deserve it.

"Ignore her," Noam ordered. His hand closed on her wrist when she moved away. "You've done nothing wrong. She has no right to treat you so."

"No right!" Mzaa screeched, but she was in tears. Hadhi was struck again by the sadness her father spent his life cultivating in those who loved him. Could such sadness ever be escaped?

"You destroy my family, but I have no right?" Mzaa collapsed on Nuru's bed, glaring across the room at Asha.

Hadhi was paralyzed, her mind at war over the desire for the comfort Noam was offering and her growing guilt.

"You only had to wait a little while." Mzaa sighed. "Enzi will forget about you and move onto his next challenge as soon as he has had you."

Hadhi jerked involuntarily, and Noam ignored her resistance, pulling Hadhi against his chest. He must be unaware, but in his desire to protect her, he was nearly as rough as her mother. But Hadhi was strong. As much as she craved and marveled at Noam's care, she did not need it to shove aside her revulsion or her fear. Her own love would do that. She pulled her arm from Noam's grasp, carefully, laying a soothing hand on his shoulder.

She had been selfish. She had seen what she wanted and embraced it with all her heart. But it only took the thought of Enzi's hands on her, of him trying to break her; it only took remembering that her mother would allow this graciously, for Hadhi to realize she had a right to be selfish. She was right to grab hold of any joy life offered her.

From the corner of her eye, Hadhi saw Sabra standing against the wall in the next room. She was wearing a chiian for the first time since she was married. Hadhi supposed it was a statement of her strength, her independence. But Hadhi saw Sabra's hesitance still. Hadhi felt oddly old. She understood her mother better than ever before, and Asha. Even her Mzaa Sabra. She was married and a mother, and all against her will yet somehow the world failed to kill her sweetness.

"It might have been so with Enzi." Hadhi dragged her gaze back to her mother. "But it will not be so now."

"Not if he finds out! How could you be so selfish?"

"King Enzi will not find out. You will not tell him, and I certainly will not. It will not be because," Hadhi glanced to Asha, unconscious because she tried to do the right thing, regardless of the cost to herself, "King Enzi's next challenge will be in need of protection. And I mean to give it."

Noam jerked slightly, likely thinking Hadhi should not have shared this.

"What does that mean?" Mzaa buried her face in her hands as Hadhi settled on Nuru's bed next to her mother.

"King Enzi is an evil man, Mzaa," Hadhi said softly, trying to soothe even as she spoke horrors. "I must stop him. Or he will find all the happy, innocent creatures, like Asha and Nuru, and destroy them."

Mzaa's eyes were red and held so much fear, such age showed on her face. She had never looked more beautiful in her daughter's eyes.

"I will marry him at sundown," Hadhi said, carefully, risking her entire future on the hope that she truly did understand her mother now, when she never had before. "And I will do what my father taught me—wait for my moment to strike."

Hadhi felt Noam flinch from across the room. Felt his frown though she did not look. He would not understand this. There must be limits, even to his understanding. But she thought, *hoped*, he would care for her anyway. Mzaa drew her shoulders up. With a delicate hand, she wiped away her tears.

"You were an innocent creature once," Mzaa said, as though the memory confused her. "Before she came along. Before Zuberi let you see Enzi—" Her words just stopped, so casually casting sun on Hadhi's darkest demon. She knew? "I had hopes for you. But afterward, what hope was there?"

Hadhi swallowed. Her mother knew what happened. Knew and because of it, because Hadhi was no longer happy or innocent, she had ceased to hope for her. Ceased to love her.

Must you ruin everything?

Hadhi supposed she had ruined everything. Her head began to pound with unshed tears. She did not dare look Noam's way. She wanted to crawl in a hole and hide. She had ruined everything for her mother. She could have been queen, the realization of a dream her mother had not even dared to have. But if Hadhi killed Enzi—

"Asha will be queen," Mzaa said before Hadhi's mind had worked that out.

"Maybe she should be."

"Why?" Mzaa charged to her feet. "Why should she have everything? You were Zuberi's eldest. It is your right! You deserve just as much as her. *More!*" The word rumbled violently.

Hadhi chewed on the inside of her cheek to restrain her growing rage. Her mother knew. Knew and did nothing, but it was Hadhi who had ruined everything?

"She was his beloved, and now she will be the beloved of all Maltuba! Don't you want more? You should hate her."

"No!" Hadhi rushed past her mother to stand over her sister. "No, I should not. I never should have. The blame does not belong to her." Hadhi snarled and the monster leapt to its feet, bore its teeth in warning. Mzaa cowered back. But it was not enough, Hadhi's rage wanted blood. "In this vision you have where I am queen, do you see where you are?"

Mzaa stared at Hadhi as if she had gone insane.

"I have hated her," Hadhi confessed in a teary snarl. "And *you*. If I were queen, you would remain in this hut forever. I would *never* have you near me again, because you speak to me and I feel small and ugly." Hadhi forced her voice lower and lower, because all she wanted to do was scream. "But if Asha were queen," Hadhi smiled brittlely, "she would have you in her palace. She would care for you. Because you are her family. We are her family!"

Noam's hand came to rest on the small of Hadhi's back, offering comfort, but not forcing it. Hadhi watched her mother cowering away from the monster. Like a mirage, Baba's spirit entered the room, smirking at all the pain.

Hadhi shut her eyes, and the silence expanded as she breathed in and out. Over and over. When Hadhi opened her eyes her father's ghost was gone. But his legacy, the pain, the anger, the self-loathing, that was everywhere.

"Baba was an evil man." Hadhi walked to her mother, taking her hand gently, but Mzaa pulled away.

Hadhi let her go. It was not her fault. "He stole all of our happiness, all of our hope. I understand. I forgive you for not loving me. I know he stole that from you as well." Hadhi choked a bit on the words. "But I can still love you. But I will not apologize for grasping onto any joy I find. Nor will I allow you to make that ugly," Hadhi whispered, embarrassed even to say this.

Noam stood halfway between Hadhi and the doorway. He was watching her with all his muscles clenched. He wanted to fight for her, but he stood by and listened as she spoke. He loved her. He valued her.

It was startling. Beautiful beyond understanding.

Mzaa opened her mouth but stopped short, glaring at Noam. After a brief nod from Hadhi, Noam stepped through the arch, giving them more privacy. Though he was bound to hear all.

"I have...loved you, Hadhi," Mzaa said haltingly, the words apparently forced to claw their way out of her. "You were a sweet child. Then you grew hard, and every day your father held her higher and—" She cut off her own bitter snarl and became the indifferent mother Hadhi had always known. "I only wanted to give you your birthright."

Hadhi recognized in her mother the same kinship she had seen in the nymph, sour-faces all. But it was not a sourness of resentment or ugliness, as she had always thought, it was sourness of longing. Longing for love you were never to feel.

Hadhi could not speak anymore, so she wrapped her mother in a tight hug. Mzaa clung on as well, tighter even than Hadhi. But so quickly she let go, shoving Hadhi away.

"I might dissuade Enzi from marrying you," Mzaa offered, cleaning some invisible dust off her wrist as she spoke.

"He must be stopped," was all Hadhi could managed as her every impulse leapt at the idea of avoiding this marriage.

What would become of her? Hadhi had no illusions about Azize's plan. It would not work. His men were too few, and Enzi would see them coming. If they had shared it with her father's spy, Enzi might already know. So Hadhi would be married and wait for her moment to kill the king.

If they were lucky, Enzi might only punish Azize's friends, but leave his son and Asha alive to take the throne once he was dead. But what of Noam? Could she convince him to hide? To leave? She could not bear it if he died. Even knowing this road ended in death for her. Killing a king was treason, no matter what your reasons. It must be met with death.

"We had best prepare for your wedding." Mzaa swept from the room. It was clear Mzaa knew Hadhi's intent was to kill, but she made no more objections, seemed unconcerned that this would destroy her daughter. That it was murder.

Hadhi released a little breath. She felt oddly better. Perhaps she had been loved all along and never realized. She cast one more nervous glance at Asha, dim and still in the shadows. Asha was always burning with life before. Something must be done.

Hadhi walked after her mother. She crossed the threshold and Noam caught her arm, swung her against his chest. He sealed his lips over hers, holding Hadhi tight against him.

I don't think I can ever let you go.

Don't.

When he drew his head back, Noam's grip relaxed around her and he stared into her eyes.

"The plan will work, Hadhi," he reassured her. "Enzi will be imprisoned. You will not be anyone's sacrifice."

Hadhi lifted a hand to his cheek, memorizing Noam, as her heart broke. He did not know that.

"Hadhi." Noam leaned close, whispering with a fierceness not suited to a man such as him. "Enzi will not be yours to kill. If the plan fails—"

Hadhi lay a hand on his lips, silencing the promise she knew would come next. She could not have that for him. He could not turn murderer for her. She would hate herself if his soul had to hold the ugliness hers did.

Hadhi's fingers traced the drying skin of his lips. Poor man, he was unsuited to this dry place. Not knowing why at first, Hadhi pressed those same fingers to her own lips, but when she felt the surge of love and comfort within, she understood. Just like the Maumai did with their loves, she was guarding his beautiful, tender heart within herself. She needed this tender man, and so did the world.

The peace that filled her made Hadhi wonder if that feeling was the very reason her father fought so hard against any kind of faith. His whole world built around a violent, vibrant hunger for more power when surrendering to the understanding that you could not control all, to the understanding that no one was all powerful, and asking for help was such a softer feeling. He was the sort of person who would mistake softness for lack of strength. But it was not.

Look at Noam, so tender, so kind. His words and his actions gentle, but his love strong enough to withstand her doubts and the ugliness she had shown him. Softness could be very strong.

Hadhi needed to do more things like this, follow her gentler urges. Because this little superstitious action, guarding his soul within herself if only in symbol and treasuring what she loved, gave Hadhi a bit of peace she had been needing.

"Let us prepare for it not to fail," she whispered. "My father had a spy among you, I think…" Hadhi broke off. Would he believe her if she insulted one of his friends?

"You think the spy is Kane," Noam said when Hadhi hesitated.

She met his gaze in surprise.

"I didn't like the way he spoke to you. It made me suspicious. I have mentioned my suspicions to the others. They will be on their guard and I can look after myself." Noam smiled fondly.

Hadhi wore a tiny smile of her own, but for entirely different reasons. "You noticed how he spoke to me?"

"I noticed everything about you. I noticed you before we were even introduced. I was constantly torn between watching you watch the dancers and watching them myself."

Hadhi beamed. She loved this man. She wished she could have forever with him. Not just all of their time, but unending time.

But the monster was prowling inside her, and she felt no hope that this would turn out well for her, only that she might protect others. This, here was the end of all time for them.

But she was not even allowed to dwell. Was not allowed the hours she needed to find all the words he deserved. All she could do was try to see everyone she could safe and hold on to the memory of that other world she and Noam had made.

"I need a promise from you, *please*. If the plan fails, my family will surely be killed. Promise me you will guard them while the others take the palace and get them away if things go wrong."

Noam raised a brow, clearly interpreting her words for the protection they were. "I will not leave you."

"Please, Noam. I can protect myself, but they cannot." And Hadhi did not want to have to choose between stopping Enzi and saving them. Did not want Noam seeing her a killer. Or him dying for the cause. "Promise me, please."

"I will get them to safety," he promised hesitantly. "Then I will be coming back for you." He pulled her face to his, her lips to his, holding her so close they might meld into one being, for all time.

Noam set her away, and his eyes fastened on hers, commanding her understanding. "I love you, Hadhi, *iooni.*"

Hadhi drew the words into her, resisting with all her might the need to point out that he barely knew her. He smiled.

"Even the parts I do not know yet." He did not wait for a response, rushing out of the house.

Hadhi stared after him, the words he deserved poised on her tongue, too cautious or too slow to dive out after him. Sabra emerged from her hiding spot against the wall. She smiled, letting her eyes trail after Noam.

"Where is Nuru?" Hadhi asked, her voice thread thin.

"I am not sure," Sabra answered. "You are always surprising me, Hadhi."

"And me." Hadhi sighed, wearing the beginnings of a grin. She caught sight of her mother and snapped back to the moment. "I cannot wait. I must tell you and Mzaa. Asha needs our help.

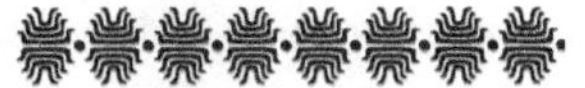

BENEATH THE TIDE

Asha woke with tears dripping down her face to pool beneath her head. She felt so many hearts breaking, crying out in agony, begging for help, for time, for love they'd yet to feel. Crying in rage at a life cut short, wailing against their murderers. The world was so large and its sorrows so loud. Asha rolled over and wept silently.

It was more than just the Battle Born she felt. She felt people the sisterhood had avenged, people dying right now, even the sorrowful souls alive in the world drew Asha's attention. Did Zawadi feel this always?

Asha moaned, longing to take back her promise. No. Not that. But— what she wouldn't give for the power now. She felt so weak, so unlike herself. The power would make her brighter. Free. She *needed* to be free.

From some distant part of her mind, Asha noticed a hand soothing her forehead, cooling her with a damp cloth. Someone promising it would be alright, urging her to drink, asking her to say she was well. It was so far away, she couldn't tell who spoke. But she felt safer for the presence.

She lay, for little bits of time, at sea in the swelling tide of sorrows. Then an emotion so large or so desperate that it couldn't help but shake the world would wake her. She didn't open her eyes; she just lay and felt.

She felt a burning knotted stomach, all fear—Hadhi. Asha had always considered Hadhi a steady presence unmoved by the world. Fearless. Not so now.

"I do not know how to help." Hadhi's voice was as steady as ever, but her heart wasn't beating. It was clenching, like a fist, over and over, clenching, unclenching. Hadhi truly did care, didn't she? It was so new.

"Whatever you do, do it quickly." Jauhar's indifferent voice barely reached Asha.

"Hadhi," Sabra's voice came from at Asha's shoulder. It was her hand at Asha's brow, her offer of solace. "This creature...could you perhaps...capture her? Make her free Asha from this wish? You are a great hunter."

Asha fought to rouse enough to stop them. But Hadhi was already revolting. Sorrow, confusion and rejection overpowering her fear.

Hadhi whispered, "I *will* not."

"But you said..." Sabra began hesitantly, feeling incredibly torn herself.

"He killed them," Hadhi snapped. "Killed nearly all of them, and you want me to find the last, and do what? Torture it?" Hadhi was shaking from her core out, her soul begging to be good, to protect instead of harming. Begged not to be her father's monster.

It was such a different meeting Asha was having with her sister today. Hadhi was all fear. Fear and sorrow and desire. What *power* the Battle Born could have of her.

What power Asha could have. If she could find the strength to lift herself, Asha could reach out. She was certain if she touched Hadhi she could take some of that glorious, explosive power. Then Asha could fix things, set right all the pain. She could do it if she only had the power.

She had tasted Zawadi's power twice, felt how it could connect her to the world, give her power over it, lead her through it. Remake her. Now, without the power, with only the emotions, Asha was coming to understand what Battle Born truly were. They were emotion transmuted to power.

Other people's emotions.

And Hadhi had so much coursing through her. Sorrow, and guilt and fear, even joy, everything in Hadhi was mountainous, volcanic, untamable. She *was* power.

It made Asha hungry, but not all of her. Her body, every sinew and thread that had been changed by the magic longed to feel that power again. But her mind had never been altered by it. It remained her own, and it worked now, questioning. It wondered why, when Hadhi held so much power within her, Zawadi had come to Asha first?

He spoke of his best beloved...said she was his own self reborn, his legacy.

Asha let out a little moan, fighting the hunger, wanting to sink beneath the sorrows and never be heard from again. She was the beloved of a monster. She was like him. *I understand, you are Zuberi's daughter.* Asha refused to be like him.

"We must find a way to help her that does not involve the creature," Hadhi went on, relentlessly. "It might not even be safe to seek her help. Wishes made of such a creature...lead to one's death."

"Then why does Asha yet live?" Jauhar sounded bitter and impatient. Asha was not loved by this woman. It ached, far away in Asha's being, but she barely felt it.

"I do not know," Hadhi answered her mother's bitterness with concern.

"You don't know anything," Jauhar snapped. "You are taking the word of a woman you saw carrying Asha. Why should she be believed?"

"It was not her word that told me such wishes lead to death. Nor hers that told me she would come for revenge. Those words were my father's."

"When?" Jauhar snarled.

Sabra tensed, such a timid creature still. Asha had thought she developed more fire over the years.

"Before he left." Hadhi's heart was pounding so hard it drowned out all the sorrows that had woken Asha. Asha pried her eye lids apart and watched her half-sister silently. No one realized Asha had woken; all eyes were on Hadhi.

"He warned me they were coming. Said I must protect everyone and make sure we made no wishes." With her eyes open, Asha nearly forgot the turmoil within Hadhi. She appeared so certain. Hadhi could lie? How had Asha never noticed? "He said the nymph was coming to kill him, but would kill us for revenge."

"This beast killed him?" Jauhar raged.

"No." Hadhi's voice was hesitant, but certainty radiated off her. What did she know?

"How would you know?" Jauhar snarled.

"I..." Hadhi's insides paused, held in some internal struggle. Then Hadhi expelled the breath. "Why would it kill him, then wait a year to come after us?"

The room was silent for far and away too long. Asha shifted her gaze between them all, soaking up their private sorrows. When her eyes fell on Hadhi again, their gazes caught.

"The nymph did not kill him," Hadhi insisted, her eyes on her sister. She seemed to want Asha to understand something.

Asha tried to reach out, to feel what Hadhi wanted her to know, but Hadhi's feelings were not so enormous any longer. Crawling away to cowering in caves and peeking furtively into the world. Asha was starved by the retreating power. Hadhi regarded Asha a moment longer, then all of the sudden jerked aside, hiding, as her emotions were.

"I should prepare for the weddings. Make no wishes, even to yourselves," Hadhi ordered, taking charge. "We will wait for the hours to be up and hope Asha is herself again. If she is not...I will do whatever I have to." Hadhi spun on heel and fled the room, and Jauhar followed, silently seething, at the creature, at her dead husband, Asha, even her own daughters. Was there no one Jauhar did not hate?

Sabra remained beside Asha, her hands clenched in her lap.

"Am I everyone's fool?" Asha croaked.

"Asha!" Sabra jerked a hand against her chest.

"I knew you were unhappy, but I didn't understand it," Asha whispered. For this moment, the sorrows were an ocean at an even tide, too deep to find her way through, but calm enough to breathe. "I thought you were angry with me because you felt yourself so much better than me, now you were married. But you were angry with me for another reason entirely, weren't you?"

Sabra bit her lip, and tears built in her eyelids. For a moment, Asha thought she wouldn't answer. Sabra nodded. "I hadn't any right to be angry with you, but yes, I have been."

"What did he do to you?"

Sabra looked away. Her sadness rose to the surface of the ocean Asha floated on. Sabra was lost—searching for herself. Only certain of one thing, one love, Lin. She was sadness and rage and a strange sort of joy and growing desire to know herself.

"Zuberi made it clear I was not to be your friend or influence you any longer."

"Why?"

Sabra took to her feet and paced the tiny room, stopping to tower over Asha. She wore a look of such disdain Asha wondered if Sabra even knew how much resentment she carried. There was power here too, in anger, in resentment, in sorrow.

Have a care with that hunger, dear.

"You listened to me. You left his side—for mine. You loved *me*..." Sabra drifted off, her next words a whisper. "He feared you loved me more than him." Sabra drew in a deep breath and her face twisted into a hard smile. "But he was wrong."

Asha wanted to roll away and hide, but the tide was rising with Sabra's rage, with the rage of all the murdered women.

You wanted to feel it, now you will not hide from it.

Asha shook but she did not back away from the truth. Her father, *her* best beloved was a monster and she never knew.

"Your father, Asha," Sabra said with false sweetness, "would have turned the world inside out to see you happy. But only if you were happy *at his side.* You were the place he hid from his own evil, and he couldn't risk losing that. Had he lived, you would never have adventures, never be married, you would never have anything but what he allowed you. You would have planned, and hoped, and stretched on forever with the dreams he fed you. But none of it was real."

Sabra was shaking as hard as Asha. Her hands were fisted around her silk and her teeth clamped across her tongue. She wept as she watched Asha, waiting on something from her.

But Asha couldn't respond. The rage, the resentment, it was all so strong in Sabra. Next to her love for Lin, her hatred of Zuberi was the largest piece of her soul. And so much of Asha wanted a taste of that power, though the rest of her railed against being anything like the father everyone but Asha had known. Had he understood this hunger in her? Nurtured it?

Hadhi should feel this, should see the monsters Baba had made of all of them. But perhaps not, it didn't make Asha feel any better. It frightened her. Hadhi was a monster of self-loathing, Asha of hunger, and Sabra... such rage as she felt could do terrible things.

"Did you kill him?" Asha whispered and more tears raced down her cheeks. Perhaps it had been for all of them, to free them. The thought shouldn't hurt this way, Asha's soul wailing in despair and betrayal, that Sabra would have killed Baba.

He must have hurt her terribly. She would only have been protecting herself and her child. She might have known by then that she was pregnant. But no matter what excuse she gave, Asha couldn't help feeling betrayed by this girl who had been her friend.

Sabra just stared at Asha, a steady, unshaken regard.

"Did you hear what I said, Asha?"

Asha nodded, her hands dragging at the blanket like a claw till it was crowded around her middle in a little heap. Inside Asha, all the women Baba slew snarled and hissed. Made her feel each individual slice of his sword. She was bleeding inside; she felt his twisted hunger and ugliness. Felt the Battle Born cry in agony. Every cry building on the last, until they were so loud she could barely see Sabra.

"I know he deserved it," Asha sobbed, louder than she intended. Shouting over the pain. "He was awful. But he was my father."

"And you were his best beloved," Sabra spat. And every other pain sunk beneath the onslaught of Sabra's anguish. She gave a helpless sob and rubbed her hands across her face. "I have resented you, and *myself,* for resenting you. One moment we were girls together, laughing, playing, dreaming, and before the night was done, I was his wife. Given no choice, no chance even to *breathe.* I was gone from my family though they lived only steps away. They dared not speak to me for fear of angering him. I was more alone than I had ever been, and you were—*thrilled.*"

"I thought it made us family," Asha cried out, reaching for Sabra. Sabra jerked back and Asha wobbled. The world spinning around her and the pain so large and heavy she thought she might die of it.

No more wishes.

Why did she never listen to Hadhi?

"I know what you thought!" Sabra shook with the exclamation. Everything shook. "I wanted it to be true. I wanted it so much. At least that way I would still have you. But..."

"He wouldn't let you." Asha's head fell against the bed. She hadn't even the strength to hold up her neck any longer.

"No." Sabra laughed. "Before I was married, I thought you knew everything. I thought more of you than myself. *Loved you* more than I loved myself. But you didn't see me! Dying, Asha. I was dying a little more every day I was with him. And it was," she laughed and tears sprayed the air, "*Jauhar* who helped me. Not my friend. You didn't see me anymore. Just like he wanted."

The words struck Asha, no, struck the surface of her ocean. She was already sinking into it, hiding from the pain, from the hunger, so she barely felt the disturbance.

"Yes, you were everyone's fool." Sabra bit her lip and glared. "But we all loved you. I did not kill your father. It would have hurt you too much. But I celebrate every day I am free of him."

Asha closed her eyes and let the ocean of sorrows rise up over her. She could barely breathe for all the suffering. Maybe she shouldn't. What had she ever done but cause pain? She was just like him. Even now her skin tingled, her stomach growled, and her muscles coiled all calling out for one thing—

Power.

If she had the magic, she could be free of this, free of the pain, and the past. Free of being Zuberi's daughter. She could be...

It will consume all that is human within you.

Asha pulled her knees up to her chest and held on, a tight little ball shivering and alone, waiting for the hunger to pass.

ZUBERI'S WOMEN

Jauhar had never felt so displaced. Not when Zuberi brought home his second wife, his forceful beauty conquered in battle, and Jauhar was replaced in *everyone's* affections. Not when she was forced to care for the dying woman, at once wanting her to live, because there was nothing about her to hate and wanting her gone so Zuberi would be Jauhar's alone again. Not even when she'd seen Hadhi's eyes after she followed her father.

Her daughter, the sweet little girl Jauhar had loved, the girl she'd dreamt for, died that day. And for weeks after, Jauhar tried to bring that Hadhi back. But she would not confide in her mother and was afraid to be touched. There was no going back. Jauhar had hated her husband for it, but she'd loved him too. So she'd tried to make Hadhi what he wanted, even if that meant her being nothing her mother wanted. But Hadhi would disappoint them both.

Today was worse than all of that put together. She wanted to let loose her fury and ravage the world. She wanted to kill this creature threatening them. To kill Noam for giving Hadhi hopes and desires. She wanted to strangle Azize for picking Asha. She wanted Asha to suffer the slow heavy grinding of her heart, knowing she was unloved. But—more than any of that, Jauhar wanted Hadhi back. The child Hadhi. And since she could not have her, Jauhar wanted the obedient, sour-faced daughter of two days ago.

Hadhi stood in the center of the room with a hand bunched around her dress and a far off look on her face. She looked almost pretty. Her eyes would darken with worry like they did every day, but before her sour-face could emerge, something would tickle her from within, quirking up the corner of her lips.

Thinking of her lover.

Jauhar yanked Hadhi's head back by one of her fraying twists to snap her out of her fantasies. One could not live on fantasies.

Sour-Faced-Hadhi understood that. She would have taken the rebuke with a cringe or a look of shame, but not this new woman. One taste of passion and Hadhi thought herself her mother's equal. Hadhi pulled her mother's hand away and met her eyes coldly.

Could she not have even Sour-Faced-Hadhi back? Without Zuberi, Jauhar was nothing.

Jauhar felt a bellow of rage, powerful enough to crumble the earth, begging to get out of her, but greater still was her desire to sob. She would have nothing of this new Hadhi, not even the deference she'd shown when her innocence was first lost.

"Go wash," Jauhar snapped, her eyes raking Hadhi from head to toe. "You have a wedding shortly."

"Nuru has not re—"

"You do not want the king smelling another man on you. Wash!" Jauhar stomped towards the exit.

"I..." Hadhi began with a hesitant voice. Jauhar couldn't help stopping. "Is it so unforgivable, Mzaa? You would prefer it had been Enzi?"

Enzi was a disgusting man. No mother wanted her child anywhere near him. Were she speaking to Nuru, she would know her answer. She would rather kill Nuru than let the king defile her.

But Hadhi was not like other girls. She was not even like a daughter. Just another of Zuberi's women, twisted, and ugly, and—in Jauhar's way.

"It was selfish and thoughtless. What if you have that man's child?" Rather than looking suitably chastised, Hadhi's lips notched up. She had no right to such hope. "What if the king knew? What would become of your lover then? Your family? Your child?"

With every word, Hadhi crumbled further. Not since she was ten had she looked so vulnerable. Not even shaking and dripping with her own blood. Jauhar should want to pull her close. To be her mother. But as vulnerable as Hadhi appeared, Jauhar still saw the woman of Zuberi's creation.

"You've had your passion, now wash off any sign of it and prepare for your husband. Before everyone suffers for your mistake."

Hadhi ran out the back of their home. Jauhar watched her go with breaths that stabbed at her. And an essence longing to go after her daughter.

Did it never occur to you to build her back up?

NO! Jauhar's mind shouted at Noam's echo. What would have been the point? Zuberi crushed all opposition. He always won.

I will do what my father taught me—and wait for my moment to strike.

That was no one's little girl. Hadhi didn't need any of them. If she had ever been her mother's daughter, she was not now.

Jauhar pulled in a deep breath, ignoring the pain. She turned gracefully and left the hut in the opposite direction from Hadhi. It would just be Jauhar and Nuru now. Asha would marry Azize, Hadhi would marry the king. She would kill the king.

She must be put to death for such a crime.

Jauhar walked, unseeing. She had to get Nuru. She could protect Nuru. Nuru was still her daughter. They would be pariahs after Hadhi's crime, but they would have each other.

Hadhi would be killed.

I will do what my father taught me.

Zuberi always had designs on the throne. He hadn't shown Hadhi the truth only to steal her innocence. He wanted her to hate Enzi. He wanted a weapon. Jauhar's steps began to drag through the sand. Over her shoulders, she saw the clouds of sand rising in Ether but couldn't rouse enough feeling to care.

Zuberi wanted a weapon he could cast aside when the thing was done. Hadhi would always have been killed for the crime.

I will do what my father taught me.

The words struck Jauhar with such force she stumbled, barely managing to catch herself on her knees.

Zuberi had it all planned. Hadhi to kill the king. His *beloved* to marry the weak-willed prince. Zuberi would be king without the name, but all would know. Having served her purpose, Hadhi would be killed, so she could never speak of it.

Zuberi never meant their daughter to survive what he raised her to do. Never. And Jauhar had helped him.

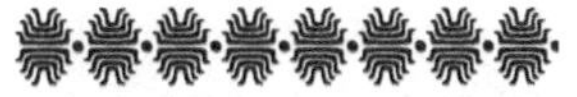

THE LUCKY ONE

et her be blessed instead.

That was Noam's wish, that Hadhi have his luck, have his blessings. And what was the first thing she heard when she returned home? Her mother calling her selfish and the cause of all her suffering, heaping blame and responsibility on her. He tried so hard not to hate that woman but...she had no right to the name mother. Clearly his wish had not worked. No one could call someone with two such parents blessed.

The Battle Born was right. Noam's life had not been free of rejection or pain. He remembered once, just before they realized his mother was sick. Noam was...perhaps nineteen, courting a local girl, he'd received such glares and snide remarks over his shoulder, but he'd felt hopeful, because that seemed to be the worst of it. Her parents were not thrilled with him as a perspective husband, but they were not opposed either. Then came his birthday and he realized they had only been waiting for the chance to do the most damage.

He'd woken to their yard littered with dead mayflies again but refused to let it stop him going to see Danna. Only to have her brothers attack him on the road and have Danna say she'd never wanted him to court her at all. Noam had returned home with his nose bloody and his hands bruised, with his heart bruised, but the only member of his family home was his father.

"They would stop if you would stop antagonizing them," his father had raged, shouting down at Noam from the porch with the neighbors who had attacked his son still within earshot. "Stop moving among them. You have no right to call on them."

He was so angry with Noam, just for existing. For reminding him, every day, of his mistakes. Noam had known his share of rejection. But he'd still had such love. *The three shield*, his siblings with their arms locked on either of his. Shiraz always leaping to his defense with words or with retribution.

Ethan always with a smile at Noam's presence or an arm slung around Noam's shoulder as he called him his *favorite little brother*. And his mother...

Noam's mother was a bright, kind, loving woman who would wrap her arms around him and call Noam a miracle. She would slip onto the bench beside him in the meeting hall and nudge him in the ribs asking in a whisper if he was paying attention to the sermon or just looking at the girls in the choir. His mother who laughed when the children taunted them with that infernal song, and lifted her son into the air, to swing him around shouting *"you can fly if you want, but never away from me."* That was a mother. That was the sort of love Hadhi deserved, the sort of love that might have protected her and kept her from believing her father's lies. But she had lies and pain flung at her from both her parents. She deserved so much more.

So Noam wished again as if saying the words enough would change things.

Let her be blessed instead.

Wishing wasn't enough. He needed to make sure Azize's haphazard plan worked. He had to—

zzzz.

A bug flitted by his ear. A mayfly. He quivered, and then nearly laughed. Why was he letting this tiny thing rule him? He thought of Hadhi's take on the song, that it was a beautiful love story. For the first time, he wished he hadn't been so afraid of breaking the bond with his siblings that he'd never asked his mother about that man. Had it been a love story for her? He knew she cared for the man who he'd called father, but was she ever loved as she deserved?

He hoped so. But what he had to make himself believe right now was that he was not a mayfly. Because Noam wanted more than one month with Hadhi. Hadhi deserved more than a secret affair. He wasn't going anywhere without her. Wish or no. Whether Azize's plan failed or succeeded. Noam would fight with everything in him to stand beside Hadhi. And...he was lucky. He was blessed, it woul—

zz—

Thunk.

Noam felt more of a jolt from watching the mayfly fall through the air than he did from the blow to the back of his head. The stick must have struck the mayfly too. Must have killed it.

Noam stumbled, dazed, but not hit hard enough to be knocked unconscious. He turned wobbly, his gaze drifting up from the dead bug to the stick raised again to strike.

Noam just managed to catch the improvised weapon, though the action made him slip around.

Kane looked a good deal worse for wear, his gaze was crazed, he had several cuts, his clothes were ripped, and there were welts around his neck as if someone had tried to choke him. But still he grinned.

"Not so lucky anymore, are you?" Kane taunted.

Noam shook his head to clear the haze and yanked hard on the stick, pulling Kane forward. He kicked out, but Kane was faster. Releasing the stick, he leapt out of Noam's reach.

"Why are you doing this?" Noam tried for reason, though he expected nothing positive from this man.

"Because I choose to. I make my own destiny." Kane kicked out.

Noam stumbled out of the way of Kane's foot but was too unsteady. He braced himself on his knees to keep from landing in the dust. He swung the stick, but Kane grabbed it. He stood above Noam, vibrating with the intensity of his anger. He held the stick between them, glaring as he swung out suddenly with his free hand and punched Noam under the jaw.

Noam fell, his consciousness blinking in and out. His head hit the ground beside the mayfly and he saw it twitch, heard a soft *zzz* as it tried to stir.

"I make my own destiny," Kane growled, holding the stick high to hit Noam again.

Noam blinked and the last thing he saw before he lost consciousness completely was *Hadhi*—standing in the cave amid the willoomi.

"We walked together, straight into the brightest, fiery heart of Ether. We found a world all our own." Her echo assured him. *"We are still walking there."*

She turned away from him, and Noam stretched out a hand to stop her. Wait, he tried to cry out. *You can fly if you want, my love, but never away from me.*

Hadhi's echo turned back, smiling sadly. *"Now I can live there, on my dark days, instead of in the pit of rage with the monster."*

Darkness devoured Noam's vision from edge to center, until all was black.

The others Kane had deposited in the dungeon or told soldiers where to find, but with Noam, it was a pleasure to drag him into the king's study and throw him at his feet.

King Enzi laughed at the sight of Noam's bruising face and unfocused eyes. "Had a bit of trouble with this one, did you?"

"No trouble," Kane replied honestly. "Just fun."

Enzi chuckled all the harder. "Ahhh. Now I hear Zuberi's man in you. You were so serious before. But now I see him in you. What happened to this magic being you promised me? First you claim to have killed Zuberi yourself, then you tell me you found his killer and promise to present her to me and yet," the king stretched his arms wide, "all you bring me is a kitchen hand you yourself said was no one. Not up to the task?"

"I have trapped fey before," Kane answered smugly but something compelled him to also destroy Enzi's smugness. "And this kitchen hand is someone to your future bride." Kane meant it to sound like a light taunt, but he could still hear the echo of Zuberi's ghost telling Kane he wasn't strong enough to create his own destiny. And the echo of that fey woman saying the same, and his words came out sharper than intended. "I found them together."

"Is that so?" Enzi asked, bending towards the only half-conscious Noam for an answer. Noam didn't make a noise until the king's foot connected with his stomach. Even then it was just a groan. "Interesting information indeed." Enzi turned away from Noam. He waved for a guard to carry Noam to the dungeon, but it was clear he was nowhere near done with him. But nor was he done with Kane.

"That doesn't answer my question about the creature I was promised," the king remarked once Noam was gone.

"She got away, for now. But...as long as you have Noam, we can lay a trap for her. She likes him, many fey things do."

Enzi smiled genially at him. "Isn't he the lucky one, to find favor with so many interesting women?"

Kane remembered thinking the same thing when Noam had joined Azize's crew. Kane had traveled with Azize for nearly a year before then, and the prince had treated him as just another of his father's men until mere weeks before he met Noam. But Noam wasn't on the ship for five days before Azize knew his name, and a week later, he was asking for him as his constant server. A week after that...when by pure *luck,* Noam was the closest man at hand when Azize was knocked overboard, he dived in to rescue the drowning prince, and Azize removed Noam from service entirely. Made him practically his shadow.

Laughed with him, shared secrets with him, and suddenly, as if Noam's arrival was all he had been waiting for, Azize opened up to Kane as well, began gathering more men, became easy and open, lived each day for the adventure! It was as if Noam's luck extended to those he befriended. In every new land, Azize found one more man to add to his growing army. And always with his faithful shadow at his side.

Noam was lucky.

Or he had been. Before today.

But Kane had never needed luck. Kane worked for what he wanted and he achieved it. When they reached Feather, though none but Kane had been observant enough to notice it, a tiny fairy began following Noam around. It looked more like a ball of light than a being, but unlike Azize, Kane actually spent his years of travel learning. He'd heard about pixies; he even knew the ways to trap them. So Kane set a trap and caught what was generally considered to be the most powerful fey being in a tiny vial he wore around his neck.

He had meant to use it against Enzi and Zuberi when he caught it. Had marveled at the short sighted hubris of the man to send Kane into a world to learn new ways to kill him. But Kane made his own destiny. If Enzi's death wasn't at his hand, with the king's look of fear pointed at Kane alone, what was the point?

Kane made his own destiny. He didn't need luck. He didn't even want it!

"Tell my soldiers what you need for this trap, and they will give it to you. And bring me the rest of your companions. I want them all in my dungeon before sunset."

"I need nothing from your soldiers."

Enzi smirked. "Oh no, not Zuberi's man. You need nothing."

"Well, one thing. It is a gift for Your Majesty." Kane pulled the vial up by the long chain that hung to the middle of his chest. "But if I might borrow her to place a trapping spell around Noam's cell, you will have two fey creatures in your possession." He handed the vial to the king, and the stones on his sword flared to life, sucking power from the creature so even trapped in the vial, she shrunk further still.

Enzi's breath caught, fear and excitement mingling in his eyes to make him look nearly wild.

"It is called a pixie. The most powerful of the fey. She can put a spell on the dungeon to make it as tight a trap as this vial."

"Ahh," Enzi sighed with his fingers closed around the vial. "I can see you will be a most interesting man to have at my side. Zuberi loved the hunt, but so rarely did he bring me anything truly special alive enough to add to my menagerie." He waved at the nearest guard. "Diji, tell the others you've a new commander."

King Enzi slapped Kane on the shoulder and Kane felt electric. Power and pride coursed through him. He'd done it. *He made his own destiny.*

And he didn't need luck to do it.

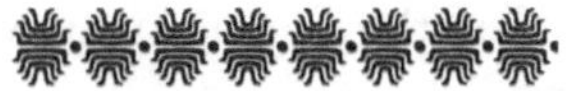

FRIENDLY SKIN

"Do you make it? Or do you let Zuberi choose a destiny for you?"
The words she'd taunted the young man with ran over and over in Zawadi's mind. Oriole's mind. With each passing second, she was becoming more Oriole, the broken, frightened, vengeance seeker who knew that the person she truly needed to punish was herself. All of the plans Zawadi had come with were unspooling, leaving chaotic mounds of agony. She should be punished.

Perhaps that, Oriole's crimes, and not the perversion she had made of Dove's blessing was the true reason another of her order was near. Perhaps she was here to punish her. Perhaps Asha was dying of the sacrifice she had made for Zawadi, and Dove would come to grant her death wish. Surely she had been wronged by Oriole's plans. Wronged enough to earn Battle Born interference.

Oriole could no longer excuse herself.

"Do you make it? Or do you let Zuberi choose a destiny for you?"

She couldn't recall ever having said she made her own destiny, but in the back of her mind now, she wondered if she had not existed with equal self-importance as her enemy. Whether she had or not, she had certainly allowed Zuberi to frame her destiny when she came here. She had never been a vengeance seeker, only justice, only balance. But she knew the man to be dead and sought out those who loved him to make them pay for his sins. That could never be justice.

Zawadi shook and her heart still raced over what she'd nearly done. It wasn't that the young man didn't deserve to die. She could feel such terrible deeds on his skin, had felt the mixture of blessing and curse that Dove had left upon him. But...Oriole would not have been killing him for his crimes, or for a death wish she was fulfilling. She would have done it for herself alone. For the...*joy*...of it. For the feeling of power. It was not even about him. As she choked the life from him, she did not see that boy or his evil; she saw only the man who had created him. The man who had created the monster she was as well.

You would not be happier if she were like us. It would only make you sick inside, if he had made her a monster.

She was so right. How could one so angry and so...self-loathing understand so much? How had she seen the monster in Oriole before she recognized it in herself? Oriole meant what she said to Zuberi's eldest, to *Hadhi*. That impenetrable soul she had was the kind over which Battle Born magic had no power. Yet she still wanted to find her alone. Wanted to offer her a gift and see what...pain it could draw from her. That made Oriole such a monster! Her similarities to her father were not the reason she wanted to hurt the girl. She just...She reminded Zawadi of all the times when she had wanted. Wanted love, wanted independence, wanted family, wanted individuality.

Zawadi didn't *want* anymore. Not anything. Her curiosity was so small it barely nudged her. Her thoughts of death merely pouts, her being had no will to bring anything about. She didn't want anything. Or she hadn't, until she'd hit the ground on that hillside and her thirst for vengeance had been wetted. And that quiet, angry, twisted girl was—Hadhi was want—walking and talking and moving about the world. She did not belong to her father or Noam. She was nothing but a swirling empty well, calling out to be filled.

She made Zawadi? Oriole? Mother Bird? whoever she was now ache with the need to feel.

She leaned against a tree in the jackal enclosure beside a trio of chained and sleeping scavengers. She'd come to the king's menagerie to hide from Dove. She should flee this place and the monster it was rousing in her, or take back the wishes she'd granted, every one. But she couldn't bring herself to do that. There was choice, wicked choice in all of the wishes she'd granted. But she also felt another force at work, be it the spirits of her dead or magic itself and she...didn't know if it was right to stop it. So she just... watched the animals. How long had it been since she'd watched animals simply for the pleasure? This was no pleasure.

Most of these animals were long since broken. They had given up. Like her.

The room was stunning. Outside, the building was formed of sand-colored walls, built in a hexagon with six cylindrical rooms at the meeting of each palace wing. The menagerie was held in the northeastern most cylindrical room. Along the wall at seemingly random intervals were hexagon shaped windows each with a different color pane of glass. The light fell many colored through the windows and across the ground, decorating the already lush room. There were jungle plants and a mossy floor, and the sounds of birds in the trees. Though it was not the largest or most complete menagerie in the world, there were several monkeys, one cheetah, three jackals, a few meerkats, some sheep and rabbits and various other small creatures. The cheetah was the largest animal by far and it lay stretched out on a tree branch, bored and broken. Despite its beauty, it was a thoroughly depressing place. She wasn't certain why she stayed, until she watched the prince rush in looking sweaty, harried and near tears with frustration shouting for Asha.

She'd not seen him alone since she urged him here, needing something to stir up this settled community. Something to threaten his father with. Though she had not had to use him so.

The boy was fraying. He collapsed against the wall beneath an uneven pair of windows of green and pink. Beside the monkey enclosure, he rubbed his face.

"I thought she was just hiding from me." He spoke to the animals, reaching a hand through the bars, only to have it slapped away. "But what if something has happened? What if Jauhar is right, and my father is holding her somewhere to make an example of? Or...she had magic, she said she'd wasted it spending her time with me when she should have been nations away. What if she went? What if when the magic left her, she had no way to return?"

Oriole snorted. That boy did like to give himself reasons to give up, didn't he? He hung his head a while longer, feeling sorry for himself.

Like you?

Just as Oriole was beginning to resent him as much as anyone else she'd met, Azize pushed off the wall and walked into a beam of blue light. He pulled out Asha's slipper, twisting it and turning it and squeezing it in his hand. He shoved it into his pocket and fisted his hands before him.

"Zawadi," he shouted.

It startled a squawk of a laugh from the colorful quetzal body Zawadi was borrowing. Quetzal's bird body, not her fairy one. Even among this menagerie, Quetzal stood out, coming from such a different part of the world with lush rainforests and such color even in the air...but the prince did not see her. So Oriole had a chance to sit back and amuse herself with the realization that the prince didn't just know her from Noam's warnings, he also knew her by the name she had given only to Asha. Would it have occurred to him that it was she who led him here?

"Zawadi. Battle Born. I know what you are. Come to me."

Ha. Oriole watched the boy sweat, running his hands up and down his pant legs. Watched his hand inch towards his pockets, then yank away like it held a snake. Hmm.

Distracted, Oriole looked around the menagerie. It had an absurd lack of snakes. Were they kept elsewhere? Or was the king just wily enough to be aware that with the hatred his people carried for him, a snake from his own menagerie getting loose would make an excellent mode of execution?

"Zawadi! Come to me," Azize shouted at the top of his lungs. He ran his fist up and down over his pocket, fighting against his urge to touch it.

What did he think to achieve by standing in the middle of the room shouting her name? Asha had done similar things yesterday. Zawadi would not have known they wanted her if she had not been there waiting. Some fairy could sense other's needs, but only those they were close with. Could humans just feel when other beings wanted them? She'd never heard tale of it. Or was it just that they thought of her like a servant they could summon at will?

"I'm not touching it, and you're going to show yourself. I am prince of these lands, and I order you here. Come to me."

Order her? Oriole rolled her eyes and let out a high pitched squawk of warning. She waited until she had his eyes. Waited until they widened in awe of her astounding beauty, Quetzal was always a stunning creature. Even in the robes of the order she stood out. When Oriole held his eyes, she tilted her head and her power flashed within them, the boy prince took a step back from an entirely different sort of fear.

Oriole leapt from the branch, throwing her wings wide, her long curved tail brushing the branch of the tree for a moment, then a mist of magic swirled between them, concealing her as she took on yet another form. Swiftlet.

"I don't care if you touch the slipper or not, that is not my spell." Oriole's derision emerged a bit incongruous from the other woman's body. Swiftlet had been quiet, sly, and possessed a wide sense of humor. But rarely was she anything but kind. She was one of the shorter women among the order but had a deep well of loving comfort to offer the dying.

All the order dressed in dark grey or black fabrics and covered themselves from shoulder to toe, as well as covering their hair. Some went further, covering everything but hands and eyes, while others preferred more free moving attire like the high slits and loose leg coverings Pintail wore. Swiftlet was a bit of an outlier. She was covered from shoulder to toe, but her gown filled out as wide as two other women's together. And though she covered her hair in a scarf, it was folded to look like a flower emerging around her high bun.

"I need the extra height, or no one will ever notice me in this flock of cranes," she'd said when Oriole was younger, not yet mother bird, still learning her place among the flock of magnificent and distinctive women.

Oriole remembered laughing. No one would miss Swiftlet. She was quiet and short, but you would see her grin from the corner of your eye and watch it vanish when you looked at her directly. She lingered in your mind. She beguiled.

Oriole brushed aside a tear and focused herself on the here and now. On the distraction of the prince before her.

"Where is Asha?" Azize blurted out.

Swiftlet's smile tickled her lips for a moment but disappeared as Oriole grew at home in her friend's skin. "Demands? So quickly after you begged my presence, it is unwise."

"I ordered your presence." Azize's eyes grew round, and Oriole wondered if he was pleased or frightened to hear his father's tone from his own lips. She knew this boy to be one who had lived in fear of his father, and in hatred.

"I cannot be ordered by you, princelet," she dismissed. "I came for curiosity's sake. And will depart when bored, which approaches rapidly. I've few hours left of weightlessness. Why should I waste them here?"

It wasn't true. He was a welcome distraction from her self-pity...and fear. It seemed weightlessness didn't sit well with her.

"Did the magic take Asha away? Did it consume her? Have you killed her?" Azize rushed desperate words into the world.

Did it consume her? Oriole was curious about that as well. She'd warned Asha that the magic would consume all that was human within her, but she wasn't entirely sure now. It was surely changing her, one thread at a time. Her body fighting both to have the magic and to cling to her human soul, to...improve it. In Oriole's experience, few and far between were those who worked to truly be better than they were. Many wished for it, many wanted it, but it was not simple to do; most gave it up. She wondered, if given the choice between polishing that soul and having the power again, which Asha would choose. What would the magic would make of her?

Bluebird?

What choice would you make? her mind taunted her.

"So inquisitive suddenly," Oriole commented sarcastically, to distract from her punishing mind. "Why stand here with me? Go find your answers."

"That's what I am doing. Why are you after her?"

Oriole sighed, her breath shaking the trees, she walked towards the cheetah resting sullen across a branch. "I have not killed her. Nor has the magic, as far as I know." When she was just before the tree, the limb was far above her head. Oriole laughed. She'd never thought of Swiflet as *this* short. She reached above herself and ran a hand over the cheetah's head. It didn't stir.

"I am after no one," Oriole lied, stepping back. Or did she lie? She couldn't tell anymore. "In my younger days, I knew all, I led the magic. Made my vision and my designs manifest through its power. Not so any longer." She said it all as if to herself, or to the friend whose body she was inhabiting. Azize was here, but with her unable to feel his deeper emotions, he was a good empty vessel to speak into. An echo chamber.

"Do you know where she is?" Azize demanded.

Oriole narrowed her eyes at the man, annoyed with him for breaking the silence. "I know where I left her."

"Where?"

Magic billowed out from beneath the bubble of her skirt and pinned Azize to the ground like the chains around the necks of all these animals. Oriole advanced to stand over him, baring down at him with all her rage and power. All her pain. "Do you know what your father is, son of Enzi?"

Azize sunk under the weight of the magic and the rumble of Oriole's voice. He nodded.

"How long?" Her voice was everywhere, waking the animals so they mewled and screamed and squawked.

"I've known since I was a child," Azize admitted.

Oriole nodded her head slowly. "Do you approve of his mode of rule?"

"No!" Azize struggled against her hold, trying to rise, but it was not to be until she was through with him.

"Then do you care nothing for your people, son of Enzi?"

"Of course I care," he shouted, enraged. "I'm trying to stop him!"

That didn't suit Oriole. Rage meant he felt powerful. It meant he was missing the larger lesson. Still trying to use Oriole to fight his battles. Oriole left the weight of her magic upon him as she slowly drew the air around him into the widening sleeves of her gown. She let him see the air departing, let him gasp and grow frantic, let him begin to wonder if he would survive this moment.

"Are you really? Or are you only trying to appear to have tried?" Oriole pressed.

Azize's eyes were wide and terrified, but she could tell he was hearing her.

"You sent Noam to me, to beg me not to interfere. Would not a man who truly wanted another stopped welcome my assistance? Or seek the assistance of a people he knows have long suffered at that man's hands? Or are you, like your father, terrified of those people? Afraid if you let them turn on your father, they might turn on you as well. Afraid that, even though you do not want the throne, they might not want you on it."

Azize gave up fighting. He lay against the ground and took in the words. Oriole observed him with only a fledgling's worth of pity. She released the air, allowed him to breathe again.

"You should ask yourself, *daja fa Enzi*, why now you want to stop him? And what truly will the world look like for this nation when you do?"

Oriole turned back to the jackals. She could hear the boy pushing to his feet behind her. Heard his breathing evening out.

"Noam, Asha, even Sabra, they all keep needling me, pushing me to be here for a reason. But I am not. I don't even know why I came."

Oriole looked over her shoulder and nearly laughed. She'd forgotten again how short Swiftlet was. The prince was a head and a half above her at least. She shrugged. "I nudged you here. I needed something to shake things up, so I could watch them all."

"I didn't even come of my own will?" Azize shook as he spoke, and his hand retrieved the slipper once more. "Was anything real?"

"Everything was real," she snapped impatiently. "*You* felt an urge to know if you were strong enough to face him. I made it stronger. *You* were drawn to Asha the magic gave you the space to feel it and the...all consuming need to pursue it. For the most part, magic only accelerates or amplifies. It can create, but so rarely is that required that most call that a dark art, bygone and forgotten."

"So you don't create all these different bodies you inhabit?" He threw off the angry question.

Oriole raised her hands before herself and felt the ever increasing bellow of missing with her heart. "Her name was Swiftlet. She was born a fairy of the water. She came late to the sisterhood of Battle Born, well into her fortieth decade of life, with a human wife and a child gone to plague. We had come to grant her son's last wish, that his mother find a family. We had not expected it to be us, but it was." Oriole let the story sit between them. She lowered her hands and met Azize's gaze. "I make none of the forms. I only slip into the skins of old friends. Friends lost at the hands of your father and his man."

Azize swallowed his anger. He stared down at the shoe before him and shook his head.

"I think when I was little, my mother hoped that I would grow up and... take the nation from my father. That I would free them all. But I never lived up to that. When I received word, she was dying...I knew I had failed her. I decided to never come home. But the longer I went, the more I wondered if..."

"You wouldn't be stronger without her here to fail," Oriole completed the thought for him. She knew.

The boy nodded. Such a lost boy still. Oriole would not call what was inside of her pity. She didn't know what it was. But it compelled her to speak.

"When she lay dying, she had only one wish. It was not for her own freedom; it was for yours."

"She didn't want me to come back?" the boy asked.

Oriole shrugged. "She wanted your choices to be your own. And when I nudged you here, I made myself a promise that I would not allow Magpie's blessing to be perverted. So you will be free, no matter what man must die to protect you, whether you stay or leave. Know this, every decision you make, or have made thus far, is your own. The spell of that shoe cannot steal your will; it can only amplify it."

"I..." Azize opened and shut his mouth multiple times, finally growing bold enough to ask. "Is Magpie one of...the sisterhood? Where is she?"

"Dead, along with all but twelve of her sisters. Dead. So one man could rejoice in his strength and another could marvel at his own power. You might consider, if you chose to stay, that the rule of any leader affects far more than just his own people. Our every choice, even just for ourselves, affects the entire world." She wished she'd understood that when she led her flock.

Azize stepped forward, reaching out.

"What are you?" he asked hesitantly.

"Bored," Oriole snapped and with a flash of power was consumed in dust and rainbow lights. She flapped into the trees in Magpie's bird body and watched the boy a few moments longer.

He stared into his hands for the longest time, tilting the slipper into different strands of colored light. Then a smile painted his features. Oriole could nearly hear his mind working, hear the shoe speaking to him.

Come find me.

With a sparkling golden mist of sand and light, he vanished. Off after his love apparently. Oriole didn't know what she expected; it was not as though he would march up to his father and demand the throne. And honestly, Oriole was no more certain than others that it would be a good thing if he did. But it didn't matter. None of it mattered. What would come would come, and with so many dangerous men roaming the world, and so many of her cursed wishes working, she doubted it would bring much joy.

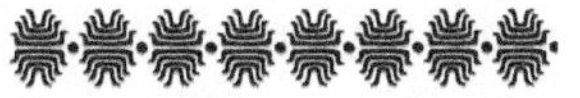

MADE OVER

The water in the bathing hut was from yesterday, but Hadhi did not think there was time to fetch more or heat it. She should wash. She knew she should before her mother said it, but now she did not want to. She wanted to preserve any remnant of that moment, even if it was only dirt and sweat.

You've had your passion, now wash off any sign of it.

Mzaa had not meant any physical remnant. At least not only that. She wore the same look her father had so often—jealousy. Mzaa wanted Hadhi's joy washed away, as her father would have done had he lived. She wanted Hadhi stripped of any hope or love, of any sign that she was someone other than Sour-Faced-Hadhi. Mzaa had done a good job of dragging Hadhi back into the anger, and fear, and guilt. With her eyes traveling over Hadhi as though she were a rotting carcass and her voice full of disgust. The parts of Hadhi that wanted her mother's approval and love, the bits that worried Noam was a nymph, the unlovable parts, all crawled out of their corners. They took over, so Hadhi felt ugly all over.

It did not help that Hadhi knew she had been selfish. The guilt wanted to eat away at her and make her sour, angry and alone. Always alone.

But Hadhi wanted to be better than herself. She wanted to be the sort of person who could truly believe in a brighter future. She wanted to be hopeful and beautiful, the sort of person who deserved Noam's love, the sort of person who knew that. Not the sort whose lack of faith hurt him. He had looked so betrayed when she failed to believe him. She did not want to put such a look on his face ever again.

She wanted so desperately to just do away with that part of herself, to drown it in love. But Mzaa had a talent. Mzaa spoke and Hadhi felt like every time she ever managed to protect herself or someone she loved, another person paid the price. Who would pay next?

What if she did have a baby? Noam's baby.

Hadhi's hands slipped down, covering one another, covering her belly as if to protect a child that her imagination alone brought forth. She would not have even thought to wish for such a miracle, if her mother had not mentioned it. But now her mind called forth such beauty. They could be happy, Noam, Hadhi and their child. They could laugh, and love and...dance! Hadhi's breath popped into the world. She expected a laugh at her fantasies, but the sound was closer to a sob.

Dancing through life, starting over, being happy, those were fantasies. She would be married at sunset, and not to Noam. If she were pregnant, it would not be joyful but frightening. If Azize's plan failed, Hadhi would turn killer again, rather than let any child near the king. But what would become of her baby? It might be killed or taken, Hadhi would never forgive herself. Noam would never forgive her. And the baby... She could imagine such horrors, but selfishly, the worst of all in her mind was her child growing up and feeling towards Hadhi as Hadhi felt towards either of her parents. What if it hated her? Or felt unloved by her?

But Azize may yet succeed!

Hadhi nearly cried in relief; her mind was no longer only a sour pit. It may not be wholly positive, but it could save her from pain with hope.

Hadhi had never thought well of Azize. She knew growing up with Enzi he had many reasons to fear, and she could empathize with that. But nothing she knew of him recommended him as a revolutionary, nor as a new king. She did not know that she trusted him to make Maltuba better, or that she even thought such a thing could be achieved with a new king. But she did not know what would and Azize was Noam's friend. Noam believed in him. Maybe Hadhi could still be happy if she learned to believe as well.

Hadhi closed her hands around each other. She could not do as her mother wanted. She could bathe. She could prepare to be queen. But the defiance, the slowly growing self-confidence, even the hope would not be washed away. They were not Noam's doing alone. He started it, but not this morning. He started her changing by giving Hadhi permission to be herself. He had started it, but it was Hadhi who kept it going. Pride grew up from her toes, strengthening her muscles all the way up her neck. She was the one who chose not to be the monster, not to hurt the little girl she thought was the nymph. It was Hadhi who took the opportunity to see Asha, to love her. Hadhi who decided to embrace her love for Noam. She would keep making such choices, keep changing. She had to.

She was not born Sour-Faced-Hadhi, was not born a monster, but the world had made her over. She could change again. Not the world's doing this time, but her own.

Hadhi took a clean cloth from the little covered basket in the corner, dipping it in the water. She removed her gown and cleaned as best she could, then she doused her hair to make it easier to comb, unwilling to waste a moment more on her mother's concerns. She had a revolution to take part in. She might have to marry Enzi, but it would not last forever.

Noam would be forever. This slowly emerging new Hadhi would be forever.

She returned to the hut, with her old dress slung around her for modesty. The sandstorm was growing closer, to bathe fully might have been pointless anyway.

Hadhi rushed down to her mother's room. There was a wooden box at the far wall, covered in beautiful carvings. Mzaa kept her favorite things inside it. No one was allowed to touch it. When Baba died, Mzaa tucked what few things Uncle Kafil let them have of him into the chest, as though he had belonged to her alone.

Asha had railed against the unfairness; even Nuru begged for some piece of him. Hadhi's only regret was the dagger. It was found with his body. Hadhi wanted it burned with him, but Mzaa kept it, tucked it into her box. Hadhi could not pass the box without thinking of it. Remembering the way his blood had clung to the blade and to her hands. How spots of it had sat under her fingernails, shouting her guilt for months after.

Hadhi knelt before the box and threw back the lid. The knife lay atop the pile of silks and other treasures, such an ugly thing the prize of her mother's collection, because Zuberi had loved it. Because it was the last thing he touched.

It seemed, staring into the wealth of color, blurred beneath the ugly stained weapon, that this one weapon had begun all the madness with the nymph. How might things be different if Hadhi had never picked it up from the dust?

It would feel somehow fitting to gift it to the nymph, let her hold the instrument of Zuberi's demise. But Hadhi did not touch it. If she touched it, she would kill again. She knew it. Predators had their teeth for feeding.

She wanted to be more, and that meant surrendering her teeth.

There was a vibrant silk beneath the dagger, many shades of green with flares and explosions of purple, and gold, and a trim from the pelt of a cheetah. It was a queenly silk, one of Aunt Lolia's making. Mzaa guarded it jealously; she had worn it only once. Hadhi recalled how her hand had longed to reach out and brush across it, to see what beautiful felt like. It was marvelous. She had known from the moment she saw it that she could never touch it; such riches were not meant for ugly people.

Hadhi let her fingers glide across the silk, and a smile tugged at her lips. She was not ugly today.

In a rush, half excitement, half fear of Mzaa catching her, Hadhi cast aside her own damp silk and pulled her mother's silk from the box. The knife tumbled off it, down further into the box, but Hadhi barely noticed. She snapped out the silk, shaking off the wrinkles and dust from laying unused. Hurriedly, she tugged the silk around her.

"Don't rush, you'll rip it."

Hadhi startled at Sabra's voice. She walked to Hadhi and lifted the ends from her, tying them securely around Hadhi's neck. Then she led Hadhi to a little stool against the wall. She took the damp cloth from around Hadhi's hair and dipped her fingers into the jar of Mzaa's oil to help her finger comb Hadhi's hair, spinning and fluffing up the coils rather than pulling them apart as Mzaa would have her do.

Hadhi was too startled to speak. She sat stiffly and let Sabra go about her work. Sabra bent to the chest, and pulled out a much smaller silk, a head wrap, not a chiian like she wore. Those covered one's hair, these just embellished it. Mzaa never allowed Hadhi to wear them; she said they drew the eye to her scars. But Sabra just set about wrapping the scarf from the base of Hadhi's skull up to the crown of her head, pulling a few curls out the front, and leaving an explosion of them above. Then she twisted the remaining fabric together and looped it around her head in a gentle rope.

"You are lovely, Hadhi," Sabra said quietly.

Hadhi bit her tongue to hold in the snide comments of doubt. Doubt not just of Sabra's words but that anyone ever really meant such things. She needed to kill those doubts, but knowing she needed to was easy, and actually doing so seemed to be a constant challenge. But she had met challenges before.

"I have wanted to tell you for sometime," Sabra whispered, looking anywhere but Hadhi's face. "I am sorry I ever called you sour-faced."

Hadhi was taken aback. She did not hate Sabra any longer. She knew Sabra felt...sorry for her, since joining this twisted family. But Hadhi always expected the old Sabra was somewhere in her, waiting to become friends with Asha again, so they could pick on Hadhi together.

"I..." Hadhi had no idea what to say. She felt an odd urge to cry, as if from the old hurts. But today was not a day for that. Yet she could not simply say all was forgotten when it still hurt. "You will raise Lin better. Better than any of us was."

Sabra regarded her with a steady searching. After a few moments, Sabra nodded, as though this had been an order.

"Is Asha any better?" Hadhi changed the subject.

Sabra nodded and shrugged. She looked away, searching Mzaa's little pots for the gold, blue and green paints and the brushes. Hadhi did not know why she continued letting Sabra tend to her...except...it was what was done. Mothers and sisters and aunts all gathered around a bride. They adorned her hair and her skin, they dressed her with rings and silks and paint, but most of all—with love. Hadhi had not really thought she wanted this, but she sat quietly, sipping up the attention as Sabra painted the cluster of dots for the jungle on her cheeks, and the single strip of blue for the sea through the center of her top and bottom lips. Aunt Lolia would have been here with her if she lived. Hadhi could almost feel her. Perhaps this was why little girls looked forward to becoming brides, waiting to be welcomed among the women they loved, who loved them. Welcomed and called one of them.

"She is awake." Sabra chewed on her lip as she painted the golden sweeps of the desert above Hadhi's eyes. "But barely strong enough to lift her head." Sabra retreated to examine her work. She returned, and Hadhi felt the soft brush of golden paint gently tracing the edges of her scars. She went stiff, unsure if she was thrilled to have her battle wounds decorated, as warriors did, or ashamed because none of her battles past brought her pride.

Sabra stepped back and her eyes traced Hadhi's face. Her lips shifted from her soft smile, opening to speak.

"She will recover," Hadhi blurted out, afraid of what Sabra might say.

"Wait here," Sabra said with a sudden spark of enthusiasm, rushing from the room. "I have something for you."

Hadhi forced her muscles to unknot. No, no battle of her past was one of pride, but the battle she was waging with all the ugly voices inside— that would be. And the scars represented all the anger inside her as much as they did the hunt that formed them. Decorating the scars only honored that struggle.

Sabra rushed in clutching something in her fist and beaming. "After your father stole me, I was crying, your mother and I were alone." Sabra stopped before Hadhi, hiding her secret. "She comforted me, much more sweetly than I would have expected. I always thought she hated me."

"Mzaa hates everything," Hadhi accepted quietly.

"Well, she gave me these." Sabra opened her hand to reveal three rich strings of shining beads. Nothing like the painted wood beads Hadhi and her sister's wore, even finer than what Mzaa wore herself. These were real gems, dark green with such luster the light just danced across their surface. Hadhi caught her breath. Why had Mzaa hidden them?

"Your mother said the queen had given them to her when Rama became pregnant, as a bribe to treat the new woman and her child well."

Hadhi felt another of those twinges of sympathy for her mother. Replaced in her husband's affections and in running her home, and the woman who replaced her had been friends with their queen. Of course she felt the lesser.

"Jauhar said the queen needn't have bothered, she had no intention of harming Asha's mother, and that Rama was well able to fend for herself. But the bribe infuriated her. When she gave me these, she said I was a good girl, and if I respected her place, she would always look after me. She has even kept her promise."

Hadhi felt a curl of unworthy jealousy. Sabra needed someone to care for her and protect her from Zuberi, but that it should be Mzaa—who could not protect her own daughters—it stung. Hadhi took a deep breath. Jealousy was what her parents lived by. She would not be ruled by it.

"You should keep them," Hadhi began, but Sabra cut her off.

"No. Don't you see?" Sabra lifted the beads to Hadhi's neck and tied the ribbon tight. "These were a symbol of one woman's protection, the queen's protection for Rama, then your mother's for me. Now they will be a symbol of our protector." Sabra stepped back, dropping her hands to her sides. "I know that is what you are."

Hadhi held a hand to the beads, shaking her head.

"I have never protected you, Sabra. The night my father took you," Hadhi explained, ashamed. "It was I who had pointed out that Asha was not home. I told him where she was because..." Hadhi shook her head, hated admitting she had sent him Sabra's way only so she and Nuru could be free of him a while. "It was my fault."

Sabra laughed, she reached out and she squeezed Hadhi's hand. "Hadhi, I was not married to him long, but your father never once decided a thing on a whim. What he did very well was wait for just the right moment to inflict pain on as many people as possible." Hadhi caught her breath as Sabra's words rang true. "It was not your fault, but I am certain he wanted you to think it was."

Hadhi let out a little breath of laughter, and her hand slipped from the necklace. That sounded exactly like her father.

Still, Hadhi had never done much to protect Sabra. But she meant to protect them all now. That was what being made new meant, starting from this moment and being better each one after.

"Thank you," Hadhi whispered with tears in her eyes. "I regret the method, but...I am glad we are family now."

Sabra pulled Hadhi into a brief hug. "As am I."

"I should go." Hadhi's stomach dropped with the fear she had convinced herself she was not feeling. She wished she could see herself. There were mirrors in the mansion, but none here. Hadhi would have liked to see herself when she was not ugly. Would have liked to see her scars painted as though they were part of her beauty. She thought it might make her feel more confident. But Sabra's words and her soft smile were helping.

"I wish I knew where Nuru was," Hadhi blurted out. "I need to speak to her, I... Please keep her near you." Hadhi had never thought to marry or to leave Nuru. She was not truly leaving, not really. But it still felt wrong. It felt like an end, like if she did not see Nuru now, she never would. They had not spoken once today, and the last things Hadhi said to her yesterday had been in anger.

"Tell her I am sorry for being angry yesterday. Tell her I understand," Hadhi implored.

"You will tell her yourself. You are not dying, Hadhi. The king is a terrible man, but he will not kill you."

"No," Hadhi agreed. The king would not kill her. "Tell her all the same."

"Alright." Sabra searched Hadhi carefully. She glanced over her shoulder, stepping closer and lowering her voice. "You have always been the strongest among us." She weighed her words heavily. "I thank you. For myself. But mostly, for your brother. Lin can be his own man, because of you." Sabra was in tears, and Hadhi—could—not—breathe.

Hadhi curled her fingers around the silk and fought the urge to hide. It had eaten at her for so long, wondering how the evil did not show, how no one saw her for the murderer she was. Now that someone had, Hadhi did not know what to feel.

Sabra looked down shyly. "Before I was married, I was angry with you for what I perceived as...a lack of love, and a desire to make others miserable." She looked ashamed, though her assessment was not entirely unfair.

"But I understood you after," she continued. "Before he was even found, you were different. Quieter and shattered. When he was found, I understood."

Hadhi had an overwhelming urge to apologize, though Sabra had no love for Zuberi. But before she could speak, Sabra went on.

"I think," Sabra faltered. "Wait a moment." She rushed out of the room again, and Hadhi held herself tight, waiting for Sabra to drag Asha in and force Hadhi to admit the truth.

But Sabra rushed back in with *Lin* in her arms. She stopped before Hadhi, holding the baby boy out. Hadhi stepped back, bumping against the stool she had just vacated.

"Please, hold him. What you did, you did for us all. It does not make you like your father. I am sorry I asked you to trap the nymph. Hold Lin. You almost never touch him."

Hadhi was braced against the wall. She did not want to harm that baby. He was sweet and good and unsullied. But once you were touched by a monster, you were changed.

"He should know you," Sabra insisted, stepping even closer.

It felt wrong to be near him most days. But—she was *different* today. Hadhi breathed out shakily. She chewed her tongue as she hesitantly reached out for her baby brother. He was so light and soft. He cooed and reached up to tug at the gems on Hadhi's throat. Hadhi sighed and lay her cheek against Lin's head. She held him close as he began gumming at the gems and felt the simple contact lightening her from within.

With one hand, he tugged at the gems and the other lay against Hadhi's collarbone, warm and comforting. He made a little humming noise as he played, and Hadhi felt like rocking from side to side, like spinning around the room with the child.

She closed her eyes, unaware that she *was* rocking. In her mind, she saw the sort of life she had never dared to hope for before today. Noam with his hand at her waist, their child in her arms. It was bright before them, the baby hummed, and together they all swayed. Surrendering to the dance of life.

Hadhi breathed the promise deep within. When she breathed out, the promise stayed inside her and gave her strength. Everything could still be alright.

Carefully removing the gems from Lin's mouth, Hadhi handed her brother back to Sabra. He grinned up at Hadhi from his mother's arms. Hadhi gently lay her fingers against his head and brought them to her lips.

That smile was well worth protecting.

Sabra's eyes were wide with shock, but they drifted closed, and tears wet the corners as Hadhi repeated the motion with her, protecting her Mzaa Sabra's spirit within herself.

As her hand fell to her side, Hadhi cast a glance sidelong into the box. To the knife. If she was going out as a protector, she would likely find a use for teeth. Killing the king might not be beautiful, but it could prove necessary. Yet Hadhi felt not the slightest desire to hold that weapon.

She lay a hand on Sabra's shoulder, in gratitude, then forced herself to move. If she did not go now, she might let her fears take over, might revert to old ways. So Hadhi fled the room, with a hand clasped around the beads and her heart full of certainty that though the paint would eventually wash from her skin, and the gown and gems as well would leave her body, the beauty and the goodness in her heart were growing. And those things she would make certain lasted for all of time.

SOURCES OF STRENGTH

CHEETAH

A vicious mewl and a loud crash startled Nuru. Her eyes shot towards the menagerie.

She must be dreaming! Animals of different species were racing out of the palace, headed south, towards the jungle, jackals, monkeys, meerkats, birds, cheetahs.

Nuru's breath caught.

A single dark grey coated cheetah set its claws on the ledge of the broken window the animals were escaping through and yowled after the others like a threat. The animals took off even faster, even the other, lighter cheetah. Then the animal in the window shifted. Her gaze fell directly on Nuru. She gave a quick high chirp, startling a shiver down Nuru's spine. The cheetah stepped carefully out of the window, its eyes never once leaving Nuru.

"There's no reason to worry."

Nuru heard Hadhi's voice from the past in her mind as the cheetah came nearer.

"Cheetahs do not want to hunt us. They are afraid of us alone."

"What if it isn't alone?" Nuru had hissed, latching onto her sister's arm, trying to drag her away. "Like the one that mauled you."

They had gone together to hunt fish for dinner. And they'd spotted a single cheetah across the river. Nuru had never been scared before, but since Hadhi was mauled, these beautiful creatures seemed more frightening. But Hadhi had taken Nuru's hand in her own and pulled her slowly to the ground, so they were both sitting. She was watching the cheetah out of the corner of her eyes, but she hadn't looked directly at it, scanning the brush along the shore instead.

"That was my fault. I was not paying attention. I am now. Do you see how big it is? That is a grown cheetah, a male. They like to stalk their prey. If it was after eating us, we would not see it until it attacks. But this one...I think he is just hot. Look at his eyes, see the way they keep drifting up and down. We woke him from a nap. He is not here to kill us. And we do not need to kill him just because we are afraid. We have frightening teeth and claws too. We just call ours weapons."

They'd watched it until it climbed up a little dip and back into the tree to resume napping. Then Hadhi and Nuru finished fishing and went home. Safe. And Nuru had begun to see the animal's beauty again. The memory drifted through Nuru, and she slowly settled herself in the dust, breathing slow and calm as Hadhi had. She was afraid, but she also wasn't. She watched the creature, marveling as it came towards her.

Nuru had never seen a cheetah with grey fur. The spots on its back and the rings on its tail were grey as well, or maybe silver; they seemed to sparkle. And she watched Nuru with as much interest and caution as Nuru was watching her.

The cheetah came nearly up to Nuru, then sat her rump in the dust as Nuru's was and glanced back at the palace. Nuru was suddenly revived from the fear and the exhaustion that had held her right here before the palace when there was so much she ought to be doing. She was exhilarated, her fear and caution transforming into excitement. It was just sitting here with her. Like they were friends. Wasn't that amazing? Wasn't it beautiful? Hadhi should see this. She would be so proud of Nuru.

The cheetah turned its calm soft gaze back on Nuru.

"Are you going in then?" it asked in a curious feminine voice.

Nuru sputtered unable to find words. Unable to move.

The animal before her raised a brow and smirked at Nuru. Smirked. Animals were not meant to have expression, but this one did.

"What are you?" Nuru breathed, frightened and intrigued and slightly... amused. Had she just politely asked something of a cheetah?

"I've been asked that a few times today," the cheetah remarked philosophically. "I can't say I know at the moment."

"Are you not always a cheetah?" Nuru grinned as the words left her lips. This should be impossible. How was this possible? In the back of her mind, she heard Eshe speaking the words of the old legends while the spirit dancers performed them.

"Gitonga, the great spirit of the jungle, came to Sekou and sat beside him in the sun for many hours teaching the boy the way of the animal, until evening was upon them. Then the Great Spirit picked up his cat skin and slunk off through the shadows."

Perhaps Nuru was like Sekou. A Great Spirit left in the body of a human so she might stop them warring with the animals. Only Nuru was here to lead her people out of war with themselves.

The cheetah took her time responding, eventually shrugging her shoulders. "I come in what form your mind will best understand."

Nuru was fascinated. Perhaps this truly was the way. She'd known there must be a way for all this mess to end peacefully. "So you have no form of your own?"

The cheetah scoffed. "You've a bit of your sister in you."

"Hadhi?" Nuru raised her chin, smiling broadly.

"Asha," the cheetah corrected and laughed, if you could call its mewling growl such a thing. "Don't scowl. You like Asha well enough. The ways you are like her are good. As far as I can say, from so short an acquaintance."

Nuru supposed she ought to be skeptical or afraid. She was speaking to an animal that clearly knew who she was and knew her family. Even if she was speaking to Gitonga, who the legends described as a man, there was no reason to assume she was benevolent. But Nuru felt peace filling her body as she had when Hadhi took her hand and sat her down to watch a predator. This time it would be Nuru doing the comforting. Nuru doing the protecting. She wasn't afraid, because she had known there was a way to protect her sister, and her nation, and now it was before her. So she would do what the heroes in stories resisted until the very last moment; she would take what was laid before her with gratitude and see where it led her.

Nuru tilted her head up inquisitively. "Which bits are like Asha?"

The cheetah smiled toothily. "She is curious, as you are, more intrigued than concerned for her safety. Like you."

"I am safe with you, I think," Nuru said softly. "For I respect your great power and wisdom, and I am honored you would bestow a visit on me, Great Spirit."

The cheetah laughed, a mewling rumble interspersed with chirps.

"Great Spirit, is it?" She shook her head amused. "Tell me something, daughter of Zuberi, why are you so like but so different from your sisters?"

Nuru opened her mouth to respond but paused. Was this not the spirit of the jungle? Who was she? Why was she here?

"What do you mean?" Nuru asked slowly.

The cheetah rose and padded back and forth, before Nuru, examining her. "Your sisters, for all that they are different, are both filled with burning passions. Bright with joy or dark with longing, both are full to the bursting with it. But you." She padded right up to Nuru's face, making her breath catch. Having those teeth so close was startling. The cheetah pressed her nose against Nuru's and stared into her eyes, searching for something. Such lovely, unreal eyes she had, silvery dancing pools. How could she be anything but a great spirit?

"You are something else." The cheetah finally backed away. "Neither full of joy, nor full of longing. You are open to seeing both the wonder and the mundane ugliness of the world. What was so different for you?"

Nuru shook her head, shrugging. "I am just Nuru."

But as the words left her lips, Nuru felt more than just the power in the air, felt more than just the wonder at this creature and she knew her own answer had been wrong. That made her...cautious. This wasn't the spirit of the jungle, was it? Or if it was, she wasn't here for gentle purpose. Something was terribly wrong.

"Hadhi protects me," Nuru answered correctly this time.

"Hmm." The cheetah meandered away; it looked like she was dancing. Nuru shifted back onto her heels preparing to...she didn't know what, there was no way she could outrun a cheetah, and a magical spirit wasn't likely to be more vulnerable than an animal, was she?

A woman of Maltuba can marry a cheetah or a gazelle.

She'd come out of the palace, and she certainly sounded like a woman to Nuru, but what if this was the king somehow? Or what if he had some magic, and Queen Imara had never died, just been transformed? What if this was the old queen, come to protect her territory? It sounded fantastical, even to Nuru, but nothing made sense. She was talking to a cheetah.

"Yes. I sensed this in her," the cheetah spoke to the distance. "Not goodness, but dire, unshakable *vigilance* over those she loves."

"Hadhi is good," Nuru snapped, too offended on her sister's behalf to remember the lessons from the old tales and mind her tone when speaking to beings of great power. "Why shouldn't she protect the people she loves?"

"She should." The cheetah sounded confused. "Of course she should. But...perhaps she should love more. Or perhaps she should *be* more. What would she be without you to guard? Without you to avenge?"

Avenge? How could Nuru have so mistaken its intent? "Who are you? Why are you talking to me?"

"Ah, caution at last," the animal chuckled but did not bother looking Nuru's way. "Is Hadhi cautious? We've not spoken much."

"Who are you?" Nuru repeated. "Why would Hadhi need to avenge me?"

"Avenge you?" The cheetah turned to stare at Nuru as if she were insane. Then understanding fell across her face, and she shrugged. "Oh. I don't imagine she will. I was only wondering."

"I don't understand you, but I think maybe I should go." Nuru began edging backwards.

"And do what? Kill the king?" The cheetah shook her head. "You are not up for that, I think. And he is not the sort of cheetah you can ask a favor of," she said ominously. Nuru's stomach grew knots. Then the cheetah hid her teeth and nodded coaxingly. "I am."

Nuru took one step back and another. Hadhi's voice rising in her mind like she was just behind her.

Wait, you have no idea what dangers are out there.

"I don't think I should, thank you." Nuru walked backwards, keeping the cheetah in sight.

"Don't you want a favor? I can grant you any one wish." Her tone lowered to an enticing mewl.

Nuru stopped. *Any one wish.* That was quite the offer. Hadn't she just told herself to accept what was laid before her? Hadn't she been seeking a peaceful way to free Hadhi from the king? To free the nation from him. Maybe this was that way. She wanted to leap forward and beg this creature to free Maltuba from the rule of kings, but Hadhi was in Nuru's mind, cautioning her.

"Why would you offer me such a thing?" she asked. "You don't know me."

The cheetah had been stalking Nuru. At those words, she stopped and stared off, perplexed.

"Do you know, you're right." She shook her head. "I've felt so much from so many, thought sure I knew all, but I know so few people. I most often meet new people at their end. But the ones who go on living, go on changing and—wishing. I did not expect that. How long do you imagine it takes to know a person?"

Nuru shook her head.

"Asha, for instance! She surprised me, when I was sure I knew her, whole and all. Surprised me, gifted me. There is a bit of me that wanted, in that moment, to run away and never return. But I couldn't bring myself to leave." The cheetah plopped onto its behind in the dust, looking uncommonly human. "I *cannot* leave. The gift will be gone soon, would have been even if I ran, but at least if I were gone, I would not have to see what it costs her."

"What does that mean?" Nuru shouted. Frightened for herself, and her sisters, and even this sad, powerful creature before her.

What was happening? Where was Hadhi? Hadhi was always near when Nuru needed her. But ever since they'd fought last night, something had changed. Nuru had hurt Hadhi, and she wasn't sure she could ever make it right.

The cheetah shook her head. "I do not know. That is the worst of it. I never know exactly what the magic does once gifted. My power is only in the feeling, in the carrying of pain. My power never kills, never gifts, never does a thing but absorb and redistribute."

The cheetah bared her teeth, hopped onto all fours, and advanced on Nuru. "But it can do more. What would you have of me? I want to gift you. It is only me offering you this gift."

Nuru didn't like the feeling coursing through her that she should have been more sympathetic to the heroes of the old tales all fighting against fate, too scared to see it was there to help them. From one moment to the next, she didn't know what was right, if she was safe or in danger. If this creature was friend or foe, benevolent spirit or a dream Nuru couldn't wake from. All she knew was her world was coming apart and she wanted to fix it, but she didn't know how.

"I will not hurt you," the cheetah said, its powerful teeth visible as it spoke.

Nuru shook her head. How was she meant to believe that? How was she meant to trust it? She might have trusted it ten minutes before, but now she was hope and fear twisting together, becoming entirely confused. Rising up above all her other worries, over all her other loves, was one tiny image of her sister, sitting blistering in the sun, with no food, only allowed to move to relieve herself, swaying but silently resolute. All to protect Nuru from another cheetah. And Nuru hadn't even thanked her. She had resented it. She'd been protected and Hadhi was hurt for it, but she'd been angry with Hadhi.

Nuru stared at the cheetah before her, she might be in terrible danger, but all Nuru could think was, *someone needs to protect Hadhi.*

WORDS OF COMFORT

Hadhi was just making her way out when Azize tried to march in. He was not even pausing at the threshold. Hadhi knew her place and would usually cede the space to him, but she did not back down today, her momentum forcing him back into the sunlight.

She was stronger today, emboldened by every soul she had pressed to her lips and offered shelter within herself. Even Asha. Perhaps she was just a bit more like her sister for having gone in to see her when she'd left Sabra. Now that her sister's spirit was guarded within herself.

She had hoped to find her awake, to speak with her before she left, but Asha was tossing about on the bed, speaking in her sleep. She always tossed in her sleep so it ought to be comforting after her stillness earlier, but the sight was not comforting. And all Hadhi could do was press a kiss against her sister's head and whisper her love, hoping Asha might hear her.

"I love you, Asha." Her sister had settled a little at the words, shifting still but no longer thrashing. And that was enough. "I will make this right," Hadhi promised and raced away from her. Charged forward as Asha might, and here she stood, forcing a prince to cede space to her. How new it felt, every small bold step making her bolder after.

"Hadhi," Azize exclaimed, examining Hadhi in shock and appreciation.

Hadhi ticked up and impatiently inquisitive brow.

"You look different, "Azize fumbled.

He was among those who could not imagine her being lovely, apparently. Hadhi had been among them herself, but it annoyed her to feel his shock. Were a fine gown and gems what made the difference? Truly?

Hadhi smiled defiantly. "A king's bride is not married in her sister's adjusted gown." Her voice was meant to sound condescending, but it quivered when she mentioned the king. She heard it and stiffened. She needed to be strong. "I understand I am part of a plan."

"Noam told you?" Azize demanded, apparently enraged.

"Has he not found you?" Something twisted in her stomach. Noam had left over an hour ago; he should have found Azize by now. Had something happened to him?

But while Hadhi was worrying over Noam, and awaiting Azize's response, Azize was squeezing the slipper in his hand. Asha's magic slipper. Hadhi looked from his hands clenching around it back to the prince's face. There was a look there that Hadhi did not like. A look that reminded her of her father. Fear and hunger twisting together. Something was wrong with him.

"Azize," Hadhi snapped to get his attention.

He woke from his fixation with the shoe, but for a moment could do nothing but stare at Hadhi. After a long moment, his face softened and his hand loosened on the shoe.

"I am sorry," Azize said, seemingly sincere. "I should have been the one to speak to you. We were becoming friends."

Hadhi smirked, incredulous. Friends? She had made him laugh twice. Pleased him. But he made no effort to do the same with her. Was that friendship in his eyes? Did he not offer care and companionship to Noam?

"I have been impressed with your desire to care for your family," Azize rushed to explain his sentiments. "Your honesty, even your willingness to go along with this plan, knowing what it would cost you if we fail. You impress me."

Hadhi smiled gently at the words for she realized just how vastly his lack of understanding stretched.

"I will not be given a choice in marrying your father, Azize," Hadhi explained in a comforting voice as she might use with Nuru. But she did not conceal any of the truth from him, as she might with her sister. "He knows I am unwilling. It is part of what pleases him."

Azize looked away.

"But knowing me for a hunter, I am certain he will be watching for some attack. My only options are to marry him, hoping to gain my freedom if your plan succeeds. Or telling him your plan and solidifying my place as helpmate to an evil man." She shrugged.

Azize shivered. The hungry fearful look enveloped his eyes again. That look her father had always worn before he did something evil.

"I will help you," Hadhi informed him. He seemed to need to hear it. "Because he must be stopped. But the effort is not so great. I would only have been doing it unwillingly otherwise."

"You could run," Azize pointed out. "I have run my whole life."

"That is allowed—for *princes*."

Azize was uncomfortable being confronted with the truth. He would not meet her eyes and seemed to be trying to come up with a way to make it all less unpleasant.

"Noam would run away with you, if you asked." Azize tried to shift the conversation again.

"Yes," she nodded. "And I would leave my family here to suffer for my offense."

"Exactly!" Azize shouted, grabbing onto her arm. He spoke with an intensity that bordered on frenzy crushing the magic shoe against Hadhi's left wrist. "You were the daughter of an evil man too. You knew what he was. You could have been like him, but you aren't. You impress me."

Hadhi slowly drew her arms away, surprised to be moved. People kept complementing her today. She did not know what to do with it. It did not feel true. It was not true, not really.

Hadhi had not planned on killing her father, as Sabra's words implied. It was a reaction. A vicious instinct that he had trained into her. Once she had struck, she chose not to...waste the impulse. Not to give him any chance of survival. But she had not killed him to protect her family...or if she had, even she did not know it. And as much as she would like to believe Azize's praise Hadhi knew herself to be a murderer, a liar, and a sister who had so failed to love another that she was dying. There was no way such a person could ever be described as good. But what she could be—what Hadhi would be—was better.

The thoughts rumbled through her, shaking something. Before she could figure out what that something was, a rumble aloud pulled her focus. The desert was moving closer, roaring with the voices of the dead. She should warn Sabra, but as the thought occurred, Hadhi saw Sabra inside shuttering anything that would be open to the storm.

"That is very kind." Hadhi forced her eyes back to Azize. He continued to stare at her intensely. Taking a deep breath, Hadhi shut away all her hopes and fears, and breathed out, pulling her shoulders up, with her heart beat quiet in her chest and her mind cleared for the hunt. "I must go confront your father."

"Why?" Azize demanded, frightened again.

"If I do not go to him, he will send men to find me. And then I will be brought to him in chains. I am a daughter of Zuberi, and I have made my disgust of your father known to him. Daughters of Zuberi are not taken. I must see your father, fight for myself, and let him bend me to his will with threats and violence and..." Hadhi did not say what she was thinking. But it did not appear to be necessary. Azize seemed to know as well as she that the king enjoyed forcing himself on the unwilling.

Hadhi pitied Azize again, wondering what he had suffered at his father's hands to send him running. She did not blame him for that. She was a bit envious, but she had no desire for anyone to be trapped with King Enzi. Still, Azize was not the only one in need of protection from the king. And it seemed unlikely he would be the one to offer that protection.

"The plan will succeed," Azize said by way of reassurance.

Hadhi smiled fleetingly. "Asha is not well," Hadhi said firmly. "Be careful with her. Being the daughter of an evil man has a price."

"The nymph!" Azize raced inside.

Hadhi breathed out as he passed and turned away from her home. She walked towards Jaccada. It was several miles; if she walked slowly enough, she might not have time to truly confront the king. A shudder raced down her spine, and she wondered if she had been taking her time hoping for just that. Hoping that the king cared enough for his schedule that he would drag her to the desert without having time to break her.

She wished she had not been so forthright with Azize, for her own sake. She wished she had allowed her mind room to think of something else. Now the fear began to consume her. She kept having flashes of Enzi forcing himself on Kiho. She would shake them away by imagining the king dragging her out to the desert and Azize's bit of a plan somehow being successful.

Then the twisted angry—*frightened*—part of her mind would whisper that she did not deserve a reprieve. She had not saved Kiho. She had not done a thing to stop Enzi or protect the other victims she was sure existed. She deserved to suffer; they did not.

Hadhi stopped. Just stopped in the middle of the road.

zzz.

A little bug like the one that had been following her lay on the ground, battered. Hadhi crouched, running a gentle finger over it, wishing she had more to offer it than comfort.

There were hills on her left and tall grasses on her right. In a little while, this whole way would be lined with people on their way to the desert, to witness her marriage. But now it was empty.

zzz.

The bug nuzzled her finger, then flapped into the air as if restored. She followed it with her gaze as it flew towards the desert and the storm. Yes, the bug was clearly a kindred to her.

Hadhi sent her mind walking into the desert with it. Sent her mind to that place burning with love, hers and Noam's. Her mind could live there, it needed to live there. So that she could be loved for all of time.

She shut her eyes and felt from the tips of her fingers radiating through her whole body the shock and the brief flash of joy that had consumed her when Noam walked by her family in the line and squeezed her fingers. It was such a brief moment. Nothing compared to their conversations or the warmth and love of them together in that cave. But that moment, his fingers locking around hers, his need to touch her simply because she was near— that moment drew her over and over. That moment was so full of love, before either of them had said it.

She pushed off her knees, standing tall. She could do this. She would not live in the fear as her father had. She—

"Hadhi?" Uncle Kafil's voice startled Hadhi's eyes back open.

He was up ahead on the road from town. There were a few people with him, rushing to be the first to the desert to see her married. Hadhi shook off the thought. Her uncle moved away from the others to meet Hadhi. She walked to meet him.

"Uncle." Hadhi nodded her greeting. They had barely spoken in the year and a half since Baba died. Since Aunt Lolia died. He seemed as uncomfortable as she.

After a moment, he fingered the gown. "Lolia was so proud when she made this for you."

"For me?" Hadhi gasped, her hands tightening around it. Taking in the gown again, she wondered why she was surprised. These were Hadhi's favorite colors, and the patterns was the symbols of all Hadhi's favorite things, the golden dunes of the desert, the many greens for the jungle, and the swirls of purple for the willoomi. And the gown was trimmed in the fur of the cheetah Hadhi had killed. The bounty Baba sold and gave to anyone but her. Aunt Lolia would have known how much that hurt Hadhi, not because she wanted the pelt, but because...she could not escape the scars, so she wanted her skill acknowledged as well.

Uncle Kafil's voice was quiet. "Your father said you wouldn't want it and gave it to your mother instead. But Lolia made it with only you in mind. She said she wanted you to see all the beautiful things about you, even your scars." He smiled softly, his eyes tracing her scars and the golden paint adorning them. "I...am sorry. I have been angry since she died. I was angry that you were not there to see her spirit released."

Hadhi bit her lip, heedless of the paint, and felt a few tears rush down her cheeks.

"I was angry too," Hadhi whispered.

"I know." Kafil nodded. "I should have known then, but I do know you would have come if your mother let you." He nodded behind him. "The king will not be allowed to marry you."

Hadhi looked at the odd gathering and saw some of them ducking into the tall grasses or tiny caves on either side of the road, saw the youngest girl among them, who was likely little older than Nuru, lift the blankets covering the camel's back and remove weapons to pass among the others. She saw Sade at the back of the gathering, directing others. Sade sensed Hadhi's gaze and looked over with a smile of love and friendship as they used to share. She nodded once and went back to her work.

Hadhi squeezed her uncle's hand as she shook her head. "You could all be killed. Even if you succeed you could be killed."

He nodded. "We know. But he must be stopped."

"I know." Hadhi leaned closer to her uncle, speaking in hushed tones. "There is another plan. A plan to...capture the palace and imprison Enzi as he returns."

Uncle Kafil looked as skeptical as Hadhi felt about that plans ability to succeed. "Your plan?"

Hadhi laughed. "No. The prince's."

He raised his head and his eyes hardened. "We are not entirely sure we think he should lead us, Hadhi. Are you?"

Hadhi shook her head. "No. But I cannot say I know who should."

Uncle Kafil smiled. "We have discussed letting the tribes divide."

"You nine?" Hadhi asked softly, raising a brow. "You are nine adults and three children nearly grown. This is a nation of thousands. What makes you think they will agree with you? What makes you think this will not lead to years of war and the deaths of your children?" Hadhi shook her head. "I do not like Azize's plan either. But if it fails...it leaves me married to the king. I give you my word he would not survive the month," Hadhi promised flatly.

Uncle Kafil breathed out what sounded like a laugh. "All my life, I loved my brother."

Hadhi's heart clenched waiting for him to say he knew she was Zuberi's murderer. Waiting for him to say he despised her. But...if that were so, why try to rescue her? Perhaps they just did not want the king having another heir.

"He protected my father and I. Raised our fortunes when we were cast out. He never rested. Made himself the best hunter, the best soldier, tricked and charmed his way into Enzi's attention until he was his closest companion. I thought it was love that drove him, until I saw him with you girls. It wasn't love. It was hunger, and he tried to beat or manipulate that same hunger into all of you. But you, Hadhi, you protected your family in secret, your cousins, your aunt, your sisters. Your actions are driven by love. But what you learned best from your father was to count on none but yourself. Others will help you. Others love you. Take the camel, we will follow our plan, and if you must, you will follow yours. Nuru is hiding your cousins. I do not want them to die, but I want them to see their father showing what love looks like. Go on now." He lifted her hand and kissed the back of it.

Hadhi watched her uncle take a few weapons off the girl and disappear into the long grasses as did she, leaving Hadhi alone on the road with the camel.

Was that truly what she had learned best from her father? To be alone? She did not truly trust anyone's plan but her own. That was fair. She had not expected anyone to care to...protect her. Had she learned that from Baba? All she knew for certain was that she did not want others to be hurt in her defense.

Hadhi walked forward. The camel was well trained. She convinced it to kneel, tapping the back of its forelegs twice. She sat on its back. When it rose, she guided it to turn around with a gentle hand. The sandstorm was growing closer. She could all but feel it, feel screams and sobs and so many heartbroken spirits calling out to be heard. She thought she might even hear her own sob in that mess of wind and sand and souls. Her sob as her father's body was burned. Her sob of guilt and anger and—love. Her sob that begged to be forgiven, to be made over.

"Mind the storm," Hadhi called out. "It does not look like it will let up. If you must stay, the caves are safer or our family hut."

Hadhi shut her eyes, begging any ancestor in that storm not to harm these people who were willing to brave danger or even death to guard her.

A BETTER WORLD

"Asha! Asha?" Azize ran through the house, past Sabra, not even acknowledging her.

Sabra yanked Lin off the ground where he was crawling into Azize's path. The prince tore past them, unaware. He looked terrified, but that did nothing to lessen Sabra's rage with him. She crossed to the main entrance, shutting it up and stuffing rags around the edges to keep the sand out. It seemed he would be stuck here with them until the storm passed.

Sabra doubted there would be any weddings today. The goddess Ether did not approve.

Sabra set Lin back on the ground as he began to fuss. Silently, curiously she moved to the edge of the stairs so she could listen to Azize and Asha. The lower part of the house was well fortified from sandstorms, provided nothing came in through the upper layer, and Sabra had shut up every hole she could find. It amused her only slightly that Jauhar having Asha patch the hole in the roof turned out to be quite necessary.

Sabra didn't hear their greeting, but from the sound of Asha's voice, she was not much recovered and in tears again.

"Oh, Azize, he was such a bad man," Asha sobbed.

There was a long quiet stretch of just Asha's tears and Azize's rapid desperate breaths. It seemed he was unsure of what to do with a tearful woman. Like so many men before him.

Sabra scooted down the stairs and sat on the middle step. From here, she could keep one eye on Lin trying to pull himself up to stand against a stool and spy on her old friend with the other.

Asha was trying to sit up, but without the strength, she kept slumping against Azize. It didn't look a bit romantic, just worrying.

Asha looked drained, nearly on death's door. The sight of it sucked at Sabra's insides. How could she have fought with her in such a state? She shoved away the feeling and latched onto the rage. The rage had been keeping her moving since last night. She couldn't let it go now.

"I didn't see any of it." Asha sobbed. "He did so many terrible things and I thought he was perfect."

Sabra saw Azize's lips pinch with rage, but he shook it off. "You didn't know."

"I didn't even try to see. I just wanted to be happy. I wanted him to be perfect, and to have adventures, and…"

"Asha, you must not make yourself ill. You are not responsible for what he did. No one blames you."

"Hadhi blames me. Sabra blames me, and Zawadi, and *especially Jauhar*," she gurgled as her tears streamed down her face and into her mouth. "Even you blame me! You said I couldn't be the only person in Maltuba not to know what he was."

Sabra looked up the stairs to her son. *Sabra blames me.* She did. She kept blaming Asha. Her friend. Sabra blamed her for all her suffering, even knowing it was not her fault. She blamed her, because she was the only one Sabra could punish for it, the only one who could be made t—

Sabra gasped and let out a tiny laugh. Lin was standing. He gripped onto the stool moving his feet, not walking, just feeling out steps. He was so lovely. So precious to her. She wished he'd come to her a different way, from a different father, but she wouldn't give up this love for anything. And she was, in quiet moments, glad that this was his family.

Sabra blames me.

Sabra watched her son release the stool and take his first step, so proud, so fearless. He took one step, two, then he stumbled and fell on his behind with a little squeal of laughter.

Sabra needed to be more like him, fearless, open, and loving. She had blamed Asha because it was easier to be angry, but she needed to let go of the rage and let love hold her up. Love was the power of her goddess. Rage was what weaker beings used.

Sabra walked to the doorway, she didn't enter the room, or she wouldn't be able to see Lin, already trying to stand once more. But she needed to be better.

"Asha," Sabra said softly and waited until her friend turned against Azize's chest and looked her way. "I am sorry that I blamed you. It was easier to feel anger than to feel helpless. But it was never your doing. Your father went to great lengths that you wouldn't know."

"I am sorry as well." Azize held Asha to him with a hand at the back of her head. "Please let me help you."

Sabra looked away from that hand, not sure she liked the possessiveness of it. But perhaps he was just trying to help. Sabra needed to be rid of the rage. She saw Lin walking again. Every few steps, he fell.

"It's my turn to help others," Asha insisted. Sabra returned her focus to the room in concern.

"What does that mean?" Azize squeezed her intensely.

"Five hours," Asha said through another bout of tears. "Just like before, but this time, she has only the magic, and I have only her pain."

"No!" Azize exclaimed.

She has only the magic, and I have only her pain. Sabra thought of that woman she'd spoken to, the first time so benevolent, and the second so sinister. She knew Hadhi had taken her request to capture the woman for something worse, but truly Sabra just wanted her...held. Questioned and her intentions discovered. Sabra couldn't decide if she was friend or foe, but even if she was a foe, shouldn't such an offer from Asha be enough to free her from the woman's vengeance?

"It will help me to make up for the past."

"Asha, you have nothing to make up for!" Azize insisted.

"No?" she asked, hiccuping. "Not even for hurting you, Azize? Not for hurting Hadhi? Or ignoring Sabra's pain? Nothing at all?"

"I knew my father was hurting people, and I ran away. You have nothing to apologize for." Azize swallowed looking smaller for his guilt. "I have a plan to unseat my father," Azize went on, looking between the two women for approval. "I will replace the palace guard with my men, then take my father into custody. All that is required is to get my father and a large portion of the guard away. So I thought we should be married. I want to marry you, Asha," he whispered, his eyes clearly avoiding Sabra. "I want a promise of happiness with you, forever." He swallowed. "But...without finding you, or asking, I announced that we would be married today."

"You did?" Asha sounded merely intrigued.

Was anger at such an action merely Sabra's response to her own experience? Was it acceptable to have your choices stolen, if it was by someone you cared for? Sabra didn't think she could accept that.

Azize nodded. "And my father...announced he would be married today as well,"

"To whom?" Asha demanded, breathy but growing suddenly stronger.

"Hadhi."

"But—" Asha pushed back from Azize's arms, shoving herself fully up on the bed. "You are afraid of him. No, he cannot."

Sabra moved closer to the stairs, feeling that fear in Asha, like she'd felt it in herself when Zuberi took her. She didn't want Hadhi forced anymore than Asha did, but Sabra wasn't sure there was such reason for fear. Hadhi was stronger than them. *Hadhi isn't you, Sabra, there is no breaking her will.*

"Asha, Hadhi is prepared to help," Azize reproached. "I am sorry that this happened. But when my plan succeeds, he will be king no more. He will be imprisoned, and I can do away with the marriage."

"And when it fails?" Little lights jumped in the room, drawing Sabra's gaze. Had that come from Asha?

"It won't fail." Azize released Asha's shoulders. She was standing on her own now but was nearly as wobbly as Lin. "I am sorry the plan requires Hadhi, but she wants to help. She is proud to protect others."

Sabra could tell Asha heard the censure in Azize's tone. As if to say Asha would not do the same. Was he not listening? Asha had done the same. Asha was taking on the pain of a stranger. It didn't lessen Hadhi's sacrifice, but if Azize truly loved Asha, he should recognize Asha's sacrifice.

But Asha didn't address that. "You haven't felt what I have. You don't understand. I let this happen to Sabra. I cannot let it happen to Hadhi too. Not now that I know."

"You didn't let anything happen to me." Sabra stepped forward, defending her friend.

Asha looked over her shoulder, with so much love in her eyes. "I didn't see it either. We have to help her. We have to protect her."

"What would you have me do?" Azize demanded. "I cannot force my father to give Hadhi up unless I am king."

Asha shone with a new sort of light. It was not as bright and playful as when they were girls, when Sabra first fell in love with that magnetic brilliance. But she shone with loving certainty. And it was...beautiful.

"Do not dance around stealing power that belongs to you already."

Azize looked as doubtful as Sabra felt. She had loved and liked and been enraged with Azize, but...Asha was endowing him with more abilities than he had.

But Asha shimmered in a cloud of blue light. She was dazzling. She was impassioned. And just like when they were children and she invented adventures, she was *magnetic*. Who could blame Azize for wanting to live up to the faith she was expressing?

"Take what is yours, Azize. You are a threat to Enzi's power. If you speak for them, your people will stand behind you. I will stand behind you."

She eclipsed the world with her impatience, pushing, fighting, demanding. Always Asha forced a being to be more than they thought they had inside. She stood tall like a queen demanding her due when only a few moments ago she had been helpless. There was truly no one like her. She was even defending Hadhi, as Sabra had hoped she would one day.

Again, Sabra wondered if the creature stalking them was really after vengeance. Or simply after a better world.

A WOMAN'S DOWNFALL

Jauhar expected to be led to the throne room when she requested an audience with the king, or to one of the gardens. Places of splendor, intended to overwhelm. Instead, she was led to the interior courtyard, a place where servants and guards mingled, where animals were butchered, and laundry washed. It was no place to meet the wife of your closest advisor. The only reason the king would be there was because it held the entrance to the dungeons beneath the palace.

Jauhar should not be here. As she went seeking Nuru, her plan had made sense. They had to be stopped. Asha and her mother couldn't win. It was not as though Hadhi had ever needed her mother. She had not even consulted her about her plans. No one did. Everyone underestimated her, even Zuberi. But Jauhar had learned. She had watched. She knew how to foil a plan. Asha would *never* be queen.

Jauhar ground together the beads of the shoe. She had not meant to take it, it was just in her gown, because she had not changed since the night before. But she was glad she had it now. She smashed the beads together and let it remind her of all the punishment Asha deserved for her pampered life and the adoration heaped on her. For the displacement she and her mother had cost Jauhar.

For three long years, Rama was Zuberi's favorite wife. Her iron will and refusal to bend to him ate up all his attention. She'd befriended Jauhar's daughter at a time when Jauhar was at her lowest. Then Rama had birthed Zuberi's favorite child and Jauhar vanished. Jauhar had longed for the life she'd had before that woman came along. She'd wished and wished to be rid of her. Wished so often and so strongly that when Rama fell ill, it felt as though Jauhar had made it happen. She couldn't countenance the thought.

She nursed the woman as though she were her own child. Held her, cared for her. But Rama was too ill, her body too wounded from days as a soldier and her battles of will with Zuberi. And when she was gone, Jauhar was changed. Hardened. She knew she could live regretting the woman's death, resenting her husband and her own jealousy. Or she could go forward and be all Zuberi needed. She could reclaim her place and be as powerful as her husband. But only if she learned to ignore the pain. Only if she were impervious.

She couldn't kill her love for Zuberi, but she could kill her desire to get love back. She made herself a pillar of strength. She truly thought she had succeeded. She gave him what he wanted, never asking a thing for herself, but to know his plans. And he'd given it, shared things no one else knew.

I will do what my father taught me.

Jauhar's hands clenched into fists, and she fought to calm her rapid breathing. Now was not the time to fall to pieces over one more betrayal. Zuberi had his reasons. He always did.

"Three men now you've turned away; do you want Hadhi to rot here at our sides?" Jauhar had demanded. She had made Hadhi presentable, desirable, no easy feat with a girl who was scarred, sour and reserved. But Jauhar had found men to want her and presented them to her husband and Zuberi had changed their minds.

"Jauhar," Zuberi laughed at her anger. She wanted to rage all the more, but nowhere in the world was there a man of such beauty when he smiled. Nowhere else were their eyes that pulled one in, made one beautiful simply by falling on you. "Those men are not good enough. I am the right hand of the king. My daughter will be queen."

"How? Azize has run off. And he never paid Hadhi any mind when he was here. You said yourself she is no great beauty."

"No, she isn't." Zuberi shrugged. "We must hope Nuru has more of her mother as she matures." He threw off his compliments so casually, for a moment her body would sing from his appreciation then he would turn away, and Jauhar was bereft again. "My man assures me Azize has not favored any particular woman in his travels. He may not like his home, but Maltuba has him in its clutches."

"So she is to wait indefinitely?" Jauhar asked with a bit of a bite. Zuberi never minded her passion or her rage. He walked to her, smiling. He knew how it affected her, when he was right before her. Zuberi slid the back of his hand down her cheek, to her neck, and her arm. He wrapped it around her waist, pulling her near.

"Do you doubt me, my love? I always have a plan."

Jauhar leaned into her husband and let her voice fall low. "I only want to be a help to you."

Zuberi chuckled. "Imara is ill, unlikely to survive. Azize will return." Jauhar nodded, not sure why she felt excited. She should not feel excited at the prospect of one more motherless child, but it was not as though Zuberi had arranged for Queen Imara to fall ill. Even he was not that powerful.

"Asha will nurse her—"

"Asha!"

"Yes," he cooed. "The queen is fond of her because she was Rama's daughter. But we will send Hadhi to help. Azize has never liked Asha; he will see Hadhi being a good nurse, obedient and quiet. Beside her sister, she will appeal to him."

It hadn't made much sense. Beside Asha, Hadhi might as well be a wall for all the attention she attracted.

But Jauhar hadn't seen it.

"The only trouble is Asha's friend."

"Sabra?" Jauhar fought the urge to growl or claw. She'd seen his interest in the girl for some time now. She had wondered why he didn't just take what he desired. Now she knew. Sabra was part of some plan.

"Azize was infatuated with her before he left, and she has only gotten lovelier. If she follows Asha, Azize may notice her and not our daughter."

Jauhar swallowed her tongue, giving herself a moment to become composed. "Then you must remove her from his reach," Jauhar remarked, knowing how he would do this. "Only your daughter has a right to sit beside the king."

"Yes," he agreed as though he had waited on her input, and she believed him. Hadn't she? "You must help Hadhi to be more lively. No man wants a little statue for his wife. Think of it, Jauhar." He grew passionate in his excitement, spinning her around, his eyes sparkled with power and hunger. "My daughter, queen of Maltuba. No one will ever be our equals."

She'd wanted that so badly, wanted his joy so completely that she forced herself not to care for another thing. Zuberi always knew best.

I will do what my father taught me—and wait for my moment to strike.

Jauhar wanted to bellow. Wanted to march into the desert and collect all the bits of dust that were her husband and stitch him back together so she could *rip him apart*. He'd made a fool of her. He'd *used* her! Like he did every other woman. She wasn't special, wasn't necessary for his plans. Sabra with her pouting and tears had been more use to Zuberi.

The betrayal filled Jauhar with a rage matched only by her hatred for Asha. It was all, always about Asha, his best beloved. In her pocket, Jauhar yanked at a single strand of beads in the slipper. She felt the band stretch tight, nearly ready to snap. Her rage powerful enough to sever even this magic her husband had left to his favorite child.

That was the worst of it, the most enraging aspect of nymphs and rebellions and Hadhi finally coming into her own. Though he had not lived to see it, though it was not his plan making it come to pass, though it would *all be Hadhi's doing*, Zuberi would still win! Asha would be queen. Hadhi would die. Jauhar and Nuru would rot at the mouth of the desert and—

Zuberi would win.

He'd made a fool of her too many times. Jauhar would not allow him to win again. She could not allow Rama to win. Rama's daughter would die, not Jauhar's. Hadhi would be queen, she would mother the royal line, and Zuberi and everything he'd loved would simply be forgotten. Jauhar released the slipper; she couldn't afford to sever the magic and risk the shoe vanishing.

When King Enzi finally approached, he walked up from the dungeon, wiping blood from his hands. Jauhar's stomach clenched, fear skating through her. She knew he did it intentionally, meant to frighten her, but it still worked. She had no recourse. But she also had nothing left to lose.

All Jauhar had left was revenge.

"Jauhar," King Enzi greeted her brightly. "How intriguing to see you still in last night's gown." Enzi tossed aside the cloth he'd cleaned his hands with. It had barely touched the ground when a servant slipped from the shadows and yanked it up. Her eyes darted to Jauhar's, a warning? As quickly as she appeared, she slid back into the shadows, leaving Jauhar all but alone with the king.

"Are you come to beg I leave your Hadhi with you?"

"No." Jauhar straightened. Zuberi was never frightened of this king. But he was not frightened of anything. She would best Zuberi, she had strength he had not even begun to tap, because he never saw her value.

The king turned away. "I always admired your husband. He was so… ambitious. No matter what power I gave him, no matter what title or how much trust he always wanted more. And he had the skill to get it."

Jauhar took a step back. The king was not looking at her, but the absence of his gaze did little to comfort her.

"It made me cautious. A man like Zuberi might have designs on my throne."

"No, never," Jauhar sputtered. She should not have come.

"He seemed well satisfied when I agreed to make Asha my son's bride." Enzi spun around, examining Jauhar. "He never told you, did he? He let you think it would be Hadhi." Enzi chuckled, "I did admire the way he kept you all on his string. Zuberi and women, no other man had his skill."

Jauhar's spine stiffened at the insult. Even now, with Zuberi dead a year and a half, he still had the power to rouse her envy.

"Your Majesty, there is something I must tell you," Jauhar spoke between her teeth, enraged and desperate.

"Caution is one of the better lessons your husband taught me, Jauhar. And suspicion. Azize was never a bright boy, seemed likely to make a poor leader. He is so hesitant. But he made friends in his travels, and all of them soldiers," Enzi laughed. "It makes a man suspicious."

If Enzi knew the plot, Jauhar's speaking of it could do nothing to help her. He would see it as mere self-preservation.

"I've kept careful watch of his friends since they entered Maltuba. All his friends."

Jauhar sucked in a startled breath. He knew about Hadhi and Noam. Her last hope, undone by a man and a bit of lust. Was that worth *dying* for? Hadhi would be killed for the betrayal and her family would suffer. Did she not see that?

Jauhar forced a breath. Zuberi could not handle deviation. But Jauhar was not so limited, so Hadhi could no longer be queen. No matter. As long as Asha never was.

Jauhar gripped the king's wrist fervently. "Then surely you know what Azize is planning." Jauhar sighed as if relieved of a great weight. "I overheard him discussing it with Asha this morning."

"Only with Asha?" Enzi smiled, amused. "Is your Hadhi not involved?"

Jauhar's heart stopped. Hadhi would die, was dead already for her selfishness. But...in her mind's eye, she saw her daughter with such a glow on her face, beautiful, if only for that moment.

You will not be anyone's sacrifice...I love you, Hadhi, iooni.

It was a lie, all men lied to get what they wanted. But Hadhi had believed. And she had been transformed. No longer one of Zuberi's women. Jauhar was so jealous. She wanted her daughter punished. She'd wished Noam dead for freeing Hadhi so completely.

There was a fleck of blood on Enzi's hand, a tiny spot, he might have missed it. Or he might have left it, meant it as a threat. Meant to assure Jauhar saw it.

She had wished Noam dead only an hour ago. Was she so powerful?

"Jauhar," Enzi prompted. "Was Hadhi part of the plot?"

"I...I do not know," Jauhar whispered. She didn't know what she was doing anymore. She needed her revenge, but she wanted Hadhi alive. She wanted to be her mother again. "She wasn't with them. She had not... returned yet," Jauhar said, not meeting the king's eyes. A bit of truth fed a lie well. "I do not know where she spent the night."

"That is easily told." Enzi grinned. "She was with her lover."

"Lover?" Jauhar gasped, shrinking to the side prettily, hoping to fool him once more.

"Indeed." Enzi stretched out his blood spotted hand for Jauhar's. She placed her hand in the king's hold and followed him reluctantly into the palace. "Come, Jauhar, tell me what you overheard, and I will reward you."

"But..." Jauhar forced her feet forward. "Surely you were mistaken, Hadhi has no lover."

"Oh, but she does." Enzi tightened his grasp. "He is luxuriating in the dungeon as we speak."

"A...a...alive?"

"Of course. What sort of wedding present would he make dead?"

Jauhar's heart sang. He still meant to marry Hadhi! Jauhar still might have it all. A daughter queen, Zuberi's best beloved punished, her place acknowledged. She would win all!

"Alive, he can be beaten," Enzi said casually. Jauhar let the words float over her. Hadhi had made her choice. "Again and again, at my pleasure," Enzi continued. "Alive, he can quite thoroughly punish your daughter, for her youthful and foolhardy passion."

Jauhar's free hand fisted at her side. There was no reason for the fear trying to claw at her gut. Hadhi was strong; it would not affect her.

"You see, no matter how much caution I was forced to use with Zuberi," Enzi spoke on, oblivious to Jauhar's inner turmoil, or perhaps more likely, pleased by it, "I was rewarded with so many intriguing lessons. It is always love that destroys a woman."

Jauhar bit her tongue to suppress a whimper. She had never heard a thing so true. But it wouldn't matter, it couldn't matter. There was no breaking Hadhi.

She already has been...That she picks herself back up does not mean she hasn't been broken, it only means she keeps living.

"Your daughter's lover has not been helpful as yet. Tell me, what has my son planned for me?"

Jauhar met Enzi's eyes. She could barely think past *it is always love that destroys a woman.*

"What destroys a man?" she asked without meaning to. "A dagger kills a man. Even one as powerful as Zuberi. But what destroys a man?"

The king released Jauhar's hand. She saw the curiosity in his eyes. He had expected threats to Hadhi would destroy Jauhar, as love must? Jauhar nearly laughed. There was nothing left to destroy. Zuberi had taken it *all*.

"Would Zuberi have been destroyed or proud seeing Asha convince Azize that he must take your throne and your life?"

"Asha?"

Jauhar did not let him speak. "Asha has always hated Hadhi. At first, she merely meant to catch Azize and best her sister." Jauhar slowly slipped her fingers around the shoe, letting each word build on the next as she revealed it. Enzi gasped. "She never wanted Azize before, but Hadhi might have become queen. Zuberi would not have allowed it of a sibling."

"He would not," the king agreed, but his voice was distant, nearly wounded.

"Asha is her father's child." Jauhar had to work harder than ever before to make her tone soft and unassuming. Enzi was too stupefied to speak, eating up her words in fear. "When she learned you meant to marry Hadhi, she pounced on your son and dug into him. Poor Azize, he never stood a chance. Just as Zuberi intended, I suppose."

Jauhar wanted to crow. Love might destroy a woman, but it was vanity that destroyed men. Enzi thought himself so clever. Like Zuberi thought himself. And all of them would be undone by a wife, a mother, a tool to be used then cast aside. A woman.

CHILDREN OF THE MONSTER

"Who are you?" the child asked again, and just the asking revealed what Oriole needed to know: the girl would stay. And she would wish.

But there was no answer to her question. Oriole could no more remember who she was today than she could when she first told Asha her name was Zawadi. What a bitter joke that was, calling herself a gift knowing she had come with such a darker purpose.

She could lie, even to herself, and say the magic brought her. That she didn't have hopes when she came. That she had not envisioned every one of Zuberi's women suffering violent painful deaths, as though it would make up for the lives he had taken. She could lie. She had. Had all but convinced herself that she only followed the magic now, that she had no will in all of this. But it seemed the one being she could not lie to was Zuberi's eldest.

Her eyes haunted the Battle Born, would not leave her mind for an instant. Not because of the threat inherent, or the power she sensed behind them. No, those eyes were haunting for their recognition, and their understanding.

If you destroy her, offer her joys and then rip them away, correcting scales that can never be balanced, you are as bad as he was.

That girl...in another life, when Oriole had been sure of who she was, when her name was one she had chosen, when she was whole. Before she'd allowed herself to become a monster. In that life, Oriole would have brought Hadhi among the Battle Born. Would have blessed her thrice, with magic, with sisterhood and with purpose. Hadhi had such a lonely, hungry heart and an oddly loving one for the child of such a monster.

But that was true of all Zuberi's daughters, wasn't it?

This one even. Only a child but so desperate to help, so willing to trust a stranger, and in the body of a predator no less. Where did she come by such trust?

"Hadhi protects me," the girl whispered, as if reading the Battle Born's mind.

"You've said," Oriole replied, disinterested, annoyed really. She couldn't make it fit. Someone who thought so little of themselves, who doubted every love, someone such as Zuberi's eldest daughter should not be able to raise one as trusting as his youngest.

"*No one* protects Hadhi," the child said with a bit more bite, making her point.

"Ahhh, yes." The truth of Nuru's words skittered through the Battle Born's bones. It was not quite true today, but all her life she must have been undefended. All her life alone. Oriole quivered in fear and empathy.

What she wouldn't give to be as solid, as sure, as immutable as a stone. Because, with nothing more than Nuru's words, Oriole felt herself changing again, softening. Her heart was opening to the children of her enemy. The children of her destroyer.

Oriole had known who she was before Zuberi. Known her place, her purpose, her worth. Now all she knew was rage and vengeance and—

Emptiness.

Such—utter—absence.

Nothing.

Filling her up.

Filling the world.

Mountains,

Oceans,

Galaxies of—

Nothing.

"Hadhi's different since Baba died," the child's voice broke into the silence.

The Battle Born was so relieved she nearly cried at the sweet salvation of this child's wondering, awakening mind.

"Baba used to call me his little jungle cat. I knew he loved Asha best, but he liked me. I was never near him for very long though, Hadhi would shoo me away, or find a way to nudge Baba out the door. I thought she was jealous, because," her voice dropped to a whisper and she could not meet the eyes of the cheetah before her, "he didn't love Hadhi. Not at all. He called her ugly or monster, and he prodded Asha until she called her Sour-Faced-Hadhi."

All at once an active mind was not enough for the child. She began to pace, wringing her hands and shaking her head back and forth as if in answer to some question no one had spoken.

"She should have been happier when he died. I didn't want her to be, but...I would have been if I were her."

The Battle Born nodded; she would certainly have been happier with Zuberi dead were she Hadhi.

"But she isn't happier. I don't know what to do. She always protected me. Even when I didn't want it. Why didn't I protect her?"

Oriole's sigh dragged her to the ground where she lay beneath all the misery. "I have found in life, one often doesn't see what is before them, until it is far behind."

Nuru collapsed to the ground as well, staring off at the palace. She should be staring firmly at the animal before her, the real threat. Hadhi would be. Hadhi was one who saw the threat of the moment, perhaps only the threat of the moment.

"I did see." Tears slid from the child's eyes, shamed and remorseful. "I just..." Her eyes latched onto Oriole's, begging her to understand. "I didn't want him to call me ugly. I didn't want Mzaa to slice me with her eyes the way she does Hadhi. I wanted to be a little jungle cat." Her eyes slid over the cheetah with a heavy sort of clarity. "Wild and free," she finished, but her tone implied she was growing to a deeper understanding even of animals.

Oriole lay her cheetah head upon the sand and startled, finding it wet. Was she crying? It didn't suit her. Empty things hadn't feeling enough to cry. But she was, and she couldn't stop.

She could feel Dove nearby, feel her wanting to come to her, but knowing Oriole would not stay. She could not—had no right to the comfort of old friends, because like the child before her, some part of Oriole had seen Zuberi's evil and wanted what he offered all the same.

"To be loved for yourself, it is such a beautiful, powerful weapon," Oriole growled. The girl looked startled, but she didn't speak. "Zuberi knew that weapon well.

"I was called Oriole, among the Battle Born," Oriole found herself speaking truths to this child that she could not with anyone else. "I had been with them for so long, been loved as a sister, a friend and a leader. But to be Battle Born is to give up bits of the self, to surrender to the sisterhood. He must have studied us for ages, your father."

It was subtle, but a slight crinkling at Nuru's eyes and the sudden stillness of her hands betrayed that Nuru had indeed heard her. She was frightened now. Asha knew next to nothing of her father's evil, and Hadhi all. Oriole knew the child had overheard some last night, but she wondered what all she knew. Oriole's mind wanted to linger on the questions and pick them apart, but her heart, that angry empty thing she'd rather thought was dead, was demanding other things. Demanding truths confronted and freed.

"I met him when seeking a missing Battle Born. He'd found her, saved her, it seemed. But for this...miracle, for saving one of my girls, my Magpie, he wanted nothing. Saving her was reward enough. Meeting us was reward enough. Meeting me." Oriole scoffed, and her eyes darted to Nuru's looking for equally cynical amusement, but her face betrayed only her wholly intent focus.

Hadhi would have been scoffing as well. Hadhi understood the weapon of love.

Oriole licked her snout and shook her head. "I must have gone twenty times to meet him. He wanted nothing, would say it again and again, nothing but to speak to me, to see me. And I had not been seen as separate from my sisters in so long. He played on vanity I did not even know I had. Until I wanted it to be true. I would hear his stories about you and your sisters, and I thought how lovely it must be to have such a life. To be singular.

"I knew," Oriole growled, at herself, but the girl shivered. "Knew from a life of watching humans. There is no unselfish desire. There had to be a reason he wanted me. But I didn't care. I wanted to be wanted for me alone. So I ignored the bits that didn't fit. I ignored the coldness in his eyes, and the twisting feeling in my stomach that whispered if I could not sense a desire from him, there was something very wrong. I didn't want to see. So when he finally asked for what he wanted, all I wanted was to please him. And my family are dead for my mistake. And I am here."

Oriole rose onto all fours. Nuru rose as well, backing slowly away. Oriole tilted her head up, sniffed the air, the terror wreaking from the child. A day ago, she would have rejoiced, but she was changed. But that didn't mean she knew what to do.

"I am here," she whispered, and Nuru flinched. "I am here," Oriole cried, unable to force clearer words from her lips, but she saw the girl understand.

Nuru crouched before the cheetah. Reaching out, she ran a hand from the crown of Oriole's head, down her neck, comforting her. "Singular," Nuru whispered. Her tears fell to join Oriole's on the ground.

After a moment, Nuru sat again and lifted the cheetah, the Battle Born, the enemy she did not fully recognize, into her arms holding her close. Saying not a word but offering more comfort than Oriole could ever deserve.

ETHER RISING

Asha didn't know if she was absorbing power from Azize, or if some shift in her thinking made the Battle Born she carried give her strength, but she was standing. She didn't feel weak, she didn't feel hungry, she felt...

"Ether," Asha whispered, turning away from Azize. He let her turn but slipped his arm around her to hold her steady. She faced the wall of the room, but she saw far beyond it. Heard beyond it. A cry of anguish was drawing nearer, so wrenching and so familiar and so powerful, it was dragging every other soul with it.

"What of Ether?" Azize asked hesitantly. She felt it all over him, hesitance. Fear that he wasn't enough, that he couldn't care for his people alone.

All her life, Asha had looked on her father, strong, confident, powerful and thought that was what a man should be. But she was wrong. She wasn't sure what the right way was, only that it was not Baba's way. Though she was beginning to suspect that Azize and all his doubts might have the right of it. At least his doubts were for what would become of his people, concerns that he might fail them. Wasn't that better than facing the world absolutely confident that it could take nothing from you?

Asha swayed, but she was feeling better, so much better. Power, like she had not even experienced the first night, was coursing through her. Ether was waking up, the spirits within roused, and she felt them all. She took a step towards the swirling sands, each grain a soul. They were infinite and powerful.

Asha bumped some obstruction in the living world and pitched forward. Azize caught her around her waist and pulled her back against him, easing her back so her head rested on his shoulder.

"I do not think you should be standing. Lay down. Let me care for you." Azize might not be a beacon of confidence, but he could be strong for her. He was lovely, now she'd taken the time to see him. "I will find a way to help Hadhi. Please rest."

"I can't." Asha rolled her head against his shoulder to stare up at Azize. He looked different now, his inner being showing through in soft soothing tones. If only he could see what she did. "Ether is calling me. It's rising."

"The sandstorm?" Azize asked. "I think I caused it with this." He leaned up awkwardly, angling his right hip into the air, and pulled something from a pocket.

"My slipper." Asha reached a hand up through the air, through the sand she saw dancing around her, and slid it across the sparkling beads of the shoe. Her spell. She tingled from the touch. It raced from her fingertips to the center of her being, digging up—her hunger.

She curled her fingers away.

"Yes. It's magic," Azize said, intent on the shoe, unaware of Asha's inner fight. "Every time I touch it, it gives me power and confidence. It led me to you."

No. It would make him as hungry as her soon.

Asha wrapped an arm around Azize, holding onto him with all her strength; she couldn't let him change. She felt Sabra leaving the room, giving them privacy.

"I let it bring me here, and the sandstorm came with me," Azize explained.

"So powerful, Enzi's boy?" Asha startled at the familiar voice. Baba!

He stood before her, tall and confident and so beautiful. Asha's hand itched to reach out and feel him. He looked so alive. Nothing but sand and a slipper stood between them. Baba smirked superiorly at Azize, winking at Asha, waiting for her to join his teasing, as she always had before.

Asha's heart twisted, and her body trembled. Baba. He couldn't be here. Unable to resist, Asha reached out a hand for his once dear face.

"Asha, what is the matter? You're scaring me." Azize pulled on her shoulder, but Asha barely felt it. Baba was here.

"That boy couldn't raise a sandstorm if he possessed every magic on the earth," Baba joked, looking slightly hurt that Asha had yet to join his teasing.

Her heart longed to make him smile. Longed for him to tell her everything she'd learned was a lie. But she wasn't alone. The women he'd slaughtered were inside of Asha, whispering, nudging, urging Asha to see the truth.

Her hand dropped.

Baba's gaze fell to the slipper, and his eyes sparkled. "But my girl," he said with covetous glee.

"He is not here for you, child," Wren's sharp voice poked at Asha's mind. Asha didn't know how she knew the nymph's voice, or why the command of it felt more like solace than censure. But she felt understood, forgiven even, for still loving Baba.

"You could raise the whole of Ether if you wanted." Baba beamed, as unaware of the Battle Born in Asha's head as Azize was unaware of Baba's ghost. What world was she in? "Couldn't you, Beloved?"

Asha flinched. How she'd longed to hear him call her that, just once more. But it ached now. A dainty, comforting weight settled on Asha's arm, like a hand, offering strength. A tiny brown and white bird sat on her wrist. "Sparrow?"

The world tilted, the slipper fell from her view. Asha didn't understand until she felt Azize's arm beneath her legs. He was lifting her. He lay her back on the bed and placed the slipper beside her, crouching so their eyes were level.

Asha raised a hand, reaching out to touch Azize. Every moment, she felt further away from him. She needed to touch Azize, to feel reality. He would hold her here, help her do what she needed to do. Save Hadhi. Stop Enzi. Help the Battle Born find peace.

She needed to do it all, and Azize would help, but Baba's ghost slid between them.

Asha whimpered, pulled her hand back to the bed.

"Have you been listening to liars, beloved?" Baba's eyes turned cold.

"Ethee Oxita!" Asha couldn't quite make Azize out. She felt him jump to his feet, leaving her alone, and wanted to call him back. But Ether had her.

"Asha," a friendly voice poked at Asha's consciousness, Emu. "Tell him you are stronger than him. Just turn away, child."

"I always knew you would bring me power." Baba was fixated on the shoe. He stretched a hand towards it. Asha was terrified. He was dead, couldn't touch it, couldn't take the power. He was dead, but—

Asha was not in Ether, and still she saw the rage of its sands. She could not make out the room for all the waking souls. What if Baba could grasp it here, in this half world? What if he could come back?

Asha watched, torn up over the bit of her that wanted him back. Was she awful? Even knowing his evil, she wanted him back. She wanted to feel as safe and loved as she felt while he lived.

"LIVE." Nighthawk shouted the word so loud Asha shook with it. The bed shook. The slipper tumbled to the ground.

"You wanted to see." Sparrow's soft peck of a voice wondered at Asha. The little bird climbed her arm, coming to sit beside Asha's face, on the pillow. "You wanted to see the whole world. Did you not understand there was ugliness for every beauty it holds?" she questioned gently. "Do you still want to see? To be Asha, only more aware?"

Asha's heart paused, and the sands, and Baba, and even the Battle Born paused with her. Everything held, glistening, poised on a moment. Did she want to see it all?

She had not noticed Baba as Sparrow spoke, but now she saw his hand all but wrapped around the pulsing bead of power that was Asha's slipper. He wasn't here for her. Would he call the power beloved? Had he ever, even for a moment, meant the word?

"I shouldn't love him," Asha whispered. "He's evil."

"Your father?" Asha searched the frozen sands and just made out Sabra's shape in the doorway. She had a large bulge on her shoulder that must be Lin covered up in a cloth.

Asha nodded. "I must be as evil as him."

Sabra sighed. "Evil and love cannot exist in the same place, Asha." She came closer; her voice was muffled but grew louder as she approached, clearing away the sands with every step. They fell to the ground in little piles around her. "Evil is a choice, made every day. If you can love him still," she shook her head, and the last of the sand fell away. Sabra had her face covered with a thin veil, and a scarf of similar material lay over Lin's head, protecting him from the sand.

Was it not all a vision? Had Ether actually marched into Asha's home?

"If you love him still, you are a greater good than I ever knew. Do not be afraid of that."

Be you, just be more aware.

"Only think what could be done with power like this." Ether moved again, and Baba had the slipper in his hand, light permeating the skin of his palm, letting the slipper show through.

Asha felt drained. Was he stealing the power from her?

"Live," Nighthawk said, more gently this time, and her voice took on a shape. A shadow of a bird beat its wings behind Baba's head, sweeping up sand in billowy curtains. Slowly, the shadow transformed, growing larger, becoming a woman. She had huge brown eyes, thick dark lashes and brows, a rounded nose and chubby youthful cheeks and wheat golden skin. She looked about Asha's age. She stood just behind Baba, watching Asha as though she loved her. "You are not meant to be among us yet, Bluebird." She smiled a sad smile, her eyes full of entreaty.

"The Battle Born?" Asha sighed the question and her heart beat wildly. Until this moment, she did not realize how much she wanted to be a part of something larger than herself. To have a family again. One she understood. One where there was no doubt she was loved.

Nighthawk shook her head slowly. "The dead."

"Asha?" Sabra settled on the bed near Asha's waist and lay a hand on Asha's shoulder. "You seem so far away. You are frightening me. And Azize. He looked half-mad when—"

"Where is Azize?" Asha demanded urgently.

"He ran into the middle of the sandstorm. Said he had to protect you, or it wouldn't stop."

"No," Asha sobbed. "No, we have to stop him. Call him back."

"We cannot. The storm is still raging, can't you hear it? Look at all the sand he let in only from walking outside."

He could die.

"You have to decide which world to fight for," Nighthawk said gently. "The dead?" She looked around, grains of sand sparkling under her gaze. "For so long, I fought only for the dead. It was only as I faced death myself that I understood my error. Do not make that mistake."

"But..." Asha sobbed the word. She was so weak. If she fought for this life, it meant laying here, waiting. It meant not latching onto that power that would allow her to help, but would drain her to death in the end. "I can't let Azize die."

"Then fight for him." Nighthawk's eyes flashed. "Use every bit of who you are, for the right reasons this time."

"You," Sabra spoke so slowly, hesitantly. Asha barely heard her. "Will be no help to him in the storm."

Asha's eyes fell on the slipper, and Baba. He was all made up of bits of sand with light stitching them together; every moment another sand vanished, and the light took over. She saw his core, his hunger. Like an endless pit, it devoured the magic but was never filled.

His eyes flashed up, sparkled as they met Asha's. "Are you sure you want to see more, Beloved? You won't like it. You never understood this part of the power. Always hungry, but never ravenous. Not enough to see the truth." He scoffed, then as if sorry for treating her so, he reached out a hand and ran it down Asha's brow. "I taught you all my tricks. My best beloved. Gave you everything you needed to see the world, but you're still right here, in the same place where you were born, living on scraps. What use is power for someone so ordinary?"

The words slammed into Asha, making her want to hide. But she didn't. She felt the Battle Born as one closing in around her, closing their arms around her. And a new presence flapped into the room, beating up great wrinkles of sand, nearly a storm all its own.

The creature had pointed ears like a hyaena, hundreds of teeth, and a scaly body. The monster Asha invented!

It beat its wings so hard, Baba fell backwards, trembling.

"Leave her be," it shouted, with Hadhi's voice.

Baba's monster.

Asha cringed, suddenly afraid.

Baba wore a sneer, but he trembled as he faced the Hadhi monster. "A fine show, Sour-Face, but what will it gain you? Already your sister cowers from you, and she hasn't seen half your ugliness."

The Hadhi monster landed between Baba and Asha, curling her wings against her sides. She stood guard like she would over Nuru, fierce and fearless. But Asha knew that wasn't true; she'd felt Hadhi's fear earlier. The Hadhi monster wouldn't look Asha's way. It was afraid.

She hasn't seen half your ugliness.

"Hadhi?" Asha spoke in a small voice, but Hadhi shook at the sound.

Wren's voice floated through Asha's ears. "It is not an easy choice, to know or to hold onto the joy of ignorance. But she..." A little woman appeared beside the Hadhi monster. The woman had heavy eyes, not much used to smiling, and a face wrinkled from a long life. She was the first form Zawadi had visited in. A comforting presence. She reached out slowly and smoothed a hand down the monster's shoulder.

"Your sister believes in you," Wren informed Asha. "She believes you are capable of both the joy and the knowing. Are you?"

Asha nodded, stretching her hand out to touch Hadhi. Hadhi trembled as she turned. She had her own face now.

"I'm sorry," Hadhi pled for forgiveness. "I never meant to take him from you."

"Ha," Baba startled Asha's attention off her sister. "You were always jealous, monster. Ravenous."

Hadhi shook her head, tears scattering from her eyes. "I never meant—"

"She'll hate you, monster," Baba growled. "No one ever lo—"

"Stop it!" Asha shouted. The Battle Born each cast off feathers. They raced across the room, covering Baba's mouth and cutting off his hateful words.

I thought it was impossible to love me.

From far away, Asha felt Sabra shaking her body, saying something. But Asha couldn't make herself stay in that world. She needed to see what Ether was showing her.

"I love you, Hadhi," Asha promised.

"You don't know me yet." Hadhi shook her head, barely able to meet her sister's eyes. "I never meant to take him from you."

Asha did not understand.

"It is in you to understand," Sparrow pecked at Asha's ear, more insistent than patient now. "Do you already know? Is that why you shy from the truth?"

She didn't want to see, did she? Even Hadhi had said so.

TO LOOK ON DEATH

"When the thunder came and shook the trees, shook the mountain and scattered the leaves, when flames grew high and ate the sky, when water fell down and slipped the ground, when all was chaos, screams and pain, what steady presence would remain? What force bore with you through every fear, through every sorrow, joy or tear? What name do you cry, to the darkening sky, when the life is fading from you? What name do you bless when with tenderness she gathers your loved lost to greet you?" Ayinde had his eyes closed and his foot scuffing the ground when he came to the end of his invented song of praise for Ether. He was shy of hearing what she thought, so it was really very mean, but also very necessary to tease him.

"Mzaa?" Arya guessed, teasing her brother.

But really it was his own fault. She shouldn't have had to come to the palace this early to bring him food. The vaashta were challenging him, not allowing him to eat food from the palace and telling him he could leave to eat if he wanted, but implying his apprenticeship would end if he gave in. It should not fall on his family to prove Ayinde's devotion. It should not fall on anyone. They should *see it*, but with every passing day, Arya grew less impressed with the voices of the gods. They seemed to her to think more of themselves than the gods they were meant to serve. Not like her brother.

Ayinde had wanted to be the voice of the desert since she could remember, anytime mother told the story of their joint births, and how Arya had nearly died he would run out to the desert to make offerings and pray.

It was annoying. But she could see the way he ate at his own lip worried that Vaasht Bakari would not appreciate his song, and she relented. She understood fear of rejection.

"It is beautiful, Ayinde. You should give it to Eshe first, perhaps she will prepare a dance for it."

"I thought maybe...Nuru. Maybe if she makes a dance for it and shows Eshe, she might join the dancers."

Arya rolled her eyes. She'd noticed his changing interest in Nuru, but she had not seen anything similar from their friend. Ayinde was always racing ahead of everyone, so determined to be the first at things, but she did not think it would serve him well as far as Nuru was concerned.

"Nuru is not one of the dancers because no offering was made on her behalf, not because she isn't great. Eshe needs the offerings to give to the vaashta, or they are not considered dances of worship. Although, the vaashta were the ones to make an offering for Neema. Perhaps if Nuru shows her devotion..."

Her brother turned away, crumpling the sheet he'd read off in his hand and doing nothing to hide his sudden agitation. "No."

There was much more to that no than just the word; Arya could hear it. She pushed off the low wall where she was sitting with one crutch and crossed to him sharply. What was he hiding?

He felt her behind him. She knew he did. But he just kept walking, out of the garden and into the open courtyard. It was oddly empty for this time of day. And there was blood dotting the ground up ahead, leading towards the dungeons.

What exactly had Arya missed at last night's ball? She hadn't particularly wanted to be at that ball. She enjoyed spending time with her friends, but in that situation, it seemed boring. But as she'd stood in the line, watching the shoe in the prince's hand change size for different women, choosing some and rejecting others...well, she supposed she'd started wanting to be picked. She'd wanted to be wanted, not because she liked Azize, but the slipper falling off her foot, so wide there was no question that she would be welcomed, that hurt a little.

Most days, she didn't feel all that different from her friends. But then Ayinde would rush out to the desert to thank Ether for sparing Arya's life in birth, if not her legs. Or magic slippers would reject her and welcome every beautiful, amusing—exceptional—woman in line. And she felt—

"Do you think when the gods bless a king's rule, that they bless *all* he does?" Ayinde's whispered question dragged Arya back into the present.

Arya was not fond of the king. Twice in her life his eyes had fallen on her, and both times she felt shriveled up inside, ugly and afraid. Yesterday in that line was one of the times, and his eyes and the slipper stretching wide put together made her feel uglier than she ever had before. She didn't like that feeling. She didn't think the gods had blessed his rule. Only the vaashta. None of the old stories treated kings as if they were ordained by the gods. If a king's rule was in service to the people and the gods, it was blessed. But that was very different from the gods blessing every king's reign.

But before she could launch into the tirade that her brother, and probably the vaashta should hear, she saw something unsettling and slapped her brother's leg with a crutch to draw his attention.

Together, they ducked behind the fountain in the center of the court as guards came forward, led by one of Azize's guests, dragging two other badly beaten, bound and gagged friends of the prince. Ones she'd met, Massahiro and Tareek.

Once the leader ordered the guards to "put them with the others," and waved into the dungeon, he remained outside, smiling and wiping blood off his hands with his robes.

This wasn't good. Seriously, what had she missed? She turned to her brother and watched as his face was transformed from the weight and fear of a few moments before to a look of awe. She glanced back into the courtyard in time to see the remnants of a glistening light fade into a woman who'd appeared in front of Azize's friend. Or...betrayer as the case may be.

She was short enough that the twins could see Kane's nose and eyes over her head. He raised a brow that looked mocking.

"I know my mother is dead, using her face will not help you. I know what you are," the man remarked coldly.

"I'd no doubt you knew. You watched her die."

"*Ether,*" Ayinde breathed, barely more than a whisper, and with such reverence. She could feel him trying to start forward, desperate to see the goddess's face, but Arya pulled him back.

"It was one of her more profound regrets," the woman, perhaps the goddess, continued. "That the sight might scar you, that she was not able to save you from the wicked men who took you. That you might die, and if not, might live in the pain and forget the love."

The man gave the woman such a look of anger, of hatred, Arya shivered and gripped her brother tighter. She didn't know what was going on, but if that was Ether, and they looked on her face, that meant they would be welcomed among the dead, and she wasn't about to let her brother rush out and face death like that was a good thing. The goddess was good, meeting her in your time was good. But if that was Ether and she'd come for this man...he must be very bad. Ether had not interfered in the human realm since she stopped her brother Urgongmok from destroying humanity and split him into the first sands of her endless desert.

"My mother was weak," the man scoffed. "My father was weak. They could not survive, but I did. I made myself strong, and I made myself right hand of the king! I make my own destiny." He turned away, but not fully, one eye watching the magic woman. He slipped a hand into his pocket as he moved.

"No. You do not. But you can, if you choose a path other than the one that was made for you by your mentor. And that wish you made unknowing. Wish again; take it back."

Bodiless screams rent the air and such heat consumed the courtyard that the fountain began to hiss and steam. The man opened his mouth as if to scream then grit his teeth. He lashed out at the woman with a knife and Arya lost her grip on her brother as he raced forward to save the goddess. But the woman, the goddess, whatever she was, transformed into a dove and flapped into the air, but her voice lingered.

"Not one of your dying neighbors blamed you. You can still embrace the blessings they sent to you. But it has to be a choice."

Ayinde skidded to a halt just out of arms reach of the man. "Ether," he called out.

Arya was afraid that man would attack her brother. She pushed to her feet and moved as fast as her legs would carry her around the fountain. But she was nowhere near them when he turned away, stomping down into the dungeons.

"Leave the courtyard. It is off limits. And don't be such a fool. None of your gods are real. Or if they are, none of them care for you."

Arya stopped. For a while, she'd struggled with wanting to say similar things to all of her family. Her twin most of all. She'd been struggling to believe, and it almost felt as if Ayinde had pushed and pushed to have this apprenticeship to prove to her that the gods were real. And all it had done was made her doubts stronger, because of the men he learned under. But now...was that what doubt looked like?

Arya followed the bird's path with her eyes and saw clouds rising in the distance. Clouds of sand. And she flew right towards them. Was that Ether? Ayinde was on his knees with his head bowed and words of prayer falling from his lips, but Arya watched the storm, watched the bird, saw other birds join it. She didn't believe that bird was Ether. Nor that the rising storm was the work of the goddess. But she did believe that something bad was happening. She was suddenly quite glad that the vaashta were uzaoka, because she had a feeling her faithful trusting brother was going to have some need of her doubtful caution.

A GOOD OMEN

Hadhi saw Nuru before she reached the palace. She was sitting on a little hill near the north-eastern entrance with an animal in her lap. It was a sign!

She had needed to see Nuru and speak her love before she could commit herself to any plan.

"Nuru," Hadhi called, urging the camel on faster.

Nuru looked up. "Hadhi," she gasped and set down the animal to stand. It was a cheetah! A dark grey cheetah.

"Nuru!" Hadhi shouted terrified. "Do not move." Hadhi raced towards her sister, hoping the commotion would scare the animal away. The cheetah raced towards the palace. When it was a few yards away, it leapt into the air and with a flash of light transformed into a large buzzard and flapped its mighty wings towards the wall. The nymph.

Hadhi slid off the camel's back with fear still racing through her. "What were you thinking? How many times must I tell you, this is a dangerous place?"

Nuru smiled fondly. "You think everywhere is dangerous. You look beautiful, Hadhi."

Hadhi's head pounded as painfully as her heart in fear. That animal had clearly been the nymph, come to offer Nuru some twisted wish, to leave her weak and broken like Asha. But even were that not the case, what was Nuru doing holding a predator like it was a pet?

"Every place *is* dangerous." Hadhi grabbed Nuru to her holding on tight. "Tell me you did not make a wish," she begged.

"No."

"No?" Hadhi pushed her sister back to stare into her eyes.

"I made no wishes," Nuru explained and glanced towards where the animal had vanished. "But, Hadhi, I think I should. I do not want our uncle to die or for...anyone to be hurt again. But I do not want you to marry a cheetah either." Nuru's eyes were red and swollen.

"Marry it?" Hadhi shook her head, then comprehension dawned. Hadhi lay her forehead against her sister's and sighed, wishing she had a way to reassure Nuru that was not a lie. And so...warmed from the knowledge that Nuru worried as wildly for Hadhi's safety as Hadhi cared for her. Hadhi pulled back, her heart slowing now she knew Nuru was safe. She had made no wishes. What would Hadhi have done if she lost her? "Nuru, you must be more careful. You stop my heart taking such risks."

"I think you should run away," Nuru whispered rather than answering Hadhi's plea. But her arms locked tighter around her. "If you run away, you can be safe. Then Uncle Kafil and his friends can have time to find more support or a better way to stop the king."

Hadhi shut her eyes and held her breath. She would have kept all of this from Nuru if she could. She did not like to see her sister frightened or angry. Did not want her involved in an uprising that might see her friends and family killed or might make them killers. It was very easy to think yourself capable of killing, very easy to see yourself as right to do so, because someone else was so wrong. But then came the quiet afterwards, when the world had not changed because one monster had simply taken another's place. She did not want that for any of them.

She did not want the feeling that had lived in her since killing her father for anyone else. The king needed stopping, but she did not think more death was what would serve Maltuba or any of its people. Maybe Azize's plan was best...or maybe not. But it would leave her in the perfect position for hunting the king. She could be the only one to feel this ugliness inside her. Perhaps she would not in this case, knowing all the people she would protect and choosing her course.

"I am the way to stop the king," Hadhi whispered after the long silence. "The king is not the cheetah, Nuru. He is a scavenger, a jackal at best. I am the cheetah. But...I would never leave you forever," Hadhi said. It was more a wish than a reassurance; she knew death would likely take her from her sister very soon.

"You should." Nuru began to sob. "I'm sorry I said you see all men the same! I should have asked if you wanted to marry Azize. I am sorry I let Baba hurt you."

"Nuru." Hadhi squeezed her sister's shoulders and set her away so they could see each other eye to eye. Hadhi's gut twisted. In her sister's eyes were remnants of that same sorrow she saw in her own face. Not so much sorrow perhaps as guilt. "I should not have been so angry with you. I should have just told you how I felt. But I did not know how to say that...I did not want to marry Azize, when my doing so was meant to protect you. I should want to do anything that protects you." Nuru shook her head like she would interrupt, but Hadhi kept right on talking. "But you did not allow Baba to do anything. He did what he pleased. He was..." she did not want to tell her sister; it had nearly destroyed Asha to hear it.

But Nuru deserved to know.

"Our father was a bad man."

Nuru nodded towards the ground where she had been sitting. "I think Baba did something to Oriole and her family. Something bad."

There was no doubt that he had; that animal was surely a nymph. "He killed them."

"Oh." Nuru sunk a bit at the shoulders, more from acceptance than surprise. "Please let me find Oriole and make a wish. You should not marry the king; he is a bad man too. You know these things and you do not tell me because you think I am not strong enough—"

"No," Hadhi interrupted. "I do not tell you because I do not want you to have to know how bad the world truly is."

Nuru stepped back, shaking her head. "Maybe that is why you should tell me! So I can show you how beautiful it is too," Nuru argued. "You never see the good things people do for each other. The things people will do for you!" Nuru shouted. "Uncle Kafil and his friends are doing something right now, to protect you."

"I know." Hadhi nodded, a bit flabbergasted to hear her sister speak so maturely. "I saw them."

"So see the beauty along with the bad. See it all, Hadhi," Nuru insisted. "And...run away. Noam will take you. He said he loves you. Let him take you away."

Hadhi smiled. She wanted to know when Nuru had spoken with Noam, when she had gone from calling him just Azize's friend to trusting his opinions. She wanted to bask in all the outpourings of love and support she was finding today. She wanted to know why today was so different. Had she not been paying attention before? But Hadhi saw the guards at the towers noticing her. Soon, they would be sent out to bring her in.

She could not run away. Nor could she walk in there and do what she must with Nuru at her side. But she could not tell Nuru all. Here she was within view of the palace, openly discussing their uncle's plan to overthrow the king. She was too foolhardy, too confident. Hadhi loved that about her, but now it would not serve them well.

But Nuru's words played through her mind, mixing with her uncle's, and Hadhi began to wonder...began to feel that perhaps they were right, and perhaps she had known they were right all along but been unable to find the words in her mind to understand it. Why else would she have come toothless if not because she understood that this fight, this moment, was about more than her alone? It belonged to them all. Her's might still be the hands to end Enzi's life, but first she would fight to give them all time to find better ways.

"If the opportunity presents itself, I will run," Hadhi promised. "But... today, I will trust to other people's plans. As you must. Hide our cousins, keep them safe. But if Noam comes for you, take them all and run."

"Hadhi," Nuru began, but Hadhi was not finished.

"I saw the sunrise." Hadhi beamed at her sister, raising Nuru's chin with a hand beneath it. Then she raised her fingers to her sister's forehead and brought them to her lips with a smile of pride for her sister's heart. "It told me the only way Maltuba can ever be what it deserves is if we make it so. We cannot go on forever living at the edge of Ether, as though unsure which life we belong to. I choose this life, and I do see its beauty. I love its beauty. I love you and Asha and Lin and Sabra and Mzaa."

"And Noam?" Nuru asked slyly.

"Oh yes. Very much. I love you all and that love makes me strong." The word vibrated through Hadhi, she knew somewhere her father's spirit was scoffing, calling her a fool, calling her weak. But he did not understand as much as she had always believed. Love made her strong.

"I will marry the king, or...pretend that I will do so. And give other's the chance to make this place that we love better than it is now."

Nuru's eyes overfilled, showering her cheeks. "But I want you to be happy. No one ever protects you, Hadhi."

Hadhi yanked her sister tight against her chest again. Too tight, crushing them together. "*You* protected me. You are *my* most beloved. Every day you smiled, every day you held my hand or laughed with me or came to me with your tears. Every day you were you, I was protected. You are my joy, Nuru. Since Baba died, I have not shown my love very well. But there was never a day or even a moment when I have not loved you."

Nuru clung on tight. "I wish you would just be safe. You always protect me. But I can be strong now, and you can be safe."

Hadhi saw the pride in Nuru's expression. She might have some of her sister's guilt, but it did not hold her down; it just folded into her and made her want better for the future.

"Did the animal offer you anything, Nuru?" Hadhi asked, desperate to understand more of her sister's innate confidence.

Nuru nodded. "Any one wish."

"But you asked for nothing?"

"You would have told me to be cautious." Nuru shrugged. "You would have wanted to know why she offered me a wish."

"I would," Hadhi agreed. "But...is there nothing you want regardless of caution?"

There were certainly things Hadhi wanted that desperately.

Nuru began to nod, but it became a head shake and a shrug. "I would have wished that you never marry the king," Nuru confessed. "But she began to cry, and then you were here."

"I am glad you made no wishes. Everything will be alright now. We will make it so. There is power in a people coming together to make the world safer."

As much as Hadhi's newfound confidence made her feel stronger, she knew there were still dangers in the world. Enzi was not likely to be easily stopped. She wished she could keep her sister entirely from the fray, but somehow, when Hadhi had not been looking, Nuru had become a woman. There would be no hiding her from the danger now.

There was a dry wind coming from Ether. The sandstorm was growing closer. She hoped her uncle and his friends had found shelter. Such a storm could consume them.

"Nuru, where have you hidden the children? Are they safe from a sandstorm? Be sure. And if Noam comes, take them all with you and run. Promise me."

Nuru stared at her sister defiantly a moment. She searched Hadhi's expression; it was clear she knew Hadhi had a secret. She must want to know what it was. She was curious, like Asha. But Nuru had one thing Hadhi doubted anyone else had, absolute faith in Hadhi. After a long stretch of silence, Nuru hugged Hadhi once more and whispered resolutely into her shoulder, "I promise we will *all* be safe."

She kissed Hadhi's cheek and ran off towards the center of town, leaving Hadhi alone before the palace walls. Hadhi waited for her sister to be out of sight. Taking the extra moments to guard her heart, her loves and shut them away in the cave within, where she kept all her beauty. Where they would be safe as she went to face the ugliness of the world.

On the ground at her feet, she saw another of those unfamiliar bugs, a cluster of them. All dead. *It is based it on bugs that live for only a day, but... magical.* Were these those bugs? Hadhi crouched. Were these mayflies? Had they lived their entire iooni already?

Hadhi felt her heart catch with a sudden fear. *But when May is over, he's gone forever. Doomed to love for only one month.* No. It was just a story. No. Hadhi stood with her shoulders back and her head high. She had made the mistake already today of doubting Noam's love; she would not do it again. Even if these were mayflies, Noam was not. He was a man. A man she loved, a man who loved her. He would not be dying today. She had caught his soul beneath her fingertips and pressed it to her lips. He was guarded inside of her. They would all be safe, just as Nuru said.

She heard the howl of the approaching sandstorm like an affirmation from the goddess and that too gave her comfort. It was a promise, that howl, an answer to her prayers. They would *all* be safe.

THE SHIFTING GROUND

Oriole fled Zuberi's children on shaky wings. Everything inside her was unstable ground, shifting, rolling, and changing shape in ways she didn't even understand yet.

She could still feel the press of Zuberi's youngest girl's arms around her, Nuru's arms. Oriole felt her grasp and the swell of beauty that had been rising within while she was held so securely. Hope and understanding, forgiveness. It felt so like peace to be in that child's hold. Felt so like herself.

Asha had taken her pain. Nuru had offered her forgiveness. And Sabra had implored her to let the rest of this family be free. All these women were so different from what she would have expected to find in the life of such a monster.

With the space from her pain, Oriole could see how right Sabra was. They all deserved to be free.

But even knowing that, even free of the pain, even knowing her magic could not touch that girl, she still wanted something from Hadhi. Zuberi's legacy. She wanted to punish her. She wanted to destroy her as she would have done to her father had someone else not beat her to it.

Oriole wanted her suffering, even knowing it was wrong. And her mind filled up with voices urging her away from such impulses.

She is the only one of his children I am certain was beaten by his hands and scarred by his words.

He didn't love Hadhi. Not at all. He called her ugly or monster...
Why would you delight to see her suffer further?

Oriole flapped into the air in Osprey's body with no thought but to flee the parts of herself intent on vengeance. But something stopped her before she'd even put the girls fully out of sight. Just two mayflies had woken a shiver inside her that felt like a swarm last night. But now she watched as a true swarm crested the palace wall, all of them converging on one spot.

The door to the dungeon.

Oriole released a heavy sigh and glided along in the wake of the swarm. She didn't want to follow where they led.

It seemed he was wrong. All that belief and boundless hope for nothing. She had no magic but the kind that led to death any longer.

What a horror she was, absent a purpose in life. Why hadn't she died?

LIVE! Nighthawk's dying wish screeched, momentarily loud enough to drown out the din of insect wings and even the raging winds of the sandstorm drawing nearer.

She paused, momentarily torn as she heard so much more in that storm than just Nighthawk, so much sorrow, so much power, so many wails of love and agony. She felt drawn to it. Felt safety in it.

Wasn't that odd? A thing composed of such pain and destruction, but Oriole was certain if she could make it into those winds and that sloshing sand, that altering landscape, she would be guarded. What could have woken such a force? Was Ether truly a goddess who tread upon the earth to guard her followers?

Oriole didn't know. But she saw from behind the approaching wall of dust...above it, wings. Birds of different shape and size but all of such beloved familiarity. The rest of the flock. *Her daughters who lived.* They were coming. A wave of fear fell over Oriole's wings, urging her to flee in the opposite direction to flee not just the parts of her soul still hungry for revenge, but also the daughters she had no right to face unless it was in punishment.

She should flee. Go before she had to face them and see their scorn for what she had become. But as yet more mayflies flew past her, woozy with their already fading existences, she knew she would stay. Couldn't help it. Couldn't help but wonder if she had meant the wish she'd granted Noam exactly as it was working. She knew her magic could not touch Hadhi. But—to lose Noam—that would touch her. That would scar her anew. That would be a punishment.

Why would you delight to see her suffer further?

How much of her really was Oriole any longer? And how much was the monster that girl had seen? Had she done this?

She didn't know. She had no answer to so many questions, most of all— Why would you delight to see *anyone* suffer?

WITH THE FACE OF AN ANGEL

The door to the dungeon torture room was shut, throwing the room into darkness. Noam fought what felt like the weight of the entire castle, trying to rise.

He should have realized he was being watched; he deserved to be caught with how little attention he'd been paying. The Battle Born had warned him. Hadhi had warned him. He should have been prepared.

Noam dragged himself across the dirt floor towards the bars. His right arm was heavy and limp; it made a deeper trail in the dirt. One of his eyes was swollen shut, his head ached, and everywhere little bits of dirt struck stung the cuts all over his body. The king was a thorough man. At least two of Noam's ribs felt cracked; he could barely get in a breath.

He was underground and there were no windows, but Noam heard the rising buzz of a swarm. As if every mayfly alive was covering the door to the outside. A few had followed him in, fading already from their one day of existence they had ridden in on his person. They made his gut clench with fear, but he could not bring himself to harm the dying creatures further, so they lay on his clothes, occasionally shifting their wings and making him shiver.

Even when he'd wished to give his luck to Hadhi, Noam hadn't truly believed that he was lucky. Hadn't seen how many ways the luck protected him. Noam had thought all the Battle Born meant by luck was...ease of spirit. A freedom from carrying the burden of his past.

He'd wanted that for Hadhi. Now he hoped it protected her as thoroughly as it had protected him in the past. He would take any beating for the chance to see her safe.

Noam wrapped his arm between two of the bars and reached up from the outside, using the leverage to help pull him up against them. A searing pain scored his lungs. He wasn't sure he had the strength to lift himself, but he had to try.

As if of one mind, a bug on his shoulder lifted itself and flew on wobbly wings. Its uneven flight towards the door stopped suddenly as it crashed to the ground. Noam jerked when it landed, twitched, then moved no more.

They lived a lifetime in a May,
But dawned the June, he'd flown away.

Noam dragged his gaze away from the dead bug and shook the bars of his cell. The king must know all by now. He would be rounding up what was left of Azize's friends, then Azize, and Hadhi. Unless the luck protected her. She deserved so much better than this life. He should have run away with her from the moment he realized how sad she was.

To be happy would be to go somewhere else.

He should have paid more attention to her doubts, should have listened to her and asked her advice. He'd seen it in her eyes, that look of knowledge and resignation. Hadhi was well used to having no say. Well used to knowing better but not saying a word. He should have paid attention. But Noam had been as arrogant as he'd thought his friend. Thinking it was only sadness that made Hadhi look so. Thinking he would show her the way and make her happy. Give her luck and that look would be gone forever.

It would never be gone. Not as long as she was forced to silence her thoughts. Even if it was for one who loved her.

The dungeon filled with soft pockets of light. They grew slowly together, giving Noam's eyes time to adjust. He lay his head against the bars, staring up as a woman formed out of the light. Not a woman, an angel. Her eyes fell on the doomed bug before returning to Noam with a look of such sorrow.

"Moth—" Noam coughed, before he could form the word. He spit blood onto the ground and tried again. "Mother?"

The vision shook her head. "You know better than that."

She was right of course. The Battle Born had taken his mother's body, her height, and the gentle way her long hair tumbled past her waist, even the way her gaze at once soothed and challenged him. But she did not have his mother's warm brown eyes with flecks of grey. Or her presence. Whenever she was near, Noam felt joy in his heart, even when he was crying. Not so now. Yet still the form comforted him.

"Time and again, I leave you with all you need to take your love and flee, Noam, but time and again, you stay. I did warn you."

Noam opened his mouth to speak and found himself coughing again. His chest pinched, and he fought to stay awake as the exhaustion and pain wanted to drag him into oblivion.

"There is only so much luck can do for one determined to be a hero. Taking her away would be saving her, you know?" The words emerged from his mother's mouth in a tight, frustrated tone.

"No, it wouldn't." Noam's hand loosened around the bars, and he slipped down, but he was not in control. He closed his eyes, and his mind drifted to all the things Hadhi had stopped herself saying, all the things trapped inside her.

I never have the words to be understood.

And what had he said in return? Don't talk, stifling her voice like so many others.

"She needs to stay. She needs to do something before she can be free."

"What?"

Noam shook his head. He didn't know, he hadn't let her speak.

Or maybe she had, and he hadn't really listened.

"She needs to save her." Noam forced his hand into a fist around the bars to keep himself awake, clenching his teeth against the sting of the metal clawing at his skin. "The girl she didn't save as a child."

"Avenge her, you mean." The Battle Born nodded sadly. Did she think she knew Hadhi? Did she think they were the same?

They were surely similar, but there was something, despite her cynicism and disbelief, something more hopeful in Hadhi.

She still had people to love, Noam realized. People who loved her.

"No, I mean save her," Noam corrected. "It will not be the same girl, but Hadhi needs to save something of her, before she can move on."

His mother—the Battle Born who wore his mother's face—spun away, moving about with a jerkiness that spoke of unrest. She paced the length of the room, never once looking Noam's way.

"Just as well she stays," the woman hissed between her teeth. "I would only have had to search for her otherwise, to exact my—"

"Who do you think you are fooling?" Noam asked. "You wear my mother's face to chastise me for failing to run away with the woman I love. Hadhi terrified you, but still you made no move to harm her. You granted my wish to help her. You don't want Hadhi harmed any more than I do." Despite the pain and the weight of his exhaustion, Noam felt stronger.

"You do not want to harm any of them, do you?"

She stopped at the end of the dungeon, too far away for Noam to see clearly with his swollen eye. But the light around her dimmed.

"She should go on, never saving her, carrying the guilt, letting it make her speak for others. But never freeing her of the weight."

"Why?" Noam demanded, horrified.

"Because she will not know herself," the Battle Born spoke listlessly. "She will not know her mind, or where she belongs. Without the weight, she will be a foreigner in her own soul."

"No," Noam groaned aloud as he forced himself onto his knees. "Not Hadhi."

"NO?" The room shook with her rage, sending bits of rock chipping off Noam's cell. Tiny pieces of gravel struck Noam's sore body and felt like the pounding of Enzi's fists again.

That man was oddly fond of doing his own beatings. Another king would force others to torture for him, but Enzi took delight in inflicting pain.

"Was it not your love she questioned only moments after declaring her love for you? She is a being composed solely of doubts. In herself, her value, in everyone around her. Did your luck cause such a profound transformation?" the Battle Born demanded.

Noam had no good answer. His wish had not changed Hadhi. But he hadn't wanted it to change her. Only to protect her. To enrich her life. But it had not even done that as far as he had seen. The things Jauhar had said, the guilt she lay at Hadhi's feet, could not be called luck.

What if all his wish had done was take away his luck? What if none of it had gone to Hadhi?

"She will be at sea with no rudder if she rights her wrongs," the Battle Born said when Noam made no reply.

Noam shook his head. There was more to Hadhi, so much more. Even under her mother's censure, she had not simply taken in the guilt. She had declared her love, her right to be loved, offered her mother forgiveness. She would not sparkle and smile and laugh at life. As Noam had. Not his serious Hadhi. But she would not lose herself either.

"She will be made new."

"She asked if you were one of my *punishments*," the Battle Born interjected. "Tell me that didn't fill you with rage and betrayal and self-loathing. She caused that. Tell me I am wrong."

Noam was on his knees, his head held up more by the bars he leaned against than his own strength. His good arm was braced against the ground, while the other hung uselessly, its weight dragging him sideways. Everything ached and stung and dragged at him. He didn't want to think about that moment.

She had warned him. Hadhi had said she didn't deserve him and could not keep him. He hadn't really listened to that either, too caught up with her. She loved him. It was all he cared about, but she deserved more, they both did. If he'd listened, he might not have felt the punch of her mistrust from his body all the way to his soul.

"Tell me it wasn't that old desperation for love you could not have that drove your wish." She rushed to his side and gazed at him imploringly. "You can still take it back. I will return your luck if you ask it."

Noam startled, appalled. Surely she didn't mean it. She wanted Hadhi safe. Didn't she?

She knew so much. The Battle Born saw the way Noam had wanted to shout, to shake Hadhi and tear apart her doubts, demand she love him. Saw how Hadhi's doubts had made him want, even if just in that moment, to turn his back on her.

Noam had waited his entire childhood for his father, just once, to see only the strength of Noam's love for him, not the betrayal that gave him life. He'd waited, and offered, and never been given the love he knew he deserved. And he could see it all happening again with Hadhi. So he wanted to turn away.

But then Hadhi said the words that broke his heart—for her.

Did you make him feel this way?

And Noam remembered all the moments when his father would smile at him and some seed of hope would spring up, grow leaves and flower, in mere moments. He would build such hopes on tiny little offers of...not even love really, just appreciation. Eventually, his father remembered to hate him, and Noam was left feeling worthless again.

Hadhi knew that pain. And in that moment, it became more important to love her, to stay and say the words again and again, to show her his love, until she came to expect love as she already expected rejection. It was more important to give her love than to feel it in every moment.

It didn't stop the pain, but it made it worth the while. It made the wish not so much a choice but an inevitability.

Noam was lucky, and that luck led him here, to Hadhi. If for no other reason than so he could give her the thing he'd wanted most, all his life. A love, free of restrictions.

"Love drove the wish." Noam spoke softly, still frightened that he had already seen Hadhi for the last time. But no less certain of her love for him.

He felt her love. She'd given him things too. Noam lifted one of the bugs still stuck to his pants and let it rest in his palm.

It is impossible not to love you, she'd said and held him tight, promising him that even his father loved him though he had not shown it.

Hadhi's love wasn't as loud as Noam's. Nor was it a thing free of doubt. But Hadhi's love was beautiful. It offered him peace and perspective with things he had pretended not to care about, that drove him nonetheless.

That it is temporary does not change that it is love.

Szo ethuri, zyid qi.

"I could never take it back," Noam told the Battle Born. "Hadhi will become someone new, someone of her own making. She will always have doubts, but she will find her way through them."

The Battle Born leaned heavily against the bars, her eyes full to bursting with tears. They begged Noam, held him in a question she had yet to voice. Slowly she wrapped her hands around the bars, shaking them with the depth of her emotion.

"How?" she sobbed.

Noam shook his head. This was not his mother, but he still wanted to reach out to her. Wanted to heal her. This woman knew others so well, for one who did not seem to know herself.

"Perhaps you should ask Hadhi."

She looked aside. Noam felt a stab of terror that she would leave and never return. He threw out his good hand, covering hers on the bars, and falling against them from the sudden motion. Noam gripped her hand tight.

"Did you feel my mother's last wish?" he begged.

"It was not mine to grant, but I know it."

Noam's gut twisted. His mother had always been so lovely, and strong, a force, but a gentle one. But in her last months, she'd tried to send them all away, Noam and his siblings. And though each of them wanted something from the world, none went, and none knew why. Then she began fading, exhausted after only a few moments standing, could barely breathe without the sound of it scraping the air. They understood that some part of them had known what was coming.

He'd never felt so helpless in his life. Even now, locked in a cell and beaten, he felt there was still something to be done. Still hope. He'd had none then. And she died. Left him, with his father, without her to stand between them.

He could have stayed longer; his father had not sent him away. But Noam had come to realize that when his father saw Noam, he only remembered his mother's betrayal, not her love. He'd left, thinking it was the kindest gift he could give his father. But what if it wasn't what she wanted?

"She wanted only love, for each of you. For her children to be loved as you deserved," the Battle Born whispered, and Noam sighed, his heart releasing a delicate, relived beat.

Hadhi, his mother had sent him to Hadhi.

"Thank you!" He wasn't sure if he was speaking to the Battle Born or his mother.

"If you had only one wish," Noam asked, wanting to offer her the comfort she had given him. "What would you ask for?"

The Battle Born shook her head, tears sputtered from her eyes, and the room shook with her once again.

"I would not even know where to begin," she whispered. Light slowly suffused her being like she would split apart, but it stopped, diving back into her, and she remained in his mother's form with a look of fear and confusion.

THE MONSTER'S ECHO

The Hadhi monster flinched, shrinking as if to hide. Beyond her, Baba continued to tremble, no matter how Hadhi shrunk. He was afraid of her.

Do you already know? Is that why you shy from the truth? Asha heard an echo of Sparrow's voice, and so did the Hadhi monster.

"I never meant to take him from you," Hadhi repeated.

No.

Not Hadhi. She couldn't have.

She loved him. She had said so. Asha had seen her grief!

Hadhi buried her face beneath one of her wings. Baba coughed, gurgling on blood. He was on the ground with a hand over his side and blood seeping between his fingers.

All at once, the Hadhi monster stood over him, with blood on her hands. Baba's monster, with its hideous hyaena face stared down at their father. Asha curled away from the sight.

She killed him. Hadhi killed Baba. It made no sense. Not from the sister Asha was getting to know, but from the monster...

"A monster? Hadhi?" A voice Asha did not recognize emerged slowly from behind her. The woman was lovely. With deep brown skin so dark it glistened against the whites in her eyes. Her hair was twisted into a maze of tiny knots and her face was familiar and strange at once with her high cheek bones and a wide sloping nose and the gentle intensity of her expression. She walked with a sideways jerk of the hip like she had to twist her whole body just to step. Asha felt that twist from somewhere in her memory. She *knew* this beautiful woman; she just could not think how.

"I remember Hadhi." The woman stopped between Baba and the monster. With a gentle finger, she raised the monster's head and winked at her. "She had bright eyes then, burning with all the love she had to give."

The woman shifted her gaze to Asha with an expression of such love, Asha's heart stopped. Longing to live in that expression forever. To soak in it. To exist in it and nothing else.

"She used to lay her ear against my belly and listen to your heartbeat."

This was her *mother*? Asha recognized bits of herself in that face now. Their noses were similar, and their cheeks, but Asha would never have imagined herself looking so...warrior like. Her mother had such muscular arms and legs, and had such intensity in her every move. Those parts of her were more reminiscent of Hadhi. Hadhi who was not her daughter, but who had spent so much more time with her.

"It's so fast." A child's joyful voice came from the monster. "I think she's running."

Asha's mother laughed and ran a hand down the hyaena's head. "She is excited to meet you."

The monster raised its head proudly. "Baba thinks she's a boy, but we know better."

"We do," Asha's mother agreed. Her mother, she was so bright and determined. She was always vague in Asha's imaginings. It had never occurred to her that Hadhi might have remembered, might have known Asha's mother. "We'll show him," Mzaa winked.

The Hadhi monster giggled. Asha was beginning to soften towards her when something small and rotten flew through the air, smattering on the back of the monster's head.

"Why so sour, sour-face?" Asha heard the echo of her own childhood voice.

The monster growled, clawing at the ground, and a snarl curled up its lip. Asha jerked forward to protect her mother, but Mzaa halted Asha with a disappointed glare. She framed the monster's face in her hands and raised it for Asha to see.

"This isn't rage you see, or a monster preparing to attack. This is pain that you caused." Gently, Mzaa turned and rubbed her cheek against the monster's. "Shhh, child. It's not one bit true."

Asha chewed on her tongue, wanting to cry or to argue. She and Hadhi had already addressed this! It was a long time ago, and Asha was sorry. Now, the first time she ever saw her mother, she was defending Hadhi. Making Asha feel like maybe she was the monster.

Baba jumped into the fray, peeling the feathers from his mouth. "Rama doesn't know the half of it. Does she, monster? But Asha sees the real you. You're nothing but the mon—"

"Stop it, Baba! Just stop," Asha shouted, trying to cover her ears, her eyes, still aching from her mother's disappointment. Would she have loved Hadhi better?

Baba stared at Asha as if she and not Hadhi had stabbed him. He lay down, gripping his wound. Asha fought the desire to run to him, to comfort him. Nothing made any sense. Why? Why did she have to see? Why did she have to know? How was she meant to be...joyful, or light, or anything but tortured ever again?

Hadhi changed again, no longer the monster. She was a little girl with tight black curls clinging to her scalp and hungry quiet eyes. She curled up on the ground, covering her head in her hands, rocking back and forth with her ears covered. Asha's mother knelt beside her, gathering Hadhi into her arms, but her eyes found Asha.

"A sister can be your truest friend and guardian. I remember when Hadhi was that for you, when she wanted to be that always. But your father didn't want such things for either of you. So he taught you both to see lies. You do not have to see them now."

She stood then, leaving Hadhi where she was, and walked to Asha. She slid her hand around Asha's face, marveling at her. "Be you. Just be more aware."

"It doesn't make sense. I loved him, and she killed him."

Mzaa nodded. "Yes." She settled her lips on Asha's cheek softly. "What else did she do?"

In hundreds of flashing puffs of sand, Asha remembered; Hadhi nursing her when she was ill, comforting Asha when storms came, guarding Nuru, watching Lin play as though he were the most amazing thing in the world, comforting a strange girl at the ball. Hadhi. Offering comfort to what she thought was her enemy, carrying her sister home though she was tired and soaked. Watching the sunrise as if it would save her. Hadhi, thanking Asha for showing her who she was, loving Asha, ordering her to be herself, telling Asha it was alright, to love the monster.

Beyond her mother, Asha watched the child Hadhi crawl over to her bleeding father. She lifted his head onto her legs, soothing his forehead.

"My monster," Baba laughed. "My own image reborn."

Hadhi cringed but didn't abandon him. She continued to soothe his brow.

She was beautiful, wasn't she? Despite the blood. Loving, even in her most monstrous moments.

Asha tore her eyes from them, looking into the eyes of the woman she had always wanted to know. The woman whose love she had always longed to feel.

"I am sorry. I will make you proud."

"Oh, Asha." Mzaa knelt, wrapped both arms around her daughter. "You already have. That I am disappointed by one failing doesn't mean I cannot see all the beauty and goodness in you. It means only that I want you to feel the full potential of this heart." She lay a hand over Asha's heart and stared at her with all her love.

Asha nodded, her eyes stinging and blurry. Already, Ether was moving on. The room grew more distinct.

"Love," her mother insisted, and she faded into a swirl of sands.

"Live," Nighthawk commanded.

Ether faded from Asha's gaze, but sand floated still in the air. Asha saw the room, saw Sabra rocking anxiously, Lin wriggling trapped a bit too tightly against her. She saw the slipper lying on the ground. Waiting for her.

"No point granting wishes to the dead," Asha whispered. "They're never there to see it."

"Asha, you are not talking like yourself."

Asha met her friends gaze as her hand stretched out for the slipper. "Yes, I am. I understand better now. The power is only as good as what it does, only as powerful a hunger as you let it be."

She closed her fingers around the slipper. Power raced beneath her skin, through her veins, up her spine, curling her neck and startling all the hairs on her skin awake. Her entire being tingling, Asha rolled her neck as the magic eased away her aches and her exhaustion. She sat up.

"What do you mean?" Sabra asked.

Asha blinked, and her eyes flashed blue.

The door to the dungeon screeched open. A mayfly flew in looking vigorous until a hand swung out—*crushing*—the creature against the wall. Noam's heart constricted as Kane stepped in.

"I've a suggestion of where to begin wishing," Kane taunted. "Why not wish for your freedom?"

The Battle Born jerked forward to attack but could not seem to move. As if there were an invisible cell within this room, she could raise her hands, could beat against it, but could not move more than a foot in any direction.

"What have you done?" she cried out.

"Made my own destiny." Kane wiped the remnants of the dead bug on his clothes and laughed. "Just as I said I would." His attention shifted to Noam. "I heard a story about you before you joined Azize," he said conversationally. "A song. Perhaps you've heard it as well. *As doomed as mayflies are their gifts, they gleam in May, in June cause rifts.*" Kane laughed hard. "And you go and wish to give her your luck, on the—*last day*—of May! Do you think she's as doomed as you now?"

Noam's fingers curled softly around the mayfly in his palm, protecting it as his heart pounded. He'd built this tiny blameless creature and someone else's song into such monsters in his head, let them rule his life though he'd smiled over the fear. And now...real threats loomed over all the people in his life, and Noam had no means to protect any of them. The mayfly in his palm was doomed already, the Battle Born with his mother's face was trapped by magic. Kane was a traitor to Azize and all of his friends, risking all their lives. And Hadhi was out in the world preparing to face an evil man with no idea that he knew their plan already.

No matter what Noam tried to tell himself. That he'd wished her his luck. That he'd seen now how powerful a force that was. That he—was—*not*—a—mayfly. That the poem was a love story, not a curse.

No matter how he tried to comfort himself he could not escape the doubts, the fears. He could not escape the certainty that love story or no, The Mayfly's Visit was most certainly a tragedy.

Fear had been the defining characteristic in Oriole's makeup since Zuberi destroyed her home. Fear of the monsters in the world, fear of her own wants and desires, fear of her continued existence. Every moment, whether she was playing Zawadi, the mysterious magical being with secret vengeful intents, or dressed up in Asha's skin and slinking around the palace to play with her victims, all she'd really felt inside was fear.

And here she stood, trapped in a cage of magic, watching the boy whose ugly wish she had blessed vibrate with power even his predecessor had not shown, sparkling with rage and with magic, taunting lives, destroying hopes. She looked out of this box at him and felt what Hadhi must have when she threatened Oriole—recognition. He was composed of fear alone as well.

Made my own destiny, just as I said I would.

I make my own destiny.

The words, the men, their ugly angry, frightened spirits layered over one another in Oriole's mind. Here in this quiet box awaiting her death. He would kill her now, deliver her to his king, and kill her. Or try to use her to kill others.

Oriole felt them growing nearer. Finch and Needletail out ahead of their sisters. Headed right for her. This man would finish where Zuberi had failed. He would kill them all. As Oriole sat here in her fear and waited to die.

But she felt the ground shifting again. Not in the physical world, but the ground within herself. Parts of her buried under the cave-in of her fear shook loose. The parts that wanted to live—even if only to set right what *she* had done wrong.

She heard a scream, a bird's high pitched cry. That call that had drawn the flock to her before she was one of them. She heard the anger in it, the demand for justice, for balance, for the power to set right the wrongs of the world. All of it rose within her and cried out for help that she didn't deserve, but help her daughters did.

She expected the answer to come from the others who lived, or even from Asha out there in the world, feeling with Oriole's power. But what she felt building in her was so different...it was not just power, it was hunger, and love, and wild, untamable, *insatiable* empathy.

It felt the magic that made this cell, felt the trapped creature forced to make it. It felt the pain Oriole had given away, and the bits she clung onto. It felt her fear. It felt her regret, and it felt her growing understanding, her changing form. It recognized both her monster, and her fight against it. Felt her wish for help.

And it opened its arms.

It offered her anything in its power to give.

Winds beat against the outside of the dungeon, shaking the building, shaking the walls of Oriole's cell. It did not shatter it, but it fed the power of the cell into Oriole's starving being, one bit at a time.

The room shook. And Oriole's eyes flashed.

Before Hadhi reached the gate, their were soldiers surrounding her. Four of them. Two took up Hadhi's arms, one stood behind her and another in front. They said nothing; their leader merely jerked his head towards the palace as they led her forward. She knew every one of their names, but she did not say a word either. What was the point? They were taking her where she meant to go.

Hadhi's heart pounded harder the further they walked and her stomach twisted. Servants darted out of her path, and other soldiers looked on, every face either blank with resignation or cold with fear. Some just looked away. So many looked away. She did not deserve anything better.

But she did have better. Her uncle and her neighbors were preparing to ambush the king to save her.

They're doing that to help themselves. Hadhi heard her father's voice like he was whispering in her ear. Like she was ten years old again and he was crouched next to her, teaching her to hunt.

They could help themselves other ways, Hadhi's mind argued back. They could wait and gather more supporters. They were on the road for her. Uncle Kafil had said so. And Sabra had helped Hadhi dress, to give her confidence, to remind her of what she was fighting for, to—

To sate her guilt. Baba's echo scoffed. *This was always your problem, Hadhi, you wanted to make sweet motivations for every action. You want it to be love. But I told you—there is no such thing.*

Hadhi clenched her fists. He was wrong. It did not matter if no one else felt love for her. She loved them. She was here for love. She had come without a weapon knowing what Enzi would do. *What would appeal to King Enzi is the challenge—of breaking your spirit.* He wanted to take her apart a piece at a time as Baba had Sabra. He wanted to hurt her, weaken her, force himself on her.

Hadhi knew all of that, but she came weaponless.

To sate your guilt. Baba laughed.

Hadhi jerked to a stop, and the guards stopped with her. She bent forward, braced her hands on her knees. The guards let her be. She could feel them unsure what to do. She could feel concern, even regret. But in a moment, they would force her forward. They did not think they had any more choice than she did. Her breath was gone and her eyes flashed with painful lights and her mind worked, wondering if those were not the truest words her father's ghost had ever spoken. Truer words than her father had ever spoken while living.

She had felt to blame for Kiho's suffering for so long. Felt guilty for every moment of freedom she had. She had been terrified of the future, of marriage, of being touched and taken and owned. She had pretended that she was impervious, that she was only angry. But she had been guilty.

Had she come without a weapon, knowing what Enzi would do because...his forcing himself on Hadhi as well would somehow make them the same?

I taught you how to avenge her. I want you to have your vengeance. Take it. Steal one of their knives. Prove your strength. Or are you as pathetic as Ahon's girl?

His question rang unanswered in her ears. It was always unanswered. Her mind wanted to search for her father. To look in his eyes, but she knew he was not here. It was memory, and it was doubt. Always her doubts were in his voice. She wanted to answer him aloud now. To ask why he had never said Kiho's name. Was it because he did not know it? Or was it fear?

Fear that saying her name would make her real, would make her pain crawl inside him. He always hid from the pain, and he had tried to make Hadhi do the same. All he had done was teach her to hide her pain *from him*. She still felt it. She still lived in fear.

Yes! She was as weak as Kiho.

If it was weakness to be afraid of someone intent on harming her. Yes, if it was weakness to want to hide. Yes, if it was weakness to shudder and shrink inside. Yes, if it was weakness to cry out for help when you needed it. YES. If it was weakness to want to be your own, to want to decide how your body was used, to decide who you were.

In every way—*yes*. She was *weaker* than that child had been. Because hiding from her fear had left it still a ten-year-old clutching a rock as she hid and listened to another child's screams.

But—Hadhi pulled in a deep breath and held it within. When she released the breath, the guards on either side of her closed their arms around Hadhi's again, pulling her up. Without a word, she walked with them. Her head was high, and her muscles coiling for a fight, and her shudders were banished within. Not because she was stronger than Kiho, but because unlike that little girl, Hadhi knew what was coming. And because her father *was a liar*.

He did not want Hadhi's revenge. He wanted proof of his superiority. And Hadhi had not come here to sate her guilt. She had come here to protect other children, because she could see beyond this moment, and she was done hiding from the fear.

It would not make it better. But this could be her past, one day. Ugliness would be her past. She had a future waiting for her, people were rising up to defend each other. They would make a lovelier Maltuba. Hadhi would be part of that. Love would be her future, love from this community that her father had taught her to ignore, but she would ignore no longer. Love from Nuru, and Sabra, and Asha—*and Noam*. They would love her and she would love them and it would make the world more beautiful.

Killing was Baba's way. It had been the only way Hadhi knew, but she could learn a new way. Protect with a different kind of strength.

It was time for her to face her greatest fear—toothless—but strengthened by love and by the power of all the wounded souls screaming to be freed.